About the Author

Born Glasgow, Scotland in 1929. Grew up in Peebles in the glorious Scottish Borders. Educated at Peebles High School.

Started work at 17 as an apprentice in the Woollen Industry.

Interrupted by National Service in the RAF between 1947-49 and on demobilisation became full time student at the Scottish Woollen Technical College in Galashiels, graduating in 1952.

Retired in 1996 after 50 years' service in the textile industry, including a spell of 10 years in Quebec, Canada.

Elected a Fellow of The Textile Institute in 1986 for his contributions to the industry.

Married in 1954 to Rhona, and have raised one son and two daughters who have long since flown the nest. For the past 22 years they have resided in Swansea where they enjoy an active life covering sporting and musical activities. Ken started his first published work at the age of 14, supplying the local newspaper with reports on soccer activities, and during his adult career in textiles had over 50 articles published in textile magazines with international circulation.

He plays the piano, and is a member of the Morriston Orpheus Choir, one of the leading male voice choirs in Wales who performed in Carnegie Hall in October 2001, a mere 5 weeks after the 9/11 tragedy to show support for the people of N.Y.

During his 10 years in Canada, Ken was a prominent member of Toastmasters International and became a champion speech contestant. He was a winner of 21 out of 25 contests and only failed by the narrowest of margins to qualify for the Toastmasters World Championship Finals in Toronto in 1968.

ADDITIONAL INFORMATION ON PUBLISHING ACTIVITIES

Over 50 articles published between the following International Textile Magazines.

1. Textile World of Atlanta, Georgia. Two articles subsequently reprinted in Asian Textile World.
2. World Clothing Manufacturer.
3. International Dyer
4. Knitting International
5. Wool Record
6. Laundry Cleaning International.

Two part article on How to Win Speech contests published in the Speakers Association magazine in the 1970's.

Commissioned by BBC Radio Wales to prepare programme for transmission in August 2004 to commemorate the 75th anniversary of the closing of the most unique Chapel in Wales. A Chapel constructed 650 feet below the ground in a coal mine. For 85 years the miners held a weekly service underground in the Chapel. This pit had the best safety record of all pits in the area, and the miners believed their prayers helped protect them. Narrative and hymns feature in the programme, the hymns being sung by the Morriston Orpheus Choir.

E-mail: kennedy.scott@sky.com

To my mother, Emma Maxwell McCone, who died age 37, victim of a national epidemic of TB in 1931, and for my father William Gilmore Scott, Second Engineer in the "Baron Erskine", sunk by a German U-boat, in the North Atlantic, March 1942.

Emma Maxwell McCone

THE WISHING BOY

AUSTIN MACAULEY
PUBLISHERS LTD.

A CIP catalogue record for this title is available from the British Library.

ISBN 978 1 78455 065 3

www.austinmacauley.com

First Published (2015)
Austin Macauley Publishers Ltd.
25 Canada Square
Canary Wharf
London
E14 5LB

Printed and bound in Great Britain

Acknowledgments

My gratitude to Catrin Collier, well known Authoress, who presided over an evening class of budding authors, in the Miners Library in Swansea that I attended 10 years ago. It was there that the ambition to write a novel was inspired.

Also gratitude to my friend Alan Lewis for his assistance in editing chapters of *The Wishing Boy*.

Chapter One

The horseman came from the West, like an apparition from the dark shadows that still clung defiantly to the rocky moorland that stretched back to Connemara. The dawn was already alive with golden tints as the new day appeared in the East.

It hinted at a fine soft morning, but the rider had no interest. He was too tired to care. His grey Cob picked its way over the stone pitted ground with the delicacy of a dancer, despite the handicap of the donkey tethered to the saddle and trailing behind it.

Seamus slouched in the saddle, coat buttoned to his neck, his cloth cap pulled well down, and beneath its brim, his eyes struggled to stay open. He was physically exhausted and mentally drained. The events of the night would haunt him forever. Over and over in his mind, he fought to justify his actions. He had manipulated a disaster into a triumph, and made his father a hero in the process, but where was the glory when you had to murder him to do it?

In a few minutes he would reach the farmhouse where Catrin would be waiting. How would he be able to console her after the traumatic events of the night?

Suddenly his nostrils twitched. An acrid smell of burning drifted on the light morning air and forced him to open his eyes. Against the light, beyond the rise he was approaching, there appeared to be a dark cloud. As he concentrated his gaze, he saw it was not a cloud. It was smoke, spiralling upwards in uneven gusts, glinting with fiery sparks, and it was coming from the direction of Ballanalee.

He cast the donkey free and dug his heels into the flanks of the Cob, forcing it into a gallop and racing to the crest of the rise. His worst fears were realised. The farmhouse was ablaze and burning fiercely. The alien odour that had roused him came from the black oily smoke of the burning thatch. He lashed the cob and set it to clear the stone dyke that enclosed the field behind the house. He slithered to a halt at the gate and dismounted on the run, dashing into the yard and calling for Catrin. But there was no answering voice, only the noise of the flames.

The outbuildings had not yet caught fire, although sparks were flying towards them. He noted the doors of the hay shed were wide open and Catrin's little trap was gone, nor was there a sign of her pony.

The front door had been left open and a strong draught whistled through it to help fuel the fire. The earthen floor was a carpet of flames, a constant stream of wood and clumps of flaming thatch dropping from the loft, each impact throwing showers of sparks upwards.

In the middle of the inferno he could make out the stout bog oak table around which generations of O'Farrell's had sat. It was besieged by a ring of fire, and on the table top something burned with great intensity.The hissing sounds of the burning thatch grew, and a mass of it descended with a roar into the room below. The table collapsed sending a cascade of sparks flying, and the black smoke surged skywards, to hang like a spectre of evil in the morning air.

He fled to the earthen bank behind the house. The lean –to that formed the storeroom was cut partially into the bank. Its turved roof was already aflame, and above it, the loft window belched fiery tongues that were rapidly blackening the whitewashed walls. The heat was unbearable, his lungs gasping for air, and his eyes streaming from the smoke. There was no point to remain. No one could have survived the inferno.

He stumbled blindly across the bare grass of the knoll that sloped downwards to the thickets and then through the grove of trees that fringed the strand of the river estuary. He flung himself down on the damp sand, and lay on his back drawing gulps of the cool air to bring relief to his tortured lungs. For the first time in ten hours he relaxed. He lay still, his mind blank, his eyes gazing hypnotically at the sky, until he drifted into a deep sleep.

Something was tugging fiercely at his shoulder, and a hysterical voice was shouting. He reluctantly shook himself free from his slumber, his hand automatically seeking his revolver, but it was not there. That was enough to waken him in a flash.

As his head cleared he saw his assailant was only Michael, the lad from the village, the one they called Michael the eejit. A poor, harmless soul, the butt of many a joke, but an observer of much.

Dev. and himself knew him well. Michael regarded them with hero worship and was forever hanging around Ballinalee.

"The house, Seamus. The house! It's on fire. Quick, quick, git up an' put it out." His little twisted mouth showered him with spittle as his voice rose, and he continued to pull at his coat.

"Ach, it's just you Michael, so 'tis. Keep yer hair on. There's nuthin' we can do gone. Leave it be.

"Did ye see where she went, Michael?" he had him by the shoulders trying to calm him.

"She went off. She went that way," he pointed towards the East.

"She didn't see me," he laughed at his cunning, "but I see'd her, an' she did it. Will ye catch her an' kill her?"

"No, no, Michael. Not at all. It's alright. I know why she did it. She meant no harm."

It was good thinking on her part. The evidence would be destroyed and neither the Army or the Garda would ever know the true facts.

"Dev will be angry, won't he?" Michael remained agitated.

"No he won't, Seamus assured him. Anyway, Dev won't be comin' back."

Michael's face twisted. "Why?"

"He's gone to another place, that's all." There was no way he could tell the whole story. He put his arms around the bony little shoulders and spoke to him in a fatherly way.

"Michael, me boy, you're a fine runner are you not?"

Michael nodded vigorously.

"Run to the village an' tell Constable O'Leary to git on his bike an' come out here. He'll need to know about the fire. Will ye do that fer me?" He fished in his pocket.

"Here's a silver sixpence. Go as fast as your little legs can take you." He spun Michael around and gave him a push. Michael ran a few steps and then turned, waving his arm, clutching the sixpence firmly in his hand and with that sped off towards the village.

Seamus was relieved. He had given Dev a solemn promise to make sure Catrin was alright. She must have taken the pony and trap and returned to Dungannon House where she would be safe with her grandfather. Daniel would understand her grief and would comfort her. Just to be sure, he would call in.

He retraced his steps into the yard. His horse had moved uphill, well out of reach of the blaze. The fire had settled into a subdued crackling but the sparks had eventually succeeded in setting the pig sty on fire.

His father's car was still parked in the yard, close to the new outbreak, and it was time to move. He yanked the door open and saw the keys were in the ignition. His father had evidently thought he would not be staying long.

He started the engine and reversed to drive out the yard, bumping wildly along the dirt road as he accelerated. He wanted to avoid the possibility of meeting the constable, for that would destroy his alibi.

As he drove along the main road, his eyes squinting against the sun, he felt more able to reflect on the situation.

The Dublin Command would take the glory. Two more martyrs to add to the role of honour, and a show of defiance that would be put on at a remembrance service with full military honours. The thought of it made the bile rise in his throat.

He would have to find a safe house and lie low for a while, but he would be back. There was still a fight for freedom to be won and, despite the crime he had committed, he owed his father that much.

Catrin would return to Dublin and get on with her life. She was young and had spirit. She would get over her loss in time. He sighed.

She had brought a new awareness into their lives, and there had been times when he wished it was he and not Dev who was the object of her purpose in coming to Galway, but it was a feeling he could never tell her.

He wondered if she had finally found all the answers to the mystery surrounding The Wishing Boy. He had never understood her obsession.

Now that her curiosity had been fulfilled, could she possibly be happy now that the full costs of her obsession had been met? He pondered the thought. There was one thing she would never know.

There was another Wishing Boy.

As he continued to drive into the full light of day, he cast his mind back to the events of a year ago, when Catrin had first entered their lives, and tried to imagine how it had all begun. He could speculate all he liked, but one thing he did know for sure...

The Wishing Boy had a lot to answer for.

Chapter Two

The day The Wishing Boy came to Dublin was nothing out of the ordinary. The early Spring of 1937 produced many such days. Unsettled weather in a city also unsettled by the political climate.

A mottled mass of grey cloud scudded overhead, and a chill wind funnelled up the Liffey all the way from Dublin Bay, sending the early morning shoppers in O'Connell street scurrying for shelter to escape it's vindictiveness. It was a morning to stay indoors and bask by a blazing fire. A time to read a good book and sip tea. Catrin Kilpatrick was not so inclined. She had a regular Saturday morning schedule, and weather would not be allowed to detract her from it.

She would meet with Cara, her best friend and confidante, and have morning coffee in the Gresham, after which they would shop. On this particular morning her father had given her twenty-five pounds to spend on something for her forthcoming birthday, and she was determined to spend it.

For the umpteenth time she inspected her appearance in the large gilt mirror in the hall. Her titian, shoulder length hair had been taken up and coiled neatly under her hat, hiding its glory, but practical for the windy conditions.

Her dark green woollen coat with its fox fur collar not only looked elegant, but would keep the chill wind at bay. She tilted her head to admire her profile, and smiled in satisfaction. How many heads would she cause to turn today, she mused?

Megan Kilpatrick stood at the living room door watching the mirror ceremony. She never ceased to wonder at her daughter's rituals whenever she was going out.

"Time you were gone from here, Catrin. You're Da'll be wondering what on earth's keeping you."

"Don't fuss, Mam. He's busy enough, warming the car. I'm ready. See you about one o' clock then." She kissed her mother and sped out the front door, slamming it behind her and sending a draught of cold air sweeping inside.

Megan sighed. Himself sitting in the cold to warm the car for her. Making a rod for his own back, she had told him many times, but it made no impression. Catrin could manipulate him without him even noticing. She shrugged and made her way back to the comfort of the living room fire.

Roderick Kilpatrick watched his daughter flounce down the steps from the front door. He should have been irritated, for the engine had been idling for more than five minutes, but he found it impossible to be mad with Catrin. She was the apple of his eye, and as his only child he considered it his duty to provide all he could for her.

She was a picture of elegance, worthy of all his indulgence. He leant over and opened the car door.

"Thank you, Da", she said with a dazzling smile. It's lovely and warm. Mam says you spoil me, but you don't mind, do you?" She pecked him on the cheek and flopped into her seat. Roderick smiled and put the car in gear.

On an overcast day, Lower Fitzwilliam Street was robbed of its splendour. The elegant line of Georgian houses, the longest of its kind in Europe, looked best when bathed in sunlight. Otherwise the red brick was dulled, the wrought iron balconies that graced the first floor windows looked in need of paint, and the pillared doorways with their decorative fan light windows lacked distinction.

It had been a proud day for the Kilpatrick's when they moved from their modest quarters in Kingstown to the splendour of Fitzwilliam Street, a direct result of the family printing business prospering. Roderick had even greater ambitions, and he looked forward to the day Catrin would assist him in the enterprise.

"So, where's it to be?" he asked. "Swizers or Brown Thomas, or is it straight to the Gresham?"

"Gresham first," she replied. "We'll have coffee and then we plan to see an exhibition of Irish crafts at the Parnell Gallery. Might find something new there. I've seen everything there is in Brown Thomas, or the rest of Grafton Street for that matter."

"It'll take some doing to find something you haven't got," sighed Roderick, "but it's a good thing to support the crafts. You might see something useful."

He drove carefully through the morning traffic, skirting the slow moving dray carts, anxious not to startle the horses, and patiently allowing the tram cars to load and unload their human cargoes as they jerked their stop-start way into the city centre.

He drove to the top of Upper O'Connell Street, passing the rows of Hansom cabs waiting patiently for fares, the horses with their backs into the wind, and the cabbies stamping their feet to keep warm. He drew up at the impressive entrance to the hotel and let Catrin out.

The Gresham or the Shelbourne were the places to be seen, and he was happy to provide her with the best places. For him, Saturday morning was another working day, and once he had seen her disappear inside, he made his way to work.

Cara was already seated at their usual table. Smaller than Catrin, her short dark hair and glasses gave her a secretarial look. She had the potential to be pretty, but lacked the expertise. She had always been in awe of Catrin and content to follow in her wake. Their friendship dated back to the days when both families had moved into the area at the same time, and had continued through school and college.

"You're late," Cara exclaimed. "I was beginning to think you weren't coming. The waiter keeps asking me if I want to order."

"Oh Cara. Pay him no heed. That's what he's there for. We've plenty of time."

"I'm looking forward to the exhibition," Cara was excited, "but do you think you'll find something to spend your birthday money on?"

"When it's a miserable morning like this, I feel like buying something, even if it's just for the sake of buying. It makes me feel better." She beckoned the waiter and ordered. Cara continued the conversation.

"I've heard the Celtic jewellery is very good, but a lot of the exhibits are either pottery or paintings. That's not you, is it? Are you sure you don't want to have a look in Grafton street?"

"There's nothing of interest there. I'm hoping the exhibition might inspire me. It's different."

They lingered over coffee, chatting amiably and gossiping when Cara suddenly lowered her head and whispered excitedly.

"Don't look round, but there's a man in army uniform who's been gazing at us for the past five minutes. He's just smiled at me."

Catrin lowered her cup and whispered. "Why didn't you say something before?"

"I wasn't going to pay any attention. But he keeps smiling at me."

"What's he like?"

"He's really handsome. Very smart in his uniform. I think he's an officer."

They finished coffee and signalled the waiter.

"No need to pay anythin', Miss," he told her "the officer gentleman over there requested the bill an' he's takin' care of it." He indicated the table behind them.

Cara bubbled. "Fancy that! Bet it's you he's after. He is handsome, take a look."

Catrin rose, gathering her handbag and fussing unnecessarily with it as she dared raise her eyes in his direction. He sat alone, lounging in his seat, his right knee crossed arrogantly over his left, stubbing out a cigarette as he returned her gaze. She felt the fine hairs on the nape of her neck rise and colour flooding to her cheeks.

The nerve of the man! What gentleman would dare such a thing without an introduction? She strode over to his table aggressively.

"I don't know who you are sir, but your generosity is misplaced. We can take care of ourselves, thank you."

"I insist you allow me to return the money." She fished a pound note from her handbag and proffered it, but he made no move to accept it.

"I couldn't possibly accept money from a lady," he spoke with a refined Dublin accent. He had a disarming smile.

Cara was correct. He was handsome, in fact devilishly good looking. His dark brown hair was neatly trimmed with just the hint of a kiss curl fringing a broad handsome brow. A fine pencil slim moustache gave him a rakish look, and the turned up corners of his mouth suggested mischief. When he smiled his teeth looked perfectly even and white, a rarity for a Dublin man. That smile could weaken the knees of many a woman, but Catrin was not one to be lightly disarmed.

"I apologize for not having the pleasure of an introduction, but I had hoped my gesture would give me the opportunity. I didn't mean to offend you. Won't you join me?"

"I'm afraid we can't." Catrin had made one of her rapid assessments. Good looks or not, he had an arrogance that displeased her.

"We have to be off. We're late as it is. Thank you for trying, but"... she tossed the pound note casually on to the table, "you'll have to excuse us." She stalked off beckoning Cara to follow.

Cara could only stammer "Sorry", and with a faint smile hurried after Catrin.

Lieutenant Anthony Dillon watched them go with a wry smile. He should have known the Gresham was not the place for such a crude approach. The titian haired girl had taken his eye as soon as he sat down. She was very attractive and his curiosity was aroused. Her rebuttal merely increased his interest. He signalled the waiter and waved the pound note she had tossed on the table.

"These ladies seem to be regulars. Tell me who the red haired one is."

The waiter eyed the note. In his eyes it was almost half a week's wage.

"She's the daughter of Mr. Kilpatrick. Well known man o' business in Dublin. I believe she's called Catrin. Bit uppity, but a cracker right enough." He pocketed the pound.

"Do you know where they're going?" Anthony queried.

The waiter hesitated. He was on to a good thing here. Anthony extracted a shilling form his pocket and slid it under his saucer.

"As a matter of fact, sir, I did hear them mention an exhibition. Something about paintings. Probably the one that's just opened at the Parnell Gallery. You might find them there."

Anthony made his way out, collecting his greatcoat and peaked cap from the hat stand. He checked his appearance critically in the ornate mirror and, satisfied with himself, strode through the foyer and into the blustery morning outside.

The exhibition hall was within walking distance and the breeze did not bother him. He wanted another chance to engage this fascinating young woman. The fact that she had snubbed him was of no consequence. On the contrary, it made the chase all the more exciting.

He quickened his step and strutted boldly in pursuit of his prey.

Chapter Three

The exhibition proved to be a disappointment. They had worked their way through most of it and Catrin had seen nothing that fired her imagination. It was Cara who persuaded her to view the one remaining room they had not seen.

First impressions were that it was more of the same. There was only one other person in the room, a man at the far end who was restlessly pacing back and forth. He glanced briefly in their direction and then sat down on a bench, legs stretched out, hands clasped behind his head. She could tell he was bored.

Catrin dismissed the pottery in the first section, but was intrigued to see that the next items were most unusual pieces of driftwood. It was not ordinary bleached driftwood, but pieces that had been turned into shapes that were recognizable as animals, fish, reptiles, and even human figures. Skill and imagination had capitalized on the natural shapes and some had even been tinted with pigments to highlight their characteristics. Driftwood was of no interest to her, but she had to admire the artistry.

She proceeded to a selection of paintings that occupied the upper part of the room, a pleasant selection of landscapes and seascapes, quaint Irish cottages by the lakes, old churches and mountain scenery. She was about to declare she had seen enough when Cara called out to her from the other side of the room.

"Come look at this, Catrin," she said excitedly, "isn't it beautiful." She gestured to the painting in front of her.

It was the largest canvas of the group, distinguished in a splendid gilt frame, and completely different from any of the others. Two lovers, in elegant Edwardian costume sat in a leafy bower sharing a moment of bliss. Their faces radiant and close to each other, her hands clasped in his, and such adoration captured in their eyes. He, handsome and dark haired, she fair and petite with a radiant smile. It was obvious that they worshipped one another. It was a picture that captured the emotions of all lovers.

The strangest thing of all was, that despite the enchantment of the lovers, her eyes were drawn to the other figure in the picture, a young boy spying from behind the hawthorn hedge that hid him from sight.

"Look at the expression on his face," Cara was lyrical, did you ever see such adulation?"

Catrin agreed. She guessed the boy to be about twelve or fourteen years old, the age of puppy love, when spying on lovers is a common mischief. But this boy was no mere Peeping Tom. His arms reached out as if trying to draw the lovers to him, his mouth like a red cherry, puckered as if begging a kiss. It was a brilliant portrayal of the human emotion of love. Whoever had captured the moment understood the feelings of love. This was the kind of inspiration she had hoped to find and she immediately set her heart on acquiring it. "Who's the artist?"

Cara peered closely at the corner. It's someone called Devlin O'Farrell.

"That's incredible. The same artist who painted the others. But this is so different. This is something special."

"It must be, Cara continued, it's got peculiar little things under the signature. They look like little hearts."

Catrin made a closer inspection. Below the O'Farrell signature, a little to the right, were three little red hearts, each of which had a faint little jagged line through them.

"They are little hearts, but why the lines through them? Are they meant to be broken hearts? There is something indeed unusual about this painting. I like it. It would look wonderful in my room. I wonder how much it is? All the others have a price on them, but not this one. What a nuisance!

She looked around for an attendant, but the only person in sight was the man on the bench. He remained in the same bored position.

"Excuse me, she called out, do you happen to have a catalogue?"

He rose and came towards her. Fine looking man in a rough sort of a way, she thought. Pity about his suit.

"I haven't," he replied, "didn't need one. Whit wid you be after knowin?" The broad accent, and the soft, lilting brogue suggested he was from the West.

"Would you know something about this painting?" she asked.

He appraised it for a moment. "Indeed I do. I know a lot about it." The authority in his voice surprised her.

"Do you happen to know the artist?"

"Indeed I do." He was enjoying teasing her, and Catrin began to bristle.

"In that case, do you know how much he would sell it for? All the others have prices on them, but not this one."

"That's because it's not for sale."

"Then why doesn't it say so? Why are all the others for sale and not this one?"

"If you'd bothered to buy a catalogue you'd have seen it wasn't for sale. As to why, that's personal to the artist."

Catrin bridled at his impertinence. She was not accustomed to a perfect stranger winning a war of words.

"Who are you to know so much?"

"Himself. Devlin O'Farrell." He laughed at the look of consternation that appeared on her face

"You? The artist?" she said in disbelief. She judged him to be in his late twenties, a rough diamond in an ill-fitting suit of grey Donegal tweed. A mischievous smile played around the corners of his mouth, and he did not appear upset at her outburst.

He was slightly taller than herself, stocky in build, with dark tousled hair framing a tanned face. Obviously an outdoors man. His eyes were dark, and he sported a small neat moustache, and on the strong rugged jaw a fringe of neatly trimmed whiskers.

"I really like this painting," she said demurely. "It's the most exquisite expression of love I've ever seen. It radiates emotion. I can feel it."

"High praise, indeed. Thank you."

"I would like to buy it."

"There's twenty pities for you. You could have anythin' else in the collection, but not that one. I've already told you. It's not for sale."

"But why not?" She was really angry. "I would give you a very good price."

He shook his head. "Anythin' else but that one. I'd even throw in a piece o' the driftwood for free."

"I don't' wish anything else. I want that one," she stamped her foot.

"Then it's more than twenty pities," he began to get heated, "I'm not after partin' with it." He started to walk away.

"Wait!" Catrin ran after him, "at least tell me more about your work." She had decided to modify her tactics.

He halted and turned in his tracks. "What wid you be after knowin?"

She assumed the plaintiff look that had so often won over her father.

"Has the portrait a name? And why are those three little hearts painted beneath your signature? What do they mean?"

"That's a lotta questions. I'd rather not say."

"Oh please. I like your work. It's only natural to want to know more about it."

He looked at her coldly. The faint smile had gone. There was a glint of anger in the dark eyes. Somehow it gave him an air of pride that made him attractive.

"Flattery'll git you nowhere wi' me, but your persistence is worth somethin'. All I'll tell ye is that it's called The Wishing Boy, but that's all. The reasons I'm after keepin' it are personal. I don't have to tell you or anyone. No disrespect, but money can't buy everythin'. I'm on my way now. Enjoy the rest o' the exhibition."

He walked off briskly, leaving Catrin speechless and angry. She would have paid her twenty five pounds and more. The very fact that she couldn't have it despite her wiles made her all the more determined to have it. It was unique, a talking point, so unusual and skilfully painted. And those little hearts? There had to be an intriguing story behind them.

She walked back to Cara who had remained near the painting. She looked at the face of the adoring boy and could see what inspired the title. The sublime expression on the face and the pleading mouth could so easily be recognised as not only craving for affection, but also as a wish he was making. But what was his wish?

She made up her mind. She must have it and learn what it was.

"Let's go home," she motioned Cara, "He's not seen the last of me. I'll have this painting if I have to track him down and pester the life out of him. You see if I don't."

Cara saw the determined look and the thrust of the jaw, and a shiver of fear passed down her spine. There was something unusual about this painting, and for some unaccountable reason she felt afraid.

At that moment there was a confrontation at the exit. They looked at each other and ran to the scene of the disturbance. There were voices raised in anger, one of which was unmistakably Devlin O'Farrell's. The other was also vaguely familiar.

Chapter Four

Had Devlin O'Farrell not been in such a hurry to flee from the fiery young woman who posed questions he did not wish to answer, and had Lieutenant Anthony Dillon not been in such a hurry to pursue the same young woman, fate might not have intervened. But they were, and it did.

Anthony hurried through the first three rooms and feared he had missed his quarry. He was rushing to enter the last room just as Devlin O'Farrell came bustling out of it. They collided like rugby players, the impact knocking each of them off balance. Anthony was first to recover.

"What the hell d'you mean charging out like that? You eejit!" In his anger the refined Dublin accent vanished.

"Who's an eejit?" Devlin challenged. His anger increased as he saw the military uniform. "Why don't you look where you're goin?"

Anthony stepped forward menacingly. Devlin held his ground. They were about to exchange blows when a slim elfin figure thrust herself between them.

"This is not the place for a scene," she said sharply. "You," she addressed Devlin, "were in such a hurry to leave, since you did not wish to do business with me, so I suggest you get on your way." She turned to Anthony.

"I can't imagine what you are doing in an art exhibition. I think you are out of place and should leave, too."

The men continued to glare at one another, but the artist was first to give way.

"Beggin' your pardon, miss. It was an accident and this fellah should have been more of a gentleman to say so. Sorry about the business matter, but I told you I had reasons. No offence intended. Nice meetin you." He tipped his cap and walked off.

Catrin looked at the lieutenant inquisitively. She had no doubts that his presence was no coincidence.

He read her thoughts. "Why shouldn't I be at an exhibition? I like artistic things."

"Are you sure that's all you came to see?" Behind her Cara cringed.

"Well, not quite." He hung his head in mock shame, like a puppy being scolded.

He looked at her appealingly, and smiled. It was the smile of a skilled charmer.

"To be honest, I had hoped to catch up with you."

"I thought as much, Catrin" said smugly, "you don't shake off easily, do you?"

"Not if the goal is so worthwhile. I believe persistence eventually wins reward."

Catrin beamed at the flattery. His motives were exposed and it would be a pleasure to lead him a dance.

"I think persistence can be a nuisance," she said icily, "it may work for military objectives, but not with us." It was a cutting way of ending the conversation and leaving him frustrated.

She took Cara by the arm and led her away leaving him "We're leaving now. Enjoy the rest of the exhibition. With your interest in artistic things, you'll find this room interesting."

He could not help being bemused as he watched the trim figures disappear, his eyes focussed on the beauty in the long green coat who moved with such elegance.

A thoroughbred filly. Beautifully formed, high strung, skittish, and with energy and spirit. As an accomplished horseman he recognised the characteristics that placed her above the field. The challenge was impossible to resist, but he had to find a way of getting to know her. A straightforward solution eluded him. He made his way from the gallery deep in thought, little dreaming that fate had more tricks to play. Catrin 's disappointment at the exhibition was soon dispelled. Cara's parents were holding a house party that evening, and there would be dancing. Catrin loved to dance. She had a natural gift for movement, light on her feet and beautifully balanced, and she was in her element flouncing around the dance floor, well aware she would draw the attention of every man in the room.

As she prepared herself, she waltzed around her bedroom, humming a melody and periodically pausing to glance in the mirror. She had wheedled her father into buying her a new cocktail dress, black satin, simply styled, which clung to her hour glass figure like a second skin.

With long narrow shoulder straps, the cut exposed a daring amount of cleavage which caused an argument with her mother. Her earrings, necklace, and bracelet were a legacy from her late grandmother, and made a sparkling combination that pleased her.

The McAulliffe house stood in Meirion square, directly opposite the Kilpatricks. It was one of a number of imposing Georgian houses facing each other in Fitzwilliam Street, but separated by the dainty Fitzwilliam Park that divided the streets from one another. The park was an important status symbol, for it was private, for the use of the residents only. It was where Catrin had first met Cara, a petulant meeting with each disputing the other's right to be there.

From such an unlikely beginning, their friendship had solidified into a relationship that strengthened through both school and college years. Cara was her confidante, and they had no secrets from one another.

In the early days, Catrin had been jealous.

The McAulliffe's house had been the home of a foreign diplomat at one time, and had facilities for splendid entertainment. This was a valuable asset, for it was the custom during the winter months for the residents to take it in turn to host parties. But none of the other house possessed a ballroom with a splendid sprung dance floor. Catrin had often wished it was her house.

By the time the Kilpatrick's arrived, there were guest congregating in the large lounge enjoying drinks. A barman and two maids were busy ensuring every guest was catered for, and the noise grew as conversations developed and inhibitions were shed.

Inevitably, the men formed one group, expressing their opinions on politics, business, and the state of the country. The women gathered at the far end of the room, intent on discussing the latest fashions, scandalous gossip, and how well their children were doing. Catrin preferred to circulate, and Cara dutifully followed. Her fiancé, Roger, was in the group of men and would eventually join her.

Catrin's inspection of the crowd was primarily to seek out who would be her most likely dance partners. She intended to spend most of the evening on the dance floor and she wanted only partners who could match her abilities. She was unprepared for the surprise that suddenly materialised.

Two men detached themselves from the group and came towards them. She knew Roger, Cara's fiancé, very well but the other... she was lost for words. He had shed his uniform and was dressed in a smart navy blue suit, extremely handsome and unmistakably the same officer she had dismissed so abruptly at the gallery earlier in the day. She looked to Cara for an explanation, but she was just as mystified.

"Good evening ladies," Roger gushed, "I'd like you to meet an old friend, Anthony Dillon. I bumped into Tony this afternoon. We haven't seen one another for a long time. He's joined the army, and just had a promotion. He wanted me to celebrate with him so I suggested he come here."

Anthony stepped forward and shook hands with them both. His handshake was firm and she thought his hand lingered just a little too long.

"At last. A formal introduction. I ran into Roger just after I left the gallery. There wasn't the time for a long conversation and there was a lot to catch up on. I appreciated his offer. What a wonderful place to have a party."

"Let's have a drink to celebrate," Roger suggested, "it won't be long before the music starts." They made their way to the bar.

"I've got to warn you Tony, Catrin's a fiend on the dance floor. Can wear a partner down to his knees if he's not careful." .

"Oh Roger. Don't go on with you. Perhaps Tony doesn't dance." Cara was jumping in before Catrin had a chance to retort.

"On the contrary," Anthony broke in, "I'm pretty good. I'd be delighted to partner Catrin, if she'll allow me." He looked at her with a challenging smile.

He's baiting me, Catrin thought, but she rose to the bait.

"Of course I'd be delighted. But keep in mind Roger's advice. I don't suffer fools gladly. Does military training include dance instruction?"

"You might be surprised. Anthony looked pleased with himself. He had the fish on the line. His smugness annoyed Catrin and it made her want to cut him down to size.

The dance floor would make a good battleground. But the evening did not work out according to plan. He proved to be an excellent partner, adept at every type of dance the musicians could offer, reels, polkas, quadrilles and especially the latest ballroom dances.

He matched her step for step, perfectly timed, and frequently forced her into hurried movements as he produced variations no one else had ever challenged her with.

At the outset it was a contest of wills. He held her tightly, moving with grace and confidence, light on his feet, and in perfect rhythm to the music, He spun her deftly, circled gloriously, and swayed with such balance. It was almost like flying.

At first he said nothing. He steered her through the maze of dancers with consummate ease, occasionally gazing into her eyes with an intensity that made her quiver. Her willpower was under siege and as the night wore on, she could see she might lose the battle.

When the interval for refreshments arrived, she was glad to excuse herself and seek out Cara.

"I can't get over him," she enthused to Cara. "He's a fantastic dancer. I've never had such a good partner. I can usually manipulate them, but not this one. He's shaken me."

"I can see you're impressed," Cara said, "great change from this morning I must say."

"Don't be silly. I never thought a soldier would know much about dancing."

Catrin was intrigued. She always was with the unusual. But Cara's disclosures matched some of the "There's a lot you don't know about Lieutenant Dillon."

"Has Roger been telling you something?"

"He says Tony's a real ladies man. A bit of a rake. Expelled from a private school over some scandal. His father is high up in the Civil Service and managed to get him into Military College. He seems to have settled into a military career successfully.

She could almost hear her grandfather saying — 'he could charm the hind leg off a donkey, so he could.'

He was waiting for her with a glass of wine, and led her to one of the small tables at the side of the room.

"To the most beautiful woman in Dublin," he raised his glass in a toast, and also the finest dancer."

"Thank you, she replied sweetly, "I now see what you meant by persistence."

"But is it succeeding?" he asked, "Do I detect a breach in the defences?""

"I'm sure I don't know what you're talking about. I'm very surprised by your ability to dance so well. I never imagined soldiers had time for that. How did you learn so well?"

"It's really a military secret, but I can tell you. One of my colleagues at Military College was an ex dancing instructor. He told me it would come in useful for social functions."

"It looks as if he was right."

"He was. At staff dances it comes in very handy. I have made a few useful connections through it."

Catrin decided not to probe further. Cara's information seemed to be well founded.

"Roger says you had a promotion to celebrate."

"Yes. My commission as a full lieutenant just came through. I've been expecting it for some time."

"So why are you celebrating here, and not with your family?"

"Let's just say I have some problems. My father and I don't exactly see eye to eye. I haven't spoken to him for a long time. I didn't see the point in trying to celebrate with him." He finished his drink and glanced in the direction of the musical trio who had resumed playing.

"It's a waltz, my favourite. Would you like another dance?"

For the first time all evening there was no trace of arrogance in his voice. It sounded like a plea and she nodded an acceptance. In the next instant his arm was around her and she as swept to the dance floor and circling the room in glorious style.

By the end of the evening Catrin was captivated. She had never enjoyed an evening more and she was glowing with pleasure as they rejoined Cara and Roger who were bidding farewell to the departing guests.

"You two seem to have hit it off," Roger quipped.

"Couldn't have celebrated my promotion better," Anthony enthused. Never had such a beautiful partner. She was terrific."

Cara looked at Catrin. She had a dream-like look in her eyes. It must have been a good evening.

"Pity you're being posted," said Roger," where are they sending you?"

Catrin suddenly came out of her trance. "You're going away? When?"

"I would have told you before the night was over. I'm being posted to Galway, the back of beyond. It takes the gilt off the promotion, but I have no choice. Now that I've met you, it's going to be a real chore."

"You're a dab hand with the blarney, so you are," Catrin laughed. "Galway's not the end of the world. It's a lovely place. My granddad lives there. We visit him often."

"Really? So you might be able to visit me, too?" Anthony brightened visibly.

Roger caught the eye of Cara and signalled a tactful withdrawal.

"Listen you two. We're going. Best of luck, Tony, and keep in touch. See you soon Catrin."

They left with Cara giving a backward glance at Catrin with a look of warning in her eyes. Catrin ignored it. She had her partner to thank for a wonderful evening and she felt flirtatious.

At that moment Roderick and Megan appeared and called out for her to join them.

"I'll have to go," she said with a trace of sorrow, "let me know how you settle in Galway. I'm sure we'll be there soon. My granddad's always asking us. Thanks for a lovely evening. Sorry about this morning."

She stood on tip toe and kissed him lightly on the cheek, a look of mischief in her eyes. It made his pulse quicken.

He watched her disappear through the front door and then returned to the lounge and sat down at one of the tables. He drew a gleaming gold cigarette case from his inside jacket pocket and extracted a cigarette. He made a great play of tapping the end of it several times on the case, as if showing off, before lighting it.

He sat back, totally relaxed, blowing smoke rings in the air and reviewed his evening's work.

He was well pleased. He had broken through the defences. Given more time he was sure he could affect a conquest. He cursed his posting, for it would make the challenge more difficult. On the other hand he was sure she had been hooked, and she might come to Galway a lot sooner than she imagined. He would have to think up ways to entice her.

He stubbed out the cigarette and sauntered towards the hall to bid goodnight to the hosts. He was genuinely grateful. They had provided an unexpected opportunity for another conquest, and he looked forward to taking up the challenge.

Chapter Five

Catrin had risen late and was having a leisurely breakfast when the phone rang. She had been awake since eight, but lazed in bed recalling the excitement of the previous night.

Despite the caution given by Cara, she had to admit that lieutenant Dillon had made a distinct impression, and he was certainly the most handsome man at the party. She heard her mother ask the caller to hold the line, and anticipated the call was for her.

She picked up the receiver expecting to hear Cara's voice.

"Good morning, it's Tony. I would have rung earlier but I wanted to make sure I didn't rob you of any beauty sleep. How are you?"

"Just about recovered. And you?"

"I'm still flying. What a celebration!"

"Get on with ya," she mimicked a broad Dublin brogue, "You're full o' Blarney, so you are."

He laughed uproariously, and changed to become serious.

"Listen Catrin. I haven't got much time. I'm using the CO's phone and he's liable to come back shortly. Can you meet me for lunch to-day?"

"To-day? You don't give a girl much time."

"I'm sorry. I would have liked to make it a dinner date, but I'm off to Galway in the morning and there's a lot to do before I can go. It may be the last chance to see you for some time."

"Is it so important?"

"It is to me. I was hoping you might feel the same."

"For goodness sake, Tony. We've only just met."

She suddenly realised she had called him by his first name. It had tripped off her tongue quite naturally.

"Let's talk more over lunch. Do you know the Royal Hibernian in Dawson Street?"

"Yes I do. My Da often takes business clients there."

"Good. Can you meet me at one o' clock. I've booked a table."

"You do assume a lot. It's after ten now."

"I know, but that's not a problem to a girl with your energy. You can be ready in no time.

"Oh, God! I have to hang up. I hear the CO coming. I'll be waiting." The phone clicked and left her in wonderment.

She did not like being pushed into any situation, but she had to admit the nerve of the man excited her. Her mother watched the rituals of her preparations with interest.

"Are you sure you should be encouraging him?" she asked.

"It's only a lunch, in broad daylight and in public. What's wrong with that?"

"Nothing. But he might get the wrong impression. It might be wiser to leave things as they were, or is this just another heart you want to break?"

"I don't go around breaking hearts," Catrin protested, "at least not deliberately."

"Maybe you don't do it deliberately, but I've seen quite a few fall by the wayside when you've finished toying with them, and pretty miserable they've looked."

"Oh Mam! All men are like that. Don't go on so. I have standards and if they don't match up I see no point in dragging on, that's all."

Megan sighed. "I sometimes wonder if you'll ever find a man at all. You'll never find perfection in a man no matter how many you try."

"So? I'm prepared to keep looking. Lieutenant Dillon can have his chance. At least he's different from the rest. He stands up to me and gives as good as he gets. I look forward to cutting him down to size. It's all part of the learning process. Don't' worry about it."

She checked her appearance once more in the mirror, and as she ran her fingers through her hair and patted it into place, she requested Megan to call a taxi. She would be a few minutes late, but she regarded that as a woman's privilege.

There was barely five minutes to spare when she clambered into the taxi and ordered the driver to head for the Royal Hibernian. What had seemed an anti-climax of a day had suddenly become exciting.

Chapter Six

"You've had a lot of experience then?"

"How lovely." Catrin glanced at the surroundings of the Buttery. The restaurant was well filled and there was a steady buzz of conversation that supplemented the ambience of the Art Deco décor and created the atmosphere for a pleasant lunch.

"I knew you would like it." I'm a good judge of taste. It was pure arrogance, but Anthony was thrilled that she had agreed to meet him at such short notice. The signs were encouraging.

"You've had a lot of experience then?"

He smiled at the obvious implication "I suppose I have, but there's always more to be learned."

"Does that mean I am very interesting?" She was enjoying the flirtation.

"Very much so. But there's more to it."

Before Catrin could pursue the flirtation further the waiter appeared and requested their order, which effectively broke the thread of the conversation. The meal turned out to be as excellent as he predicted.

Anthony was in his element in good company and the ambience to compliment it. He amused her with some of his army experiences, and she related some of her childhood memories of Galway.

"I'm sure you'll find it a lot better than you think," she consoled him, "my grandfather has a lovely big house there, on the side of the river. I spent all my summer holidays with him, and I loved every minute."

"It seems like the back of beyond to me. I'll miss the hustle and bustle of Dublin, and now that I've met you, I'll miss it even more."

"Oh, Tony. You're full of the Blarney, right enough. There's lots of pretty girls in Galway."

"There won't be one to match you. I'll be miserable wondering when I'll see you again."

"Don't be silly! I'll write to you. There's the telephone. We'll be able to keep in touch."

"It's not the same. You can't maintain a love affair by letters or phone."

"Since when did this become a love affair?" Catrin felt flattered, but at the same time annoyed that she was being taken for granted. Never before had a flirtation turned serious in such a short time.

"You must admit we hardly know one another, and I've told you already I'm not one who jumps into a relationship."

It was time to put him in his place, but Anthony was not put off.

"I knew as soon as I saw you. I could tell you were something special. I wouldn't have followed you to the gallery otherwise."

Catrin felt her cheeks colouring. She accepted he was a real charmer, but this was serious and more than she had bargained for. She recalled Cara's words of warning. She looked at her watch.

"It's after two. Didn't you say you had sneaked out? Won't they be looking for you?"

He looked at his own watch. "Damn! You're right. I'll have to get back otherwise I'll be in trouble." He reached across the table and clasped her hand. "When will you come to Galway?"

"We always come to the Galway races."

"That's not till the end of July. That's months away!"

"Don't be so impatient. There's only one thing I can think of that could make it sooner."

"Tell me. Can I help in any way?"

"As a matter of fact you could. She explained her encounter with Devlin O'Farrell and her determination to track him down.

"That's the fellah I almost had the fight with?"

Catrin laughed. "Yes, that one. Good job I intervened, otherwise you might have come to the party with a black eye."

"He looked a bit of a bruiser right enough. So what do you want me to do?"

"I've found out he lives in Galway somewhere, but I don't know where exactly. Perhaps once you're settled in, you could scout around and locate him. If you let me know, I'd try and arrange to visit my grandfather."

"If that's a promise, consider it done. You promise to come?"

"Yes, of course. I want that painting before anyone else buys it off him."

"It's a deal then." He rose and signalled the waiter for the bill. He came round the table to assist her with her coat and surprised her by kissing her firmly.

"Tony," she blushed. "Not in public. You're like a little boy with a new toy, so you are." He laughed and escorted her outside.

He hailed a taxi close at hand and held the door open for her. As she made to step inside, he pulled her into an embrace and kissed her again. The intensity of it took her breath away. She pushed him away gently and administered a light peck to his cheek.

"Thanks for a lovely lunch, but don't get yourself into trouble. A newly promoted officer can't afford to get on the wrong side of his CO."

She lowered the window and waved to him as the taxi sped off. She sat back, flustered by the attention. She could imagine what Cara would say. Strangely enough, she had the feeling that she would miss him, but it was a happy coincidence that Galway was also the home of Devlin O'Farrell.

She would be very happy to twist her father's arm and arrange a special visit, and she would know better by then just how she should continue the relationship.

It was a thought that circulated in her mind for the rest of the day and she began to scheme how she could persuade her parents to plan a trip to Galway. Daniel, her grandfather was the key. She would telephone him and ask him to invite the family.

Daniel loved fishing and so did her father. Why not suggest they get together?

Chapter Seven

Major O'Brien was furious. He had been the victim of a stormy session with the Commandant immediately after lunch, and as a result was suffering from indigestion. He blamed his discomfort on the young upstart of a lieutenant who stood before him.

"At ease," he ordered. "I've been looking for you for the past half hour. Where have you been?"

"Sorry sir. I had to pop out for some last minute things I needed."

"Why didn't you inform me?"

"I tried, sir. But you were in with the Commandant." It was a blatant lie but he stared the Major straight in the face.

"I've got your rail warrant". He handed it over. "You'll catch the train at 09.00 hours. My driver will drop you off. You should be in Galway by 13.00 hours. A sergeant from the barracks will pick you up. Any questions?"

"What about Private Cunningham?"

"Your batman? He'll follow with the rest. They'll leave in the lorry I'm allocating you. There's another truck at the barracks and also six horses stabled there. You might find them more practical for the area."

"How many men will I be getting, sir?"

"You will have a corporal and eight privates. There's already a sergeant and two privates at the barracks, so you've almost half a platoon. That's more than you'll need, but there's a reason for being generous."

The major was annoyed at the instant disappointment that registered in Anthony's face. The way the army was being dismantled, he was lucky to be getting so many.

"I have your orders here," he indicated a manila envelope lying on the desk, "Better sit down. There's some things you may not like."

Anthony pulled up a chair and sat down, one leg crossed over the other in a challenging pose. It did not improve the Major's temperament.

"I want to emphasise something of great importance. I know what you young upstarts can be like, and I don't want any trouble. You will be in command of the Lombard street barracks, but you will actually be subordinate to the Chief Inspector of the Garda Siochana." Anthony gave a gasp of surprise.

"I stress that," the Major continued. "Your unit is only there because the Gardai have requested support."

"They are aware of unrest in the local Republicans, and suspect trouble. They lost two constables recently in a bomb explosion, and there have been other nuisance raids on Post Offices and government property. The Gardai are responsible for law and order enforcement, not the Army. You will only be asked to help with that if the Gardai request it. I want that perfectly understood."

"But sir, what will we actually be doing?"

O'Brien picked up his pencil and idly twirled it through his fingers as he gathered his thoughts.

"There are a number of things, but there is something else I'll come to in a minute. As you are aware, the government has officially banned the IRA, and is cracking down on them in Dublin. In Galway, the enforcement is not so strict. Your presence will show the people that the government is very determined to keep the peace. You will train your men daily to deal with subversive activities, and let the public see you doing it. But that's as close to military action as you get. Is that clear?"

Anthony mumbled agreement but inwardly he was fuming.

"You will assist with the transfer of prisoners to and from the courts. You will provide escorts for payroll personnel, and you may be asked to house and guard prisoners in the barracks on occasions."

"Taking these chores off the Gardai will free them for other duties."

"With respect, sir. I think this is a complete waste of our military training. We've been trained for combat. These duties could be performed by reservists."

The Major sighed, and tapped his pencil on his desk to relieve his irritation. For the first time in the interview, he felt sympathy for his junior officer,

"I appreciate how you feel, but that is the way we are structured at the moment. There are no reservists. You must know the strength of the Army is being reduced by the government."

Anthony looked glum, but suddenly remembered the Major had said something. "You mentioned another matter?"

"I was coming to that. It's important and you may find it more to your liking. I'm taking a risk telling you, and it must remain in confidence. Have I your word on that?"

"Yes sir." He uncrossed his leg and leaned forward with new interest.

"I take it you know what is going on in Europe?"

"You mean the Spanish Civil War?"

"That, of course. We have a direct interest since both Republican and Blue shirts are fighting in it, but it's not that I was thinking of. People in the know think Germany is re-arming for another war. There's a leader called Hitler who appears to have an ambition to take over all of Europe."

"I thought that was just sabre rattling." Anthony made the remark tongue in cheek. Politics was not one of his interests, but he liked to give the impression that he knew something of current affairs.

The Major was warming to the discussion. "A lot of people think that, but I think there's a lot of truth in it."

"Surely someone will put a stop to him?"

"Who?" the Major smiled coldly. Anthony fidgeted uncomfortably. He had no idea.

"I don't know either," admitted O'Brien, none of the big countries seems to want to fight. Ireland certainly can't. We haven't even the men and equipment to defend ourselves."

"Would Germany attack Ireland?" Anthony was now very interested.

"It's not impossible. If they want to attack England, it would make a good base. The High Command has given it some thought and if a war should come, the responsibilities of the Gardai will change, and the Army will take over the military defence. There is a plan to create a body called the Local Security Force that will combine the Army and the Gardai to enforce law and order."

"Which is why this posting has a great many implications. Can you see what I'm driving at?"

"It puts a different perspective on it," Anthony felt more enthused.

"In a sense," the Major continued, "you are an experimental unit. A lot of people are going to be watching how well an Army unit can work hand in hand with the Gardai. Make it work well and it will smooth future operations if and when the positions of control are reversed. Does that make the posting more interesting?"

"It certainly does. It makes a lot of sense, too."

"That's what I like to hear," the Major was relieved. "First thing you have to do is to make contact with the Chief Inspector. His name's Gallagher. Treat him with respect. Remember there's no love lost between the Army and the Gardai. There's rivalry and jealousy and they won't relinquish authority easily. Earn their respect and prove to me your promotion was justified. That'll be all. I'll see you in the mess this evening and we'll give you a good send off."

Anthony rose, saluted smartly and marched off. He was already dreaming. If this posting was a success he would be in line for promotion to Captain, and before long he would be sitting in the Major's chair.

A relieved O'Brien watched him go. He yelled at his orderly to bring him tea on the double. As he sat sipping it slowly, he relaxed and congratulated himself in dealing with his problem so effectively.

It was a feather in his cap to get Dillon out of the way by actually motivating him. Stringing him along with the purely speculative plans of the High Command was much better than the alternatives. The blistering words of the Commandant still echoed in his ears.

"Get that over-sexed young devil out of my sight. My wife's been showing an unhealthy interest in him. I just found out she bought him a gold cigarette case last Christmas. Can you believe that? The best part of fifty pounds? Well, he's not going to cuckold anyone else. He's got his promotion so get him out of here. Post him as far from Dublin as you can, and do it now!"

It was not such a difficult problem. The Commandant wanted him posted, someone had to go to Galway, and he had engineered it very nicely.

The danger of a scandal was avoided and the Commandant would be off his back. He drained the last of his tea and opened the bottom drawer of his desk to locate the hip flask he kept for special occasions.

As he felt the warmth of the spirit draining into his gullet, he could not refrain from a smile.

A gold cigarette case! The Commandant himself did not possess one.

His smile broadened into a laugh.

Chapter Eight

No one was more surprised than Roderick Kilpatrick himself to be coming to Galway. He had been surprised to receive a phone call from his father, requesting him to come and join him in a spot of fishing. Their next visit was not planned until the Galway Races.

He was reluctant to take time away from work, but pressure from both Megan and Catrin forced his hand. He toyed with the idea of driving down, for his father had not seen his brand new Austin, and it would have given him pleasure to show it off in Galway, where there were relatively few cars in comparison to Dublin. But a drive of one hundred and twenty miles was a daunting task, and although Catrin was capable of sharing the driving, he felt it was too risky. So they travelled by train as they had always done.

It was late afternoon when they arrived and found Daniel waiting at the station with his pony and trap. As if to bid them welcome, the rain clouds parted and a watery sun appeared. Daniel welcomed them with his usual enthusiasm and wasted no time in loading the trap and setting off for home. They travelled along the main road up the western side of the Corrib towards the lough, and about two miles from the town, turned off on to a dirt road which ran for about two hundred yards through dense trees before emerging into the clearing that fronted Dungannon House.

Stately, yet unassuming, the house stood two stories high and was regarded as one of the most imposing in the county. Named after the armed volunteers of a convention held in

Dungannon in 1872 to protest about English interference in Irish affairs, Daniel had let the name remain.

It was the gardens surrounding the house that softened the austere grey building and bestowed grandeur to it. There was no season of the year when there was not a flower, shrub, or tree which did not display colour. Most of the flowering plants had been planted and nurtured by Catrin's grandmother who spent her happiest days in the garden, taking great pleasure in the hundred and one aromatic fragrances that were created as a result of her labours. Sadly her enjoyment was cut short when she had died suddenly from a heart attack when Catrin was only twelve. Daniel drove into the courtyard and pulled up outside the front door. He led the way up the steps leaving Roderick to bring the luggage and bellowed for his housekeeper, Mrs. Donavan to get the kettle on and make some tea.

She was disliked by Catrin and was often the butt of jokes between herself and her father.

She was an austere grey haired widow with a hard set face, devoid of a smile or warmth. Dour and critical of anything that interfered with her established routine, she served Daniel with the minimum of effort on her part, and she skimped on the house-keeping.

As they sat having tea and chatting in the front sitting room, Daniel appraised Catrin with enthusiasm. He doted on her as much as Roderick.

"Saints be praised. I'll swear you're prettier than when I saw you at New Year. Mind you, you've your grandmothers colorings, and it suits you real well, Have you found yourself a young man yet?" He loved to tease her.

He was interested in all the family news but eventually fell to discuss business and the gossip in Dublin with Roderick. Megan retired upstairs saying she wanted to rest for a while, leaving Catrin to do as she pleased.

She decided to take a walk around the house since there was plenty of daylight left and it was a pleasantly mild evening. The surrounding woodlands were alive with the sounds of blackbirds, thrushes and doves, and in the meadows across the river she could hear cattle lowing. It was peaceful, a complete contrast to the noise in Dublin, and it brought back memories of many happy childhood days.

The early Spring flowers were past their best, replaced by hosts of daffodils, hyacinths, and a few tulips and pansies had appeared. In the woodlands the trees appeared to be planted in a sea of bluebells. As she walked around the side of the house she could see the wisteria that climbed the wall was not yet flowering, nor was the rose that was trained to climb the solitary yew tree that stood like a sentry at the side of the large wooden door that led to the walled garden at the rear of the house.

She retraced her steps to the front of the house and crossed the road to the field that bordered the river. She made her way to her favourite spot, a sheltered glade on the side of the river.

She stood on the patch of gravel that had built up along the bank watching the water flow lazily on its way to Galway two miles downstream. The Corrib was deep at this spot, and it was here her grandfather had taught her to fly fish, and to row.

She looked for his boat, and found it under the same clump of bushes where it had always been hidden, and the oars were under another bush close at hand. If the weather stayed fine, she would row up the river as far as the lough, or perhaps to the old ruined castle that was another of her favourite haunts.

She sat down on a tree trunk that had been washed up by a high water and quietly meditated as dusk started to fall. She planned to go into Galway in the morning and start enquiries to find Devlin O'Farrell. She had been disappointed to have received no information from Anthony, but accepted his excuse that he had been too busy settling in to his new position.

She felt guilty at not having told him she was coming, but she wanted to surprise him, and she had not wished her grandfather to think that it was Anthony behind the real purpose of her visit. If she had told Tony, he could have embarrassed her by turning up at Dungannon House.

How he would react when she suddenly told him she was in Galway would be interesting, but she would make her enquiries about Devlin O'Farrell first before springing the surprise.

She was tired after the long journey and went to bed shortly after returning to the house. Her mind was seething with activity with the result she was a long time in falling asleep.

Two miles downstream, in the Lombard street barracks, Lieutenant Anthony Dillon also had a restless sleep, but it was not through worry. On the contrary it was due to excitement.

Chapter Nine

He stood in front of his shop in Eyre Square and ranted and raved to himself. He had one of the best locations in the Square, and he deserved better. The window display looked unappealing, and the wrong type of goods appeared to have been flung into it at random.

He stormed into the shop bellowing for attention. His temper flared again when he saw no one in sight.

"Eamon! Eamon! Where the devil are you? Git out here!"

The office door at the rear of the shop burst open and a young man raced out. He stood nervous and apprehensive in front of his father.

"Sorry Da. Didn't know you were coming to-day. It's been quiet all day. I thought I'd catch up on the paperwork." He looked down to his feet, to avoid his father's hostile gaze. Maguire could smell a lie a mile away.

"I'm surprised you have any feckin' bookwork to do. Who's gonna be attracted by a window display like that?" he gestured to the window. It looks like a tip. Book-keepin' you say?" He pushed past Eamon and made for the office. Eamon scuttled to the front of the shop anxious to distance himself from the tirade that he knew would follow. Maguire appeared from the office brandishing a book in his hand and halted in front of the cowering Eamon.

"Book-keepin' is it? I thought as much. Bliddy poetry of all things." He threw the book in disgust, catching Eamon a sharp blow on the chest. It clattered to the floor, spine up, and the pages spread-eagled. Eamon looked at it sorrowfully but made no move to retrieve it.

"How the hell d'ye expect to do business reading that tripe? Bad enough hidin' in the office, but to be reading' that!" He gave the book a kick that sent it sliding along the floor.

"These kinda' books are for silly women. Read somethin' more manly if you have to read. I sometimes wonder if you really are a son o' mine. Thank God Seamus is no' the same."

His maltreatment of the book brought out a faint spark of rebellion.

"Mam used to read that book. She wasn't a silly woman. She loved poetry." It was a daring statement for he feared his father.

"That's enough, Maguire warned, keep that mush outta my sight. Don't let me catch you neglectin' your job for that tripe. Maura should know better. Where is she, anyway?"

"She went out to bank some money and get stuff for tea.

"How much has she banked?" he barked."

Eamon darted to the till and produced a sheet of figures that Maguire glanced at quickly. His face froze.

"God almighty! Is this all you have to show for the past three days?" He flung the sheet at Eamon.

"You'd better pull yer socks up the pair o' you. Just twenty pounds and a few coppers? That's not good enough!"

His tongue lashing was interrupted by the appearance of a young woman who bustled into the shop. She had overheard his outburst and leapt to the defence of her younger brother.

"What's the matter Da? Why are you so angry?"

Maura Maguire was more experienced in dealing with her father than Eamon. She would bear the flow of insults and criticism stoically, and then calmly pick up the pieces when he was finished. She was tactful and acted as her father expected of her, obedient and subservient, but deep within her a flame of resentment burned. The only sign of her feelings was the sorrow reflected in her large dark eyes.

Maguire respected his daughter. She was more attractive and smarter than other Galway girls. As beautiful as her mother, God rest her soul, and just as pretty. She had that same type of Catalan nobility, too.

She was one of the jewels in his possession, and he guarded her jealously.

"I came round to see if you knew where Seamus was, an' I find the shop empty an' his lordship here sittin' in the office readin' poetry. Not even Irish! Then he shows me your takin's fer the week so far. Jaysus Murphy! It's a disgrace. An' no wonder. Look at the window. It's like a jumble sale."

The place is not even clean, he swept his finger under the ledge of the counter and held up his hand to show a small grey smudge.

"It's not good enough Maura. I want it sorted out by the mornin'. I'll be in to check it an' I better see an improvement. I wis askin' about Seamus."

"He's off with Dev some where's across country. He said he'd be back for tea".

Seamus was her older brother, often a protector of both herself and Eamon when Maguire's temper got out of hand. Three years older than herself, he was tall and lanky, a quiet but determined man who obeyed his father but was not afraid to clash swords with him. Like herself, he had dark brooding eyes, but unlike Maguire, Seamus was heavily bearded. He seldom smiled, and his feelings were locked away in the deep recesses of his mind.

He had been brought up in the difficult times of the twenties had been brainwashed since infancy to fight for Irish liberation.

"Good. I've something important to talk about. I'll be off then. Jest remember what I've told you, an' pull yer socks up. I'll see you later." He stomped out the door, leaving it wide open. Maura stood on the step watching him out of sight. He'd be making for Rafferty's to check on his haulage business.

Rafferty was the Quartermaster of the Brigade. They were always planning something.

Eamon had retrieved his book and nursed it to his chest. Maura put her arm around his shoulder and comforted him.

"C'mon Eamon. I'll give you a hand to sort out the window. I should never have let you do it on your own, anyway, but you have to learn. Next time you'll do better. We'll give the place a good clean in the morning. And I'll stand in the doorway and welcome the passers by. When he comes to inspect us the place will be buzzing."

"You don't hate poetry, do you?"

"Of course not. Mam used to read it to us. I loved it. She read it so beautifully. You could almost see the pictures in your mind."

"Why did she have to die?"

"I don't know. She was there one day and gone the next. Seamus knows something, but he never talks about it. He's always been closer to Da." She patted him gently on the head, "c'mon now. We have to get this window sorted."

Seamus appeared in time to join them for supper. Maguire sat in his accustomed place at the head of the table. He proposed the blessing and signalled to Maura to pass around the bowl of steaming potatoes whilst he proceeded to carve thick slices of cold bacon to be placed on each plate.

There was no conversation. It was the custom to wait for the head of the house to speak first. It was half way through his meal when Maguire paused and laid down his knife and fork.

"Maura says you were across country wi' Dev," he addressed Seamus.

"Aye. We were checkin' old man Murphy. He's startin' his still to-morrow an' Dev wanted to make sure he was OK."

"Was he?" Maguire resumed eating.

"Sure. But he's moaning like hell. Reckons he'll finish for good after this year. Narry enough money in it. Thinks you should be payin' him more. He's heard a rumour that the Excise is callin' in the Army to help them stamp out the few stills that have survived the last purge."

"It's more than a rumour. This bloody government!"

He banged his fork on the table. "They've reduced the tax on whisky so our stuff can't compete. Not content to let it rest at that, they've promised to drive us outta business. What do these feckin' politicians know?"

"There's loads o'folks prefer our precious to real whisky. They've already closed down all the bad stills in the country. Why can't they rest at that? Ours is top quality, better value than whisky.

"You can get drunk quicker, that's for sure", laughed Seamus.

"It's nuthin' to laugh about. That Poteen Murphy turns out is the best there is. We've got to try an' keep him sweet. I've got feelers out in Belfast. Better prices for it there. Maybe I can spare him a copper or two more. I've still got a good market for the stuff, so I'm not lettin' any rumours about the army put me off. I'll pay Murphy a visit myself and remind him o' a few things."

He pushed his plate aside even although he had not completely finished.

"Belfast? That's a long haul," Seamus was impressed.

"Not for us. Rafferty has several lorries in and outta there every week. Picks up stuff at the docks an' delivers it all around. There's still a crew operatin' in Mayo. They want the best grain, an' that comes into Belfast from Scotland. I've got the market cornered so you tell Murphy from me that there's still money to be had. What about Dev? Is he still behavin?"

"Doesn't touch a drop now. But he's a bit tetchy at the moment. Didn't like that last job you gave him. He knew one o' the constables."

"It wasn't his fault. If those two had followed instructions, they'd still be here. Anyway, this isn't the place to talk about it."

Maura was about to open her mouth to speak but Maguire cut her off. "Make the tay, Maura. Take Eamon with you. Seamus an' I have business to talk about."

Maura signalled Eamon to join her in the kitchen. They both knew Devlin did special work for their father, but they were never allowed to be present when Republican business was being discussed.

Maguire waited until Maura had brought the tea before he began his discussion. He took a few sips and waited until he was sure she was out of ear shot.

"You'd better watch your movements from now on," he warned Seamus.

"For why?"

"You know there's soldiers arrived in the barracks?" Seamus nodded.

"Gallagher's just told me that they've been authorised to run horse patrols over parts o' the county as of next week. They have a right to question if you look suspicious." Maguire sipped his tea as Seamus digested the information.

"I thought Gallagher assured you there would be no trouble from the army. Is it because o' the last job? I told you it was risky. There was every chance someone would get hurt."

"Shut yer gob about that!" Maguire set his mug down heavily sending a slop of tea on to the table. "If those two gobshites of constables hadn't been so damned nosey they wouldn't have got themselves kilt. Anyway, It's two less to trouble us."

He swept the spilt tea off the table with a sweep of his hand.

"Gallagher assures me these soldiers are jest a cosmetic exercise forced on him by Dublin. But don't get careless, an' stick close to Dev. Keep your guns handy. There's plans in the offing, and Dev is very important. I've already put the word around that anybody tryin' to get to him is to get short thrift."

"Don't worry. Dev an' I know how to take care o' ourselves."

"Fine then, but watch out for the smart aleck of a lieutenant in charge. Gallagher doesn't trust him. Thinks he's ambitious an' might try to do more than he's officially allowed. If he does, we'll plan something for him."

"I'm off to the pub now. I've left Brendan long enough. He'll be wantin' off home. I'll see you in the mornin'"

He donned his jacket and made for the door calling out to Maura that he was on his way to relieve his barman.

The front door slammed behind him and as the echo of his footsteps died away, Maura and Eamon emerged from the kitchen and joined Eamon.

For a short time they could exist together as a family and converse about pleasant things. From Seamus they could draw strength.

Flann Maguire would have growled displeasure if he had known, but his mind was on other things as he drove back to his pub in the village. Extra troops in the barracks was not something he had anticipated, and he had unhappy memories of his last encounter with the Free State Army. He had no intention of another period of detention in the Curragh.

He had the advantage of knowing the territory and had numerous powerful contacts in strategic places. The new officer would have to start from scratch, and he would find the locals hostile to his presence. He certainly could count on Gallagher to see that the Garda would offer him little help.

The thought pleased him and a fleeting smile crossed his lips, but his eyes quickly resumed their normal baleful look. He imagined the new lieutenant strutting around the barracks twiddling his thumbs whilst the Galway Brigade carried on as normal.

He'd soon tire of nothing to do except spit and polish and might be tempted to stick his nose out. That would suit him fine. He'd happily give him a bloody nose. The cold smile returned.

Chapter Ten

The drive into Galway was delightful. It was a fine dry morning with the hint of a fresh wind blowing up the river, and the pony and trap bowled along with Catrin and her mother revelling in the serenity of the countryside.

No rattle of tramcars, or noxious petrol fumes. It refreshed the senses and brought colour to their cheeks. It was a wonderful contrast to the stinks of stale urine and horse dung that clung to the city streets.

Catrin loved the countryside, and her annual visits to Galway had always provided pleasure. Her vocation probably lay in the city, and she had a love of Dublin, but that was largely due to the relatively good fortunes of the family. Had she ever explored the other side of the Liffey and experienced the dreadful slums of Gardiner and Gloucester streets, she might have revised her opinion.

They found O'Brien's livery stable and left the trap there whilst they explored the shops. Catrin's plan was to start her enquiries at a central point and work her way around until she found the information she sought. She left her mother in the aptly named Shop Street and made for Eyre Square.

Maguire's Gift and Craft shop seemed a logical starting point for there was a display of driftwood figures and paintings in one window that looked similar to the work she had seen in Dublin.

She pushed open the door and walked in. A few tourists trawled the variety of ware that was on display on counters that stretched to the rear of the shop, which went surprisingly far back. At right angles to the entrance, a large glass topped counter held a selection of Celtic jewellery, behind which a young man stood, rather pale and self-conscious. He smiled nervously and bid her good morning. He had long black hair and his dark eyes had a deep sensitive quality. His hands rested on the glass top and she noticed how long and slender his fingers were. The fingers of one hand tapped on the glass top, as if he was playing an imaginary tune. She smiled a greeting in return.

"Can I wander around and browse?" she asked.

"Certainly. Call me if there is anything you want to know."

She made her way towards the display of paintings at the rear, hoping The Wishing Boy might be on display. She had a nagging fear that the artist might have changed his mind and decided to sell it. But there was no sign of the painting she sought.

"Are these the only works of Devlin O'Farrell?" she asked the young man.

"You know him?" he asked as if he was surprised.

"I saw some of his work recently at an exhibition in Dublin. I actually spoke to him. I presume you know him?"

"To be sure. We know him well. He works for my father."

"You mean he does other work as well?"

"Oh yes. The driftwood is seasonal, and he fits in the painting amongst other jobs. My Da has lots of work for him. He can turn his hands to many things."

"That's good. You might be able to tell me where I can find him."

A frown crossed the young man's face. "That's rather difficult."

"Why?"

"He's a bit of a tinker, so he is. He works at things all over the place. Sometimes he's away from Galway for days at a time. It's difficult to pin point his whereabouts."

"But he must have a home somewhere nearby?"

"He lives outside of Galway. Out in the country somewhere," he was beginning to stammer.

"Where exactly?" Catrin's patience was becoming exhausted.

"I can't tell you. As a matter of fact he doesn't want strangers coming to his house."

"I can't accept that," Catrin was getting angry, "any artist interested in selling his work would be glad to see someone who wanted to buy it. I would like to see the manager," she snapped, "is he about?"

The young man turned beetroot red and did not know where to put himself. He was saved by the sudden appearance of an attractive young woman who entered the shop. She had heard Catrin's request as she entered and immediately sensed trouble. She placed the shopping bag she was carrying on the counter, and turned to Catrin."

"Can I help?" she said pleasantly. "I'm Maura Maguire. I manage the shop. This is my brother Eamon who assists. What seems to be the problem?"

Catrin explained the nature of her enquiry and explained it was specifically the painting of The Wishing Boy that she was interested in.

Maura knew immediately what she wanted. "It's certainly the best work he's ever done, but there's a sentimental value to it. You'd be wasting your time."

"I'd still like to meet him," Catrin remained determined.

"That's very difficult. At this moment he's gone to do a job in Connemara. But in any case, I can say quite definitely that he won't wish to sell it."

Catrin gave a sigh of exasperation. She would have to continue enquiries elsewhere, but this shop was obviously a base he might visit.

"If I leave you my address, will you please contact me if he shows up? I'll be in Galway for a few days."

Eamon picked up a pencil and prepared to write. "What name, please?"

"Miss Catrin Kilpatrick. I'm at Dungannon House. Telephone me if you could."

Dungannon House?" Eamon glanced at Maura, "you must be related to Daniel Kilpatrick?"

"I'm his granddaughter."

"Of course! I should have recognised you," Maura exclaimed. "I used to see you sometimes, rowing on the lough. That was a long time ago."

"You were on the one side, and we were on the other."

A bitter memory flashed through her mind. The other side of the lough was for the rich – they were on the poor side. She smothered the thought and smiled.

"I remember what pretty dresses you used to wear. I used to envy you staying in such a grand house."

"I'm sorry I can't recall." It was a curt reply. Catrin could not fake sympathy.

"Please call me if Mr. O'Farrell shows up. I'll drop everything to meet him."

She flounced from the shop, banging the door behind her. She was convinced they knew more than they were prepared to admit, and she was furious. She strode angrily along the square, her face flushed and her eyes flashing, narrowly avoiding a collision with a couple as she turned into Shop Street and located her mother.

"Let's have some tea before I explode," she commanded, and piloted Megan into a nearby tea shop. She related the events over a pleasant cup of tea and expressed her frustration.

"There's something strange," she said. "I'm sure they were lying. But why? I only want to buy a painting off the man, that's all. I'm sorry, Mam, but I'll have to make enquiries elsewhere."

"Of course, dear." Megan was anxious to calm her daughter. "We'll ask in some of the other shops. Someone's bound to be able to help."

But she was wrong. Despite numerous enquiries, even at the Post Office, no one appeared able or willing to supply information. They returned to Dungannon House tired and frustrated.

When they were all sat at dinner, Catrin repeated the events of the day to Daniel.

Devlin goes everywhere, Connemara and Mayo quite often, and often he goes over to the west. Maguire keeps him busy, but you can bet he'll know where he is."

"But where does he stay when he does come back?"

"He has two places. There's a small farm called Ballanalee off the coast road to Spiddal. Been in the family for as long as I can remember. He has another place not so far from here. Up the lough a bit."

"It's not visible from the road or from the lough. It's too well hidden by the trees."

"Has he ever done any work for you?"

"Not work exactly. But I see him now and again. He brings me a supply o' Irish whiskey when I want some."

Roderick laughed. "You old devil," he chortled, "it's a drop of the precious stuff you get. You've given me some for special customers. It's better than whiskey."

"That's supposed to be secret, Roddy. Don't go blabbin' it. It's true, though. Devlin acts as a distributor. I told you he was clever. He worked for a spell at the University an' knows a bit about chemistry. Rumour says he has a hand in makin' the stuff an' Maguire is the boss man"

"Would Maguire speak to me?" Catrin asked.

"No. Don't tangle wi' him, Catrin. He's got fingers in a lotta pies, an' dirty fingers at that. He rules his family wi' a rod o' iron, and he's a nasty piece o' goods. Steer clear o' him."

"Oh Danna!" she exclaimed, "I'm not going to do his man any harm. I simply want to buy his painting. I need to know the story?

"What's so special about it?" "

"I want to write about it. I've been looking for ideas for months. I just know there's something very special about this painting. I want it, and I shall have it!"

Daniel reached across the table and grasped her hand. His concern showed.

"Catrin. Let me give you a wee bit o' advice. My dear Nell, God rest her soul, used to say, **"never wish too much for something — you might get it."** She'd say it to you if she was here to-day. Heed what she said, for there's truth in it."

The subject was dropped but not forgotten. Later, as Catrin lay in bed, she found herself repeating Daniel's words. He was giving her a warning and she had a suspicion that he knew more about Devlin O'Farrell than he let on.

He should have known better how determined she could be. His warning only served to strengthen her ambition and she resolved to go into town in the morning and pursue enquiries elsewhere.

Chapter Eleven

Catrin was off to Galway as soon as she had finished breakfast. She left the pony and trap at O'Brien's and made straight for Eyre Square. Armed with new information, she was in a mood to confront Maguire himself.

She bounced aggressively through the door ready to confront the hapless Eamon, only to stop in her tracks. Flushed and flustered she beheld Anthony, handsome and smart in uniform, talking to an extremely attractive dark haired girl, the same girl who had introduced herself the previous day as Maura Maguire.

They stood close together, and in an instant she knew she had disturbed a flirtation. They moved apart the instant they heard the door open, but the girl was smiling at some remark, and his mannerism betrayed guilt. As he saw who it was, his face registered utter astonishment.

"Catrin," he exclaimed, "for heaven's sake. This is a surprise. I had no idea you were here. Why didn't you let me know?" He moved towards her.

"I'm equally surprised to see you. I seemed to have interrupted something." She turned to leave, her petulance showing precisely how she felt.

"Catrin. Wait a minute. Let me explain. I've just been asking Miss Maguire to help me select a present. A surprise for you as it happens." He indicated Maura with an outstretched arm and hastened an introduction.

"Maura, this is Catrin, from Dublin. We became friends at a house party just before I was posted." His voice had the ring of a plea.

"It was only in April," Catrin reminded him icily. She had no intention of helping him out of his embarrassment. Her attention focussed on the girl. She had been too agitated the day before to analyse her closely, but she knew instinctively she now had a rival for Anthony's affections.

She was the same height as herself, and her colouring suggested a Spanish influence. Jet black hair had a soft gleam to it and flowed halfway down her back. Her olive complexion was pale in comparison to the large dark eyes, and the bright red lips were full and generous. She was slender and moved with the grace of a dancer, the kind of girl that would attract any man. She recalled Cara's warning about Anthony.

"It's Miss Kilpatrick, isn't it?" Maura broke the awkward silence. "I didn't expect to see you again so soon."

"I don't suppose you did," Catrin's reply was blunt. "I'm sorry to have interrupted your business. I'll come back when you're not busy." She made no attempt to hide her sarcasm and turned to leave.

"Wait a minute," Anthony pleaded, "please give me a chance to explain. I was just —

"That's alright, Tony," Catrin dismissed him with a wave of her hand. "I have other things to do. Just carry on your discussion. I'm sure Miss Maguire will give you every assistance, that is, if she wants to." It was a reference to the lack of co-operation she had received yesterday.

The barb struck home and brought colour to Maura's face. Catrin sallied out the door in a temper, leaving it wide open. Her mind was in tumult. What increased her anger was the pang of jealousy that surged through her heart.

She had first claim on him, and she burned with resentment now that she had competition. She was half way along the square before she realised she was heading in the wrong direction.

Anthony watched her disappear with dismay. He cursed his luck. He had grown tired with the half promises Catrin had made about coming to Galway, and her sudden appearance had shocked him. If she had given him notice in advance, he would have ensured the situation would not have arisen.

His first few weeks in Galway had been miserable. He missed her and the social life of Dublin dreadfully, and all the passion that he nurtured for her was kept in vain. He needed to love and be loved, and the estrangement built up intolerable frustration.

One morning, as he made a leisurely patrol in the town centre, he spotted an extremely attractive girl entering the Gift shop. He was unable to resist following her and with no one else in the shop at that particular time, a perfect opportunity arose to introduce himself. His looks and professional charm did the rest. Even by his standards, his progress in such a short time had been remarkable.

She was an apple ripe for the picking, and easy meat for a charmer with his skills and experience. Her voice interrupted his thoughts.

"So you met her in Dublin? In April? You don't lose much time, do you?" Maura was piqued.

"I don't really remember much about it," he lied. "A friend of mine wangled me into a house party. There were lots of girls there. It was quite a swell affair."

"You'd like that," Maura remained piqued, "classy people and with money to boot," she made to turn away. He grabbed her shoulders and spun her round to face him. "You could hold your own with the best of them." He made to kiss her but she broke away.

"Stop that. Not here. If my Da was to come in and see us, he'd murder you. You mustn't fuss me in public. It's dangerous."

He released her. It was ironic that Maguire had a daughter who was by far the prettiest girl in Galway, and yet had no suitor. Maguire had made sure of that.

He felt that Maura and he were soul-mates, each longing for love, but frustrated. Their clandestine meetings made the liaison exciting, and added zest to their passions. It was a flame which once lit, could not be extinguished.

Anthony was infatuated with her, and she with him. But seeing Catrin again had reminded him of his former ambitions, and he was not one to abandon any conquest he had set his heart on. Besides, Catrin had class and society connections. Maura followed him to the door.

"When will I see you?" she asked. The fact that the Kilpatrick girl had known him, and was obviously interested in him, had sparked jealousy.

"I don't know," he confessed, "things might be busy for the next few days. I'll sneak out and let you know as soon as I know. O.K?"

He squeezed her hand affectionately and stepped outside. He quickened his stride and narrowly missed colliding with Eamon as he made towards the shop.

He continued on his way, unaware that it was Maura's brother.

Eamon stared suspiciously after the fast disappearing figure. He had seen the officer several times around the shop and wondered why. He made no connection between him and Maura, for he knew she controlled her emotions well, a direct result of the tyranny her father imposed on all of them.

Any thoughts in his head were forgotten immediately as Maura pounced on him as soon as he entered.

"C'mon now Eamon. We need to have everything tidy before Da gets here. Let's do the cash receipts first," she handed him the cash box, "you count up and I'll enter the figures in the book. Then we'll tidy the window display."

***

At the same time they settled to their tasks, Catrin had composed herself and cooled her anger. She had decided to call in at the police station. She now knew she was seeking an unusual character, and the Garda were likely to know anyone unusual.

The police station was an unattractive square block of a building, dilapidated, the glass windows streaked with dust and the frames needing a coat of paint. The heavy wooden door creaked as she pushed her way into the reception. A smell of stale tobacco smoke hung in the air, and she was confronted by a portly, middle aged sergeant, perched on a stool, his elbows planted on a writing desk that dominated the main counter.

"Devlin O'Farrell did ye say?" he repeated in answer to her question. "An' who exactly wants to know, an' whit wid ye be after him for, ah'm askin'?"

Catrin explained who she was and the fact that Daniel Kilpatrick was her grandfather.

"Git away wi' ye? Old Daniel's granddaughter. "Well, well, well," he shook his head in wonderment. "An' ye have business wi' Dev? Whit kind o' business?"

Catrin bit her lip. She recognised the signs. The information she wanted was not going to come easy.

"That's between me and him. Just tell me how I can find him. It seems he could be staying in one of several places. I'm prepared to visit him if that's the only way I can meet him."

"Are ye now?" The sergeant was eyeing her suspiciously. "Easier said than done. He comes an' goes from one day to the next."

Catrin boiled inwardly. His answer was a repeat of all the answers she had heard from everyone she had questioned.

"Has he ever been in trouble? Have you ever had to haul him in for something?" She decided a new tack might yield better results.

The sergeant laughed heartily. "Dev in trouble? No, no. Not him. He's too smart to be in trouble wid us. He's a decent sort. Had his share o' troubles, so he has, but never a problem to the law."

"What sort of troubles?" she asked. Suddenly she felt there might be an opening. "Naethin' serious. Hit the bottle fer a spell. He has good friends. They got him sorted out."

"What was the cause?" she felt she was gaining ground.

The jovial countenance of the sergeant faded and he assumed a stern face.

"That's somethin' personal. Sorry, miss, but Ah've given ye all the information I can.

In any case I've heard tell Dev desna want strangers snoopin' round his property. Now if ye don't mind, I've got paperwork to do."

He picked up his pen and turned his attention to the pile of papers on his desk.

Catrin marched out with undisguised fury. She was convinced there was a conspiracy to screen this man of mystery from her, and it was building a frustration she could not bear. She picked up the trap from the livery stable and headed back to Dungannon House, venting her anger by cracking the whip at the pony.

She expected another rebuke from her mother, but Megan had other things on her mind.

"You'll never guess," she exclaimed excitedly, "that young lieutenant you met at the McAullife's party came asking for you. He said he had met you in town but he hadn't a proper chance to talk to you. He seemed very anxious to see you."

"I'll bet he was." It was a tart reply, that surprised Megan.

"Well, I thought it was nice of him to take the trouble. He is such a dashing young man, so grand and smart in his uniform. Did you know his father's very high up in the Civil Service?" she gushed.

"I've invited him to come to dinner. It will be nice to have some new company to entertain, and you seem to get along with him very well."

Her enthusiasm was so great that Catrin restrained herself from blurting out her experience in the Gift shop. Her mother loved giving dinner parties, and it would help bring the old house back to former glories, and besides, it would give her a chance to test Anthony out.

She spent the afternoon helping to prepare for the dinner and she began to feel the excitement building. The only note of displeasure came from Mrs. Donavan. She was openly hostile to all the extra trouble being taken to entertain an officer of the Free State army.

Promptly at seven-thirty, a small dark green van pulled up outside and Anthony stepped out. He had changed into a dark blue lounge suit, smartly cut and perfectly tailored. Only his regimental tie betrayed his military origin. Catrin was at the front door to welcome him.

She had decided to give him a run for his money, and made an elegant picture in a pale blue evening dress, low cut, emphasising her shapely figure. She had fastened her hair up creating a regal appearance that had Anthony gazing in wonderment.

"You look wonderful," he managed to say, his eyes roving over her. Catrin's eyes glowed. It was going to be an exciting evening.

"I'm glad your mother gave me the chance to try and make up for this morning," he said as Catrin escorted him into the lounge, I felt really badly about it. I really was looking for a present for you." He reached into his pocket and brought out a small presentation box.

She opened it and found a lovely Marquisate brooch in a unique Celtic design nestling inside. She was impressed. It must have cost a tidy sum.

"It's lovely," she gasped, but she could not resist a comment. "Miss Maguire must have been very helpful."

He flushed but took his punishment nobly. "I made the choice. She merely confirmed she thought it was a good one. Do you really like it?"

"Yes, I do. I have some outfits that it will suit perfectly," she gave him a peck on his cheek. "Come and meet my grandfather. I call him Danna. I used to call him that when I was very small."

As a social function, dinner was a great success. After army rations, Anthony found the food and wines to be excellent and the conversation was intellectual and gave him a splendid opportunity to show off his skills as a raconteur. He impressed the men with tales of the army, and plied Megan with a flow of compliments. His strategy was to win over her parents first, and hopefully they would support his cause to help him regain Catrin's confidence. He had every confidence – since the presentation of the brooch Catrin had begun to mellow.

The success of the dinner and his star role of entertainer reminded her of the wonderful evening at the McAuliffe's party, and she wished there was a dance floor in Dungannon House. Nevertheless, she was not going to fling herself at him. It was Megan who suggested she show Anthony over the grounds while there was still daylight left.

"Leave all the clearing to Mrs. Donavan," she told her, "I'll give her a hand."

Catrin welcomed the opportunity. She hated washing up. Anthony was one last hope to find out the location of Devlin O'Farrell. She would remind him of the request she made in Dublin, and now that was doing penance for his flirtation, she might force him to help her.

She had shown him around the garden and was leading him across the meadow towards the river when she sprung the subject on him.

"Tony," she asked plaintively, "have you had a chance to meet some of the characters in Galway yet, I mean apart from Maura Maguire."

"I thought I had explained that. What sort of characters do you mean?"

"Don't you remember. I asked you before you left Dublin. Devlin O'Farrell, the one who painted the picture I wanted to buy."

Anthony smiled. "Oh yes. The fellah I nearly had the fight with. What about him?"

"Oh Tony. I told you if you helped me track him down I'd come down to Galway immediately. I've been asking all over the place, but nobody will own up to telling me exactly where he is. I need help."

"Now I remember. Sorry. I had forgotten all about it. I've been busy since I arrived."

"I could see you've been busy," she said sarcastically.

"For goodness sake stop bringing it up!" It was the first time he had been so curt with her. She was impressed. There was something magnificent about him with a look of anger in his eyes.

"I can understand you're thinking, but you didn't give me a chance to explain fully. I've been calling into the shop several times hoping to meet Maguire himself. He's the commander of the local Republican brigade and I want him to know I'm keeping tabs on them. I can't rely on the Garda. They turn a blind eye to a lot that's going on in Galway. I won't pretend Maura's not an attraction, I only try to worm some information out of her about her father's activities. I can assure you Maguire doesn't let any man get involved with her, and certainly not an army officer."

It sounded plausible and she decided to relent and consider a less hostile interpretation of the shop incident. He had bought her the brooch after all so perhaps his story was true.

Dusk was falling as they reached the banks of the river and there was a stillness broken only by the soft swirl of the water against the remains of a tree that lay half in and half out of the water. Catrin sat down on the upturned boat her grandfather had left out after his morning's fishing. She clasped her hands in front of her knees, gazing pensively in the direction of the lough, waiting expectantly for the first signs of an evening star.

"This is one of my favourite spots," she told him. "I've loved it since I was a schoolgirl. This is where Danna taught me to fish." She felt at peace and totally relaxed. The after effects of the wine were permeating her brain and there was a wave of warmth coursing through her body. She did not react when he sat down beside her, not even when his hand rested gently on her shoulder.

"I can understand why," he murmured softly, "it is a perfect spot. So restful. There are times I get fed up to the teeth in the barracks. I wish there was a place like this to flee to. If only you could stay. What a difference it would make."

He slid his hand from her shoulder to her neck and began to gently stroke it. She closed her eyes and nestled closer. He took it as an indication she was ready for romance and kissed her. It was a searching kiss, hoping for a passionate response, and his body tensed in anticipation. Catrin allowed it to linger a moment, but suddenly broke off and stood up.

"Don't rush things, Tony. I told you in Dublin I don't jump into relationships. I'm still not sure I can trust you. This morning really upset me."

"Forget that. I told you why I met her. I won't rush you, Catrin, but it is difficult. A letter or two isn't enough for me. I need to see you, not just fantasize. I need to touch you, to smell your perfume. Can't you find some way to stay here? I'll bet your grandfather would love to have you stay. Can't be much company for him with that grizzled old housekeeper,"

Catrin laughed. "She drives him crazy at times, but she's been with him for almost ten years. I can't get away from Dublin permanently. Perhaps I can manage an odd week-end. The Galway Race week is only a month away. The whole family comes for that. Try to be patient."

She rose and extended her hand. "C'mon. We need to be getting back." They walked hand in hand back to the house. The military van was already waiting for Anthony and he bid a quick farewell to Megan and the men. She permitted him a goodnight kiss before he climbed into the van and waved him off.

She shouted after him "don't forget about Devlin O'Farrell. I'll be sure to come and see you if you find him."

She could not be sure he heard her, but there were other sharp ears that did. From the dining room window where Mrs. Donavan was putting away the last of the cutlery, she saw the van drive away and heard Catrin's shout.

She nodded to herself. She would telephone Flann Maguire at the first opportunity and inform him that an army officer was being requested to locate one of his most trusted men.

He was always interested in information concerning the military, and what would he make of a young woman determined to track down one of his most valuable servants?

She could hardly wait to sneak to the telephone.

Chapter Twelve

The following morning was another glorious day. Catrin sat in the dining room finishing a late breakfast, basking in the sunlight that streamed through the open windows. Megan and Daniel were already in the garden, and her father had gone for a walk.

Mrs. Donavan sulked in the kitchen, annoyed at Catrin requiring a separate breakfast. She consoled herself by recalling the way Flann Maguire had praised her for delivering her information.

Catrin suddenly put down her cup and dashed to the window. Hoof-beats sounded in the court yard and she gasped as the rider appeared. Anthony, his uniform smartly pressed and his Sam Browne belt and boots polished, as high as the harness of the splendid horse he was astride.

The horse was magnificent. A golden brown gelding whose coat shone like silk, at least sixteen hands high and standing as proud as a champion. She flew into the hall and out the front door to greet them.

"What a surprise," she gasped, "and what a beautiful horse. Where did you get him?"

"Comes with the job," Anthony smiled, "there's five more at the barracks, but this one's the pick of the bunch. He dismounted as she reached up to pat the horse. "He's called Rufus, and you're right. He is a beauty."

He was hoping for a kiss, but at that moment Megan and Daniel appeared round the corner of the house, curious to see what was going on.

"Good morning Mrs. Kilpatrick, and you sir. Such a beautiful morning I had to ride over with Rufus and show him to Catrin. I believe she loves horses."

"She always has," said Daniel. "It was one of the attractions that made her glad to visit. I used to have four at one time. Irish Cobs. Strong and sturdy. They'd burst their hearts for you. Catrin used to ride them. Good little rider she was. But we've only got the pony now, no need for any more."

"Different story for us," replied Anthony, "modernisation hasn't reached us yet. My unit is attached to the Irish Lancers. In this part of the world the horse is very useful for cross country work.

"Have you any riding gear?" he asked Catrin who was still fussing the horse. "I could easily arrange for another horse and we could go for a canter."

"Wouldn't that be grand, Catrin," Megan exclaimed. "She loves riding. I'll go up the attic and see if her things are still there. Why don't you come in and have tea while I take a look?" She ushered everyone inside.

Anthony sat at the kitchen table whilst Mrs. Donavan grudgingly made the tea. It was the best tea he had drunk for ages and he complimented her. Catrin marvelled at his charm. Even the housekeeper. She smiled as she watched Mrs. Donavan refill his cup. He sat with his booted feet planted firmly under the table feeling like a lord.

"Had you made plans for to-day?" he asked Catrin.

"Not really. But it's such a fine day, I ought to spend it outside. Did you have something in mind?"

"I had intended to bring another horse, and if you had some gear we could have gone for a ride. But the horse I had in mind turned out to be waiting to be re-shod so that idea fell by the wayside. But we could do it to-morrow."

"I'd love to," she was genuinely excited. I'm sure Mam will find my old gear. I don't think my figure's altered very much. It should fit."

Anthony cast an approving eye over her figure. She was undoubtedly a catch. He could not determine whether her eyes were light hazel or pale green, but they shone like the sun, mirroring her energy and vitality. A pert nose and a wide generous mouth which indicated to him that she was sensual and sensitive. At this very moment she was the only woman in his thoughts.

"I know what we could do," Catrin jumped to her feet excitedly. "We'll go for a row on the river, maybe as far as the lough. It's a perfect day for it. We could be back for lunch. That suit you?"

"Great," answered Anthony, stirring from his comfortable seat, "but why just the morning? Couldn't we make it the whole day?"

"Not to-day. I want to go into Galway and find the Parish Priest. He's another who may know something about Devlin O'Farrell. I'm still anxious to find him."

"Why not give it a rest?" Anthony suggested. "Enjoy your holiday. I've promised to start ferreting around for you. I'm sure I'll find him for you. Trust me."

"I don't want to wait a minute longer than I have to. I must get to him first before he decides to sell it to someone else. He's a tinker. He'll need money."

"Alright, alright!" Anthony was alarmed at the feigned hysteria. "I'll start making enquiries right away. Will that please you?"

"You did promise. If you found him for me, I'd forgive you everything." It was a subtle reminder that she was still smarting over the Gift Shop incident. She skipped towards the door, pausing for a moment. "Let me get changed. Put Rufus in the stable with the pony. There's plenty of feed there for him."

Ten minutes later they were dragging Daniel's boat into the river, and with Catrin taking the oars, they headed upstream towards the lough. Anthony lounged in the stern, his hand over the side and trailing in the water. He could hardly believe his luck. Alone with this beautiful creature, rowing him upriver as if she was his slave. She was as good at rowing as he had expected and skilfully manoeuvred the boat against the current.

As she strained at the oars, and pulled faster to gain speed, his gaze was riveted to her bosom. Each stroke tightened the fine fabric of her blouse against her firm pointed breasts, revealing the outlines of her nipples. He glanced momentarily at the trees lining the banks, fearing she might rebuke him for staring at her, but Catrin was too engrossed in her labours. Had she been aware of the lust mounting within him, she might not have been so relaxed.

Further down river, in Galway, there was trouble brewing. Maguire had called in at the shop in Eyre Square to check the previous day's work. His monitoring seemed to be paying off. The window display was more attractive, the shop was better organised, and Eamon seemed more industrious.

However, he had just taken a telephone call from Dungannon House that disturbed him. Mrs. Donnovan informed him that Catrin was out with the army officer from the barracks and that she was planning to come into Galway in the afternoon to make further enquiries about Devlin O'Farrell.

"Damn the girl," he burst out as he replaced the ear piece. Maura looked up from her paperwork.

Something wrong," she enquired.

"Nothing much. Just a fiddlin' little problem. Go an' make us a cup o' tay. I could do wi' one."

It was an excuse to get Maura out of the office. He made a point of keeping as much Republican business from her ears.

With Seamus it was different. He had been literally brought up with a gun in his fist, and was a strong believer in the Republican cause. He waited until Maura's footsteps disappeared into the small kitchen.

He picked up the phone and waited for the operator. "Annie, git a hold o' Rafferty for me. He's at the haulage office. Hurry now. It's important."

"That you, Rafferty," he queried? "Anyone with you? Liam Rafferty was manager of the Maguire haulage business, and also acted as Quartermaster to the Galway Brigade. He had served with Maguire in the Limerick Brigade during the Civil War and was as cold and callous as Maguire himself.

"Ah'm on me own. Whit ye after?" Rafferty was on the alert. Maguire usually came to see him in person.

"There's a job needin' done. Urgent. Any vans available?"

"Only the thirty hundredweight. The rest are out on jobs."

"That's all it'll take. Bring it over to O'Brien's. Ah'm comin' over to the stables me self in five minutes. Ah'll tell you what it's all about when I get there. Be quick about it, an' get hold o' Danny and Mick an' have them there as well. They'll be needed."

In the meantime on the river, as they progressed towards the lough, Anthony was enjoying himself. He had already found the heat of the sun too much, and had removed his tunic and his tie.

"Why don't you let me row," he suggested, "you must be getting tired."

"I could keep this up for hours," she laughed. "I have to row. You don't know where you're going."

"Where exactly are we going," he asked.

"Relax Tony. Won't be long." She was sculling lightly now, occasionally stopping and letting the boat come to rest in the current before starting to row again. It was tranquil, not even a breeze, nothing but the faint bleating of the sheep on the distant hills, and the wild cry of gulls that circled the lower end of the lough.

Catrin had decided it was too warm to row too far and she reduced her strokes and began to guide the boat towards the bank. As they rounded the bend and emerged from the trees, a little stone jetty came into view. A hundred yards or so behind it, stood the gaunt, grey ruins of a large building. Anthony sat up with interest.

"Welcome to my fairy castle. I used to play here when I was small."

"Perfect spot for a castle," his gaze took in its strategic position. "Nothing could ever attack Galway from the river." He was impressed.

"It wasn't really a castle. It was a fine big house. They only called it a castle because it was so tall. Come and I'll show you."

The jetty was in poor condition but she laid the boat skilfully alongside and tied a rope to the solitary mooring ring that remained. They climbed from the boat and made their way towards the ruin. She had taken his hand and he grasped it fondly, his fingers occasionally squeezing hers hoping for an encouraging response.

If she had noticed, Catrin paid no heed. To her it felt as if they were brother and sister exploring for buried treasure. To Anthony it suggested that his charm was beginning to work.

The house was larger than it appeared from the river, with long extensions running a good distance back from the ruined tower that dominated the front. It had once been three stories high, proud and imposing, but now an empty shell, desolate and forlorn. It lacked a roof, and all the flooring had gone. Every window stared vacantly at the desolation surrounding the building.

Within the walls, Jackdaws had taken possession of the empty fireplaces and had built their large twiggy nests. Their incessant cawing heightened the air of melancholy.

"Where we're walking now was once lovely gardens," she informed him as they waded waist high through the tall grass. It used to belong to one of the tribal families in Galway. It was a grand house in those days. Lots of parties, balls, picnics on the banks. Every May they used to hold a big regatta. People came from all over the country to take part."

"So what happened to it?"

"There was a terrible fire. It burned to the ground. There was a daughter and a maid lost in it. They had no money to rebuild it. Some say the ghost of the maid still haunts it."

"When did all this happen?" He had taken a firm grip on her hand, and there was a slight pressure in response.

"Before I was born. Danna told me all about it. I used to come here on my own sometimes, and play in the ruins, frightened in case there really was a ghost. Let me show you something." She pulled him strongly and he stumbled against a stone. She put an arm out to save him but with no effort he slipped into her arms.

His eyes looked into hers. They were pale green. He searched for a response, but she laughed and skilfully pulled away. It was his turn to laugh, but his excitement grew. She seemed in a mood for flirting, and he would take advantage of it.

She took his hand and led him to the front of the building and walked towards the far side where there the remains of a paved terrace were still in evidence although sadly overgrown with weeds

It would have afforded a splendid view of the lough at one time. From the front of the house, a large opening overlooked the terrace, where French windows must have provided an entrance to the terrace from the house.

"This must have been the ballroom," she pointed inside the large opening. "See what a splendid size it was. I used to close my eyes and imagine I could hear the music, and see the fine ladies and the gentlemen waltzing around the room, and then they would come out on the terrace here to cool off and take in the view, and" —

"Talk about romance?"

He took her hand in his and placed the other around her waist and proceeded to waltz slowly. Like two ghosts dancing amongst the weeds.

His gaze never faltered from her face, but her eyes were closed in bliss. Once again she could hear the music, the laughter and the gaiety. Her fairy castle was still alive in her mind.

She was vaguely aware of his lips brushing hers, but it seemed natural. As they slowly swayed together, their lips fastened to one another, and the passion that had been festering inside him all morning had to be released. He kissed her fiercely and with such intensity, it broke the spell. His hand had moved to her breasts as she opened her eyes and became aware of his movements.

"Why did you have to spoil it?" she snapped. She pulled away from him.

"It was so perfect. Now you've ruined it. I want to go back now." She made to march off, but he caught her arm and restrained her.

"I'm sorry. I couldn't help it. I got carried away. It was just as you said. A magical moment. I could hear what you heard. Feel what you felt. I was sharing everything with you. It had to happen. Can't you see I love you?"

Her anger was deflated. It was an unexpected declaration.

"You shouldn't say such things," she rebuked him in a quiet voice." It's much too early. It was a magical moment, but don't rush things. I'm not one of those foolish women who swoon and fall into your arms so easily. You've a lot to prove first. I want to go back now. Remember, I want to go into Galway. I'll let you row me back."

She made the concession in the hopes that it would soften the rebuke. His declaration was so unexpected and she needed time to digest the implications. But she also wanted to let him know who was the boss in the relationship, and who would be the one to regulate it.

Anthony was not consoled. He did his best to mask his feelings, but he felt humiliated and his ego bruised. Once the oars were in his hands, he rowed with fierce energy, venting his anger with each stroke that propelled them rapidly down the Corrib.

Catrin watched him from the stern, a mischievous smile hovering on her lips. Perhaps that would knock some of the arrogance from him and bring him to heel. It was a speculation that was naive.

Within him, the fires of lust had been fanned, and he did not know how much longer he could control the blaze.

Chapter Thirteen

Despite her petulance, and his resentment, lunch was a pleasant affair. Megan warmed to his flattery and there was no doubt he was making a good impression. As he took his leave, Catrin watched him canter down the drive and had the cheek to blow him a kiss as she waved him off. She was aware she was teasing him in the same way she had often teased boy friends, but she was clear on the strategy. If he really was in earnest about his declaration of love he would have to prove it.

Within half an hour of his departure, she had the pony harnessed to the trap and was off to Galway. She drove into O'Brien's yard and pulled up at the large double doors of the stables. The place appeared deserted.

"Anyone there?" she called out. "Mr. O'Brien? Can someone please look after my horse and trap?"

It was the first time there was no answering voice and she was puzzled. She alighted from the trap and entered the stables. It was eerily quiet. Only the sounds of the horses munching feed. She felt uneasy.

A muffled knocking sound came from a stall at the end of the stable, where the light was poor and she could not make out where the sound came from. She made her way to the rear, expecting O'Brien or one of his lads to be come to and meet her. The door of the stall was only half open. She pushed it further. As she stepped inside a figure launched itself from the shadows, and in an instant a rough sack was thrust over her head and she was thrown to the ground with her arms pinned behind her.

Her scream was cut off abruptly as a hand was clamped over her mouth. She struggled and kicked to get free, but the hands that held her were strong and unyielding.

"Git a rope on her," she heard a coarse Galway voice command and she felt her wrists being bound with coarse twine. She began to struggle and attempted to scream.

A heavy hand cuffed her ear.

"None o' that. Jest do as yer told. Give up strugglin' an' keep quiet. No harm'll come to ye, but if ye as much as squeak, I'll beat the tasty outta ye." He pushed her head down roughly. She lay still, her mind in turmoil, trying to come to terms with what was happening.

"Somebody would like a word in yer ear, that's all. Nuthin' else will happen to ye if ye co-operate. Don't do anythin' silly an' ye'll ner' see yer folks again. If ye don't, well" — he left the sentence unfinished.

She heard the sound of a vehicle coming into the yard and a squeal of brakes as it pulled up outside the stable doors. Rough hands lifted her bodily and carried outside where other hands lifted her into whatever vehicle it was. From the echo she speculated it was a covered van of some sort. She was pushed to the floor and she felt some sort of covering pulled over her. She struggled again, fearing being smothered.

The sacking was irritating her face and neck and her struggles only made the discomfort worse. Someone knelt down beside her and used his knee to push her into the side. She screamed in protest and was rewarded with a blow to her head. She blinked the tears away and lay still.

The vehicle restarted and moved off, lurching and bumping its way out the yard and gradually picked up speed. She tried to follow its route by listening for different noise that might give a clue as to where she was being taken, but gave up after a few minutes as it was too difficult to hear over the noise of the engine.

She guessed it was about twenty minutes before it slowed down and bumped over the cobbles of another courtyard. By now she was cramped and extremely hot and uncomfortable, and the dust -laden sacking was choking her. The vehicle braked to a stop and she was hauled to her feet, grasped roughly round the waist, and handed down to someone else who set her feet on the ground.

She struggled and almost broke free. "Keep your filthy hands off me," she yelled as she tried to remove the sacking. A heavy blow knocked her to the ground and she lay dazed for a few moments. She was petrified as she heard her captors talk.

"Take it easy, fer Christ's sake. Himself said no rough stuff. He wants her in one piece."

"Wid he be wantin' her fer himself? She's a good lookin' bit o' stuff, so she is."

"Shut yer gob. Git her inside."

Rough hands dragged to her feet and a strong hand gripped the nape of her neck. "Jest carry on forward, same direction as I'm pushin' ye," the voice commanded. She was being pushed into a building, an old one. There was a strong musty smell and it felt cold. Still held firmly by the neck she was pushed down a passageway and swung into a room. There was litter on the floor and she had an immediate fear of mice.

"Sit down." A chair was pushed against her legs and she was compelled to sit. Her knees trembled and she was shivering. She could feel eyes watching her, eyes that regarded her with curiosity, but with no more respect than for a sack of flour. No one spoke.

The sacking was becoming unbearable. And still no one came. She knew they were waiting for someone. She could not imagine what she was here for. Was it a kidnap and they would hold her to ransom? She heard footsteps approaching and someone entered the room. Whoever it was brought fear with him.

The door slammed shut, like the dreadful sound of a prison door closing. There were steps, heavy, measured and threatening, moving around the chair, first one way and then reversed. There were eyes, cold and merciless boring through the sackcloth, terrifying her. She drew her knees tightly together to check the trembling. She heard a chair scrape on the floor as it was drawn up close to her. Then silence. The suspense was making her sweat.

"Well then," the voice was not what she expected.

"What have we here?" It was not asking a question, but mocking her. Someone stifled a laugh.

She found courage and raised her voice. "Why am I here? What is the meaning of this? You have no right." Under the canvas hood it was unbearably hot and scratchy.

"Take this filthy thing off my head and let me see who dares do such a thing." Her temper was real and suddenly she was less afraid. Someone laughed at her audacity.

"Quiet!" The laugh stopped immediately. There was cold steel in the command.

"Listen Miss. You're not here to ask questions. You're here to answer some, an' I want straight answers. Co-operate an' ye'll not be harmed. Cause trouble an' ye'll be very sorry."

"I can't speak with this thing over my head. You'll have to take it off. I need some air."

"That's unfortunate," the voice maintained its mocking tone. "The hood has to stay on. It's customary to hold interrogations this way. The Brits taught us that. But since you're a woman, we'll make allowances." He barked at someone.

"Use your knife. Cut a slit for her to speak through. Be careful wi' that thing. You're liable to cut her nose off." The hood was seized and pulled away from her face. She muffled a scream as the point of a heavy blade slashed the canvas immediately in front of her nose. It was ripped downwards to expose a slit she could press her lips to. She could breathe better.

"What is it you want from me? Why do you call this an interrogation?

"Because that's what it is. I won't tell you again," now there was real menace in the voice, "I'll ask the questions. You just answer them. I don't intend to hurt you, but annoy me enough an' I will."

Her knees resumed trembling and she fought to keep them still.

"What are you doin' in Galway at this time o' year?"

"I'm on holiday. Visiting my grandfather."

"Who might that be?"

"I imagine you know him. Daniel Kilpatrick of Dungannon House. He's well known in these parts. He'll be most upset when he learns what has happened. He'll have the Gardai after you." A burst of laughter erupted. She calculated there must be at least three of them.

Her spirited outburst made her feel better but she was unprepared for the hand that slapped her across the cheek and made her eyes water as she screamed.

"I warned you not to be smart. Just straight answers. Understand, or do you want more o' the same?"

She blinked away the tears and they ran down her cheeks. Her mouth was so dry, she tried to moisten her tongue with the tears.

"For someone who's supposed to be on holiday, you're showin' too much curiosity for your own good."

"I don't know what you mean."

She heard the chair scrape on the floor and realised he was drawing it closer to her. She imagined his eyes boring into her and his hot breath on her face. She was frightened again.

"You're trying to be clever again. Don't. My patience is running out. You're going around askin' a lotta questions about a certain individual. I want to know why?

She suddenly knew what he was driving at, and at the same time she began to realise why she had found it so difficult to get people to say where Devlin O'Farrell could be found. Everyone was being scared off, and this was the person responsible. He must wield a lot of power.

"I don't have an interest in anyone. Why are you treating me like this?"

She shrieked as a hand grasped the hood and twisted it to pull her forward. Now she could feel his breath on her face, and it stank.

"Oh but you do," the voice hissed like a frenzied snake. "You know very well who I mean. Answer me dammit! He tightened the grip on the hood and she feared he was going to strangle her.

"The only person I've been trying to meet is an artist called Devlin O'Farrell."

"That's better. So why would you be so interested in him?"

"I saw some of his paintings in an exhibition in Dublin. I simply wanted to buy one, that's all," she was on the verge of more tears.

"Have you managed to meet him?"

"No. No one will tell me where I can find him."

She cringed, expecting another blow, but there was merely a loud grunt.

"Well now. Let me warn you. Forget all about paintings an' anythin' else, Drop any idea o' meetin' with him. He is to be left well alone. Is that plain enough?"

She sat in silence. The threat was plain enough, but she wanted to declare her defiance. But nothing would come. She did not know what to do. She heard him get up from his chair and the dreaded sounds of his steps as he passed behind her. Without warning, a hand seized the back of the hood and twisted it tightly. She yelped as her hair was pulled.

"I asked you if the warning was clear enough. I'm waiting on the answer." The grip tightened.

"Yes, yes. I heard you." She was panicking. "You're suffocating me. Please let go."

He released his grip and pushed her upright. He walked to his chair and resumed his questioning.

"Tell me somethin' about lieutenant Dillon. What's goin'on between you an' him?"

The question took her by surprise, but she found it easier to answer.

"We're just friends. I met him in Dublin quite recently. Just before he was posted. His family are friends of ours. We met up again in Galway the other day, that's all."

"Are you sure that's all? I hear he's been askin' around, too."

"Maybe he has. It's part of his job as a soldier."

"What d'you talk about?"

"The usual things. Family, friends, the weather —sport. We're both interested in horses."

"Nothin' about his work? Does he ever ask about... our mutual friend?"

"He never discusses his work with me."

"I find that difficult to believe. I've heard he boasts about it."

"He's never done that with me."

"That's even harder to believe. Why was he posted here?"

"I don't know. I've told you he doesn't discuss military matters with me. If you must know, he's trying to court me."

"Is he now? Well heed my warning Miss, for it might affect him as well. I don't want any more prying into the affairs o' Devlin O'Farrell. I want you gone from here and back in Dublin before this week is out. Stay around askin' fool questions an' you might just finish bein' fished out o' the Lough. More than that, Dungannon House could go up in flames. It's bin spared up 'till now, but it might run outta luck. Old man Kilpatrick's bin ridin' his luck for some time. It might not last."

There was a venom in his speech that brought bile to her mouth and she felt ill.

"You're gettin' away lightly this time. Wherever you go you'll be watched. If there is a next time, you'll be very sorry."

He rose from his chair and walked towards the door. She would never forget the menace of those footsteps.

"Get her back an' make sure she gets home in one piece. Don't dare lay a hand on her unless she tries anythin' funny." The footsteps retreated and slowly faded. She heard the outer door close.

The relief in the air was perceptible. But she was given no time to relax.

"Let's be havin' ye, Same as before. No funny stuff." Once again she was steered by a hand on the nape of her neck and thrust on to the same vehicle that had brought her.

She sat quietly running over in her mind all that had happened and what had been said. There was little doubt in her mind that they were Republicans.

The way he had mentioned the Brits was a giveaway, and his questioning about Anthony suggested the same thing. The

Free State Army was disliked as much as the British. The threat against Dungannon House frightened her. There was no option but to return to Dublin, at least for the time being, and her quest to find The Wishing Boy would have to be put on hold.

The truck rolled into O'Brien's yard and she was lifted down and held as it drove out of the yard.

"Yer pony an' trap's ready fer ye. I'm goin' to cut ye free. Count up to sixty afore ye take off the hood. If ye dare whisk it off afore we're clear, ye'll no see Dungannon House this night. Got that?" She nodded agreement.

She felt the knife cut through the twine and she gasped with relief to have her hands free once more. She massaged them vigorously to restore circulation. She did not count to sixty, but waited a short time and then tore off the wretched hood.

She breathed the fresh air as if it was nectar. The trap stood nearby and she climbed aboard with her legs still shaking There was no sign of her abductors, nor of O'Brien. She wondered if he too was held somewhere.

She sped back to Dungannon House as fast as she dare go, and flung herself in the door crying for Megan. The house was in an uproar until she had calmed down and was able to speak about her ordeal.

Roderick took the threats seriously enough and pulled Daniel to one side.

"We'd best get the first train back in the morning. Catrin's badly shaken and she's worried about the threats to the house. There's no point in trying to be stubborn."

Daniel agreed, but the first priority was to see to Catrin.

"Get her up to bed, Megan. I've got some pills that'll help her sleep. A good night's rest can work wonders. I'll git a hired car to take you to the station in the mornin'"

"I don't want to go," Catrin protested, "why should we give into thugs like that?"

She was still protesting as Megan and Mrs. Donovan hustled her upstairs, and within minutes the house became quiet once more.

Despite the pills Megan had insisted she take to make her sleep, it was a long time before she finally dropped off. It was a tired Catrin that got into the hired car in the early morning and took them to the station. Daniel waited until the train had disappeared out of sight and then had the car drive back to the house.

He made for the stable and quickly harnessed the pony to the trap. He returned to the house and a few minutes later emerged with a bulky object wrapped in a large towel.

He laid it carefully in the bottom of the trap and climbed aboard.

A light flick of the whip and the pony cantered down the drive and out on to the dirt road leading through the trees. Mrs. Donovan watched him go full of curiosity, but she had no idea of what he was up to. She was glad the Kilpatrick's had gone. Her routine would get back to normal and she could take things easier. She fingered the half crown in her pocket that Maguire had given her as a price for her information. She was sorry Catrin had been given such a fright, but she should not have been so nosey.

Five miles away, on the opposite side of the Corrib, Flann Maguire was in his pub close to the lough side at the top end of the village. He was at the far end of his bar talking with two customers who were drinking and conducting a heated argument in Irish. He heard the sound of someone clumping into the snug at the opposite end, but

The stained glass partition that separated the snug from the bar was closed, and he could not see who it was.

There was a bang on the counter and a loud voice called for service.

"Maguire. I'll be after some service if you please, or even if you don't please!"

Maguire was livid. No one dared address him in that fashion. He strode furiously to the partition and slid it back with a thud. He froze immediately, the colour draining from his face.

Daniel Kilpatrick stared at him, anger glinting in his eyes, but it was not the stare of hatred that alarmed him. It was the twin barrels of the shotgun, resting on the counter and levelled at his chest. He noted both hammers were cocked.

"What the hell are you playin' at you old fool? Get outta here an' take that stupid gun wi' you. You've bin at the precious again."

The two men at the far end of the bar edged their way towards the back entrance and slid outside leaving Maguire to his fate.

"You're oh so good at givin' warnin's Maguire. Well now I'm givin' you one. If you or your thugs dares harm any o' my family, or come anywhere near my house, you'll have me to answer to, and my talkin'll be done wi' this."

He banged the barrels on the counter and the clunk of metal on wood made Maguire flinch.

"What are you talkin' about you old fool? Have you lost your mind?" He licked his lips nervously.

"You know damn well what I'm talkin' about. I know it's your crowd o' thugs that abducted my Catrin yesterday an' put the fear o' God in her. You're good at that, but try it again and I'll give you this."

He elevated the barrels slightly and pulled both triggers in quick succession. The hammers fell with a dull click. He laughed at the consternation on Maguire's face and his hurried attempt to duck. He broke open the gun and exposed the empty chambers.

"Next time you try scare tactics, they won't be empty. So I'm givin' you a warnin'." He gave a final hostile glare before stomping outside.

Maguire wiped away the sweat that had formed so quickly on his brow and waited until he heard the pony canter out of the yard. He was shaken, but not for long.

"Stupid bastard! By Christ I won't forget. Your time's not long off old man. Jest you wait an' see."

Kilpatrick was an enemy of long standing. The backhand way the old man had beaten him to the purchase of Dungannon House remained an old score to be settled. He would ensure his name was pushed further up the list of offenders to be dealt with, and some day, when the uprising took place, the score would be settled. In the meantime he had succeeded in getting rid of the girl.

Mrs Donavan had reported the departure of the family a short time ago. Devlin would see to the jobs he had planned for him without the risk of her interfering.

But there remained the small matter of the lieutenant.

Chapter Fourteen

He pondered about the two women in his life. His first weeks in Galway had been miserable. Everything seemed dull, dismal, and damp. He missed the cosmopolitan society of Dublin and the many attractions it held for him. He missed Catrin, and cursed his posting to such a provincial outpost. But things had changed when he met Maura.

The opportunity to ply his skills as a seducer gave him the kind of stimulation he thrived on, and he took pride in being a master of his craft. Within a few weeks the relationship developed faster than he could believe, and he was amazed at her willingness to succumb to his wiles.

He had assumed at the outset that she was merely a shop assistant. Had he known she was the daughter of the IRA Brigade commander in Galway, he might have had more sense. But he didn't, and by the time he was aware, he was infatuated with her, and she with him.

To be able to satisfy his lust with such a beautiful woman made life in Galway bearable, and the clandestine nature of their trysts made their love making all the more passionate and exciting. Thoughts of Catrin were fleeting.

She remained desirable to him, but she was not attainable. Her letters were cold comfort, and she never seemed to be in when he telephoned. He knew she had been warming to him before Maguire had driven her off, and she was still a challenging conquest. But, as the old proverb said – 'a bird in the hand...

He could afford to smile at his dilemma. Maura had a natural beauty, whereas Catrin had the sophistication. Maura was a peasant, but Catrin had the class, and moreover, a wealthy background. But Maura was available.

It was not the first time in his life that he had plied his charms with two women at the same time. He thrived on the danger. He recalled Dublin and the Commandant's wife.

As if in remembrance, he picked up the gold cigarette case and replaced it in his pocket.

He had suspected that Major O'Brien had other motives in posting him to Galway in addition to the speculative future security control, but now he could see a definite mission to proceed with, and his spirits rose. His immediate action would be to arrange another secret rendezvous with Maura and start to pressure her for information about her father. Less than a mile away, Flann Maguire was the most satisfied. The Kilpatricks were gone and the threat to Devlin had gone with them. He was satisfied from the girl's answers that the young lieutenant knew next to nothing about him, and as for old man Kilpatrick, he would act when the time came.

He was also pleased with the improvements at the shop. His rebuke to Maura and Eamon appeared to have worked wonders. Business was up, and the shop looked better organised and much more tidy. In fact, he had never seen Maura look happier. Not only did she look more attractive, but she was actually glowing, and full of energy. She was inspiring more custom, and she had taken to making personal deliveries to outlying customers, sometimes as far away as Spiddal.

With such improvements, he was able to visit less frequently, and the business was none the worse for that. It never occurred to him that there might be other reasons why Maura looked so happy.

He was a traditional Matriarch, and guarded her zealously from being taken from him. He believed his iron will had imposed itself, and that she was happy enough to conform.

It was as well he could not read her mind. Maura's new lease of life had a simple explanation. She was in love! A joyous situation, but also one of concern.

She had literally been imprisoned by the obsessive behaviour of her father, and such was his power and influence that no young man in Galway would dare try and woo her. He had two burly men who worked in his haulage business who took care of such problems.

It made her terribly unhappy. She was a deeply emotional girl and craved for affection. She wanted to find true love, but due to her father's overzealous protection, she had begun to fear that her life would never be fulfilled.

Meeting Anthony Dillon had changed her life the instant she met him. He was the most handsome man she had ever seen, and with his film star looks he also had charm and personality. He was from another planet. He showered her with compliments and made her feel like a lady. He captivated her with tales of Dublin and other places she had only heard of. He stirred ambitions within her that she had long resigned herself as being impossible.

The first day he had followed her into the shop, his uniform should have turned her off immediately, but he was so striking in looks, so smart, so neat, so confident and smiling to melt any heart, she blinded herself to the consequences.

It may have been one of the days her romantic yearnings were high. Whatever the reason, she allowed her emotions to over-rule common sense, and Anthony took full advantage of her naivety. From then on, life had a new meaning.

He had persuaded her into meeting him in secret, hence the sudden excursions in the pony and trap on the pretence of delivering goods to outlying customers.

Such were the fires smoldering within her, that passions inflamed beyond control, and she could not believe that love could be so wonderful. Her response to his demands exceeded Anthony's expectations and surprised him, and he found himself losing control.

He was aware he was lighting a fire amongst the tinder grass, a situation he had always taken care to avoid. But he was weak. As the daughter of a hard line Republican, Maura should have heeded the warning signs

If she were to be caught, the consequences would be serious, but her need to love and be loved was too great to heed common sense, and because the relationship was with a lover who was opposed to everything her father believed in, she had no one to turn to and confide in.

It was as well that Flann Maguire slept as easily as he did, and was unaware there was a time bomb being primed to explode within his own family.

Chapter Fifteen

The Galway race week was a tradition that had been celebrated for one hundred and thirty years. A glorious sporting occasion enjoyed by the tribes and their relatives, and by others not only from all over Ireland, but also by enthusiasts from distant shores.

By far the most important week of the year, it was an annual pilgrimage, to see old faces and renew friendships. To others it was a chance to follow the horses and gamble, a time for frivolity, and get drunk.

There was a carnival atmosphere with the main streets hung with flags and bunting, banners of all sorts advertising events, and the population swelling by the minute.

The Connaught Tribune ran features on every race and was filled with advertisements and details of all the events. This year was always going to be more spectacular than the last. The pubs were well stocked in anticipation of the week's revelry, and the Garda had two extra constables drafted in to deal with any disturbances. The shopkeepers looked forward to the hosts of visitors with money in their pockets and increased sales.

Maguire's Gift shop was typical. It would open for longer, which was a disappointment for Maura and Eamon, but they arranged to work a staggered system so that they could at least see some of the festivities. They were to have the afternoon off on the second day of the races at Ballybrit, as this was the occasion of the Maguire Handicap.

Sponsored by himself, he had entered two horses, one to be ridden by Seamus, and the other by Devlin. Both loved to race, and were accomplished horsemen, and the horses had been brought in especially from Limerick.

Maguire was no philanthropist. It was an excellent form of publicity, and it gained him a prestige that fuelled his ego. He had great expectations of his riders, for Seamus had won the event the year previous. He had put up a sum of seventy sovereigns as prize money and planned to bet on his own horses and recoup the expenses.

As he scanned the confirmed entries to his handicap, and assessed form, he was intrigued by the entry of a horse named "Rufus" to be ridden by one A.P. Dillon. He skimmed over the details, assuming it was just one of several amateurs who tried their luck each year in the races surrounding the Galway Plate which was the main event.

He would have time to judge form when he saw the parade in the paddock, so he dismissed any further thought from his mind. It was to prove one of his rare misjudgements.

Whilst Maguire was making his plans in Galway, Catrin had been busy persuading her parents to maintain the traditional visit to the races. They had the desire, but also a natural reluctance to expose themselves to threat. It was a letter to Catrin from Anthony that helped convince them that they should go. He assured her that his men would give them protection, and he would personally escort them when he could arrange it.

He also told her that he had entered Rufus for one of the races, and he would be very disappointed if she did not come to support him. Catrin was over the moon.

She had fallen in love with Rufus the first time she had seen him, and nothing was going to prevent her from cheering him on. As usual, Roderick was the first to yield to pressure and Megan was left with no choice.

Catrin was more emotional. She had her father drive to Grafton Street where she bought a bright blue silk shirt and a blue and white jockey cap for Anthony to use as his colours.

She would present them on the evening before the race when they were gathered with friends at Dungannon House.

For the first time ever, Roderick drove to Galway. He wanted to show Daniel his new Austin, a sign of the prosperity the business was enjoying. It would cause a stir in Galway where new vehicles were a rarity.

He allowed Catrin to take the wheel on one of the easier stretches of the road while he sat back and enjoyed the scenery. It was late afternoon when they arrived at Dungannon House and found Daniel at the front door poised to greet them.

He fussed over them as usual and took a moment or two to look at the car and congratulate his son on a fine choice. Over tea he brought them up to date with events in Galway.

"There's been so sign o' trouble since you left. I know it's been a worry, an' I wouldn't have blamed you if you decided to stay away. But it's grand to see you again.

The lieutenant's been across to see me, an' he tells me he'll have men posted around to make sure we'll be alright. I've invited him to join us for dinner. I thought you might like that, Catrin.

He tells me he's entered for the Maguire Handicap. There's devil for you. I hope he wins an' tweaks the devil's tail." He laughed uproariously.

Anthony's transport dropped him off at seven thirty. He was in civilian clothes and looked smart as usual.

The company gathered in the front room and over drinks exchanged pleasantries and gossip, and discussed the forthcoming race meetings.

Roderick seized a chance to talk to Anthony. "I hear you're in one of the races to-morrow."

Anthony smiled. "I hope to win the Maguire Handicap. It's worth seventy sovereigns, and it would give me great pleasure to take it off him."

"That sounds rather vengeful. Is that why you're racing?"

"There is some substance in that. Daniel may have told you that we suspect Maguire was behind Catrin's abduction, but that's only partially the reason. My men got me into this. They fancy I'm a good outsider to win and could earn them some money, so they pushed me into it. The more I thought about it, the more I began to fancy myself."

"And here's your colours to make you look a real jockey." Catrin had chosen the moment to enter and present the shirt and cap to him. She kissed him on the cheek as she handed them over.

"Fabulous," he said as he tried the cap on. "Blue is my favourite colour and the cap fits perfectly. Now I know I can give Maguire a run for his money."

"Don't underestimate the man," Daniel warned. "I hear he's hired two horses from O'Leary's stables in Limerick. He's known for good horses. He'll not give up his money without a fight, mark my words."

"Do you know who's riding them?" Anthony asked.

"Probably his son Seamus. He won it last year. The other is likely to be Devlin. He's a good rider, too. That's a point, son. Watch for any skulduggery. I wouldnae put anythin' past Maguire."

"Are you talking about Devlin O'Farrell?" Catrin was suddenly very interested.

"Aye. The same fellah you've been trying to see."
"Perhaps I'll get a chance to see him?"

"That wouldna be wise, Catrin. Remember it was him you were told to keep away from. Maguire's goin' to be close at hand. Just bide your time. There'll be other chances."

"Maybe not as good."

"Listen to your grandfather," Roderick chimed in, "You shouldn't be here at all. It would be stupid to go near this fellah. You agree Anthony?"

"I certainly do. Listen Catrin. I'll personally escort you wherever you go, and I've got men who will watch the house at all times, but I won't be able to be near you before and during the race. So stick close to your family and don't take any risks."

Catrin pouted. "But I have to see him sometime. It seemed a good chance."

She sat down petulantly and assumed a sulky expression.

"Have you looked over the course?" Daniel queried Anthony.

"Haven't had the chance to take a close look."

"Try and take one," Daniel advised. "It's a fine course, but you have to watch for the tricky bit near the end.

As you come up the hill, there's two fences placed close together. Judge the distance very carefully. If your stride pattern's wrong, you'll land in trouble.

Personally I think it's dangerous. After runnin' two miles and comin' up the hill, the horses are tired an' lose concentration.

"That's how so many o' them fall there. Jest you watch out!"

The remainder of the evening passed pleasantly. The dinner was excellent and everyone was in good spirits and looking forward to the rest of the week. Catrin stayed close to Anthony, a new-found hero worship in her manner.

The whole evening was so sociable it encouraged her to flirt quite openly with him, and he responded with enthusiasm.

It was a fun evening and she was genuinely sad when it ended. They stood in the doorway, his arm around her, as his transport drove up to the entrance. The driver came forward and saluted Anthony.

"This is Private M'Garry. He's on guard duty to-night. You'll have someone every night. Through the day, I'll be with you. I dare Maguire to try anything!"

"See you to-morrow, then." He gave her a long, lingering kiss. The deepest one yet. She did nothing to break it. In fact the way she felt at that particular moment, she would not have denied him another. This would be the most exciting Race week ever.

She could hardly wait for the morning to come.

Chapter Sixteen

Seamus and Devlin stood in the stalls at O'Brien's stables appraising the horses that had just been unloaded. "Who's riding who?" enquired Seamus. He was already eyeing the black stallion.

"I'll tell you in a minute," Maguire snapped. He was in one of his moods. It had been a tiring journey from Limerick, made worse by the restlessness of the horses in the trailer. The fact that O'Leary had charged him ten pounds more than originally agreed also contributed to his bad temper.

They congregated in the storeroom that served as an office, and Maguire spread out the race programme and commenced to analyse the opposition. Most of the entrants and horses were known to him, but he paused at one of the unknowns.

"Who's this Rufus ridden by an A.P.Dillon?"

"Don't you know?" O'Brien uttered his peculiar cackling laugh.

"What's so funny?" Maguire was irritated, "Would I be askin' if I knew?"

"It's that officer at the barracks. You must'ave seen him on that gold coloured gelding. Fine horse."

"Him?" Maguire's face contorted. "Be Jaysus! The bloody cheek!"

"What's wrong with that?" Devlin asked. "There's nuthin' says he can't enter."

"Entitled or no, he's army, an' the army's no friends o' us." Maguire's morning was going from bad to worse. It didn't help that it was his mistake in the first place.

"It's only an army horse. It's not trained like these two. What you worryin' about?" Devlin was unconcerned.

"And the handicapper's put an extra couple o' pounds on him." Seamus had been looking over his shoulder at the race programme. "He'll discover what that means when he's comin' up the hill, won't he just."

"Let's hope he does," Maguire was bitter.

"Seamus, you take Black Velvet. Dev, yours is the grey. Vesuvian he calls it. O'Leary swears they're two o' his best, so I'm expectin' a winner from one of you. Whatever happens, don't let that bloody army man beat you."

"He won't," vowed Seamus, "not with two o' us against him."

Devlin spoke quietly. "I'm ridin' fair an' square to win. He won't beat me if I can help it, but if he does, it'll be because he's a better rider than me. I can accept that."

There was a deadly silence as the colour mounted in Maguire's face.

"Well I can't," he bristled. You're goin' soft, you eejit! Can't ye see what this is? He's deliberately issuing a challenge to us. He wants to get one up on the Republic. I'm not payin' fancy money for you to be a good sport. Winnin' is what I want, an' by God I'd better have it. Sort yourselves out an' make sure you do."

He bundled the race programme into his pocket and stormed out of the office. Rafferty, his right hand man made to follow, stopping only to glance at Devlin and indicate that he agreed with his master.

Minutes later the horse van rumbled out of the yard and peace once more descended on the scene.

"I still think our horses'll be better trained. All that gobshite does is to go out on patrol now an' then." Devlin was confident.

"Don't underestimate him," O'Brien warned, "I've had a look at his horse. By the looks o' it's hindquarters, there's a good jumper there."

"Even so," said Devlin, "he doesn't know the course like we do. If he goes better that we expect, we'll still catch him at the finish."

"What d'ye mean?" queried Seamus.

"Them two fences past the top. Remember? They're so close together you have to measure your stride real good. If you don't, you're in trouble. He won't know that."

Seamus was deep in thought for a minute. "So if we could force him to break stride, he might hit the second fence all wrong. That's an idea. Lot's o' horses fall there. It'll just look like he misjudged it," he smacked his thigh with his hand, "that's how we'll do it. Just a little nudge at the right spot."

"Alright then. But that's all. I'd rather win fair an' square. There's more satisfaction in that."

Devlin picked up his jacket and turned to leave. "See you here early in the mornin'. We'll give these two a light canter afore we go to Ballybrit."

O'Brien watched him go and looked quizzically at Seamus who remained seated on a bag of oats. The stableman wondered if he was thinking what he was.

"Your Da may be right. Maybe Dev is goin' a bit soft."

Seamus eased himself to his feet. "Na, na. Dev's fine. Once he's on that horse, he'll forget all about anythin' else but winnin'. He'll want to beat me, never mind some feckin' army officer. Have these pair ready for six in the mornin'. See ye then."

He left O'Brien to his thoughts and made his way into the yard. O'Brien returned to the stalls to make sure the horses had settled. As he surveyed them, he began to speculate which one he would put his money on. He could do with some extra money, and the pre-race odds were very good on the army horse, but that would be seen as treason by Maguire. His instincts conflicted with his loyalty, and as he recalled the conversation of a few minutes earlier, he made up his mind to wager ten pounds on the black.

CHAPTER SEVENTEEN

"We've combined our money, surr," McNulty told him. He had finished grooming Rufus by the time Anthony entered the stables at five thirty in the morning. The horse was groomed to perfection, his coat gleaming like polished metal in the lamplight. There's twenty pounds bet on the nose. Got the odds at eight to one," he chortled, "so it's up to you surr."

"I'll do my best," Anthony assured him. "You've done a fine job in preparing him. When they see him in the paddock, I bet the odds will shorten."

"I suppose they might. But they won't know the secret bit o' trainin' we've done up country, will they."

"Don't worry about a thing, surr. Wi' all that money on him, he'll be well taken care of."

"Get him across to the course in good time. Remember it's a 2.30 start. Make sure he's quartered comfortably and have a man guarding him at all times. This is Maguire territory we're going into, and I wouldn't put it past him to be up to mischief."

"I'm taking the small van across to Ballybrit. I need to check out the course. From there, I'm going to Dungannon House for breakfast." Anthony told him. "It's a traditional thing on race days, apparently." He left the sergeant to complete his work and drove himself to the racecourse.

It took over an hour to walk the course and inspect the jumps. The Galway Plate, the most prestigious of all the events was run over two and a half miles, but the handicap was reduced to two miles. The last part of the course was obviously going to be the toughest test for the horses. The gradient became steeper at this point and there was a stretch of uphill ground before it levelled off and gradually descended to the finishing line. Just over the hill, before the downward slope, stood the two fences Daniel had warned him about.

Anthony whistled softly to himself. They were close together, a real test for both horse and rider. The horse had a minimum of space to adjust stride between the fences, and it would be imperative to measure the stride carefully if the second fence was to be taken cleanly. He paced it out for himself and considered what it would mean to Rufus after the stiff climb uphill. As he made his way back he planned his strategy, and by the time he reached Dungannon House, he knew exactly how he was going to run the race.

He wondered how good Maguire's entries were, and whether the state of the ground would remain firm. Rufus preferred the going soft, and unless rain fell soon, he might be at a disadvantage.

Dungannon House was bustling when he arrived. Daniel had invited a host of friends to join the Kilpatricks for the huge Irish breakfast that was the essential for a day at the races, and there was a carnival atmosphere.

Catrin and her mother had been up since first light helping Mrs. Donovan to prepare the mountainous array of food laid out as a buffet for guests to help themselves. Catrin was first to grab him and led him to the buffet. A loud cheer went up from the guests as Daniel welcomed him. He introduced him to his friends with evident pleasure. The races were one of the highlights of the year for him, and it was an honour to have one of the riders as his guest.

Catrin sat with him as he wolfed the generous plateful she had made for him. She was bubbling with excitement and could not hide the thrill she felt about him competing.

"How's Rufus," she asked. "Danna and I are going to put ten pounds on him to win. I think it's' a good bet."

"My men have got twenty pounds on him, and I don't think it's just because I'm their C.O. I've had a look at the course, and your granddad is right. Those two fences he warned me about are difficult. It would be easy to make a mistake there."

"But Rufus will be alright, won't he? He's a strong horse. Oh, Tony, don't let anything happen to him. He's so beautiful, I'd die if he got hurt."

"Does that apply to me too?" Anthony was slightly piqued.

"Of course. But you know what I mean. Don't take crazy risks, will you?"

"I don't intend to, but Maguire's got two of his men in the race and I wouldn't put it past him to try some kind of trick. I'll see you before the race, won't I? Can I hope for a last minute kiss for good luck?"

"Of course. I'm dying to see you in your nice blue colours, and I'll be shouting for you to win.

She leaned forward and planted a generous kiss on his lips. There'll be another one when the race is over." She laughed and left him while she went to help her mother serve more guests who had just arrived.

Breakfast was over by ten, and the gathering started to break up and head for Ballybrit. The first race was timed for twelve o' clock and they wanted to secure a good vantage point. As he emerged from the front door, Anthony was heartened to feel a slight drizzle against his face. If it persisted, it would suit Rufus perfectly. As he made his way to the course to go through all the preparations of a competitor, he began to feel very confident.

The feeling in the Maguire camp was not so assured. O'Leary had just informed them that his horses were better on firm going, and as the drizzle turned to rain, Maguire was uneasy.

"Have you figured out yet how you're goin' to nail that gobshite o' a lieutenant," he asked Seamus.

"We'll sandwich him at the top o' the hill. If we catch him at the approach to the first fence, we can throw him off stride. He might scrape over it, but he'll fall at the second, that's for sure."

Maguire nodded. "Jest make sure it's not too obvious. Whatever way you do it, make sure he doesn't git past the post first. I'm puttin' money on you both, an' I expect to git my expenses back."

The morning sped past, and the rain continued. Despite the weather, several thousand spectators had gathered and the excitement was building. A crowd gathered at the paddock to get a first hand look at the entries as the twenty one entries for the Maguire Handicap went on show. Catrin sheltered under an umbrella held by Daniel as they scanned the parade.

"There!" she shouted, "there he is. Number seven, lucky seven. Oh doesn't he look gorgeous!"

"Are you talkin' about the horse or Tony?" Daniel nudged her playfully.

She blushed and returned the nudge. "The horse, of course. He looks splendid, doesn't he? But Tony looks gorgeous, too. I think Blue is his colour."

Daniel looked at the overcast sky. "If this rain keeps up, he won't be blue for long. This damn rain is getting' worse. I hope it's better than this for the big race."

Sergeant McNulty led Rufus around the ring and halted in front of them at Anthony's order. Catrin ducked under the rail as he leaned down to kiss her.

"Now I know I'm going to win," he laughed as he relished in her gesture. "I feel like a knight going into battle."

"Gid on with ya," she laughed, "here's another token for luck." She thrust something into his hand. "Wear it on your sleeve, just like a knight."

"What is it?"

"It's a ladies garter," she quipped, "one of mine at that. Now go and do your duty." She blew him a kiss and returned to her grandfather. McNulty resumed leading the horse, and despite being soaked by the rain, he felt jubilant. The lieutenant was threading the garter on his sleeve and it would undoubtedly inspire him. He also knew the going was getting softer by the minute, which would be good for the horse.

Closely behind Tony in the paddock, Devlin sat on the grey and watched the banter between Catrin and the lieutenant. He had not forgotten the skirmish in the Dublin gallery, and disliked him.

There was a trace of envy as he recognised the girl. He remembered the heated exchange over his painting and how attractive she looked when she berated him for refusing to sell it. He slowed up as he came abreast of her position.

"That's the opposition," Daniel told Catrin. "That's Devlin O'Farrell, the man you're always on about."

Catrin surveyed him closely. He wore green and amber colours and he looked spruce and very composed. He sat the horse well and she could imagine that they would combine well with each other. As if reading her mind, he tipped his cap to her and smiled, but had moved before she could think of something to say.

"There's the favourite," Daniel pointed across the ring. "Number nine. The black. No wonder they call it Black Velvet. That's Seamus Maguire on him. He'll be the one Tony'll have to watch. He won it last year."

Catrin appraised the horse first. Daniel was right. It would provide a test for Tony. The rider seemed a little too tall for comfort, his long narrow face, dark eyes, and bearded whiskers made him look sinister, and she began to worry.

Seamus passed their position without a glance in their direction. His mind was filled with the possibilities that could arise in the race ahead. Like Devlin, he worried about the rain. He jogged to catch up with him as they made their way to the start. They said nothing. Just a casual glance and a faint nod of the head. Their mission was understood, and they took up position in close proximity to the lieutenant. During the first mile they would keep close on either side of him and then match him stride for stride up the hill.

The riders got off to a straggly start, but soon picked up a steady pace despite the driving rain. In the soft going, the horses threw up clods of turf and mud spattered the riders in the rear, turning their bright colours into a uniform mess and making them unrecognisable.

Anthony kept Rufus away from the stand side, well clear of the first group of ten who were bunched closely. Rufus was adjusting nicely to the conditions and he was well clear of any trouble. It was a wise tactic, for three horses fell at the first fence, and two more at the next. At the end of the first mile the field had dwindled to twelve riders, and the heavy going was taking effect.

As the ground changed gradient Anthony decided to apply pressure on Rufus, and move towards the stand side. The horse responded but Anthony was taken by surprise to see a black horse come up on his inside and cut off his track. He recognised as Black Velvet and realised it was Seamus trying to prevent him from taking the inside position. At the same instant, he suddenly realised that there was a grey coming up to him on his right hand side. He straightened up to look ahead and saw they were nearing the top of the hill and they would soon be approaching the two fences.

He dug his heels into Rufus and used his whip once. It was enough. Rufus accelerated and started to draw away from the pair that threatened him, but the gain was momentary, for they came back at him and the black began to draw alongside. Seamus was using his whip and steadily inching closer, and on his right, Anthony could hear O'Farrel whipping the grey. The plan was quite clear.

They were going to try and force his horse to change stride and make the fences difficult for him. He hated to whip Rufus, but he needed to keep clear.

There was joy as he felt the horse respond with a burst of speed just at the moment Seamus swung the black to try and knock him into the grey. Had the timing been right, it would certainly have knocked him off balance and a bad clearance of the first fence would have been inevitable.

But the sudden burst of speed had taken both Seamus and Devlin by surprise and it was Black Velvet that missed its stride. Rufus cleared both fences cleanly but the effort was beginning to tell. The extra weight imposed by the handicapper was sapping his strength.

Seamus paid for his error. He scrambled over the first fence, but jumped too late for the second. Black Velvet hung for a moment on the brush and landed badly, slithering to a sudden stop and throwing Seamus.

Devlin saw the disaster but was too busy struggling to take the fences himself to do anything. He could see the gelding was beginning to tire and once more he applied the whip.

Rufus was tiring. The sudden burst of speed had taken a lot out of him, but it had enabled him to survive the jumps. Only one fence remained before the final run in, but he knew the grey was close behind. Anthony was almost as weary as the horse, but he was determined to show Maguire his dirty work had failed.

Both horses struggled to clear the last fence and each rider was using the whip heavily as they entered the last furlong. The grey was by now no more than a length behind and gaining fractionally with every stride. The spectators in the stand were on their feet cheering wildly and roaring encouragement, their feet stamping the boards with excitement.

It was nail biting. The suspense mounted to fever pitch as both horses gave their all. Rufus responded nobly and held on to cross the finishing line a mere half a length ahead of the grey. Catrin hugged Daniel and spun him around in a frenzy of excitement. Megan and Roderick were forced to dance with her. The drenching rain was forgotten and all over the course the spectators cheered and applauded what had been one of the best races ever.

Catrin hurried from the stand, rushing to greet the winner as he made his way to the enclosure. In her excitement she brushed past the burly figure of a man and woman without realising who they were.

Maguire had a face as black as thunder, and murder blazed in his eyes. Maura had been with him during the race, and had been hard put to conceal her emotions as Anthony passed the winning post. Fortunately Maguire took her excitement to be for Devlin as he made his great effort to overhaul the winner. The thought of handing over the prize money to an army officer was too much for him.

"I'm not handin' my money over to that gobshite," he spat the words out.

"You can do it," he told Maura. "I've told the Secretary you'll make the presentation. I'm not even goin' on the platform. I'll be in the first aid tent to see how Seamus is."

"I'd better come too," Maura pleaded. She was not sure how she could mask her real emotions.

"No. Get to the enclosure. There has to be a Maguire that hands over the prize. Come an' see Seamus after." He split from her and headed for the first aid tent.

Loud cheers accompanied the entrance of the winner and his horse into the enclosure. Catrin struggled to get close, shouting his name and waving desperately, but her voice was lost in the welter of cheering voices as Anthony dismounted and made his way to the platform for the presentation.

The Race Secretary announced the winner and called upon Miss Maura Maguire to make the presentation. Catrin could not prevent a wave of jealousy as she saw the attractive woman come forward to hand over the envelope containing the prize money. She congratulated him and leant forward to kiss him. The crowd roared. Catrin thought it was a kiss that lingered too long, but the crowd loved it.

Maura was thrilled. She took advantage of the kiss to whisper in his ear. "I must see you soon".

Anthony drew back in surprise. It was an unusual place to make such a request. He held the prize aloft, revelling in the cheers of the crowd. He spotted Catrin and waved, but as he prepared to climb down from the platform he managed to glance back at Maura and nod his head. She would understand.

McNulty fended off the crowd and jostled back to where Rufus stood, the steam rising from him, his flanks streaked with sweat.

"Grand race, surr. Nearly wet me self, so I did. But the trainin' paid off, didn't it? Boy is that bookie gonna be sorry the day he saw us." He rubbed his hands.

"Thanks. You did well, too. Get Rufus dried off and taken care of. He's the real hero." As they moved off Catrin burst through the throng and threw herself into his arms.

"It was wonderful," she exclaimed, "absolutely wonderful. The most exciting race I've ever seen." She kissed him several times as he stood helpless, the mud from his face transferring itself to hers.

"It was worth every moment to get a reception like this." His weariness deserted him as he wallowed in the adoration. "You're getting mud all over you," he laughed, "you look as if you've been in the race, too. I've got to go and clean up. I'll be over to Dungannon House as soon as I can. See you there." He kissed her again. It was a marvellous feeling. He no longer felt an outsider for her affections. He was a winner, and to the victor came the spoils.

"Be quick," she urged. "I'll get Danna to keep a bottle of champagne specially for you. We'll share it." She blew him another kiss and left him to fight his way back to the dressing room.

From the platform Maura watched the performance with horror. Hate and resentment seethed within her as she realised her rival had an unfair advantage. The response from Anthony was hurting. He looked as if he enjoyed it. Perhaps it was just the exhilaration of being a winner. She would win him back next time they had a rendezvous.

A tear trickled down her cheek as she made her way from the enclosure to the first aid tent. She hoped her father would take her tears as a sign of distress for Seamus, and she hoped his injuries were slight.

But it was imperative that she saw Anthony soon before that Kilpatrick woman got too firm a hold on him.

Chapter Eighteen

The races were over for another year. The Galway Plate had been won by a rank outsider and Maguire continued to nurse his wrath. The buntings and flags had disappeared as fast as they had appeared, the visitors, including the Kilpatricks had gone their various ways, and the citizens resumed their normal life.

The rain had abated after the opening day of the races and it had been a good week for the pub owners and the shops. After the excitement of the Maguire handicap, Eamon found Maura subdued and easily reduced to tears. It was difficult to attribute it to Seamus's misfortune, for he had suffered no more than a mild concussion, and was back to normal within a day or two.

Fortunately, Eamon had no suspicion of the real problem that troubled her. She had seen nothing of Anthony for more than two weeks, and she knew he had spent most of the race week at Dungannon House, living it up with the guests of the old man, and seeing a lot of the girl. She was torn with jealousy, her heart twisted with pain every moment she pictured him with her.

An unlikely source provided an opportunity for her to plan a rendezvous. Rafferty had some things that Devlin required at Ballanalee, and since all his vans were out on missions, he asked Maura if she would borrow the pony and trap from O'Brien and deliver them.

She was happy to oblige, and Eamon thought the fresh air might do her good. Business was quiet, and both Maguire and

Seamus had gone off to Belfast for an important meeting. He would have a chance to read his poetry without fear.

Maura left after mid-day. It was a fine afternoon and she had changed into a summer dress, bright red with a colourful floral pattern. She looked at her prettiest, her hair shining like oiled silk and flowing loose down her back.

Less than half a mile from the square, Anthony was making final adjustments to the saddle of his alternate horse, since Rufus was being rested after his exertions. He was out of uniform and in his polo outfit, but that was not the game he was preparing to play. Despite his instructions that she should never telephone him at the barracks, she had done so the day before, and told him she knew where Devlin O'Farrell would be the following day. She suggested a rendezvous to meet him and he would be able to question him, with her acting as a go-between.

It aroused suspicion, for he knew she disliked Catrin because of her relationship with him. She also knew that Catrin had asked him to help locate O'Farrell for her. Why should she suddenly offer to help? He decided to keep the rendezvous, but to be cautious.

From Maura's directions he was able to sketch a rough map for McNulty of the directions to reach Ballanalee, having explained he had an informant who might have useful information for them.

"I guess this might take a couple of hours, maybe a bit longer. If I'm not back within two and a half hours, I want you and Cunningham to come and investigate. If there's no sign of me, search the place from top to bottom. I don't think it's a trap, but Maguire and his crew are pretty steamed up about losing his race, so I wouldn't put it past them to try something."

"Shouldn't I go as well?" McNulty suggested.

"No. I'm sure I'll be alright." He did not want McNulty to know there was a woman involved. "Just wait like I said."

He stuffed his revolver into the saddlebag to impress the sergeant that he would be prepared for any trouble.

McNulty watched him ride off, then shouted for Cunningham to get tack ready for two horses. Barrack life was a bore and he almost wished the lieutenant would overstay his estimate. It was a fine afternoon and a ride in the country would be very pleasant.

It was a view shared by Maura. On such a fine summer afternoon, the drive along the coastal road was delightful, the road dappled by the sun shining through the trees, and the nearby sea sparkling like diamonds.

She reached Ballanalee flushed with the pleasure of the drive, and excited at the prospect of a reunion with her lover. She unhitched the pony and turned it loose into the field behind the house, pushing the trap into the outbuilding that served as a hay shed.

The door was on the latch as she expected, and she opened the top half to let in more air and light. The place was tidy save the bench near the window which was strewn with driftwood and picture frames.

Devlin had a woman who came in at regular intervals to clean and keep the turf fire going, but she would never touch the work bench.

She climbed the ladder to the loft and inspected the bed. It had not been slept in, so she merely plumped up the pillows and smoothed the covers. Satisfied that all was in order, she climbed back down and made her way to the gate of the field where her pony was grazing. She climbed upon the gate, and sat demurely on the top spar, her eyes trained on the top of the rise.

Anthony found his way at a pleasant canter. He left the road at a spot two miles further on and proceeded up an incline to the top of a stretch of moorland that seemed to stretch for miles.

He pressed the horse into a gallop and for about two miles he revelled in the freedom and exhilaration, but as he neared the top of the rise he slowed to a canter and pulled up to admire the view.

In the distance he could make out the sparkling waters of the sea. In the foreground, weaving a twisted course through the moor, a small river flowed into an estuary leading to the sea.

The remains of an old stone quarry were partly down the slope to his left full of water that drained from the hill. It looked deep.

He could see the main road running alongside a broad sandy beach and then crossing the river over an old stone bridge. About half a mile away from the road, screened from view by a dense mass of trees that grew up the side of the estuary, he could see some farm buildings.

So this was Ballanalee. The name rolled pleasantly off the tongue. The main house was less conspicuous, for the rear of it had been dug into a knoll immediately behind it, partially concealing it.

Sitting on a gate at the side of the house, he saw a figure in a red dress, and recognised her as Maura. She was waving to him. He could not resist showing off. He set the horse to clear the dry stone wall that bounded the field and charged down the field at the gallop. He slowed to a canter as he neared the foot, and eased the horse alongside the gate. He scooped her from the gate with one hand and swept her on to the saddle beside him.

It was a brilliant show of knighthood.

She clung tightly, showering his face with kisses. All the pent up emotions were released in an instant. Anthony delighted in the onslaught and then gently lowered her to the ground.

He had expected a passionate welcome, but this was almost frenzied. He had been flirting with Catrin for a whole week, but she had always kept him at arm's length. It was fun, but it left him dissatisfied and frustrated. This woman was different. For the immediate future, she was his main interest, all other thoughts were erased from his mind.

He dismounted and turned the horse loose. They walked hand in hand through the gate and made towards the house. She held his hand tightly, and there was a dreamy light in her eyes. There was no doubting what she had in mind.

He scanned the outbuildings for any warning signs, but they appeared to be padlocked except the hay shed. An unusual thing, he thought, to have buildings locked up in such an isolated spot.

The door was open as if company was expected, and the scene was one of tranquillity, the silence broken only by the soft cooing of doves in the nearby trees.

"Is he here?" he asked her.

"Not yet. We have plenty of time. An hour at least." She looked at him suggestively, and ruffled his hair playfully.

"Come inside and see." She pushed the door open further and led him inside. The dark interior was difficult to adjust to from the bright daylight of the outdoors.

She clung to him, her face upturned for a kiss. He obliged and she clung even more tightly, her tongue darting into his open mouth, searching for his tongue. His heart was racing and his breathing quickened. It was difficult to take in the surroundings when his lust was under siege.

It was sparsely furnished. A work bench, and a stout bog oak table with two chairs occupied most space. The room was dominated by the open fireplace in the far wall where a turf fire burned slowly. A recess on one side contained a small cupboard, and a high backed wooden chair sat to one side. A dresser with a china rack above it occupied the other wall. Beyond the fireplace, a dark passage led to a storeroom which was a lean-to cut into the knoll behind the house.

He noted the ladder that led to a hatch in the ceiling. Evidently there was a loft upstairs. But they were definitely alone. Maura opened her eyes and noted he was looking at the ladder.

She led him forward. "The upstairs is much more interesting."

She climbed ahead of him, allowing a daring show of ankle and leg that was designed to be provocative. His excitement was mounting to unbearable heights. She pulled him through the small opening and stood with her arm around his waist as he surveyed the room.

It was small and compact. A double bed with a plain wooden headboard took up most of the space. A woollen bedspread made up of multi-coloured knitted squares covered the bed and brought a splash of colour to the otherwise drab surroundings. The solitary window overlooked the lean-to just below the sill and had no curtains. On that side, a bedside table stood with a small oil lamp resting on it. On the other side of the bed the wall was adorned with hooks, obviously used as a wardrobe, and barely enough space between it and the bed.

Maura detached herself and lay down on the bed, her hand outstretched and beckoning him to join her.

"This is more comfortable than wet grass or the back of a van. It seems so long. I've missed you so much."

He sat down on the bed and pulled off his riding boots. She had no patience. She flung her arms around him, pulling his shirt free from his jodhpurs, and helping him over his head with it. She threw her arms around him, her right hand thrusting inside the waistband of his jodhpurs, groping for what she sought for her pleasure.

"You're a bitch in heat, right enough. Can't you wait?" He made no attempt to remove her hand. He twisted around, throwing himself on to her, spread-eagling her legs and pinning her hands above her head. The full weight of his body pressed on her abdomen and the juices began to flow.

He smothered her with a powerful kiss, held so long she had to break off to draw breath. Their breathing was laboured and deep as passions came to boiling point. At that moment any thoughts of Catrin or anyone else, vanished. His priority was to satisfy his lust and that of this ravishing creature who was so desperate to mate.

"You need to take your dress off. If you don't I might rip it off. I don't want you going back to Galway looking ravaged."

"You have to do the same," she said, mischief in her eyes. "I want to look at every inch of you, then you can ravage me all you want." He rolled over, but lay on his side.

"You first. I want to lie and watch you strip. I want all the trimmings."

He watched intently as her garments wafted to the floor, and gasped in admiration. Her breasts were no stranger in his hands, but he never ceased to marvel at the firmness and the delicate pear shapes. The nipples were erect and burning red with the passion she was so anxious to release. Her skin was white as alabaster, her body slim and beautifully proportioned, narrowing at the waist and curvaceous at the hips. The neat little triangle of pubic hair a perfect match to the magnificent black of that that flowed from her head.

"Am I beautiful?" She pirouetted to show her pert little buttocks, round and smooth as a baby's. "Now it's your turn."

He swung himself over the side of the bed and grasped her around the buttocks, pulling her in to him so she could feel the hardness and the power in his groin.

"Not yet," she chided, freeing herself from his grasp. "It's your turn to go in the shop window. I want to see what I'm buying."

She flung herself on the bed, propping herself up on one arm so as to watch him. "Hurry now. I can't wait much longer, and by the look of your crotch, I don't think you can either."

"You she devil. You'll get what you deserve soon enough."

He was out of his jodhpurs in a flash and on to the bed beside her giving her scarcely time to appreciate his lithe torso and muscular arms, but long enough to see he was fully aroused and desperate to possess her. Their previous clandestine meetings had always been in less comfortable surroundings, and the sex totally spontaneous with lots of foreplay.

There was no patience for that in the more comfortable surroundings of this haven, away from prying eyes, and in the comfort of a bed. He fell on her with an animal-like growl, thrusting wildly at her as he frantically sought the warm, wet, softness between her legs.

Outside, the stillness of the summer afternoon continued. With the incoming tide, a gentle salt laden breeze sprang up, rustling the long grass that fringed the river bank, and sighing softly through the trees.

It was a soft wind, but sufficient to rock the half open door, and in the hearth the ash from the turf fire eddied in a gentle swirl from one side to the other.

The farm cat appeared in the yard and padded cautiously through the door. It made its way to the foot of the ladder where it sat, ears twitching, as it listened to the rhythmic sounds of the creaking bed in the loft.

Satisfied there was no threat, the cat moved to the hearth and jumped up on the high backed chair where it settled down to sleep.

And all the time, in the drowsy summer afternoon, the breeze continued to sigh softly through the grass and rustle the trees, providing a gentle harmonious background for the lovers.

Chapter Nineteen

Exhausted by their steamy, passionate love making, and overcome with the euphoria of their lusts, they had drifted into a warm relaxing sleep, her head resting on his chest, his arm around her shoulder, supporting her in a comforting position from which she would never willingly move.

Anthony awoke with a start. Energised instantly, he sat up allowing Maura to slide off his chest. She gave a grunt of displeasure and stretched out an arm to recover the embrace. He shook her off and looked at his watch.

"What time did you say O'Farrell, was comin? He had no recollection of the time they fell asleep. Now that his passions had been satisfied there was his original mission to fulfil. Maura remained in paradise, still dreaming of the wonderful love -making she had experienced. She answered with another groan, and stretched out her hand to entice him to return to her.

"Maura! Stop fooling about. Tell me, dammit! What time is he coming?

He ignored her grasping hand and swung his legs over the bed, seizing his clothes and starting to put them on.

She sat up, rubbing the sleep from her eyes, watching him with a mischievous smile, and suddenly dived across the bed and ensnared him in her arms.

"There's still time," she said, a wicked glint in her eyes, "don't be in such a hurry." She pulled at his arm. "Come on, make love to me one more time."

"You told me he would be here in about an hour. We've spent at least that long in bed. He could be here at any minute.

Get up and get your clothes on. I don't want to be discovered like this. Suppose he told your father?"

"There's nothing to be worried about." She flopped back on the bed, clasping her hands behind her head, which had the effect of offering him her breasts. She was hurt when he ignored the provocation and continued to pull his shirt on.

"I don't understand. You're lying stark naked on this man's bed, obviously having been ravaged, and you don't think there's anything to worry about? If he suddenly walks in, what am I supposed to do? Pull the ladder up?"

She uttered a deep throated laugh and turned over on her stomach, arching her back to show off her buttocks, white and smooth as marble save the red imprints of the finger marks made on them at the height of their love making.

"Dev wouldn't betray me, even if he did catch us. There's no need to panic."

Anthony looked at her in disbelief. She was totally relaxed. No fear apparent of anyone disturbing them. The realisation suddenly hit him, and he was angry.

"He's not coming at all, is he? You've set this up as an excuse to get me here!"

He reached over the bed and yanked her around to face him. She squealed with pain and the expression on her face confirmed his suspicions.

"I'm right. He never was coming. You knew he was away and it gave you the chance to set up his house as a little love nest."

"Suppose I did? You were all for it, weren't you? Didn't you want it as much as me?" She was crying.

"I wouldn't turn down the chance to make love to you, but that's not the main reason I came here, is it?"

"You said O'Farrell would be here, and I wanted to talk to him. You've deceived me, and I don't like it."

"Why is it so important to meet him? I thought the fact that I was here was enough."

"I need to ask him some questions. I haven't been able to see him since the race. This seemed a good chance."

"What sort of questions?"

"Some questions about his work."

"He wouldn't tell you anything."

He seized her arm roughly and pulled her upright causing her to yelp with pain.

"I need to know more about him. I came here to-day not knowing if I was being led into a trap or not. I've got men standing by to take this place apart if I'm not back at the barracks within two hours."

She struggled out of his grip, her face red with anger. "You mean you didn't trust me? You actually thought I would betray you?

She was deeply hurt." How could you even think of it? You know I love you."

"Your father commands the Galway Brigade. I know he rules you and your brothers with a rod of iron. "You had no right to think I would set a trap for you." Her eyes filled with tears and she flung herself into his arms. "Don't let us quarrel, please. It makes me so unhappy. I'd never, never, betray you." She sought to kiss his lips, but the response was cold.

"I need to know about O'Farrell, Maura. You won't be betraying him. I'm not seeking to capture him. I just need some information."

She looked perplexed. Her loyalties were being tested, and the tears meandered down her cheeks.

"It's for that girl, isn't it? She wants to know about his painting, The Wishing Boy. That's what it's all about isn't it?"

"It had something do with that. She asked me some time ago to locate him. That's all."

"She fancies you," the tears came faster now, "I saw you together at the races. I could've scratched her eyes out. Why should I help her?"

"That meant nothing," he lied. "I was protecting her from a threat by your father. Look Maura," he changed to a condescending tone, "she's desperate to buy that painting off him. She only wants a chance to talk to him. She's tried and failed. Your father has frightened everyone off."

The tactic worked. She relented in an effort to please him.

"What is it you want to know about Dev then?"

"What sort of work does he do for your father?"

"I'm not going to tell you that."

"He's involved in distributing Poteen, isn't he?"

"Who told you that?"

"Someone with a lot of local knowledge."

"Daniel Kilpatrick, I bet. You've been mighty thick with them recently."

"He admitted being a customer now and then."

"You're not trying to catch Dev for that?"

"That's a problem for the Customs and Excise. But it's one reason he disappears so often, isn't it?"

She nodded. Her expression was sad. Cracks were appearing in her defences.

"But Poteen is only for part of the year," Anthony kept probing.

"It takes a lot of the summer," she replied listlessly, "that's when the stills are busy, but the distribution goes on in Connemara and Mayo a lot."

"Do you know his exact movements?"

"No. I knew he wouldn't be here to-day, that's all."

"But your father always knows?"

"I told you I won't say more than that. Don't ask me to betray my family. I won't do that, even for you."

He realised he was pushing her, and decided to return to his previous tack.

"O'Farrell must spend some time here. It looks clean and tidy."

"He's here a lot. Other time's my Da uses it. There's a woman from the village comes in and cleans it. He has another place he uses for his work over at the Corrib."

"Does he? He must do quite well for himself owning two places. Does the IRA pay him so well?"

Her face blanched. "What do you mean about the IRA?"

"You know fine what I mean. He works for your father. Your father *is* the IRA in this territory. O'Farrell seems to be a very important man to him, otherwise he wouldn't try to scare people away from him. That's why Catrin Kilpatrick was threatened."

"She always comes into the argument, damn you!" She was angry now. "The IRA pays nobody. They're all volunteers. They're patriots. They do their duty out of love for their country. For your information, this house has been in the O'Farrell family for a hundred years. The place at the Corrib was an old ruin that Dev restored as a work shop. With his own money!"

"I believe he does much more." Anthony took advantage of her rising temper. In the heat of an argument, she might let something slip. "I hear he's pretty smart. Worked at the University at one time. Very pally with the Professor of Chemistry. I think he's up to more devious things. This place doesn't look like an active farm. All the outbuildings are locked up. What's in them?"

"I don't know. My Da runs a haulage business. I think he stores some things here."

"Sounds fishy. Maybe my men to should search the place."

"Oh no! You mustn't do that," she flung her arms around him and sobbed on his shoulder. "Please promise you won't do that. He'll came after you for sure."

He reflected a moment as she continued to wet his shirt with her tears. "You haven't really told me anything I didn't know already. I still don't know for certain where I can track this bloody O'Farrell man down. I told Catrin— I mean the Kilpatrick girl, I would arrange a meeting. I don't like going back empty handed."

She pulled away from him. "I knew it, I knew it!" she screamed, "it's been her all along. You're doing all this for her. She's a spoilt bitch. She can go where she wants, do what she pleases. She can spend money on anything she wants. I've got nothing, but at least I thought I had you. You said you loved me. If you meant it, why are you bothering so much with her?"

"Of course I meant it," he lied again. He took her hands and pressed them to his lips. He had gone far enough. Too much and he might lose a valuable inside contact. Don't get so upset. But you must understand I have a duty to perform."

She rested in his arms, her face pressed to his chest. He allowed her a few seconds to calm down, tightening his grasp to reassure her. She looked up at him, her eyes brimming with tears, "Does that mean destroying my family? You wouldn't do that to me, would you?"

He cupped her face in his hand and kissed her gently. A new strategy was forming in his brain. "I have to my duty. Someone always gets hurt in these things. But what hopes have we got if things remain as they are?"

"What does that mean?"

He eased himself away from her and sat down on the bed. He reached for his riding boots and began to stamp his feet into them.

"How can we ever meet one another openly? How could we possibly get married? What happiness will you ever have if your father doesn't change? He'll never change. Think of it, Maura. He only cares for his cause. He doesn't care about whether you're happy or not."

She shrank back in horror. "You'd expect me to sacrifice my Da and Seamus? I couldn't do that. Never!"

"It's a terrible choice. But it's time you thought about yourself. We have no chance unless something changes. You could help me make it change. But you have to tell me more than you're telling me now. Start with O'Farrell".

"Tell me where I can find him. I have to go now or my men will be coming to look for me. Give me a date when O'Farrell will definitely be around. And you must think of how we are going to continue to meet. It's getting very risky, and God help us if your father finds out."

He rose from the bed and held her once more. He tilted her chin and kissed her tenderly, gently, and with feeling, as any lover might have when bidding a fond farewell. He lowered himself down the ladder, his last sight of her almost too much to bear.

She stood, hands by her side, tears filling her eyes, a picture of misery and despair. She heard his footsteps echo across the yard and the whistle he made for his horse. As the horse cantered from the yard, she flung herself on the bed and sobbed. "Damn you and your duty," her angry words were smothered by the tear stained pillow.

At the top of the hill, Anthony paused and looked back. He was disappointed at not meeting O'Farrell, and wondering what he could tell Catrin.

She would not be impressed by his continuing failure to track down this will o' a wisp. The only real satisfaction he had felt this day, apart from the sex, was that he had laid down the gauntlet to Maura.

If she loved him as she appeared to, it might lead to her giving him information that would help him nail Maguire. He urged the horse to a gallop.

It was vital he intercepted McNulty before he approached the farm. From now on he would have a patrol check the place frequently to see who exactly was using it. Perhaps his rendezvous had been well worthwhile after all.

Chapter Twenty

The Galway Races were a distant memory already, but the aftermath was much in evidence.

The Tuesday evening, of Dr. McCrimmond's surgery in Buttermilk Lane had been exceptionally busy. Most of the patients were suffering the after effects of too much drinking and celebrations. It was almost seven when he peered into the waiting room hoping he had seen his last patient of the evening, and was surprised to see there was a latecomer. His surprise increased when he saw who it was.

He had known Maura Maguire for many years, ever since the family had come from Limerick. A beautiful girl and a fine specimen of womanhood. By rights she should have been married by now, and producing lots of healthy babies. But he knew something of her circumstances. He, too, had reason to fear Maguire.

She looked pale and wretched, and he knew something serious must be wrong.

He ushered her into his office and listened intently as she described her perpetual bouts of sickness and a complete loss of appetite.

"Another causality o' Race week?" it was an attempt at a joke. "I've had loads in to-night that are still sufferin' the after effects of too much celebrating'.

Maura admitted at having bought shellfish and preparing a rich oyster stew. But none of the others in the family had suffered any ill effects.

"Ah then. It's possible you were the only one that got a bad one. And once that gets into your system, I can take a few days to sort itself out. I'll give you a powder I keep for just such things. It might help cure it. But I want you to come and see me again to-morrow, and bring a sample o' your water. Just a precaution. I want to make sure it's not somethin' more serious."

The following morning, she felt better, and decided to cancel the visit. She telephoned the doctor from the shop, and was surprised at his insistence that she still come and see him. "Don't forget your sample," he reminded her.

She had a great respect for the doctor and knew he was genuinely concerned, so she reneged and kept the appointment. He gave her another brief examination, including a going over with his stethoscope.

"I don't think there's anything serious, but I'd like to get your sample checked all the same. Take another of these powders I gave you and that might do the trick".

He saw her jovially out the door, but shortly after his last patient had gone, he placed her urine sample carefully in his bag and left the surgery to call at the cottage hospital.

The following morning, before he went to the surgery, he called back at the hospital. The Sister scanned the test file.

"Yes. It's here. We did it yesterday afternoon. It's positive. Quite definite." She passed him the test slip.

"I thought it might be." He shook his head.

"Oh don't tell me this is another child to be loaded on the parish. There's more than enough as you well know."

"No, no. Nothing like that, not at all." He pocketed the slip, his face sombre and troubled, and made his way out. The Sister wondered who the unlucky girl might be. She would keep her ears open for gossip.

It was during the lunch hour that McCrimmond faced up to meeting Maura. It was the quietest time of day in the surgery, a time when he usually enjoyed his mid-day snack. He did not feel like eating to-day.

"I've got the results of the test on your sample."

"Is it good, or is it something bad?"

"To some it would be good."

"Oh." She was ready to cry.

"You didn't tell me everything the other day, did you Maura?"

"I told you about the oyster stew. You said yourself it could've been a bad one." She was dabbing at her tears with a handkerchief.

"It's got nothing to do with oysters, Maura. I think you know that. It's a condition called morning sickness. It's common amongst women in the early stages of pregnancy. The test was positive. You're with child, Maura. I wish I could throw my arms around you and congratulate you. But it's not like that, is it?"

She buried her face in her hands and sobbed, babbling words he could not understand. He moved from his desk to comfort her, fearing she might faint and fall to the floor. He allowed her to cry for a few moments and then pulled up a chair and sat down beside her.

"What am I going to do?" she sobbed. "My Da'll kill me, so he will."

"Hush now, Maura. Of course he won't. I know what he's like, but he'd never do that."

"You don't understand. I tell you he will. You don't know his temper."

"Oh yes I do. I served with him in the Limerick Brigade. I saw something of his temper. But it's different with you. He loves you, even if he doesn't show it."

"No, no! He'll go berserk. I know he will. You don't understand."

"Stop saying that, for God's sake!" he could not control his exasperation. "I'll talk to him Maura. Maybe I can get him to look on the positive side. All he has to do is give his blessing to the father and get you married. You can be wed before the baby is due. That's not unusual in these parts."

"I can't get married. Even if he was willing. My Da would never accept him."

"Oh my God! What could be that bad? Be Jaysus, did he rape you?"

"It would have been better if it was," she was crying pitifully. "It was all my fault. I was in love with him. I was prepared to do anything for him. Da never gave me a chance to love anyone, then suddenly I found this person. I couldn't stop myself loving him, and then he loved me back."

"But he won't marry you? Or have you changed your mind about him?"

"No, no. I'd marry him to-morrow if it was possible."

"Be Jaysus! This is a right mess, so 'tis. I don't know what to say."

"I'm at my wits end," she wailed, "I can't think straight any more. I want things to come back to normal. I don't want this child. I wish I could just be myself again."

"Don't talk like that! It's wrong for you to be taking all the blame. The father must be made to face up to his responsibilities, and your Da must give him the chance. If he owned up and said he was sorry and would make up for it, your Da might accept him."

Maura stood up, the tears flowing down her face, and she pounded the desk with her hands.

"I can't marry this man. I would like to, but I can't. Please understand. It's not possible!"

"Oh for Christ's sake, Maura. Tell me who he is and I'll bring him to book."

She faltered, and then sat down, once more burying her head in her hands. She remained that way for a moment and then managed to stop crying. She raised her head to look at him, and his own eyes moistened. He had never seen anyone so sad.

"That I promise," he said with great conviction, "and "You're a good man, doctor. I wish it was different and we could be happy about this. It's my problem, and I'll have to face up to it somehow. Please don't tell anyone, especially Da. He mustn't know anything."

"I'll be on hand whenever you need help. Now that we know the problem, I can give you something to help. The sickness' soon pass. We'll have you right in a few days.

Before you know it, you'll be blooming again. Just you take it easy now. Try to stop worrying so much."

He ushered her gently out the front door, glad that there had been no patients to witness the scene. He watched her walk slowly down the lane with a heavy heart, and he was afraid for her.

On the other side of town, Anthony was meditating in his office. He was still basking in the glory of his achievement at the races. Even the Major in Dublin had phoned congratulations, and McNulty and the men were showing him new respect. The parties at Dungannon House had been superb. He had met people from all over Ireland and some even from London, people with real intellect and intelligent conversation. They had wined and dined well, musical entertainment, and party games, all of which had brought out his talents as the life and soul of the party.

Best of all, he was making progress with Catrin. She was warming more and more to his advances, and their little private trysts were definitely getting more amorous. It was only a matter of time, but then, as he had often thought, it takes time to school a good filly.

He had been sorry to see the Kilpatricks leave as soon as the week was over, but Roderick was impatient to get back to work and did not want Catrin exposed to more threats. Their farewell had been almost touching.

He had written a long letter to her, spinning a tale about meeting Devlin O'Farrell at Ballanalee, but that the artist was heading immediately to Donegal and would not be back for some time. He fed her with the information Maura had given him, and that O'Farrell had promised to make contact as soon as he returned.

Catrin had read the letter with great interest. The information about O'Farrell was pleasing, and now that Anthony had made personal contact, she might still achieve her ambition.

The Wishing Boy remained a priority, but she had to admit to Cara that there was also another attraction in Galway now, and for the first time there was a yearning for other things stirring within her.

Their mutual love of horses had been a big factor in making Catrin less cautious. There was an element of hero worship in her treatment of him for the way he had defied Maguire and beaten his horse. There had been no incidents to scare the family all week, and the guard duties had functioned well under his organisation. She had seen nothing of her rival, other than the presentation of the prize at the race meeting, and she was beginning to accept that perhaps Anthony was telling the truth, and merely using the girl to get information about Maguire. It was in his line of duty so she was prepared to accept that.

At the Barracks, Anthony had interrupted his pleasant meditation to smoke a cigarette when he heard the phone ring in the orderly room.

"Call fer you, surr," the orderly shouted, "sounds like yer sister again."

He frowned. He didn't have a sister. It couldn't be Catrin for she always said who it was. Oh Christ! It must be Maura, despite all his warnings not to call the barracks. He had not seen her since the rendezvous at the O'Farrell place, and in truth was glad. The longer he gave her to stew in her own juice, the more likely she was to come crawling back. Then he could manipulate her to give him the information he wanted. He shouted to the orderly to put the call through.

"Maura, I told you"... his words were cut off abruptly.

"I know I shouldn't be calling, but you haven't been to see me. I have to talk to you. I have to see you. It's important, very important. You must come!". The words tumbled out like machine gun fire, and she was near hysteria.

"Calm down for God's sake. What the blazes is wrong with you?"

"I can't explain on the phone. Just come and see me. It has to be to-night. My Da is back to-morrow. I have to see you before then."

"Alright, alright. Don't get so upset. I'll see you". If Maguire was returning to-morrow, it might be that she had something to warn him about. It was best to find out. An embrace and a few kisses would probably calm her down.

"Where can we meet, and what time?" he asked.

"Come to the shop at night. Come at half past eight."

"The shop? Isn't that too risky?"

"Not at that time. There's never anyone around at that time of night. I'll tell Eamon I'm doing some of the books to be ready before Da gets back. The shop will be in darkness, but I'll be looking out for you, and I'll let you in. Promise you'll come."

He talked to her a few more minutes, reassuring her he would be there, and that he would forgive her outbursts at Ballanalee. By the time he had finished she was calm and sounding in control of herself. He replaced the telephone and sat back in his chair to reflect on the situation.

It was a make your mind up time sort of dilemma. He could sense danger in the air. The affair with Maura was becoming too risky, and now that he had achieved his original goal to seduce her, the risks were beginning to outweigh the excitement. Nor did he believe she would forfeit family loyalties and give him the kind of information that would help him finish Maguire.

In any case, it was a relationship without a future. Maguire would see to that. In his heart he knew it was time to end the affair, to cut and run, however painful it might be to her. He would have to convince her it would be a noble sacrifice on his part in order to protect her from the possibility of discovery by her father.

Despite his self-assurance, he spent most of the day thinking about the problem, and turning over in his mind the upsetting telephone conversation. It must be something serious to have driven her to such panic. Since she obviously was infatuated with him, he convinced himself that it must be something to do with his safety. It was a reflection on his own vanity that the obvious did not occur to him.

Chapter Twenty-One

It was a dull grey evening and the rain fell steadily as Anthony made his way to Eyre Square. He wore his long trench coat over his civilian clothes. The dismal rain washed streets were deserted, silent except the noise of the rain and the splash of the down pipes as the water cascaded into the gutters.

The lights were out in the shop, but as he tapped on the glass door Maura appeared from the dark and ushered him inside. He followed her to the tiny office at the rear, a small room, barely large enough for the desk, a filing cabinet and the two chairs that filled it. The room was in shadows, the only light provided by a small desk lamp.

He shook the rain from his coat and hung it on the peg behind the door. She came into his arms immediately, clinging tightly to him, digging her fingers into his shoulder blades. She was charged with emotion. He could feel her quivering. He tilted her chin gently and was surprised by the tears that filled her eyes. He pulled a handkerchief from his pocket and wiped the tears away.

"It's alright. I'm here now. There's no need to cry. I told you to forget our little quarrel about O'Farrell. Don't keep fretting about it." He made to kiss her, but she broke away and sat down behind the desk.

"For God's sake, Maura. I only wanted to kiss and make up."

"I'm sorry, but I'm all mixed up. I can't think – I need your help to straighten things out. It's not just about me. It's about you, too."

"You're making this sound very dramatic. I've told you. Put the O'Farrell incident out of your mind. It doesn't matter anymore."

"It's not that. It's worse than that." She twisted his handkerchief tightly in her hands.

"Is it your father? Has he found out something?"

"No. He hasn't found anything out about us. But he will. I'm worried to death. He'll kill me, so he will." She burst into tears.

He moved behind her, and began to stroke her hair in an effort to calm her.

"What could possibly make him do that?" he felt a pang of alarm.

"He looks after you to the point of smothering you. He protects you from everyone. Why should you think he would harm you?"

"You don't know him. When he's in a temper, he can hurt anyone, even his family."

"I can believe that, but if he doesn't know about us, what are you afraid of?"

He began to massage her neck gently. It was one of her most erogenous zones and usually primed her for sex. To his surprise, she pushed his hands away.

"There's no need for that. It's not the time. There's something we have to talk about."

Anthony felt humiliated. His touch was usually effective, and he was losing patience.

"For God's sake, Maura, what the hell are you going on about?"

"He will find out about us. He's bound to. He'll kill me, and he'll kill you too." The words came out in a flood of tears as she buried her head in her arms.

Anthony's face turned ashen. He sat down on the other chair his pulse racing.

"Tell me then. Stop piddling about, damn it! Tell me!"

"I'm going to have a child. Your child! Damn yourself! I'm pregnant! Couldn't you see how tired and strained I was.

Didn't it ever occur to you how dangerous it was?" The tears flowed down her cheeks.

"Oh my God! I can't believe it. It's only been three or four times."

"More. It doesn't matter. I think it happened the very first time."

"For Christ's sake! I can't believe it. The first time? What bloody luck!" The enormity of the situation began to grow.

"Is that all you can say? Blasphemy and bad luck?

"Are you certain? Some women miss their periods when they've been under stress, and there's nothing wrong. You've been worried a lot recently."

"Doctor McCrimmond told me to-day. He's sure. I thought there was something wrong last month, but I just hoped it was nothing. He did proper tests. It's true."

"Why in God's name didn't you tell me the last time— the time at O'Farrell's place?"

"I wasn't sure then. I was just so happy to see you again. I didn't think. But this last week I've been sick so much, I had to see the doctor."

Anthony smacked a fist into his hand. "Christ! How can you be so unlucky?"

"For God's sake, stop saying that! "I don't know what to do. I'm all mixed up. I need you to help me. You still love me, don't you?"

Anthony's brain was reeling. The possibility of this had never entered his head. Their sex was spontaneous. Common sense went out the window when two frustrated passions clashed. He had always been lucky before. The bitter irony was it was her who became so rampant that control was taken out of his hands.

As he saw it, she was more responsible than him.

"Look Maura. I can't think straight either. This has come right out of the blue and I can't make a decision now. Give me some time to think."

"There isn't time. My Da 'll be back to-morrow. He'll know something's not right and he'll start asking questions. I won't be able to stand it."

"You'll have to say you're ill with something. Something you drank or ate. Tell him you had to go to the doctor and you've got some medicine. That will give us some time to think."

"No, no! We can't wait," she was becoming panic stricken, "we won't have any chance to meet once he's back. We need to settle this now?"

Anthony covered his head with his hands and sat bowed in thought, his brain trying to cope. Maura sat, stifling her sobs, and continuing to twist the handkerchief out of shape.

Anthony lowered his hands and raised his head to look at her.

"The most obvious thing is to get rid of it."

Her face contorted in horror. "How can you suggest such a thing? It's a human life. It's your child. It's against the rules of the Church. I couldn't do it. I'd rather die first!"

"You've already said your Da'll kill you anyway!"

"You bastard! What a thing to say. You're only thinking of yourself. Even if I did this terrible thing, how could I keep it a secret from him?"

"I could find someone in Dublin. Some of my connections will know. I'm not the only one who's made a mistake. You could come to Dublin on some pretext. It would be over in the same day."

"I can't believe you're saying this. This is our child. In normal circumstances we would be overjoyed. Now you're suggesting we murder it. I thought you loved me as much as I love you. But you don't. You're only trying to make it convenient for yourself."

"Don't be bloody stupid! It's a logical solution. I'm sorry if it hurts, but you have to face up to it. What else is there to suggest?"

"Couldn't we just run off together? Have the baby? Start afresh somewhere?"

"That's an even worse idea. I can't desert the army. I'd have them hunting me as well as your Da. We wouldn't get fifty miles from here before we were spotted. If your Da was first, he'd kill us for sure."

Maura collapsed across the desk, stricken and sobbing. Anthony was beginning to find the incessant tears too much to bear. He attempted to lift her head, but she shook his hands away.

"I have to go now," he said, "I can't help when you're like this. I'll contact you to-morrow when I've had a chance to think things out. Go home now and try and get a goodnight's rest." He leaned over and kissed the top of her head.

He took his coat from the peg on the door and slowly put it on, watching her in case she raised her head, but she continued to sob into her arms. He let himself out and strode briskly, head down against the rain, his mind occupied with the problem. He failed to notice the shadowy figure in another shop doorway who observed his exit.

As the sound of Anthony's footsteps faded, the figure emerged. Eamon Maguire was puzzled. The Captain?

He watched Anthony until he turned the corner at the far end of the square. He was about to go to the shop, but suddenly weakened, and turned to head in the opposite direction. Once again his courage had deserted him, but the presence of an Army officer emerging from the shop alarmed him.

Meanwhile, in the little office, Maura continued to rest her head on the desk, and still the tears flowed. She cried until there were no more tears left.

Chapter Twenty-Two

Elsewhere in Galway, there was optimism. Maguire returned from Belfast in buoyant mood. On his first direct contact with the Belfast Brigade, he had created a good impression. With Rafferty able to produce figures to show recruitment was at record levels, and that he had a skilled bomb maker in his ranks, he was lauded and praised.

It had been agreed that a training camp be set up in which bomb making would be a major topic. Belfast had suffered from too many would-be bomb makers blowing themselves up. There were hints they wanted to expand the bombing terror campaign, even to extending it to the British mainland.

The plan appealed to Maguire. Like many Republican supporters in the West, he had become impatient with the lack of instructions and support from Dublin.

There was a power struggle taking place between the two, and he thought Belfast offered the best chances of gaining him more rank and power.

They arrived back in Galway in the afternoon. The long drive had provided a chance to debate the matters discussed at the meeting, and by the time they arrived in Galway, a plan had been worked out. They were agreed that the training camp be located in Connemara rather than Galway. It was more remote and the territory sparsely populated.

Neither the Garda or the Army was likely to trouble them.

His first task was to locate Seamus and Devlin and acquaint them with the plan. Dev would need warning in case there were materials needed, and Seamus would have to see how many volunteers he could muster.

Rafferty dropped him outside the shop and he bustled in expecting to find Maura. He was annoyed to find only Eamon.

"Where is she?" he demanded.

"She's had to go home. She wasn't feeling well. She's been sick," Eamon answered.

"What the hell's brought that on? By God it needs to be somethin' bad to go home at this time o' day."

"She has been bad, Da. She thinks it might be that oyster stew we had the other night." Eamon had been upset to see his sister in distress and was determined to defend her.

"That's bliddy stupid! We all ate it. Have you had any problems? Has Seamus? I certainly haven't. D'ye know if she's heard from Seamus?"

"There was a message this morning. He'll be back to-night."

"Good! I've got important news for him and Dev. Get you on wi' your work. I'm goin' over to the pub an' make sure everythin's alright. I'll see you later."

He arrived home after six to find Seamus and Eamon already seated, and Maura in the process of placing food on the table.

She tried to smile but it was a faint effort. "The boys were starving so I thought I'd get started."

"You should've waited," he growled. "The head o' the house decides when we eat. Anyway let's get on with it. I'm starving', too."

The meal was well under way and both Seamus and Eamon attacked their plates with relish. Maguire raised his eyes from his and regarded Maura. He could sense something was wrong. She had hardly touched hers, and he could see she was not comfortable.

"What's this about you feelin' ill," he asked her.

"It's nothing. Just a little tummy upset," she responded. "I think it was that oyster stew we had. It seems to have stuck with me. I can't keep anything down."

"You look bloody terrible," there was no sympathy in his voice, "it must be bad to come home from the shop so early in the day." Maura sat looking at her plate.

"If ye can't eat it, don't let it go to waste. Pass it to Seamus. He watched as she scraped most of the plate on to his plate, but also saved a little for Eamon.

"I'll go and mash the tea." Maura retreated to the kitchen where she paused over the sink. She wanted to be sick, but try as she might nothing would come."I'm worried about her, "Seamus confided, "Eamon says she's been like this for a couple o' days. It's not like her."

"She's eaten nothing for the past few days," Eamon chimed in, Doctor McCrimmond's given her something to help."

"She's been to see McCrimmond? Good God! Is that right?" He fired the question at Maura who appeared with a tray and the mugs of tea.

"I asked him if he could give me something to settle my stomach, that's all. He gave me a powder to help. It's beginning to work, but it might take a day or two. He said a bad oyster might take time to get rid of. I'm feeling a bit light headed. I'll lie down a while. Eamon, will you do the dishes for me?" She left them to their tea and trooped upstairs to lie down.

"Small wonder she's light headed if she hasn't been eatin'. Somethin's not right. Maybe I should have a word with McCrimmond. Do as she says, Eamon. Clear the dishes away an' wash up. Seamus an' I have a lot to talk about."

He relayed a verbal report on the meeting in Belfast to Seamus and outlined his plans for a training school in Connemara.

"Dev an' you know the territory. Can you pick a spot?"

"Loads o' places up there. I'll talk wi' Dev."

"Is he at Ballanalee?"

"Aye. He has a few chores to catch up on."

"Well tell him not to take too long. This thing has to be set up quick. I want to impress Belfast. They're mad keen to increase the bombing campaign, and Dev's experience is a great asset to us."

Maguire sat back in his chair feeling more relaxed. The tea had filled him well and relating the success of the Belfast meeting to Seamus had fed his ego.

"Eamon, he called out to the kitchen, "fetch us in the bottle o' precious that's kept in the cupboard. I feel like a drink."

Eamon appeared quickly with the stone bottle and placed it beside Maguire.

"Get you upstairs now," he said, "Seamus an' I have some work to sort out."

Maguire watched Eamon scuttle away and sighed. "I wish that lad was more like you." He poured a generous measure of the golden liquid into each empty mug. For a few minutes, they sat in silence as they sipped the fiery liquor, and basked in the warmth of pleasure it spread through their systems.

Across the other side of Galway, however, there was no such contentment. Sergeant McNulty had seen a drastic change in the demeanour of his commanding officer. His normal cockiness and energy seemed drained, and he looked worried.

He was shutting himself up in his office a lot, and had not even bothered to check on Rufus, one of his normal daily habits. McNulty was at a loss. During the week of the races. The lieutenant had been full of life and self-confidence. Winning the handicap, arm in arm with the flashy redhead, living it up at Dungannon House. No wonder he looked pleased with himself.

The Kilpatrick girl and him made a handsome couple. Looked like a love match. Maybe they'd had a dust up? She looked the uppity type. That would explain the lieutenant's behaviour. McNulty sighed. These young bloods always took their love affairs too seriously.

Anthony sat slumped at his desk in a foul mood. He had slept little, his sleep constantly interrupted by his predicament. Damn Maura! She was the one that led him on. It was her consuming passion that made it dangerous. With her refusal to abort the baby he was caught in a diabolical trap. Whichever way he turned, the consequences were unacceptable, and he now had real fear of Maguire.

His natural inclination was to cut and run, but that was out of the question. If the army didn't hunt him down, Maguire would, and there would be only one outcome.

For the first time in his army career he needed help from his superior officers. There was one remote possibility.

Cunningham appeared with his morning tea.

"Ring the barracks in Dublin," he told him, "see if Major O'Brien's there and ask if I can speak to him. Say it's urgent."

The call came through a few minutes later, and as he picked up the receiver, he had composed exactly what he wanted to say to the major.

Shortly afterwards, McNulty was summoned to Anthony's office. He entered to find Anthony clearing his desk and stuffing papers into his brief case.

"I'm off to Dublin," he announced. "Major O'Brien wants a preliminary report on what's been happening since I took over. I may tag a few days leave on. You'll be in charge while I'm gone. You know the ropes. Just one thing.

"Keep a watch on that farm at Ballanalee and report on whoever comes and goes. Watch out particularly for this O'Farrell character. If there's anything you think I should know, leave a message at the barracks for me. I'll check with them each day.

Fuel up the small van for me. You won't need it and I'd rather drive than take the train. Any questions?"

McNulty left him to complete his packing and went in search of Cunningham to prepare the small van. He didn't mind the lieutenant going. Having no one breathing down your neck was a good thing. He might even sneak in a spot of fishing whilst keeping an eye on the farm.

Chapter Twenty-Three

"I'm sorry, Miss. Lieutenant Dillon is not available."

Maura's heart sank. "Please tell him it's very urgent."

The orderly clerk held the telephone away from him and whispered to the sergeant who was in process of posting orders on the bulletin board.

"It's that girl. The one who says she's his sister. She wants to speak with him. Says it's urgent."

McNulty took the phone from him. "Sergeant McNulty here, Miss. I'm in charge while the lieutenant is away."

"He's not there?" the voice was strained, "where is he?"

"He's had to go to Dublin. He did leave in rather a hurry, so perhaps he didn't have time to tell you. He has a meeting with his Commanding officer and he did say he might take a few days leave. I expect you'll be seeing him shortly. Can I help you?"

"No. No thank you. It has to be him."

She had passed a sleepless night, agonizing. Maura replaced the receiver. Her stomach churned as her nerves began to fray. A wave of nausea engulfed her and she ran to the toilet. She sat there until the nausea passed, her face white and sweat beading her brow. But there was nothing in her stomach to vomit. She was bitter at Anthony for suggesting abortion, but she feared her father most of all. Once he discovered the truth, she feared for both their lives.

Now her grief was compounded. He'd simply run away. All his declarations of love were meaningless. How many times had her father drummed into her not to be fooled by a lover's promise, and how many young men had he turned away when he deemed them to be only interested in her virtue?

There was a gentle knock on the door. "Maura! Are you alright? You've been in there a long time".

"Let me be Eamon. I'm not well. Just leave me be. Keep your eye on the shop, never mind me."

"Will I fetch Doctor McCrimmond?"

"No Eamon. Just do as I ask."

Mention of the doctor gave her some inspiration. She knew he regarded her as a fine young woman and she trusted him completely.

She left the shop hurriedly, pausing only to shout to Eamon that she was going to the surgery. The doctor was on the point of setting out on his daily rounds when Maura arrived on the doorstep, pale and stressed out, and terribly agitated. He immediately hustled her into his office and sat her down.

"Calm yourself Maura. I'll get the wife to make you some tea."

"No, please don't bother. I couldn't drink anything right now".

"Well just you sit there until you're ready tell me what the problem is. Relax. Take a few deep breaths. In fast, out slow. That's it."

She was calmer now, but still having problems to unburden herself.

"Is it this baby you're carrying?" She nodded, her face a picture of misery.

"I can't have it," she said tearfully. "It's impossible, and I don't know what to do.

"Why is it not possible? You're a fine healthy young woman. You're a good age, and it's time you were married. I told you already you're not the first lass that's had to get married in a big hurry. You should be full of joy, not snivelling like this."

"I tried to tell you yesterday. It's not like that. It's not normal. Promise you won't do that. Keep this between you and me."

"Is it the father or the family that's the problem? If so tell me who they are and I'll speak to them, or better still I'll get Father O'Donnell to put the fear of God into them. Why won't you tell me the name of the father?"

Maura shook her head and looked down at the floor. She could not meet his eyes.

"So how am I supposed to help," McCrimmond was losing patience.

"I can't have this baby. I can't marry the father. My Da would never let me. I want to get rid of it. I don't know what else to do." She burst into tears.

The doctor was out of his seat, horrified by the statement he had just heard.

"Listen to me, Maura. I've known you ever since you could walk. Never in all my born days would I have thought you'd say such a thing. It's dreadful! You're asking me to murder an innocent child. You call that help? I'll pretend you never said it. Get you off to the Church and say a few hail Marys."

He waited for a reaction but there was none. She sat, head bowed, and the tears continued to plop on the cold linoleum floor. "I could do no such thing,"

His anger cooled as he sought to console her. "It's against a doctor's code of ethics. My job is to save lives not destroy them. I had enough of that in the Civil War. Apart from that, it's something that could prove harmful to you. In later life you'd come to regret it dearly. I'll help you in any way I can, but don't ask me to stoop to that business."

"My Da will kill me when he finds out."

"I thought that might be the reason you're so frightened. He wouldn't approve of the father. Is that it?"

"Something like that," she mumbled.

"Well, maybe I can do something there."

"You can't. I told you it wasn't normal."

McCrimmond threw his arms in the air as a gesture of his frustration. "Be Jaysus! I can't understand. I know your Da has kept a tight rein over you, and I know what a temper he's got, but I also know he cares for you. He might even like a little grandson. Did you ever think of that?"

Maura rose from the chair, dabbing her eyes to absorb the tears. "You're wrong. He'd murder it. It's no use talking any more. I can't explain. You'd never believe me. I'm sorry I had to come to you like this. I shouldn't have asked a man as decent as yourself to do such a thing." She turned to leave.

"Wait a minute. I'll give you a sedative to keep you calm and let you sleep better and maybe then you can face up to your Da. If you feel drowsy through the day, just lie down a little."

He gave her a little pillbox. "Take one of these before you go to bed, and another one next morning after breakfast. Try to stop worrying. These things usually sort themselves out."

He watched her leave the surgery, his conscience sorely troubled. A little box of pills seemed so inadequate.

He was gravely concerned. She was hovering on the brink of a nervous breakdown. Despite Maura's plea, he still thought he could persuade Maguire to listen to reason. He had seen Maguire's anger boil over during their time together in the Limerick Brigade, and the scenes that followed were ingrained in his memory. He need not have worried. The decision was taken out of his hands.

The following day he was trotting along the coast road in his dapper little pony and trap, making his daily rounds, when he saw a motor vehicle approaching from the opposite direction. He recognised it as one of Maguire's vans with Seamus driving it, and himself in the passenger seat.

Both of them had to slow down because of the narrow road and as they came alongside one another, Maguire signalled him to stop.

McCrimmond climbed down and crossed to the other side. Maguire wound the window down.

"What's this about Maura comin' to see you," he asked in his usual ill-tempered manner? "She's lookin' bliddy dreadful. I can't have her in the shop in that state. She says it's some shellfish she ate. She's not eatin' enough to feed a sparrow. Surely you can do something better for her."

"I'm worried about her," McCrimmond answered, "In fact I need to talk to you. Not now. I have to get to Frances McCafferty. Her baby's due any time."

"Talk to me?" Maguire bridled. What can I do for her?. You're the doctor. You sort her out."

"Come and see me in the surgery. We can talk better there."

"What the hell's goin' on? Why can't you call into the house? If she's that ill you ought to put her on your rounds instead o' gallivanting' out here."

McCrimmond flushed with anger. Now he could see what Maura was so frightened of. He turned on his heel and climbed back on the trap. As he picked up the whip, he shouted across.

"Just come and see me, Make it to-morrow".

"It's important. Maura needs your help." He cracked the whip and the pony shot off leaving Maguire fuming.

Seamus had said nothing throughout the encounter. He was thinking that there must be something seriously wrong with Maura, and yet none of them had suffered similar upsets from the oyster stew.

Brendan was beginning to think there was more of a problem than an oyster stew

Whatever the outcome after the meeting his Da, had with the Doctor, he would stand by his sister and protect her from harm.

There was still the faint memory of a row he had witnessed between his father and his mother when he was young, and how much it had upset him. It was not long after that when she died. In his later years he had often wondered if there was a connection between the two.

Later that evening, when he had finished surgery, McCrimmond was making the last entries in his journal and preparing to go for his supper. He heard the outer door open and someone came into the waiting room.

"I'm finished for the night," he shouted through the door. Unless it's very urgent, come back in the morning."

"I think it's bliddy urgent!" Maguire barged into the office. "It won't wait until mornin'. I want to know what's goin' on with Maura. Why do I have to come an' see you?"

"I asked you to see me to-morrow."

"I know you did, but that's not good enough. I want to know now. You said she needed help. What does that mean? If it's only shellfish poisoning, you can surely sort that out?"

"It's not shellfish that's the problem." The words were out of his mouth before he realised the terrible mistake he had made.

Maguire froze. For the first time ever, McCrimmond had a hint of fear in his eyes. He sat down heavily in the chair in front of the desk.

"You mean it's somethin' more serious? Surely to God T.B?"

"No. Not that."

"Well, for Christ's sake what is it?"

"Have you spoken to Maura at all?"

"Not since yesterday. I've been out all day. I'm on my way home now. Since I was passin' your place, I thought I'd have a word. C'mon then. Tell me what's wrong with her."

"It would be wrong to tell you. I have to respect the confidentiality between doctor and patient."

"You feckin' gobshite!" Maguire exploded. He reached over and pulled the doctor across his desk by his tie, twisting it tight to bring the face of the doctor to within an inch or two of his own.

"You got me here on the pretence of saying she needs help, and now you're sayin' you can't tell me? I'll break yer bloody neck, so I will." He pushed the doctor back into his chair and stared at him with his grey piercing eyes.

McCrimmond was shaken. He straightened his tie and tried to regain his composure.

"I only wanted to appeal to you to be careful with Maura. She's on the verge of a nervous breakdown. Act like you just did with me, and it could send her over the edge."

"You still haven't said what's wrong. I mean there must be somethin' that's makin' her nerves bad. I'll ask you again, an' give me a straight answer, or by God I'll put you into your own hospital." He jumped to his feet and banged his ham fist on the desk to emphasise his point. The thud of the blow reverberated in the small office and unnerved the doctor.

He turned pale and swallowed hard. He had never been able to stand up to Maguire's bullying. He answered in a quiet and faltering voice.

Maguire stood as if he had just taken a heavy blow to his solar plexus. He sank into the chair.

"She's pregnant. That's why she's sick. It's a common problem during the early weeks. She begged me not to tell you. Her nerves are shot because she's terrified of what you might do. I beg you Flann. Be gentle with her."

Maguire was stunned, a picture of shock and disbelief. It was a full minute before he spoke.

"It can't be. She's never been wi' anyone. I don't believe it. What makes you so sure?"

"I had a proper test done at the hospital. It was positive. I gave her a good examination. I'd say she was about eight to ten weeks gone."

"Jaysus Murphy! I hardly ever let her outta my sight. Did she say who the father was?"

There was a vindictive look in his eyes. It was difficult to look into such venom.

"She wouldn't tell me. Said she wouldn't tell anyone."

Maguire was on his feet again. "By God she'd better tell me. I'll nail the bastard to his own front door. I've guarded that girl like a treasure, so I have. Never let anyone near her if I thought that was what he was after havin' his way wi' her. I'll have his balls," his voice rose to a shout.

"Calm down, for God's sake, Flann. This is exactly what I was trying to avoid. Act like this with Maura and you'll lose her. She'll finish up in a mental hospital."

"Shut your gob! This is my affair now. I intend to find out who's done this to my girl. Keep your nose out or I'll give you the same as I'm gonna give this bastard when I catch him." He rose and kicked the chair away from him, sending it crashing into the wall, and stormed out.

McCrimmond sat cradling his head in his arms. He was full of remorse. He had just lit the fuse of the most terrible bomb imaginable, and it would hurt someone he had the highest regard for. He wanted to weep.

He snapped out of his anguish as he realised he must warn her. He reached for the telephone and barked at the operator.

"Annie. It's Doctor McCrimmond. You need to get Seamus Maguire for me. It's very urgent."

The call was through in less than a minute. "This is Doctor McCrimmond. Who's that?"

"It's Eamon, doctor. What's the trouble?"

"Get Seamus for me Eamon. Be quick about it. There isn't much time."

He heard Eamon call for his brother.

"Hello doctor. What's the trouble?"

"I haven't got time to explain, Seamus. Your Da is on his way, and he's in a violent temper. He's going to be nasty to Maura. He could do her great harm. Don't let him near her until he's cooled down."

"Why? What's Maura done that he should be so mad? She's only been off work a little with sickness. He can't be mad about that."

"It's worse than that! She's pregnant. There isn't time to talk more. Get her out of the house before he gets home. For God's sake protect her. Don't let him get to her."

McCrimmond hung up the phone and sank back into his chair, once again cupping his face in his hands. He had exposed Maura to violence despite his intentions of trying to avoid it.

He knew Maguire from the old days. There was a streak of the psychopath in him. Once on a spree of destruction, there was no controlling him. He remembered what happened to his poor wife.

If any harm befell Maura, he would have it on his conscience for the rest of his life. Worst of all, he was too much under the influence of Maguire to atone for his mistake. He sat alone in his misery, waiting for a call he hoped would never come.

Chapter Twenty-Four

Maura came rushing from the kitchen to see what the noise was about. "What's the matter? Why are you shoving Eamon out the door? What's he done?"

"You've gotta' get out o' here, too. Doctor McCrimmond just phoned to warn us Da's on the warpath.

"He'll be here any minute. You have to leave everythin' and go."

"Oh Holy Mother! She dropped the pudding bowl she was carrying and covered her eyes with her hands.

"He must've found out. Oh my God, Seamus, he'll kill me, so he will," she began to cry and become hysterical. Seamus took hold of her and started to drag her towards the door.

"Yes, he knows. He dragged it outta McCrimmond, an' now he's gone crazy. Eamon's gone to the shop. Off after him as quick as you can."

He had his hand on the door handle when there was the sound of a car drawing up outside followed swiftly by the fierce slamming of a car door.

"Oh Jaysus! It's himself. Quick! Upstairs to your room an'lock yourself in. I'll try an' handle him an' calm him down. For God's sake hurry," he propelled her up the stairs.

She was near the top when Maguire burst in the door. Seamus was accustomed to his father's violent tempers, but never before seen him so incandescent.

"What the hell are you doin'," he demanded. What are you pushin' her upstairs for? I want to talk to her this instant." He surged towards the stairs but Seamus barred his way.

"Outta the road," Maguire bellowed, "let me get to her. She's got some explainin' to do."

Seamus held his ground, spreading his arms at full width to bar any progress to the stairs.

"Hold on, Da. You're in no fit state to ask her questions."

Maguire made to brush past him. "I told you to get outta my way, now move aside an'let me up the stairs. I won't tell you again. Move aside!"

"I know what you want her for, Da, an'I guess she's done wrong. But she's ill Da. She's not herself. She's in a bad way. You're in no state to talk to her sensibly."

"You think I'm in a state! D'you know what state she's in? In the family way, she is. All that shite about shellfish makin' her sick. Some bliddy shellfish! I want it outta her who's responsible. Now get outta the road."

He charged Seamus and they grappled with each other. Seamus tried to pin him against the wall, and succeeded in diverting him into the living room where they broke away from each other, and stood breathing heavily glaring like wild animals at one another. Seamus had his hands raised ready to repel any further attack. Each waited for the other to make a move.

"This is not right, Seamus. The day a son raises his fists against his father in his own house is a black day for the family. There's only room for one bull in a field. Don't make it worse. Get outta the way."

"Not 'till you calm down. I'll not let you hurt her."

"I won't harm her. I just want to know who the father is. He's the one that'll get hurt."

They continued to stare at one another as their breathing slowed down to normal. Seamus lowered his fists.

"If you promise that's all, an' you don't beat her, I'll fetch her down. But sit down an' cool off an' let's act sensible about this."

Maguire reluctantly backed off and sat down at the dining table. He rested his arms on the table and stared unremittingly at Seamus with his cold grey eyes.

"Alright," he said in a voice devoid of warmth, "I don't want to have to fight with my own blood, but I'm after havin' the truth outta her. There's no bliddy eejit getting' away wi' this."

"No bliddy likely, I agree, we have a right to know, an' to see he does right by her, but let's have a cup o' tay first. That'll settle us both. Then we can talk better."

Seamus retired to the kitchen and made tea. He was stalling for time and hoping that Maura would also have time to compose herself for the ordeal ahead. He sweetened each cup generously and added plenty of milk.

"Any idea when this happened?" Seamus broke the silence.

"McCrimmond reckons she's at least three months gone. The bastard! I'll get him whoever he is. I've not been watchin' her so close lately. Everything seemed to be goin' fine without havin' to keep tabs on her."

"I've been away a lot," Seamus admitted, "But I never would'ave thought Maura would get into this mess. Maybe it was forced on her an' she was too scared to say."

"All the more reason to find out the culprit." Maguire drained his mug and banged it on the table.

"Right then. Let's be havin' her down an' get to the bottom o' this mess. I've cooled off enough."

Seamus nodded. He left the room, closing the door behind him and clumped up the stairs. Maguire sat drumming his fingers on the table as he waited impatiently for Seamus to reappear with Maura. He looked more in control of himself. The tea and the break had diminished the outward signs of his anger, but within him the fires of wrath were still smouldering and it would take very little to fan another blaze.

He could hear voices upstairs, the deep tones of Seamus and a mixture of crying and hysterical sounds from Maura. The drumming of his fingers on the table continued. His patience was wearing thin.

There were heavy footsteps descending the stairs and he sat upright and tensed in his chair as Seamus opened the door and re-entered. He was alone.

"What now?" he demanded. "Where is she?"

"She won't come down. She's too frightened. Leave her be for a bit.

She might come down later."

"Like hell she will!" Maguire rose angrily from his chair. "I want it outta her now! If she won't come down then I'll go up."

He sprang forward and shouldered Seamus aside. He had reached the door before Seamus could prevent him, and all he could do was to cling on to his jacket and try to hold him back.

"Don't go up Da. She's havin' hysterics. Leave her be." He struggled to hold on.

"Let go, you bliddy fool! Let go or by Jaysus." He swung round and struck Seamus a savage blow across the temple, sending him reeling. As he was dropping to his knees, another blow sent him crashing to the floor.

Maguire turned and raced up the stairs.

"Maura!" he bellowed, "come outta there an' face up to what you've done. I want to know who got you into this mess. You'd better tell me. I'm in no mood to put up wi'any nonsense."

The bedroom door remained shut. There was a shriek from inside as he rattled the handle in an attempt to open it. He stood back and then with a mighty blow with the sole of his boot splintered the flimsy lock and sent the door flying open.

He surged inside and saw her cowering and crying by the side of the bed. He seized her hands and dragged her to her feet.

"Did I no shout enough?" he yelled into her tear stained face. "Out wi' it! Who's the bastard that did this to you? I want to know. Who have you been whorin' with behind my back? Tell me, dammit! Tell me." He shook her violently.

"No, no. Never! I can't," she wailed, "I can't do it. Leave me, please Da. I'm sorry. I'm so sorry. It was my fault. Just leave me, please!"

He shook her again like a terrier with a rat, and she started to scream in panic.

"I won't stop until I know who the bastard is. Tell me, dammit or I'll beat the livin' daylights outta you." He released his hold of her and started to unbuckle his belt. In that instant she dashed past him in an attempt to gain the stairs.

She was halfway and could see Seamus staggering on the lower step trying to come to her aid, when Maguire caught hold of the sleeve of her dress and pulled her back. She struggled fiercely to free herself.

"Seamus!" she screamed, "hurry, hurry! He's going to beat me."

As she tried to gain the stairs, there was the sound of tearing cloth as the sleeve of her dress gave way at the seam and ripped off completely. The momentum caused by the sudden rupture of the stitching carried her into the balustrade of the landing so forcibly that she catapulted over the rail and with an unearthly scream fell headlong to the stone floor of the hall below.

The scream was cut short as she hit the floor with a sickening thud.

There was an eerie silence, broken only by the laboured breathing of Maguire as he stood motionless on the stairs, the torn sleeve of the dress still in his hands.

Seamus staggered to where she lay, and knelt down beside her. Her eyes were open, but there was no sight in them. Her head was at a peculiar angle. He felt for a pulse, and pressed his ear against her breast. He shook his head and raised his eyes to meet those of his father.

"She's dead. You feckin' eejit! You an' your bliddy temper! She's dead. I always knew it would do no good".

"You've gone too far this time." He was holding her limp hand and crying unashamedly.

"Why couldn't you wait like I told you? She might have been alright if you'd given her time. You should'ave waited."

Maguire descended the stairs slowly, his face impassive and the torn sleeve clutched in his hand. He knelt down beside the body.

"The Devil take me. She's broken her neck. My God, why didn't she just tell me without strugglin' so much? "

His eyes were moist, but no tears fell. As they continued to kneel at the side of the body, an intense silence fell over the house, broken only by the tick of the grandfather clock in the hall.

Maguire closed his eyes for a moment, contemplating what next he should do.

"Seamus, "he said eventually, "We have to move. There's nuthin' more we can to." He rose and went to the kitchen, returning with a large white table cloth.

"C'mon now. There's no use kneelin' down there. Say a prayer an' cover her up."

He thrust the table cloth into Seamus's hand. "Then fetch McCrimmond, an' if you know where Eamon is get him to fetch Father O'Donell."

Seamus spread the cloth over the body and rose to his feet. "What about the Garda? They'll need to know."

"I'll deal wi'that. Get McCrimmond first. I'll stay with her until you fetch him."

Seamus reluctantly took his jacket from the peg behind the door and put it on. His eyes were still full of tears. He started to say something, but choked on it and hurried out the door leaving it unsaid.

Maguire watched him go and then made his way to the kitchen. He opened one of the cabinets and took the small bottle of whisky he kept there and poured some into a glass and sat at the table in silence. He drank in small sips, his mind turning over his thoughts, as he sought to find answers to his problems.

He remained in a trance-like state until McCrimmond bustled through the front door along with Seamus. He immediately examined the body and as he closed his bag, looked accusingly at Maguire.

"This is what I feared. I knew you and your temper would cause something drastic. I tried to warn you. You're a bliddy fool Maguire. You've lost one of the most gentle craturs on this earth, so you have. God help you!"

"Hush up," Maguire snapped out of his reverie." It was an accident, that's all. She tripped an'fell down the stairs. Could'a happened to anyone." "Don't take me for a fool, Maguire. She wouldn't be lying in that position if it was a fall down the stairs. I also see that there's a sleeve of her dress torn off. How d'you account for that?"

Maguire's face contorted in annoyance.

"Sit down, McCrimmond," he indicated the table and the bottle that was on it. "Have a wee drop wi'me to steady the nerves. Seamus! Don't just stand there. Fetch a couple o'glasses an' join us."

Seamus brought one glass. "I'm goin' out to get Eamon. He'll take this bad. He worshipped her. I don't want a drink." He left the two men staring at one another across the table.

"I suppose you want me to cover up for you?" McCrimmond made no attempt to disguise his disgust.

"Of course. I tell you it was an accident. I never meant it to be this way. I loved the girl for heaven's sake, so I did."

"You had a poor way of showin' it. You an' your bliddy temper. You deserve to rot in hell. I watched that girl grow up. One of the bonniest I've ever seen, and so pleasant with it. Like her mother. God rest her soul. Be Jaysus, Maguire, you've a lot to answer for."

"Shut up! What is done is done. Listen to me McCrimmond, see that this is done properly. As far as anyone is concerned it was a pure accident. Nobody, but nobody is to know she was pregnant. I don't want her name to be degraded. I can take care o' the Garda, an' she'll be buried quietly without fuss."

McCrimmond looked at him in wonderment. "You're a callous bastard Maguire. You've got it all worked out and she's lyin' there still warm."

Maguire reached across the table and grabbed the doctor by the lapels of his coat. His eyes had the steely look that made the doctors face drain of colour.

"Listen McCrimmond. I don't have to take such shite from you. You an' I go a long way back. Remember Limerick? I know as much about you as you do about me, an' some of it is not very pleasant, is it? So don't preach at me. Let's leave it at that. Off you get an' deal wi' all the paper work an' make sure there's nuthin' outta place.

Just remember. You served the cause well both past an' present, but you're not indispensable. Understand?"

He released his grip and resumed his seat.

The ferocity of Maguire's voice and the cold grey eyes caused McCrimmond to blanche. Maguire noted the effect. He poured a measure of whisky into each glass, and raised his glass to the doctor.

"Here's to Maura. May she rest in peace. May God pardon her sins."

McCrimmond ignored the toast and rose to depart.

"I'll get the paper work done. There won't be any trouble, but I'll never forgive you for this, Maguire. God help you live with your conscience."

He left Maguire alone at the table, staring at the wall, his face set in a rigid mask, devoid of expression.

He drained his glass and carried the bottle and glasses back to the kitchen. The bottle was empty and the glasses drained. They were empty and no longer needed. In a symbolic gesture he threw them all into the rubbish box.

When Seamus returned they would gather over her body with Father O'Donnel and have the last rites read. Time enough to contact the Garda in the morning. By that time they'd have her laid out properly and the lock on the door repaired.

For the time being, the Belfast project would have to wait. This was one of the rare occasions when the needs of his family would be the priority.

Chapter Twenty-Five

The days that followed were days of endless grief. Eamon was worst affected. He stayed in his room most of the day, and his eyes were red with weeping. The shop was closed, the blinds drawn, and a wreath hung on the door. Maguire's pressure on the officials ensured that the tragedy was kept low key. The inquest duly recorded a verdict of accidental death and the Garda had no comments to make.

The funeral was held in Limerick, attended by only the closest relatives. It left the gossip –mongers of Galway to speculate, but it was, after all, the resting place of her mother, and it was accepted as a natural wish of the family.

The day of the funeral was dismal and grey, and the rain fell in a steady drizzle all through the churchyard service. To Eamon, it was the most miserable day of his whole life. Seamus, true to character, kept his emotions locked up within him. Only his eyes betrayed the amount of sorrow he felt.

On their return to Galway, the private group assembled in the Maguire house where there was food and drink prepared. Seamus and Devlin stood by themselves, drinking quietly and saying little. Maguire and Rafferty sat at the table, drinking steadily, with Rafferty doing most of the talking. He had the impression that Maguire's mind was elsewhere. His observation was correct.

Maguire was consumed with hate. He had become obsessed to discover who the father of Maura's child was. It was he who was really responsible for her death, and she had managed to conduct her affair so secretly, that he had no idea where to start looking for the culprit. It twisted his gut to be so frustrated. Of one thing he was certain, he would hunt the bastard down. Indeed he would, even if he had to track him right across Ireland, and there would be only one outcome.

Anthony returned from Dublin blissfully unaware of the tragedy. His leave had been fruitful. His report was accepted by Major O'Brien without comment. Hardly a surprise since the Major hadn't requested one. He was more interested in the details of the Galway races, and in his victory in the Handicap.

He stayed with one of his former colleagues who had a flat not far from the barracks, and from him obtained the name of a woman who was known to conduct back street abortions.

He spent a day of his precious leave tracking her down and made enquiries as to what was entailed. It was an unpleasant day in an unpleasant part of the city, but it gave him the information he needed, and it strengthened his belief that this was the only solution to solve his problem.

Maura would have to come to Dublin on some pretext of business or pleasure and go through the procedure, even if it was an unpleasant experience. If she refused to comply, he would threaten to leave her and deny any connection with her.

He felt in a strong position to impose the proposition. Few people would credit such an unlikely liaison as theirs, and she would be in an impossible situation to confess to such a fanatical Republican as her father.

He had not felt it appropriate to call Catrin when he had such missions to fulfil, but on the day before he was due to return to Galway, he picked up a message left for him at the barracks by sergeant McNulty, and changed his mind.

McNulty reported the patrol watching the house at Ballanalee had seen the man he was seeking, and he seemed to be busy doing chores around the house. They thought he might be there for a few days.

He telephoned Catrin and gave her the news, adding that he had come to Dublin to make a report to his CO. She immediately invited him to come for dinner and to give her all the details. It was the most pleasant event of his short stay, and it culminated with Catrin agreeing to accompany him back to Galway. She would stay at Dungannon House and ride over to Ballanalee the next morning.

The drive back to Galway seemed remarkably short. Catrin was an ideal companion, chatting merrily and laughing at his amusing comments. She was full of excitement at the prospect of meeting O'Farrell. Her obsession about The Wishing Boy had never left her.

His only worry was the situation with Maura. He had to make sure that the two did not meet. He had to see Maura immediately and convince her to obey his suggestion. If she would not agree, he would carry out his threat. If the worst came to the worst, and he did walk out, it would give him the perfect opportunity to concentrate all his efforts to win over Catrin. By the time he arrived in Galway, he was feeling much happier with the situation. He dropped Catrin off at Dungannon House and drove back to the barracks feeling he had a strategy that would solve his problem.

Immediately after breakfast the next morning he rode over to Dungannon House taking another of his horses for her, a smaller black gelding in splendid condition. Catrin fell in love with it as soon as she saw it. He offered to guide her over the moors to Ballanalee, but assured her he would keep out of sight when she met O'Farrell.

Once over the stretch of moorland, they sat at the top of the rise and surveyed the house below. There was no sign of life, only a tiny plume of white smoke from the peat fire. Catrin wanted him to leave her and return to the barracks, but he refused.

"You're in bandit country, Catrin. Don't forget the threat. I'll keep out of sight, but I'll have my field glasses trained on the house. If I see anything suspicious, I'll be over this wall and down there in two ticks."

She rode the long way round so that anyone in the house would be sure to see her entering the front yard. The gate was wide open and she rode to the front of the house and reined in directly opposite the door. The top half was open and she could see into the darkened interior.

A figure materialised out of the gloom, tall and lanky and heavily bearded. She recognised him as the man who had raced against Anthony. She had not expected to see Seamus. He leaned on the half door and regarded her with interest.

"And what would you be wantin' here," he said gruffly. His eyes were roving over her and scanning the horse. She was pretty and sat the horse well. The horse was of particular interest.

"I came to see Devlin O'Farrell. Is he here?"

"Maybe. Maybe not. What are you after?"

"I'm sure you remember me. We met at the races. I met Mr. O'Farell in Dublin. I've been trying to do business with him ever since."

He nodded. "I remember. Your fancy man's the officer who knocked me off. Could'ave hurt me bad."

"Let's just say it was an unfortunate accident." She did not want to get on the wrong side of him until she had the information she wanted. "I'm glad it was only a concussion you suffered. I did come to the first aid tent to see how you were."

"So I heard, but I don't remember. I'm sure it was Dev you really wanted to see."

Catrin laughed. "It's true. I had hoped to talk to him about his work, and also to congratulate him on riding a fine race."

"I'm impressed by your spirit, Miss, but didn't I hear you were given a warning to steer clear o' Dev."

"Did you now," she gave him a broad smile, "I can't remember. It must have been a while back. I must have forgotten. Look, I think this conversation has gone far enough. Is he here or not?"

Seamus regarded her with growing respect. This was indeed the girl his father had warned off Devlin, yet here she was, bold as brass, and on an army horse to boot. She had spunk, and he admired that.

"You're outta luck. You've had your little canter for nuthin'. Sorry Miss. He's been and gone. I can't help you."

Catrin almost screamed. "Good God! What do I have to do to meet this man? I only want to do some business with him. Why is it so difficult?"

"Maybe he doesn't want your business." Seamus was enjoying provoking her. She looked even more attractive when she was angry.

"What right have you to make up his mind for him?" she shot back. "Where has he gone now? He was here the day before yesterday." She realised her mistake but the words were out of her mouth before she could think.

Seamus opened the half door and came outside. "How did you know that?"

She had to think quickly. "My grandfather told me. He saw him around."

It was obvious Seamus had doubts. He patted the rump of the horse, running his fingers over the brand. "Fine beast. Army horse. Where did you get it?"

"A friend loaned me it. I love riding. It's my favourite sport."

Another piece of the jig saw fell into place. The army officer. The lieutenant at the barracks, of course. They must be watching the place. He'd have to warn Devlin quick.

"Well I suggest you carry on ridin' elsewhere. He's away fishing Donegal way. Don't expect him back for a few days. If I were you, Miss, I'd take your business elsewhere. Dev doesn't need it"

"That's surely for him to say," she was really angry now.

"I'm his closest friend. I know him better than anyone. He doesn't mind me speakin' for him."

"You Maguire's are all the same. For some reason I can't understand you are doing your best to keep me away from him. Even your sister wouldn't help me."

"My sister?

"Yes. Your sister. The girl in the shop in Eyre Square. Maura."

"You knew her?"

"I've been in the shop several times. She told me she remembered me as a little girl playing around my grandfather's house. She said she always loved his house. She's very attractive."

"Aye. She was. Too pretty." There was a haunted look in his eyes and he spoke almost reverently.

"What do you mean she *was* pretty? She's pleasant too, but she wouldn't tell me where to find this man either. But I won't give up. The next time I see her"— she did not complete the sentence,

"You don't know, do you?"

"Know what?" There was that haunting look in his eyes again.

"She's dead. We buried her last week. An accident. She fell down the stairs." He turned his head so that she would not see his eyes filling. He took the bridle and started to lead the horse toward the gate.

Catrin was too stunned to say anything. It was the last thing she could have expected. Such a beautiful girl. She felt ashamed she had been so jealous of her. She had posed a threat in the contest for Anthony's affections, but she had never imagined that death would be the victor.

"I'm sorry. I didn't know. I'm really sorry," was all she could say. Her shock was genuine.

Seamus shrugged his shoulders and continued to lead the horse to the gate. He paused for a minute at the entrance.

"Heed what I tell you. Leave Dev alone. Get back to Dublin where you belong an' forget him." He slapped the horse firmly on the rump and sent it at a canter down the dirt road and closed the gate.

She looked back at the forlorn figure, but he had already turned his back and was heading for the house.

She continued at a canter up the slope where Anthony would be waiting at the top of the rise. She wondered if Maura's death had been reported to him. He had said nothing on the trip back, but she did recall moments when he looked deep in thought. Could he have been hiding his grief?

She would watch for his reaction when she gave him the news.

Chapter Twenty-Six

The effect on Anthony was more dramatic than Catrin had anticipated. His face turned deathly pale and there was stark shock in his eyes

"I don't believe it. Who told you?" She had never seen him so unnerved.

"Her brother just told me. It was an accident, apparently, she was buried last week."

"I still can't believe it. What kind of accident?"

"He didn't give the details. He was very distressed. You look awful Tony, are you alright?"

"Of course I am. It's just such a shock. I saw her just before I came to Dublin." His mind flashed back to the meeting in the shop, that dark miserable night of rain and the hysteria. He gave an involuntary shudder. He had not anticipated this.

"She was about the same age as me," Catrin said sadly, "I never really knew her. You probably knew her better."

"Don't be ridiculous Catrin," He knew what she was hinting at.

"I called in the shop several times and was gradually getting useful information out of her. It helped locate this infernal man O'Farrell for you. That's all."

There was a ring of truth in that, so Catrin did not pursue the subject. But Anthony continued to express his shock.

"That swine Maguire didn't give her much of a life. He's unbelievable. Which makes me afraid for you. I think the threat he made was really meant. I'll keep a patrol watching the house and if O'Farrell shows up I'll grab him. I have authority to question anyone acting suspiciously, so I could haul him in, and possibly give you a chance to talk to him."

He spurred Rufus into a gallop and she followed a length behind him as they retraced the path back over the moor that led to Dungannon House. Each of them was deep in thought. Despite the jealousy she had once felt for the girl, Catrin was genuinely sorry. There was no satisfaction that she was no longer a threat to her.

Anthony had mixed emotions. The news had stunned him, but at the same time a tremendous weight was lifted from his shoulders. His big problem was solved, and he could breathe easier. There was only one concern.

Who else knew about her condition? Had Maura disclosed who the father of her child was? If so, Maguire would be thirsting for his blood.

He left the black gelding with Catrin at Dungannon House, and rode Rufus back to the barracks. He had turned down an invitation to stay for a meal on the grounds that he had work to catch up on. In truth, he needed time to think. There would be further opportunities for more ride-outs, and it was beneficial to his ambitions to encourage them. Their mutual love of horses was an aid to winning her over.

By the following morning he was back to normal. He had slept well and felt refreshed. He decided to take the day off and go riding. He detailed McMurty to take charge and changed into civilian clothes and rode across to Dungannon House. The pleasant early morning had developed into a fine day and by mid morning the sun was shining out of a cloudless sky.

"Why don't we make it a picnic," Catrin suggested. "We could ride through the woods and up the side of the loch. There's lots of places we could stop and picnic. You get the horses ready and I'll get Mrs. Donnovan to make us a picnic. Danna will give us some wine if I ask him nicely."

Within the hour they were on their way. Anthony had a small hamper strapped to his saddle loaded with picnic fare and the bottles of wine. Daniel waved them off from the front door, delighted to see Catrin blooming and looking so pretty.

They looked a well-matched couple, she in her jodhpurs and pretty white blouse, he in riding britches and a casually smart polo shirt. Only one thing that struck him as out of place. Protruding from the side pocket of the saddle he could see the top of Anthony's revolver holster, and it appeared to contain a gun.

They rode up the side of the river until it reached the lower end of the lough. The water was violet coloured and as smooth as glass, shimmering in the bright sun. It was the hottest day of the summer but the humidity was high and made travelling uncomfortable.

Their passage through the shady woods fringing the river had been pleasant, but once into clear space the heat became oppressive.

All of nature was drowsy, and after a further half hour, the riders were beginning to wilt. As they came into a small secluded glade Anthony drew rein on Rufus.

"This looks good enough," he said, "it's too hot to go further. Let's have the picnic here. Look across there," he pointed to the far side, "your favourite place. The old castle."

He dismounted and crossed to help her. It gave him an opportunity to grasp her waist. Any chance to feel her body close to his was an opportunity to be taken. The gesture might have warned her of the kind of mood he was in, but she considered it a gentlemanly courtesy and gave him a flirtatious kiss as a reward.

He was slow to release her. The smell of her perfume was intoxicating and there was a light of mischief dancing in her eyes. She was being provocative without knowing it, and the temptation was too much. He drew her into his body and kissed her passionately.

Summer heat encourages summer passions. She slipped out of the embrace slowly, almost reluctantly, but she was still acting flirtatiously.

"Behave Tony. It's too hot to travel, and it's too hot for that. Look at the loch. I wish I had brought my swim things. I could jump into it right now."

"Why don't we?" he laughed. Her provocation was exciting him. "What's to stop us? Who's going to know? We don't need swim things. It's more fun being starkers."

"Tony! What a suggestion! I'm not that hot! Besides, there *is* someone who might see us. Along there, look, a fisherman," she indicated a solitary figure standing on a small peninsula of land that jutted into the lough. Anthony cursed silently under his breath.

"Can't imagine him catching anything on a day like this. Anyway, he's a long way off, he won't see anything."

"He's not going to get the chance," she laughed, "and neither are you. That's for later. Much later."

It was an innocent remark, and intended for fun, but to Anthony it sounded like encouragement to the desires he had nourished ever since he had first met her. The word "later" sounded especially emphasised. His emotions began to inflame.

"Let's have the picnic now. I'll lay out the picnic. You chill the wine in the lough.

He unloaded the hamper from the horse, and as an afterthought decided to remove the saddle from Rufus. He was wary of possible danger and he preferred to have his revolver handy. Besides, the saddle might form a handy type of pillow if he could encourage Catrin to continue to be flirtatious.

He used stones to prop the bottles up in the shallows where the water felt delightfully cool. In about half an hour they would chill nicely. Mrs. Donnavan had prepared a first class selection of cold chicken and sandwiches which Catrin had arranged neatly on a large blanket. There was fresh fruit and even a slab of homemade cake. Anthony opened the first bottle of wine and praised Daniel's selection. It was the perfect complement to the food, and his spirits continued to rise.

The second bottle was even better, having chilled slightly longer. Anthony greedily imbibed more than his fair share and encouraged Catrin to keep pace with him. It was such a pleasant drink and the occasion so enjoyable, she foolishly tried to do so. The combination of wine and the heat of the day began to have effect.

As the moments passed, she was losing her inhibitions, flirting amorously in a playful way, not realising how tantalising to him she was appearing. Unlike him, whose ardour was rising to a peak, the excess of wine she had been flattered into drinking gave her overwhelming desire to sleep.

Anthony had no such desire. He could see she was succumbing to the effects of the wine and his lust was mounting. As her eyes began to flutter and strain to remain open, he made his move.

He lay beside her and eased her head on to his shoulder. She groaned softly as he began to stroke her hair, and again as he moved to gently massage her neck.

He gently nibbled the lobe of her ear and continued to stroke her neck, seeking the erogenous spot he knew to be there. His deft touches had the desired effect.

She responded by turning into him and placing her arms around his neck, allowing him to kiss her. Her eyes remained closed and she was moaning softly as if she was dreaming. He kissed her, his tongue prising open her lips and running lightly around her mouth, sensually probing and encouraging her to follow.

His pulses and heart were racing. She was offering no resistance, sighing softly and returning his advances with a rapid succession of short sharp kisses that inflamed him. His hand sought her breasts. Still there was no resistance. He fumbled with the buttons of her blouse and felt them give way one by one.

He roughly brushed aside the bodice and his fingers fastened greedily on the soft silken skin. Her breasts yielded gently to the pressure of his hand, and the nipples felt firm. His breathing was coming laboured, his lust at fever point and he could hold back no longer.

He began to try and unfasten the waistband of her jodhpurs, but the catch was difficult and he had to pull at it. Only then did Catrin open her eyes and despite her drowsiness she was quickly aware of what was happening.

"Stop that at once, Tony." It had no effect. "I said stop it!" Her protest echoed across the lough. "Get off me. I thought we were going to relax and have a sleep."

She screamed as the catch gave way and his hand groped inside the waistband. She beat at his face with both hands forcing him to let go, and with all the strength she could muster struggled to her feet. She tried to fasten her blouse, but her fingers were clumsy. He rose to his feet, his face darkened with anger.

"You led me on. You said things that made me feel you were all for it. You didn't make a move to stop when I started to kiss you. You can't work a man up that way and then expect him to stay normal. You've been leading me on for too long, denying me for months. I'm not waiting any longer."

He advanced towards her, hands outstretched, a light of pure evil in his eyes. She screamed again. A shrill note that echoed for miles across the still water, and she ran for the shelter of the trees. He caught her within a few strides and wrestled her to the ground, but she fought like a tiger, kicking and screaming, biting and scratching, forcing him to release his grip.

She regained her feet, but she was dazed and hopelessly disorientated.

She staggered towards the lough only to be caught and flung to the ground once again. Her blouse was ripped off completely in the struggle, as she continued to fight him off with flailing arms. She scrambled wildly to regain her feet and almost made it, but he tripped her and threw her violently to the ground yet again.

This time her head thudded heavily against a clod of grass that covered a large stone. She moaned once and then fainted.

He stood over her, his chest heaving with the exertion, his eyes fixed on the delicate breasts now fully exposed. Animal instincts had taken over and there was no quelling his frustration. He reached down to tug at her jodhpurs, drops of saliva forming on his lips as her limbs became exposed. He straightened up and began to unfasten his belt.

Suddenly there was a sharp zipping sound, like the buzz of a bee, and an object flashed past his head. In the next instant he screamed with pain as something embedded itself in his ear. The searing pain stung like the bite from a vicious insect, made worse by the tugging that followed, forcing him to retreat in an effort to relieve the tension that was threatening to tear his ear off.

He clutched at it with his hand trying to free himself. His hand was red with blood. He could feel a hook of some sort embedded in the lobe of his ear. He yelled with pain again as another tug on the hook increased the agony.

He twisted his head to seek the source of his torment and through the red mist of pain he could see a figure with a fishing rod, reeling him in like a fish on the line. He charged forward, slackening the line and momentarily easing the pain, but his tormentor was quick to reel in more line just as he was almost upon him. As the next pull came, Anthony was forced to stop just short of him, his hands still trying desperately to free himself from the hook.

The fisherman swung the handle of the rod swiftly in an upward arc that caught Anthony a vicious blow in the crotch. He collapsed in a heap, paralysed with pain, his face ashen and sweat flowing on his brow. He lay helpless and writhing, retching with the pain.

The fisherman leaned over him. "Keep still or I'll pull your ear off." He cut the line. "You can keep the hook."

Anthony lay still. His groin felt on fire and blood dripped freely from his ear, staining his shirt heavily.

He wanted to be sick and he desperately fought to regain his wits. How far was he from his revolver?

"Who the hell are you?" He could not see clearly, and his voice was barely audible. "Do you realise who I am? I'm an army officer. I'll have you shot for this."

"Will you now? Not if you get shot first. If this girl's father finds out what you've tried, I'd think he might shoot you. They do that in this part o' the world, in case you didn't know. Especially feckin' army officers."

He left Anthony lying and went across to where Catrin lay motionless. He pulled the blanket from under the picnic spread and covered her bare upper body. There was a large bruise coming up on the side of her head and her breathing was shallow.

As he looked for a cloth to dip in the cool water of the lough which would help keep the swelling down, he saw Anthony starting to crawl towards his saddle. He was unsure of what he was up to, until he saw him pull the holster from the saddle bag.

He was on his knees fumbling to open it when the fisherman caught him. His first kick sent the holster flying, and the second one thudded into his solar plexus. He collapsed, totally paralysed, and lay clutching his abdomen and groaning with pain. This time he did vomit.

The fisherman retrieved the holster and removed the revolver. He stuck it into the waistband of his trousers and flung the holster into the lough.

Satisfied that Anthony was beyond giving further trouble, he gathered Catrin in his arms and gently placed her on the saddle of the black gelding. He made sure she was securely held and then led the horse carefully into the dense mass of trees that surrounded the glade.

Anthony was unaware of their departure. He lay on his side, retching and vomiting for several minutes. It was half an hour later before he mustered the strength to stand up. He staggered to the edge of the lough and made an attempt to wash away the blood and residue from his face and clothes.

It required a great effort to re-saddle Rufus and set off back to the barracks. The pain in his groin was excruciating as he adjusted himself gingerly into the saddle. His ear had stopped bleeding, but the hook was firmly embedded in the lobe, and there was a steady throbbing that continued to make him feel sick.

His shirt was heavily matted with blood. He wondered how he could explain his predicament to sergeant McNulty, but at this moment in time his brain was incapable of thinking.

What he did remember, however, was the features of the fisherman. It was the lone fisherman from further up the lough. The same man he had confronted in the Art Gallery in Dublin, and the same man that had challenged him so closely in the Maguire Handicap. The same man that Catrin so desperately wanted to meet.

It was Devlin O'Farrell.

How ironic his own insatiable lust had led her to finally achieve her quest. Where O'Farrel had taken her, he did not know, but he made a vow to find out. From now on he would be the one that desperately wanted to meet the man, and the next time it would be him to exact revenge.

Chapter Twenty-Seven

Her brain was commanding her muscles to respond. But they would not.

No matter how hard she strove to move her legs, they refused. Panic began to flood through her. She did not know where she was, her head was throbbing with pain, and she wanted to be sick. Her senses were slow to clear, and when she opened her eyes, there was more panic. She could not see clearly and the light was dim.

Something cool and soothing was being pressed against her temple, and for a moment calm was restored and she felt comforted. She was lying in a bed, and she could make out a shadowy shape sitting at the side.

She moved her head to see better but flopped back on the pillow as giddiness overcame her. A hand appeared and removed the cloth from her head, and she whimpered, but a moment later it was replaced. She sighed as the coolness helped soothe the ache.

Instinctively she clutched her hands to her breast, but her panic subsided as she realised she was covered up. She should have felt fear, but strangely she did not.

"Come round now?" a man's voice, with a gentle Galway brogue made the enquiry.

"Take it easy. You took a hefty blow. You'll have a nasty bruise for a while, maybe even a black eye, but you'll be alright." The voice was reassuring, and the soft lilt made her feel at ease.

"Who are you? How did I get here?"

"You're quite safe. I brought you here, to my place, so's I could treat you better. Can you remember what happened?

"I'm not sure. I'm all mixed up. I think I'm going to be sick." She hung her head over the side of the bed and vomited. He held a basin under her chin and supported her head with the other. When she was finished, he gently placed her back on the pillow.

"Just lie quiet a while. I've a few jobs to do. When you think you're feeling better, we'll see about gettin' you home. Lie back now, and rest."

How long she had slept she did not know, but when she awoke she was feeling much better. The pain in her head had subsided to a dull ache, and her sight had returned to normal. She eased herself on to her elbows and took stock of her surroundings.

The bed was in a recess in the wall of a fairly big rectangular room, the only light coming from a large window next the door. The only furniture appeared to be a table and one chair. A bench, or perhaps a dresser of some sort was on the wall near the window, at the opposite end, a large open fireplace where a turf fire was burning.

The door opened and he entered. He was carrying a pail of water, and paused as he saw she was sitting up.

"Feeling alright now?" he asked. "You've slept for two hours so it should've done some good." He poured water from the pail into a kettle and swung it on the crane over the fire.

"I'll make us some tay, an' then we'll see about gettin' you home."

Her memory was coming back. She remembered the lone fisherman, the terrible scene with Anthony and the struggle and then... at that point her mind went blank. She covered her face with her hands and began to cry.

"You started to remember? That's a good sign. You're not too badly concussed then?"

"I think I'm alright. It came back to me just then, and it was horrible. I can't believe he did that. It was such a lovely day until"... her voice faded.

"I know who you are. You painted the Wishing Boy didn't you?"

"Now I know you're goin' to be alright. Yes. I'm you're man, and you are Daniel Kilpatrick's granddaughter."

"How did you... how did you come to... to rescue me?"

"I was fishin' a ways up from where you picnicked. I heard you scream. I think they might'a heard it in Galway. I heard the commotion an' came runnin' through the trees. I got there just in time. I could see what he was up to."

"What did you do, I mean, what happened to Tony?"

"I'm pretty good at fly fishin'. I made one of my better casts. He'll have a sore ear for a while, an' it won't improve his looks. He was lucky. If it'd been Daniel that caught him, he'd have given him two barrels o' buckshot."

"You know Daniel?"

"Oh aye. Fine old man, I like him. Sometimes we fish together. Look now, the kettle's on the boil.

I'll mash us some tay an' then we'll get you back to him. Dungannon House is not a long ways from here."

Catrin sipped the tea gratefully. She had a chance to study him more closely.

His ruddy complexion clearly identified him as an outdoor man. She noticed his mouth turned up at the corners suggesting a spark of humour. He looked strong in the neck and the shoulders. He was not handsome like Tony, but he had the rugged good looks of a rustic farmer.

"I went to Ballanalee yesterday to see you, but you weren't there."

"Did you now? What made you think I was there?"

"I've been trying to find you ever since that day at the gallery in Dublin. I eventually managed to get some information. You're a very hard man to find."

"And you're a very persistent young woman. You're still after me for that paintin', even for all the times I've said it's not for sale."

He was changing again. The tenderness was disappearing, the belligerence he displayed at the gallery replacing it.

"Is this where you paint?" she asked.

"No. Too dark in amongst all these trees. I do it at Ballanalee mostly. Sometimes I do it on the road when I'm travellin'. This is a workshop I do most o' the driftwood work."

"Where do you keep The Wishing Boy?" The question had to be asked.

He stood up and moved away from the bed. "I was hopin' you wouldn't harp on about that."

"I'm sorry. I fell in love with it as soon as I saw it. I wanted to buy it. It ought to be on display in a fine house, not hidden away in some dusty den. And those little hearts beneath the signature? I believe there's a story behind them that ought to be told. It might make you famous."

"Then you've wasted your time! I don't wish to be famous. It's not for sale an' there's no story. You're clearly alright now so let's be getting' you back. I brought you here on your officer friend's horse. I'll go fetch it." He stomped from the room clearly irritated, leaving Catrin to regret her questioning.

She swung her legs over the bed and cautiously stood up. She suddenly realised she was wearing a man's plaid shirt. She blushed as she realised he must have seen her nakedness and covered her up. She reached the table and used it to support herself as her senses slowly returned to normal. She heard the sound of a horse approaching the front door and a minute later he entered.

"When you feel ready, I'll help you sit the saddle, an' then I'll take you back." was all he said. He helped her on to the small gelding and made sure she was secure. She was shivering so he fetched a blanket to wrap around her, and then taking the bridle, carefully led them through the woods.

There were no words exchanged throughout. She was too tired to notice anything and had her eyes closed most of the time. She longed to get back to her grandfather and the safety of the old house. She knew he would be furious when he heard of Anthony's behaviour, but she would persuade him to keep quiet and not risk making a public scandal.

He led the horse right up to the front door, and gently assisted her to dismount. He knocked loudly on the door and a minute later a startled Mrs. Donovan appeared with Daniel close behind.

"In the name o' God. We've bin worried about you. What's happened?" Daniel was greatly concerned.

"Just get her into a proper bed an' let her rest, "Devlin advised, "she's had a bit o' a shake up, but she'll be alright."

He waited in the kitchen whilst Catrin was taken upstairs. He told Daniel the story once he returned.

"So help me God, he ought to be horse whipped."

"Leave him be," said Devlin. He's not goin' to feel good for a day or two, an' his ear's not goin' to be a pretty sight ever again. I don't imagine he'll feel like sex either. Best not say anythin'. You don't want Catrin dragged into a scandal."

Daniel reluctantly agreed. "But if he comes within a mile o' here, I'll see him off an' no mistake. I'm grateful you were on hand. I hate to think of what would've happened otherwise. Tell you what," he looked around to make sure Mrs. Donovan was out of sight, "I've a wee drop o' the precious stuff handy. How's about a drop?" He produced the bottle from the cupboard under the dresser and found two glasses. He poured a generous measure into each and handed a glass to Devlin.

They sat down at the kitchen table quietly enjoying the slow burning pleasure descending into their stomachs. Daniel held the glass to the light and squinted at the clear amber liquor.

"Time I had some more o' this," he said. "Enjoy it while you can Daniel. I can get you more, but it won't be around much longer."

"I've heard Maguire might be givin' it up."

"You heard right."

"That's too bad. Been a good money spinner for him. I'll miss it. Can't stand this stuff they're sellin' now as whiskey. But I'm in your debt. If you ever need a hand, you only need to ask. You're welcome here any time."

"Think nuthin' of it. Tell you what. Why not a spot o' fishin' sometime? You could get your boat out an' we could go up the lough a bit."

"I'd love that," said Daniel as he saw Devlin to the door. He watched him climb on the gelding.

"Fine horse. Are you keepin' it?" he joked.

"I wouldn't mind. But it's too well known, especially after the Races. He'd be after me with a story that would enable him to explain the mess he was in. So I'm not givin' him a chance to come after me. I'll see it's returned somehow." He swung the horse round and cantered out of the courtyard.

From her bedroom window Catrin watched him disappear. There was a touch of fate about the way he had appeared to rescue her, and she had a feeling that she would see him again soon. She would not give up her obsession to prise the Wishing Boy and its mystery from him, but she would have to devise some other feminine wile. There must be some way into his heart. She closed the curtains and climbed back into bed and was asleep within minutes.

Chapter Twenty-Eight

Mrs. Donovan stood with her back against the kitchen sink, arms folded like a hospital Matron, and watched Catrin's clumsy attempts to iron the plaid shirt. Her hardened face was difficult to read, but she gloated. It was obvious the girl had no experience in ironing a man's shirt. But she had insisted on doing it, so the dour housekeeper did not argue.

A week had elapsed since her ordeal and Catrin had made a good recovery. The only visible legacy was the yellow coloured bruise still showing on her temple, but even that she had managed to hide effectively by using make up. It was more difficult to conceal the mental scars.

She had succeeded in persuading Daniel not to tell her parents. They would have insisted on her return, and she did not want that, especially now that she had made contact with Devlin O'Farrell.

There had been a phone call from Anthony the day after the incident, full of apologies and begging forgiveness. Daniel had taken the call and left him in no doubts that he was no longer welcome at Dungannon House.

Catrin held the shirt up to the light and inspected it. It could be improved upon, but her pride would not permit her to seek help.

"Is himself comin' back for it?" Mrs. Donovan asked.

"I'm going to take it to him," Catrin announced. "He probably hasn't got many shirts so I want to get it back to him quickly." She folded the shirt over her arm and walked from the kitchen to find Daniel busy weeding in the garden.

"I want to take this back to Devlin O'Farrell, Danna. I'd like to do it to-day, but I'm not sure how to find his place."

"I don't think that's a good idea, Catrin. Why not wait? He'll be droppin' by to see how you are."

"I don't think so. I want him to have his shirt before he buzzes off somewhere else. He's likely to need it. Besides," she said petulantly, "I'm still after his painting."

Daniel laid down his hoe and sighed. "Oh Catrin. You an' this damned paintin'. It's comin' between you an' your wits, so 'tis."

"Well if you don't want to come, Danna, just tell me how to get there, that's all."

"His place is well hidden. There is a track that goes through the woods, or you can take up boat and row up the lough and land on the bank close by. Forget the horse, Catrin, you're not fit for riding jest yet."

"Then we'll take the boat. It's ages since we rowed up the lough. You know how we used to enjoy it. You could even do some fishing." Daniel smiled. He was being manipulated, but between fishing and weeding there was really only one choice.

"Alright. We'll take the boat out in the afternoon. Mind you, he might not be there, so I'll take two rods, an' if he isn't, we'll both fish." Catrin beamed and gave him a huge hug.

It was the weather for fishing. An overcast sky, but the rain holding off and the air warm. Daniel rowed steadily with a smooth and practised stroke and progress was leisurely. Catrin sat in the stern scanning the banks and looking for signs of where this hidden workshop might be.

"How far up?" she asked.

"Nearly there. See that little bit o' bankin' jutting out about half a mile ahead? That's where we'll be landin'. Then we walk through the trees 'till we come upon it."

They landed and pulled the boat up on to the bank to hide it in the trees.

"It's about a ten minute walk from here," Daniel explained as they followed a faintly trodden path through the trees.

"Why is it so well hidden?" she asked.

"Years ago there was an' old man called McAllister who used to operate a still there. Pretty crude stuff, but Poteen was big business then. Some folks were stupid enough to drink it, others used it as a medicine. Anyways, he made a livin' from it. It took the Excise a long time to find it, but when they did they smashed the whole place up an' then there was a fire.

The Excise said it was an accident, but nobody believed them. McAllister high tailed it and never came back. The place stood derelict for years an' everyone forgot about it. Devlin came across it and decided it would make a fine workshop, so he worked on it and restored it. He wanted real privacy, an' he's certainly got that."

They continued to wend their way through the dense mass of trees. Catrin had to marvel at the dexterity of this man. He seemed to be able to do almost anything.

Suddenly they were out of the trees and into a small clearing. The house stood on the opposite side, a solid grey stone built building, with the one solitary window at the front. A wisp of white smoke hovered above the chimney was the only sign of life.

Daniel shouted loudly, "Hallo the House! Anybody home?"

The door opened and Devlin emerged, dressed in working clothes, obviously busy on some form of work.

Catrin held out her parcel. "I've brought back your shirt. Thank you for using it to comfort me, it's not exactly the kind I would normally wear, but it was very good of you to loan it to me."

"My pleasure. It came very handy. It's had its day, but it's handy for working."

As he was preparing the tea, Catrin glanced around. The work bench was strewn with pieces of driftwood and he had obviously been working on them. She crossed to the bench and examined them. There were one or two pieces finished, the usual animals and fish she had seen before, but the majority were still in their natural state.

Once again she was struck by his ingenuity and imagination, but wondered why he did not concentrate more on his gift of painting. He appeared to read her thoughts. "Them's my bread an' butter".

Maguire sells them by the ton to tourists, the Yanks especially. I can turn a dozen o' them out in the same time as I'd take to do a paintin', and in the end, they're more profitable."

"Are you preparing for another exhibition?"

"Not on your life. That one in Dublin was my last. It's best to keep it local. The fellah who inveigled me to bring stuff to Dublin was full o' hot air. Told me all sorts of great possibilities, an' what happened? Absolutely nuthin'."

"You did have one enquiry."

"You're not goin' to start that again, are you?"

"No. I know it upsets you. But surely The Wishing Boy is not your final masterpiece. You have a natural gift. It's a pity to hide it."

"I don't know about that. Paintin's somethin' I do in the Spring. It seems the best time, when everythin' is startin' to come to life after the winter."

"Your life seems to be governed by seasons. Doesn't it get boring, being too rigid? I like to do things as the urge takes me."

Daniel had been silent, listening to the conversation but he could not resist a comment.

"I can vouch for that. I never know what she might be up to next."

"I can see you're headstrong, an' given to sudden whims. Bein' from you're background that's only to be expected. On my side o' the tracks, you can't afford to be like that."

Catrin bridled. She had never looked down on him.

He handed them each a mug of the tea he had been busy making while the conversation had being going on. Daniel had been an interested spectator as he watched the two of them sparring with one another.

He found it much more interesting than watching her antics with Anthony. There had always been something shallow in that affair. This was different.

He finished his tea and placed the empty mug on the table.

"Time we went, Catrin, we've interrupted Dev at his work. He'll want to get on with it"

"As you please, Daniel. Thanks for the shirt. I appreciate it." He walked with them out to the edge of the trees.

"So you used the boat?"

"Easiest way. Brought a couple o' rods for some fishin' just in case you had done another flittin'. Pity to waste the chance. Why not join us? We'll go further up, towards Oughterarder. You know a good spot there, don't you?"

"Indeed I do. How about to-morrow, if the weather's alright?"

"Suits me," Daniel beamed.

"Will Catrin join us?"

Daniel looked at her inquisitively.

"Of course. I love fishing. It would be a challenge to see if I could be as good as you."

Devlin smiled. But secretly he was pleased. Maybe he could bring her down a peg or two. It would do no harm.

Catrin was less pleased. She yanked at the oars as they made their way down the lough.

"Why is he always so touchy?" she complained to Daniel.

"I've told you, Catrin. Give up this idea about buying his paintin'. The man makes it plain he's no' willing to part with it. Why keep pesterin' him?"

"You should know me by now, Danna. If I really want something, I'll never give up. I think if I could get him to reveal the story behind it, he might change his mind. I think that's what the problem is."

"Be careful," Daniel warned, "it may be somethin' to do with the drinkin' spree he was on a year or two ago. He won't want to be reminded o' that"

"What happened?" Catrin slowed down a little.

"There was an accident. Up country somewhere. Somebody was kilt. A young woman I think. It was after that. Bad, bad it was. Hardly a day sober."

"Was it someone close to him?"

"I've never known Dev to be close to a woman. He's always been his own man. Maybe it was a relative. Anyway, it drove him off the rails for a bit."

"He seems alright now."

"Maguire got him outta it. Him an' Seamus. I hate the man, but he did a good job in straightening' Dev out. Of course after that he had him in the palm o' his hand."

"I wondered how he could work for such a man."

"Yes. Things might've been different."

They had reached the spot on the river to disembark and pull the boat from the water and hide it in the bushes. They plodded across the field and entered the house.

Mrs. Donavan had seen them approach, and the kettle was already on the hob as they made their way to the kitchen.

"Thanks for taking me there, Danna," as she pecked him on the cheek. I'll know in future how to get there."

"You're a holy terror, Catrin. Like a terrier with a bone. You never let go, do you? I wish you'd remember what your grandma used to say."

"I know," she uttered the words in unison with him, "never wish too much for something"— they both burst out laughing. It was a big joke for Catrin, but not for Daniel. He was very serious about such a pearl of wisdom.

While Mrs. Donavan prepared the tea, she was an interested party in the conversation. At the first opportunity she would contact Maguire and tell him that Catrin was defying his warning and getting too close to Devlin O'Farrell.

She regarded it her duty to keep him informed. Didn't he pay her the princely sum of ten shillings a week to give her all the gossip she could find?

Besides, Catrin was interfering too much with her routine, and the quicker she returned to Dublin, the better it would be for all of them.

Chapter Twenty-Nine

Catrin awoke from a deep sleep, disturbed by noisy voices downstairs. The clock on her bedside table showed seven thirty. She frowned and made to turn over for a further half hour, but heard the unmistakable sound of Daniel clomping up the stairs. A thunderous knock on her door followed.

"Get yerself up, Catrin," his jovial voice bellowed, "we've got company an' he wants to go fishin'."

"Who is it," she queried, rubbing the sleep from her eyes.

"Dev, it is. Don't you remember yesterday? We talked about gettin' the boat out an' all goin'? He's been on the go since sun up an' he says they're jumpin'."

She washed, dressed, and struggled to make her hair presentable in record time, and flew downstairs to the kitchen where both men sat at the table drinking tea. Devlin rose as she entered and pulled up a chair for her. The touch of manners pleased her.

"I see you're wearing your plaid shirt this morning," she smiled.

"Couldn't wait to put it on. It's the nicest feelin' shirt I've ever had on me back." It was pure blarney, but she was flattered. There was charm in his soft lilting brogue.

Daniel was looking out the window. "This is the kinda' mornin' I love. Perfect for fishin'. We're goin' further up the lough to-day, Catrin, to the deeper bits where the big ones are. Might get one o' those big pike, eh Dev?"

"It's possible. Think Catrin's strong enough to pull in one o' them?" There was a spark of mischief dancing in his eyes.

"You better believe it. Don't forget I'm the one that taught her. An' let me tell you, in case you haven't noticed already, if she hooks somethin' she won't give it up."

Mrs. Donavan had packed them a lunch and Daniel had included a billy can and some tea. The men took the oars and were pulling strongly as if competing with one another to reach the lough first. Catrin relaxed in the stern, dividing her attention between the scenery and watching them.

Devlin looked fresher and cleaner than she had seen him before.

The neat little moustache and the fringe of a beard that clung neatly to his lower jaw looked freshly trimmed. She was pleased with his shirt.

It looked much smarter than the clothes he wore yesterday. His eyes gleamed with the pleasure of the occasion, and a smile hovered about his mouth. She was aware that every so often, when he thought she wasn't watching, he glanced at her.

When she did catch him, he merely smiled. She had a feeling this was going to be a very enjoyable day.

"I'm trying to pick out where your workshop is," she called out as they neared the little promontory. "It's very well hidden, isn't it?"

"It was always intended to be hidden. The Poteen makers had a job to avoid the Excise men, so they chose well. But it suits me, too. Nobody disturbs me. Yesterday was the first time anybody's been there for a long time. But if you look very close at the tree line, you can see the barest wisp o' smoke. I put extra turves on the fire this mornin', an' the wind's so still it's not clearin' away like it often does. See it?"

He released an arm from his oar and pointed to the faintest of a haze that hung over a solid mass of trees. Had he not pointed it out, Catrin would have taken it to be morning mist.

If their attention not been diverted, they might have caught the brief glint of the field glasses that were trained on the boat from the opposite shore. From his position prone under a tree on the edge of the bank, Lieutenant Dillon noted the gesture as O'Farrell pointed to the hidden location of his workshop.

As his glasses followed the gesture, the high powered lenses easily picked out the wisps of turf smoke that hung over the trees. He nodded to himself, well pleased that his morning spy mission had been successful. He pulled a small notebook from his pocket and made a rough sketch of the locale, and an estimate of the distance from Dungannon House.

He was elated. "Now I can arrange something Mr. O'Farrell. I owe you a hook, and I intend to let you can have it back."

He kept the glasses trained on the boat, watching Catrin particularly.

She looked happy and extremely pretty, and looking at O'Farrell who was also smiling. The sight inflamed jealous rage within him, and his campaign of revenge for the pain, misery, and humiliation he had suffered as a result of O'Farrell's interference was now his main priority.

He snapped the glasses back into their case and cautiously made his way back to where he had tethered his horse.

As he rode back to the barracks he formed a plan that would accomplish two valuable objectives; his own lust for revenge against O'Farrell, and by neutralizing him, he would strike a blow against Maguire.

Further up the Lough, the fishing party had reached the spot where Devlin had predicted the fishing would be good, and they lost no time getting down to the serious business of competitive fishing.

It had been ages since Catrin last fished with Daniel, and her early attempts showed it. Devlin was quick to offer advice, much to Daniel's amusement. She was an apt pupil and improved rapidly. Daniel had the feeling that Catrin was enjoying being coached by a younger man, and she seemed much at ease with him. His observation was close to the mark.

She was in the process of a hasty re-evaluation. Despite his association with Maguire, who she hated, there was a gentle heart underneath the veneer of his hardened exterior, a gentle man, patient and caring. In those dark eyes there was a compassion that shielded a hidden sorrow. Her instincts told her that this was reflected in his painting. There was no doubt in her mind that The Wishing Boy had a tale of love behind it, and her obsession to uncover the story would never go away.

By mid-day they had a heap of fish wriggling on the bottom of the boat, including one large pike that Daniel had struggled successfully to land, and he was first to suggest they finish and have lunch.

Devlin created a fire and made a rather crude spit whilst Daniel and Catrin collected a supply of wood. The pick of the catch were gutted and roasted, and together with the food the housekeeper had packed, they had a delicious lunch.

Daniel's contribution was his tea. Once the fish were disposed of, he filled the Billy can and set it to boil on the embers.

He took great delight in handing the cups of his brew around. Nothing could beat a freshly made cup from a billy can, he boasted.

The sun made a brief appearance and Catrin sat with her back against the upturned boat, basking in the warmth. It had been one of the most enjoyable mornings she had spent for a long time.

"It was a good idea to do this," she said to Daniel, "I've really enjoyed it."

"Made me think o' the times we used to fish when you were knee high," Daniel was very nostalgic.

"It was a nice change to have some female company," Devlin joined the conversation, "especially one that could actually fish." It was a comment that brought peals of laughter.

"Normally love to be on my own," he confessed. "Gives me time to think about things. Gives me ideas of what to paint, or make. Gives me peace."

Catrin detected an expression of longing. There was something intense bottled up in this man. What was it?

The afternoon drifted by as they sat contentedly, each of them contributing a memory or a comment that sparked a stimulating discussion. She began to appreciate even more, that although Devlin appeared to be a rough diamond, he was intelligent and sensitive, possessed of light hearted charm and a wry sense of humour.

She became aware he was assessing her, too, and she wondered what his conclusions were. She had deliberately refrained from any further questions about the Wishing Boy. It was too enjoyable a day to risk spoiling it. If she could maintain this state of goodwill with him, perhaps the next time she dared broach the subject, there might be a break down in the barriers. It was a new strategy, but it might be the correct one.

Daniel had also become aware that there were changes happening. He was not unhappy. She needed to forget the ordeal she had been through, and a few days like this would be of great value. He liked Devlin. He was a man's man, and he had no delusions of grandeur about him like that other young whippersnapper.

But there was a fly in the ointment. Devlin was one of Maguire's men, and an important one at that.

The last thing he wanted was to see Catrin hurt again, and because of Devlin's association with such a man, it was a danger. Of course, Catrin had always maintained it was only the damned painting that she was interested in. Maybe if she was able to get the thing she was so obsessed with, she might avoid getting too entangled in the web that surrounded Devlin. He had a sudden inspiration.

"Why don't you come an' have a meal with us this evening Dev? Like you say, a bit o' new company now an' then's a good thing. You'd like that Catrin, wouldn't you?"

The question surprised Catrin completely, and she blushed. "Yes. Of course. There's all the rest of the fish to cook. Devlin's caught a lot so it's only right that he shares them with us."

Devlin hesitated. His natural inclinations were to fight shy of company. But this was different. Daniel was a trusted friend, and they had many interests in common, and although he would be loathe to admit it, this day had been one of his most pleasant ever.

There was a change in his assessment of Catrin. His first impressions had been that she was a spoilt young bitch, a

Lorelli that could charm the leaves off a tree, and then walk away leaving it bare. He had to admire her passionate beliefs and determination, her spirit and joy of life.

He could appreciate her natural beauty for he admired beauty in all its forms. He decided to accept the invitation.

"That's grand," said Daniel. Make it eight o' clock then. That'll give Mrs. Donovan plenty o' time to cook the fish an' prepare a first class dinner."

They extinguished the fire and set off down the lough, stopping to drop Devlin off on the bank close to his house.

Catrin took the oars for the rest of the journey back to Dungannon House. Mrs. Donavan was not thrilled to have the catch to prepare for dinner, and when she heard they would have a visitor, she was even more dismayed.

Her consolation was that it could earn her another half crown. Telling Flann Maguire that his man really was in danger of being corrupted would make his toes curl.

While Catrin and Daniel had been enjoying the afternoon, Lieutenant Dillon had been meeting with sergeant McNulty and discussing his plan for retribution.

He had not explained his real motive for the plan, and the sergeant knew nothing about his spat with O'Farrell.

When he had limped back into the barracks after the incident with Catrin, he had claimed he was the victim of a fishing accident, and the fact that the hook was still firmly embedded in his ear lent credence to the story.

Doctor McCrimmond was called in to take the hook out, and he was also given the same impression. It was not an uncommon type of accident for fly fishermen to have. The story was accepted, but with some reservations by McNulty. Why did the lieutenant arrive back minus his gun and holster, and with only one horse? He claimed to have left it at Dungannon House, so why was it found the morning after tethered to the Barracks gate?

"I'm finally laying O'Farrell by the heels," Anthony told the sergeant. "He's a key man in the Maguire camp. Without him Maguire would be badly hampered."

"Surely that's a matter fer the Garda, surr?"

"The Garda's not going to bring him in. They're not even interested. He's just a harmless tinker as far as they're concerned. But we know different. He's involved in almost everything Maguire does."

"I propose to rough him up a bit. Put him out of action for a spell. If we can do that, it'll slow Maguire up. Force him to cancel some of the events he's undoubtedly planning."

"Won't that make him mad enough to strike back?"

"So what! Isn't that what we want? Some action, instead of sitting here polishing brasses and getting fed up?"

McNulty began to see what he was driving at. He indicated his approval.

"Here's what I want, Anthony continued, "I want you to pick out two men, the biggest and roughest you've got. Get the small van ready for to-night.

"We'll drive out the Corrib road to the spot I've located this morning, and make our way through the woods to his den. We break in, give him a good going over, and wreck the place. It'll be over in five minutes and we'll be back in the barracks before anyone knows we've been out. That's all there is to it. I'll stand the men a pint when we get back. How's that?"

"Sounds like a bit o' fun to me, surr. Might be enjoyable. It's a while since I had a good fight."

"Well, this is your chance. Cunningham will drive the van, you and I plus the two others will make up the party. Everyone one in mufti, and we'll need masks to cover our faces. We'll leave as it's getting dusk so as to have the dark to operate in. Get torches issued to each man."

McNulty took his leave with a spring in his step. Action at last. Just like a good old Saturday night punch up in Dublin. There would be no trouble in getting two volunteers. They'd all want to come.

CHAPTER THIRTY

The late afternoon was blessed with sunshine flitting through the clouds. Catrin sat with Daniel on the front steps relaxing with a cool drink. She was glowing. The fishing had been good and she had enjoyed competing with the men. She had learned a lot more about Devlin O'Farrell, and her confidence was growing that she could succeed in her quest. The fact that he had accepted their dinner invitation confirmed that, and she intended to capitalise on it.

He rode into the courtyard on a grey Irish cob, almost exactly on the stroke of eight. He was wearing the same grey suit that she had first seen in Dublin, but he had made an attempt to press it into shape. She guessed it must be his one and only suit.

He dismounted at the steps and immediately delved into the saddlebag and brought out a small stone bottle which he handed to Daniel.

"Brought you a treat," he explained.

Daniel beamed. "A treat indeed. Look Catrin, liquid gold, so 'tis. Thanks' Dev. I'll keep it fer special occasions."

"Somethin' for you, too, Catrin. He produced a small glass jar. "It's rosewater. Fresh from Donegal. There's no roses smell more wonderful than them in Donegal. Good for the skin, an' a lovely perfume."

"That's really nice. Thank you," She unscrewed the lid carefully and took a sniff. "It's lovely. It's almost like holding the roses in your hand."

It was a pleasant start to the evening, and it carried on from there. Mrs. Donovan had made a tasty fish pie with a crust top pastry which was as delicious as it looked, and Daniel had pitchers of Guinness for the men, and wine for Catrin. It was a thoroughly enjoyable meal and the company sparkled.

"I can't get over how many different things you seem to do," Catrin remarked.

"You sculpt driftwood, you paint, you do other work for Maguire. How do you manage it all?"

"I take it as it comes. The Poteen business has been virtually dead for years now. Maguire's spun it out because he's always had a good product and he's got all the custom for it.

In other parts o' the country it died out years ago. It's only the old timers like Daniel that really appreciate it, and create a demand, but they're disappearing fast, too. The rosewater was payment for some bits o' jobs I do. I barter my labour for doin' all sorts o' things. I get lots that way. I got this suit for helpin' repair a wall. That's why I travel around so much. The only steady money comes from the driftwood an' a paintin' here and there. I rely on Maguire for that. It's a happy enough life.

"Why work for Maguire? Why not only for yourself?"

"I'm obligated to the man. He helped me when I needed it. I practically grew up with his boy Seamus. We've been like brothers. He got me a job with his Da when I couldn't get work. My art work is very unreliable as a steady income. I need somethin' steady to back me up. Maguire does that".

"So what made you do the exhibition in Dublin?"

"I told you already. The fellah from Dublin that gave me all the blarney. I was flattered into doin' it."

"You did have the chance of one sale," Catrin could not resist the comment.

Devlin shook his head slowly in wonderment. "You're a rare one for never givin' up, Catrin. Please stop. I thought we had a truce on the subject."

"Then I'm sorry, but you'll have to talk about it sometime, Devlin. For your own good, you have to."

"Maybe. Maybe so, but I don't want to at this time."

He rose from the table and indicated the subject was closed.

"Thanks for the meal, Daniel, an' also for the fishin'. It was a really nice day. I'll be around for a few more days, so maybe we can do it again."

"Thank you, too, Catrin," his eyes had a mischievous gleam in them, "you're not that bad at castin' a line for a woman," he laughed, "you taught her well Daniel, so you did. It was a near perfect day, but I'd better be starting back. It'll be dark soon."

"Will you find your way?" asked Catrin anxiously?

"For sure. The horse knows its way blindfold. He's bin over half o' Ireland with me."

She fondled the horse as he mounted, and walked with them to the gate, waving them off and watching until they disappeared from sight.

As she retraced her steps to the house, she was feeling pleased with herself. Things were moving slowly, but in the right direction, and for the first time she had the faint hints that perhaps Devlin O'Farrell was not an impossible nut to crack after all.

He was certainly an interesting character.

While Devlin had been fraternising with the Kilpatricks, there were others with less pleasant things on their minds. As dusk fell, a small dark green van left the barracks in Galway and made its way north up the main road that passed the track leading to Dungannon House.

Anthony sat in the front with Cunnigham the driver. Sergeant McNulty and two privates sat in the back.

Donnachie and Fallon were the two biggest men of the garrison, and known to be well able to take care of themselves in a fight. They were all dressed in mufti and wearing cloth caps.

Cunningham was ordered to drive slowly so that Anthony could compare his rough sketch against the ordinance survey map, and pin point where he thought there was a track from the road that led to the den. They had three false attempts but finally came to what looked like a bridle path that led in the right direction.

Cunningham remained in the van while the rest jumped out and dispersed themselves among the trees.

"Find a place and park. Stay with it and watch out for a torch signal. A couple of flashes and you get back and pick us up. We need to be gone quick from here." He watched the van drive off and joined the others in the wood.

"Masks on," he ordered the group, as he covered his own face with a dark woollen scarf that hid all but his eyes. He led them single file along the path which was barely wide enough for a horse and rider. As the trees started to thin out Anthony signalled a halt and ordered McNulty to go on ahead and scout the lay of the land.

"Nary a sight o' anyone, surr," he reported back, "there's a house in a clearin', but it looks deserted. There's an oil lamp in the window, but I'd say he wis out, an' the lamp's there to guide him comin' back."

"All the better then, but we'll have to make sure. Fan out and crawl towards the house. The sergeant and I will approach from the front, you two round the side and the back."

"Be careful. Remember this fellah is liable to be armed." He had a sudden horrible thought. O'Farrell had his gun.

They slithered like reptiles, keeping close to the trees and using what cover there was, and careful to avoid any noise. There was another small building on the opposite side of the house that McNulty had not mentioned. Anthony signalled Fallon to investigate whilst McNulty and he approached the front.

He saw the lamp the sergeant had reported. He was probably correct in his guess. Had there been an occupant, surely the lamp would have been used on the table. They eased themselves underneath the window and in a synchronised movement, raised themselves slowly and peered inside. All was quiet and the rest of the room was in darkness.

They moved to the door and took up positions on either side. Anthony held up three fingers to indicate a count of three, and on the silent mouthing of the count, they flung open the door and burst inside. Fallon and Donnachie had completed their approach and entered just behind them.

The group stood in the centre of the room, four pairs of eyes scanning everything in sight, but it was clearly deserted.

"Will he be on one o' his trips, surr?" McNulty was aware of O'Farrell's nomadic habits, "I don't think so. He's left a fire burning, and the oil lamp in the window. Makes me sure he's coming back. Suits us. We'll wait for him and give him the kind of homecoming he won't expect."

"That building on the side, surr, is nuthin' but a stable." Fallon reported. "There's signs there's bin a horse in it."

"That seems likely. So he's out somewhere, but probably not far," Anthony mused. "Where's the most likely spot from here?"

"Dungannon House is jest down the road. Could he have gone there?" McNulty queried.

Anthony glared at him, and the sergeant bit his lip. He remembered the red head. He expected a censure but despite a surge of jealousy, Anthony held himself in control.

It would not do to admit he had lost Catrin, especially to one of the enemy. "Not impossible," he admitted. "The Kilpatrick girl's been trailing him for weeks."

McNulty looked at him with a puzzled expression. The lieutenant seemed to be the one that was chasing her.

"She's desperate to buy some bloody painting off him, but he won't sell it." He broke off and walked over to the work bench. "Here's some of his stuff here." He indicated the pile of driftwood and the finished pieces that lay on one side. In a sudden rage he dragged the bench back from the window and heaved it over on its' side, scattering the driftwood over the floor.

He turned the table upside down and kicked the legs until they splintered and broke off. McNulty had never seen him so angry.

"Smash the whole damned place up," he ordered. "I want it wrecked completely. See if you can find any evidence of his involvement with the IRA when you're at it. Then we'll lie in wait for Mister bloody O'Farrell and wreck him, too."

He walked out into the fresh night air to cool off. He had not meant to lose his temper, and it served to remind him how jealous he was. He lit a cigarette and relaxed as he heard the sounds of the house being taken apart. The sergeant appeared to interrupt him.

"Look whit we've found, surr," he held out a large stone jug, and pulled the cork from it. "Smell that, surr. Sure ye've nivver smelt anythin' as good as that."

Anthony took a sniff, and his sudden intake of breath made him gasp.

"My God! It smells like raw alcohol."

"They calls it the precious stuff. This is the very best, I'll tell ye. Puts hair on yer chest an' fire in yer belly, so it does. Bloody sight better than whiskey."

"Go easy with it. One swig now, and you can have the rest back at the barracks. I don't want you drunk before we've dealt with O'Farrell." He raised the jug to his mouth and drew a swallow. The power of it made him gasp.

"By God! You're right. It is something special. But I mean what I say. One good swig now and that's all. You can get drunk at the barracks, but not here. Is that all you've found?"

Donnachie and Fallon had appeared and shook their heads. "Nuthin' that is anything to do wi' the IRA surr. Only the jug."

Anthony brushed past them and inspected the damage they had wrought inside. Not a stick of furniture was recognisable. Even the bedding had been shredded and scattered. He nodded his satisfaction.

"I don't know how much longer he'll be. Could be midnight, but we'll wait inside, except for you, Donnachie, go across the clearing and hide in the trees. When you hear sounds of his horse, flash your torch. One quick flash. We'll be watching from the window." Donnachie took off, muttering under his breath. He would have preferred to remain inside.

"Shut the door sergeant and blow out the lamp."

"Won't that make him suspicious, surr?"

"He'll think it's run out of oil, that's all. You stand on one side of the door, you, Fallon, on the other. When he enters, grab his arms and hold him. Belt him a good one on the kidneys and I'll go for his head. Once he's on the floor, it's a free for all. Get as many hits or kicks as you can."

"How far d'ye wants us to go," McNulty asked.

"Within an inch of his life. I'll tell you when, but I want the last punch. OK?"

The poteen had fired him up. He fingered the fish hook in his pocket. McCrimmond had given it to him after he removed it from his ear, and he had vowed to restore it to its owner. Every time his ear throbbed, he renewed his vow.

"Fallon keep watch on the window for the signal. Out with the lamp sergeant. He'll probably make for the stable first, so no movements and keep quiet."

The sergeant blew out the lamp and they hunkered down, backs to the wall to wait for their prey. Fallon trained his eyes on the far side of the clearing, his eyes straining to make sure he saw Donachie's signal. He was feeling good. The large swallow of poteen he sneaked had raised his blood and he was spoiling for a fight. A little more of the fiery liquor would have been appreciated. It would be like a good old fashioned Saturday night, a good drink and a good fight.

As the minutes ticked away, the darkness grew, and all was still. So quiet and peaceful as Devlin wound his way home, he was totally relaxed. Well fed and still tasting the Guinness on his lips, the supper had made a fitting end to a very pleasant day. He whistled the "Gipsy Rover" softly as he let the horse find its way along the bridle path. It needed no urging, for it was eager to get back to the stable and be fed.

He was thinking what a pleasure it had been to dine in Dungannon House and with such company. He had known Daniel for many years, but had never been so close to him. And his granddaughter? What to make of her?

She had been roughly dressed for the fishing, but he had been staggered to see the change in her appearance when she greeted him.

There was a classical beauty about her, an air of breeding far exceeding his own, yet she acted with a warmth and common touch that did not discomfort him. She shared his love of nature, and she was so full of energy and vitality. She could hold her own with any man, and was unafraid to express her convictions. She was not the spoilt upstart he had taken her for when she clashed with him in Dublin.

He was too immersed in his thoughts to see the brief flash of Donnachie's torch.

Inside the house, the sergeant and Fallon took up their positions on either side of the door, whilst Anthony stood further to one side. He had armed himself with one of the legs from the work bench.

Devlin frowned as he saw the darkened window. The lamp must have been less full than he thought. He trotted past the house and dismounted at the stable door. He stripped off the saddle and harness and left the horse to feed and water. Still whistling softly, he closed the half door and made his way towards the house.

Chapter Thirty-One

He was still whistling as he opened the door and stepped inside. His first intention was to refill the lamp and light it, but as soon as he entered, he knew something was wrong.

He had no time to debate. Figures sprang at him out of the gloom, pinning his arms behind his back, and as he struggled to free himself, a club of some sort crashed against his head and sent him to his knees. A boot thudded into his back and he collapsed on the hard earth floor.

He made a futile attempt to rise, but blows came from all directions, sending explosions of pain through his body. It eventually became too much. He lapsed into unconsciousness and although the punches and kicks continued, he no longer felt the pain.

"O.K., that's enough." Anthony was sweating with the exertion. He flung the blood stained piece of wood from him.

"I don't want him dead. Light the lamp sergeant and see what state he's in."

McNulty lit the lamp and brought it close to the inert figure that lay huddled on the floor, that was dark and slippery with blood. Anthony dug his boot under his victim and turned the body over.

Even McNulty cringed at the sight. The same Devlin O'Farrell who had entered the house so cheerfully a few minutes ago was unrecognisable. His face a mask of blood, nose probably broken, his eyes disappeared between huge swellings, and one ear badly swollen. Anthony knelt down, careful to avoid the blood.

"He's still breathing, thank God, "but he'll wish he was dead when he comes to. This'll keep him out of action for a while. His boss will not be pleased."

He looked up at the group for a reaction, but there was none. It had been a one sided contest, and there was no glory in winning such an uneven fight.

"Donnachie, get back to the road and signal Cunningham. We'll be there shortly. Fallon, help the sergeant drag him outside."

"Whit's next?" queried McNulty when they had dumped the unconscious body on the grass outside.

"Just one thing. Fallon, go after Donnachie and make sure he's signalled Cunningham. Quick about it!" He watched the private disappear into the trees. He brought his hand from his pocket and held up a small object. McNulty looked surprised

"A fish hook? Whit's that fer?"

"I think it'll look good in his ear," Anthony laughed softly, "it belongs to him after all."

"Fer Christ's sake, surr, ye can't do that."

"Why not. He did it to me?"

McNulty suddenly understood. He had always been sceptical about the lieutenant's story about the fishing accident. Now he knew where the bloodied ear had come from, and why he returned minus his revolver. "You did this for revenge?"

Anthony realised his mistake. He should have sent McNulty with Fallon.

"Of course not! I want to get at Maguire. It's just a coincidence, that's all, but it's a good chance to return his hook."

"You can't, surr. If ye do that he'll know who did this. Ye'll have Maguire an' his pack on us like a ton o' bricks."

Anthony cursed his stupidity. McNulty was right. He had been blinded by his thirst for revenge at the expense of common sense. He looked at the hook for a minute as if debating whether to keep it or not, and then flung it into the night.

"I guess I was carried away. That poteen's powerful stuff. I shouldn't have drunk it." He walked towards the house. "But there is one more thing to do."

McNulty watched as he Anthony re-entered and picked up the oil lamp that had been left on the floor. He looked around the room as if assessing the damage, and then flung the lamp at the hearth where the turf fire still glowed.

The glass shattered and a line of blue flames sprang up and set alight to some of the debris scattered close by. He continued to watch the flames spread as if he was in some sort of trance.

"Time we went, surr," McNulty called anxiously, "the van'll be there now."

Anthony returned to his senses and hurriedly joined the sergeant. As they made their way through the trees. McNulty was curious.

"Why torch the place, surr? There wis nuthin' suspicious there. Only the poteen."

"Because I had reason to believe it was one of the IRA's safe houses. It's well hidden from everyone. Anyone on the run from the Garda could hole up there until the fuss dies down. Well, they'll need to find someplace else now."

McNulty grunted. At least that was one answer that made sense. The van was waiting, engine running, and they drove off at speed. The streets of Galway were completely deserted and their return to the barracks was not witnessed.

Anthony kept his promise and let the squad drink the jug of poteen. As the fiery liquor dulled their brains, he congratulated them on striking a positive blow against the Maguire organisation. He did not need to share the drink to feel personal satisfaction. Not only had he damaged Maguire's activities, but he had gained his revenge.

McNulty was strangely subdued. He was thinking. Certain pieces of a puzzle concerning his commanding officer were beginning to fit, and it was making a disturbing picture. The man was not as perfect as he made out. Still, he had to agree. A jug of precious was worth capturing.

There would be no early morning parade as a further reward. The lieutenant was in an unusually generous mood. McNulty mellowed and burst into song and the rest followed. The Poteen was giving his gut a warm glow and spreading contentment through his body.

It helped dull the pain of his grazed knuckles.

Chapter Thirty-Two

Devlin O'Farrell should have died that night. That he did not was due to an extremely fit constitution, and divine providence. How he managed to crawl to the stable, drag himself on to his horse, and ride the few miles to Dungannon House was something of a miracle.

Semi-conscious, soaked by overnight rain, and still bleeding from his wounds, it was scarcely believable.

Daniel was the first to find him. He was awake at his usual time of five o' clock and on the point of rising, when the sound of a horse clip-clopping into the courtyard had him hopping out of bed and peering through the window. He was startled to see a horse he recognised as Devlin's with a rider slumped on its unsaddled back, his hands clasped round its neck, and in obvious distress.

He tore down the stairs, in his nightshirt, and rushed to catch the figure just as it was about to fall.

"Mother of God. Whit's happened?" he exclaimed as he lowered the figure carefully to the ground. It was a full minute before he recognised it as Devlin. "In the name o' God. Who did this?" There was only a faint moan in reply.

He dashed into the hall and yelled for Mrs. Donavan.

"Hurry, hurry," he shouted as loud as he could, "there's a dyin' man outside. Help me git him into the warm. He banged on Catrin's door and ran outside with a pillow and a blanket in his hands.

He slid the pillow under Devlin's head and wrapped the blanket around him. By that time Mrs. Donavan had appeared.

"Git on the phone for McCrimmond, Rose. Tell him we've a badly hurt man. He'll need to git him to hospital. Tell him he's in a bad state."

She turned to go inside but halted. "The exchange won't be open 'till seven. I won't be able to call him."

"Oh Jaysus! Damn the exchange! I'll go then. I can saddle his horse. But we need to get him inside. Where's Catrin?"

"I'm here," Catrin was running down the stairs. She screamed as she saw Daniel kneeling by the bloodstained figure huddled in the blanket.

"What's happened?"

"It's Devlin. He's badly hurt. We need to get him inside. Help me, but we need to be gentle. I'll take his head. You an' Rose take his feet. Support him as much as you can. We'll put him on the couch in the front room."

It was a delicate task, and they were painstaking in their care to move him.

Once gently laid on the couch they covered him with more blankets and Rose heated water to fill the stone water bottles that would provide extra warmth.

Catrin could only sit by his side, shocked and dumbfounded. He was unrecognisable as the man she had begun to admire. All she could do was to hold his hands, massaging them gently.

"That's no help," snapped Rose. "We need to get these wet clothes off him for a start. The poor man'll git his death o' cold. C'mon now Catrin, pull yourself together an' do somethin' useful." The complete loss of formality passed unnoticed. This was a crisis and no time for protocol.

With difficulty they managed to strip the sodden clothing from his body and wrap him again in fresh blankets, and with several stone hot water bottles placed around his body and feet.

They tenderly washed his face with a soft flannel in an attempt to clear the matted blood away. Both were horrified to see how badly he had been beaten. His eyes were mere slits, hidden by the massive swelling around him, and there were cuts on his forehead and cheeks.

Meanwhile, Daniel had saddled the horse and was galloping recklessly along the main road to seek Dr. McCrimmond. He did not know if his mission was in vain. Devlin's injuries were severe, and the overnight soaking would not have helped. More than that, the ride to Dungannon House might have aggravated any internal injuries.

By the time he arrived back with the doctor, Rose and Catrin had done wonders in making their patient more comfortable. The blood was removed from his face and head, and he was breathing more normally. Even McCrimmond was shocked. Saturday night brawls in Galway were frequent, and patching wounds was fairly regular work for him, but this was much worse.

"This is devil's work," he said as he made his examination. "Leave us a minute ladies while I take a closer look.

Brew up some tay, Rose, and put a tot of whiskey in it."

Catrin and Rose sat in silence in the kitchen. Each was unsure of what to say. Their relationship had suddenly changed. The shock had broken all inhibitions, and there was no longer a master and servant issue.

Catrin was numbed. Only yesterday they had laughed and joked with one another. Only yesterday she had begun to better understand the kind of man he really was. She had been looking forward to building on the relationship.

Daniel and the doctor entered and sat down at the table. The expression on their faces was one of concern. Rose poured him a mug of steaming hot tea and under his guidance added a little whiskey from Daniel's special bottle.

"It's a miracle he's still with us," McCrimmond said gravely. "He ought to be in hospital, but he's too ill to move. Daniel's offered to keep him here, and I think that's best. He's got a broken nose, and a broken arm plus a few cracked ribs as the most obvious. He's lucky they didn't break and puncture a lung."

"His whole system is in shock. You must keep him warm at all times. I'm worried about pneumonia. That soaking he got won't have helped. He's been badly beaten about the head so I'm worried about the effects. Right now he's under sedation so all you need do is keep him warm. When he comes to, I want you to keep talking to him. We need to know if his memory's alright. I'll come out every day, but it's a day and night job for a while. Can you manage?"

Rose nodded. "We'll cope. I've been through this before. Catrin'll learn. I'll teach her."

"That's fine then," McCrimmond took his leave. "I'll look in this evening but if there's a need before then, just call me and I'll get here as soon as I can."

He paused at the front door and spoke to Daniel. "Who would do this? They've near killed the lad. Should we be telling the Garda?"

"I don't think so. Maguire wouldn't want the Garda near Devlin. But that's a point. We'd better tell Maguire. If anyone can track down the culprits, he will.

I'll go and take a look around Dev's place an' see if there's any clues. Hopefully he might tell us somethin' himself when he recovers."

"Aye," the doctor muttered softly, "if he recovers."

Daniel left soon afterwards, riding the cob through the woods to Devlin's workshop. He could smell burning in the damp morning air long before he came to the clearing in front of the house. He reigned in and surveyed the scene.

The thatch had partially gone and what was left was still smouldering. The same rain that had chilled Devlin had saved complete destruction. Both halves of the door stood open, badly charred and threatening to disintegrate. He stood aghast at the mass of charred timber and ash that lay on the floor, some embers still glowing and the smoke rising lazily. The whole room was gutted. Nothing recognisable remained. He felt his anger rising. Devil's work indeed!

The stable had been left untouched. He glanced around and could see no damage, but as he was walking away from it, something bright in the grass caught his eye. He bent down and picked it up.

It was a fish hook. A yellow lure, although the brightness was dulled by some dark staining which he attributed to the wet grass and the length of time it may have lain there. It was one of Devlin's favourites. He put it in his waistcoat pocket and decided to keep it until Devlin had recovered. He made his way back to find another visitor waiting for him.

Seamus Maguire stood on the front step talking to Rose.

"McCrimmond told us about Dev. I came to see him, but Rose says he's in a bad way."

"I don't know how he's still with us," Daniel explained, "he's badly hurt. He's under sedation right now, so there's no point in seein' him."

"Has been able to tell you anythin'?"

Daniel shook his head. "He's had the worst beatin' I've seen since the days o' the Black an' Tans. We wonder if he'll remember anythin'."

Daniel related the pleasure they had enjoyed on the fishing trip, and the invitation he had accepted to come for dinner.

"He left here about half past ten. He was in fine fettle. He had only drunk a little. Next thing I know his cob is clopping into the yard around five o'clock in the mornin' and himself hanging on like grim death. Soaked through an' covered wi' blood he was. I'll never know how he made it."

"Be Jaysus! Someone'll suffer for this. My Da is fit to burst, so he is. We'll find the feckin' bastard an' make him sorry."

"I was expecting' Maguire to be furious. I feel the same. Whoever it was didn't content themselves with jest a beatin'. The place was set on fire as well. I've been up to take a look. Gutted it is. Nuthin' left inside an' the roof near gone. He won't be using' that again. We'll just have to wait an' see. It can always be rebuilt like he did before, but our worry at the moment is just to make sure he stays alive."

Seamus drove back to Galway and went straight to Rafferty's office, knowing his father would be there for his usual morning inspection. He relayed the information Daniel had given him.

Maguire had a face as black as thunder. "This means we're goin' to have to change our plans. Belfast are not goin' to be pleased."

"For Christ's sake! Is that all that bothers you? Dev's near been kilt, for Christ's sake! Bugger Belfast!"

Rafferty interrupted. "It's not the end of the world, Flann. The bomb makin' course'll have to be postponed, that's all. We can concentrate on firearms training. The plan can still go ahead."

Maguire shook his head. "Belfast know more about firearms than we do. It was the bomb makin' they were most interested in, especially this new fertiliser stuff Dev's been experimentin' with."

"We need to find the bastard who did this," Seamus said.

"He's not said anthin'?" Maguire asked.

"No. He's sleepin'. They're worried about him comin' out of it alright."

"Pass the word around and see if someone's seen something suspicious around his place. I want you in there every day, Seamus. I don't want him babbling' to anyone there about his work for me, especially if that young bitch is attendin' to him. She's far too curious about Dev for my liking'."

The days passed slowly as Seamus waited an opportunity to see Devlin. All his enquiries to his usual contacts had failed to come up with any information. He met with Rafferty an' his father and confessed he had found no definite leads.

Maguire was not impressed. "Dev should never have got mixed up wi' the Kilpatricks. They're poison to me, so they are. I warned him."

"For Christ's sake! All he did was go fishin' an' help them eat the catch."

Rafferty could see a father and son confrontation building.

"Flann. Seamus has a point. Lets' focus our attention on who did it. Did they mean to kill him, or was it just to put him outta action for a while?

Maguire looked coldly at them both. "I've made enquiries. It's nuthin' to do wi' the Garda or the Excise. That leaves someone who had a personal grudge.

"Be Jaysus. You might be right. Dev did beat up that feckin' lieutenant. He could've wanted to git his own back, so he could."

"My thoughts exactly. Why didn't you think o' it?"

Seamus cursed inwardly. Now that it had been mentioned it seemed an elementary supposition.

"It makes sense, but we've no proof," Rafferty pointed out.

"Well get some. Seamus," Maguire thumped the desk. "Take a look at his squad and pull in one' o' them that looks as if he's bin in a fight, or anythin' suspicious about him. Give him a the full treatment until he talks".

"If it turns out he was involved you know what to do."

A few nights later, private Fallon failed to return to barracks after a night out at his usual pub. Despite enquiries, no trace of him could be found. Pub regulars recalled seeing him with two men they failed to identify, but they were plying Fallon with beer, and apparently enjoying themselves.

A troubled Anthony reported his disappearance to the Military Police. Desertion was a possibility, but he did not believe Fallon was the type. The Army was the only life he had. He had an uncomfortable feeling that there was a more sinister reason.

Chapter Thirty-Three

Autumn was brief, and the winds unkind. By the end of September, most of the trees had shed their leaves, and the wind had changed to the North East, a wind that originated in the icy wastes of the Arctic and brought a chill that warned of the winter to come. Dungannon House lost its charm and assumed a gaunt and grey appearance.

But it was warm inside, as Catrin and Rose fought to save their adopted patient. The threat of pneumonia had been dealt with and conquered. For the first forty-eight hours after his arrival, he had drifted in and out of consciousness, delirious as he battled the fevers that beset him.

Catrin and Rose devised a shift system to compliment the services of the nurse doctor McCrimmond sent them, and the patient had a constant service, bathing him, treating his numerous cuts and bruises and endeavouring to keep his temperature steady.

Catrin relied on Rose, as she now freely called her, to supply guidance. Rose had the experience. She had nursed a sick husband for several years before he died. Catrin was a willing pupil. It was exhausting work, but she was determined, and dug into reserves she never imagined she possessed. She followed the doctor's instructions and talked incessantly to the patient, even when he was barely conscious, scarcely aware she was telling him more and more about herself.

When he was in delirium, he ranted and raved incoherently, except for one particular name she had never heard of. Daniel's self-appointed task was to keep the house warm, and to ensure there was always a supply of hot water. He replenished the stone hot water bottles when required, and every day made a trip to the fish market in Galway and brought back ice to help reduce swelling on Devlin's face and body.

Rose had a friend who made special healing ointments from plants and seaweed that she applied religiously to the multitude of cuts and bruises. It was a battle that waged intensely for ten days and nights, stretching their endurance to the limits, but it was a battle that ended in victory.

It happened as suddenly as it was unexpected. Catrin had taken over from Rose in the very early hours and was seated close to the couch as dawn was breaking.

She was watching the skyline becoming lighter, and she could sense a change. His fever had diminished and he had been sleeping peacefully for some time. She suddenly became aware that his eyes were open and he was looking towards her.

Their efforts to reduce the swelling had proved successful and she was sure he would be able to see. The rest of his face remained a mass of bruises, in colours ranging from yellow to dark blue. She moved closer to the couch almost too frightened to speak.

"Feeling better?" she dared to ask.

He lay still, his eyes moving around in his head, and then there was the trace of a faint smile. The gesture made him grimace.

"I'd like a drink o' water," he said with an effort.

Catrin poured water from the carafe on the table into a glass and supported his head whilst she held the glass to his lips. He drank greedily, but much of the water dribbled down his chin. It was too painful to drink normally and she lowered his head gently on to the pillow.

"Where am I?" he asked after he had recovered.

"Dungannon House. Remember it? Remember me? You've had an accident. You came here and we had to keep you. You were too ill to go to hospital. You've been unconscious ever since you came. You've no idea how good it is to see you awake. Can you remember anything?"

"No. It seems like a bad dream. It's all confusing. I think I must've been in a fight. I'm sore all over. I can't move for pain. My chest feels tight. What's this thing on my nose? And my arm feels heavy. What has been going on?"

Don't touch," she warned. "Doctor McCrimmond had to strap up your ribs. You had some cracked. Your nose was broken, that's been taped, and your arm is in splints. It was broken but fortunately it was a clean break. You're lucky to be alive."

He lay quiet once more, obviously taking in all she had told him.

"You're that girl, aren't you?" I know your voice."

"Are you able to see?"

"My eyes are a bit blurry, but I think you're pretty."

A feeling of relief surged through her. It was one of the nicest compliments ever paid her.

"Feeling hungry? You've had nothing but liquids since you came."

"I do feel like somethin'," he struggled to say, "but it'll have to be somethin' soft. I can't move my jaw very much."

"I had a feeling last night he was at the turning "I can get you some porridge. I'll get Rose to make some. Just you lie still 'till I come back." She made her way to the kitchen.

Rose spoke with relief. "I didn't sleep well for thinkin' about him. I thought I'd rise early an' make some porridge He'll be needin' somethin' solid in him."

Daniel appeared shortly afterwards and made his way into the living room.

"'Tis a sight for sore eyes to see you on the mend, "he told Devlin with enthusiasm, "even if you're all colours o' the rainbow. You're not exactly handsome wi' that strappin' on your nose, but you'll do."

"Don't make me laugh. It hurts."

"You have the women to thank. Catrin and Rose never left your side."

"Somehow I always knew there was someone there, even if I couldn't see. Someone that was always talkin' to me. She never stopped."

"That was Catrin. McCrimmond told her to do that."

"She's a fine girl."

"I know," smiled Daniel, "but Rose was the inspiration." He heard footsteps approaching which he recognised.

"Rose, I do believe Dev is fancyin' some o' your porridge," he greeted her as she marched in with a tray on which was a steaming bowl of porridge.

She gently helped the patient sit up, and placed a large bib around his neck and then began to spoon small amounts carefully into the bruised mouth. Daniel left them to finish, but returned later.

"Feel better after that?" he asked.

"Best porridge I ever tasted. I always thought Rose was a crusty old soul, but she's actually quite soft. I'll never be able to repay them."

"Don't fash yerself, lad. It'll be enough reward to go fishin' again once your back on your feet. Speakin'o' that, I wis up havin' a look round your place to see what the damage was, an' I found this lyin' in the grass."

He fished in his pocket and brought out the yellow lure. "Recognise it?"

Devlin winced as he stretched out his hand and took the hook from Daniel. His face screwed up in surprise and he looked inquisitively at Daniel.

"You must've dropped it sometime."

Devlin remained puzzled as he twisted the hook around in his fingers.

"It's one o' mine, right enough. You say it was lyin' near the stable?" He strove to remember, but was too confused, and the effort tired him. He closed his eyes and drifted off to sleep. Daniel tip-toed quietly from the room and left the patient to rest.

It was mid afternoon when Seamus appeared. Word had spread fast that Devlin had recovered consciousness.

"Sorry to hear about the fire," Seamus commiserated with Devlin.

"Daniel told you about it, did he?"

"Aye, he did. The bastards. They had no need to do that."

"We know who did it."

"So do I."

"You're kiddin'. How in Christ's name could you know?"

"This." Devlin held up the fish hook with its stained yellow feathers.

"What does that mean? I've seen you fish wi' that many times."

"I know, but the last time I saw it, was hooked in that feckin' lieutenant's ear. Daniel found it near the stable.

"That clinches it sure enough. We brought in one o' his men for interrogation the other night. Tough bastard. He held out for a while, but his tongue loosened in the end. He won't do it again."

Devlin looked at Seamus and read the message in the hard set eyes. One less soldier to worry about.

"So we're plannin' the next one'll be the feckin' lieutenant himself."

"Don't touch him," Devlin made an effort to rouse himself. "Tell Maguire I want him."

"Don't be daft, Dev. It'll take weeks before you're back to normal. He might have another go at you."

"He could easily have kilt me if he wanted. Lay off him. He's mine."

"I'll tell Da, but he won't like it. He's mad at all his plans being thrown up in the air. The Belfast lot are givin' him stick."

"I'll be outta this bed jest as soon as I can. Never been sick like this, before, an', I hate it."

"What's to complain about? You've never had such a good bed. And having two nurses fussin' over you? By God, I'd suffer a few bruises to have that pretty red head look after me."

Seamus blinked. It was rare for Devlin to rebuke him. "Treat her with respect. She's helped save my life, don't forget."

It had been a long time since Devlin had championed a woman openly. As Rose entered with a drink for her patient, he deemed it a good time to finish his visit.

***

Autumn continued to fly. With each passing day, Devlin made progress. They moved him upstairs to the spare bedroom where the bed was more comfortable and there was privacy.

Inactivity was his main enemy. He had always been engaged in some work or other, and it was difficult to adjust to convalescence. His bruises took time to come out, and at first even his movement around the house was agony. His sight was back to normal and the strapping on his ribs and nose had been removed, and also the splints from his arm. He was eating much better and gaining weight, and if he had been forced to admit it, the pampering was beginning to grow on him.

He had completely revised his impressions of Catrin. She was not the little stuck up snob he had supposed. She was good company, easy to talk to, and an avid listener. She sat enthralled as he told her of the experiences of his countryside travels, and the quaint customs and work habits he had encountered.

She was unlike other Galway girls who were always subdued in the presence of men. She was vibrant, and full of energy, eager to learn more about his nomadic lifestyle. She told him of her desire to travel and to write about her experiences.

"Things are changing in Ireland," she said, "the old ways and customs that you've experienced will soon be forgotten as the new generations arise. I'd like to chronicle as many things of the old days as I could so that they could be preserved for posterity."

"That's a strange ambition for a beautiful young woman," Devlin commented, "but it's a noble thought. What sort o' things were you thinkin' about?"

"Some of the things you do. Poteen for instance. The history of making it, all those stories of incidents with the Garda and the Excise, and the many different characters involved with it. You could almost write a book on that alone.

There's the things you've told me about harvesting the seaweed for fertilizer, cutting peat and transporting it by donkey. How people scratched a living from the bare fields. There's hundreds of things, and some of them I haven't even heard of. Don't you think it would be a good idea to write about them and provide a record for posterity?"

"Of course. Mind you, Ireland's full o' people who want to write its history. But a fresh approach might be welcome. I'll gladly help you as much as I can. "

He was impressed by her attitude. He had seen and done many of the things she mentioned and he began to look forward to their daily conversations.

She had tactfully refrained from mentioning The Wishing Boy, but deep down he knew her obsession to obtain the painting was merely hibernating.

As the days passed by, and he became more attached to her, he began to realise that he would like to open his heart to her, and if that meant revealing the mystery behind his painting, so be it. It had been a cross he had borne long enough. But the timing had to be right. His instincts would tell him when that might be.

Catrin knew nothing of the changes taking place in Devlin's mind, but found him interesting and very intelligent. She had a great respect for his experiences in a rough life, and his practical philosophy. His physical appearance was improving day by day, his scars healing well under the treatment of the herbal ointments Rose applied daily.

Considering the severity of the beating he had endured, the improvement in his appearance was credit to their nursing. He was a better looking man than she had first imagined. She knew his soul ran deep, and that there were dark secrets locked within. Whatever secrets lay behind the creation of his masterpiece was of great significance, but she would never draw it out of him unless it was voluntary on his part. It tried her patience sorely, but she knew she would win in the end.

It was a further week later when Devlin announced he felt well enough to leave. The legacy of the bruises was still plain to see in the various colours that adorned his face and body, but they were much less painful.

His nose and ribs felt fine, his arm freely moving, and he was walking firm and steady. Doctor McCrimmond agreed that he was fit enough to go, as long as he was cautious in his movements.

Daniel had Rose prepare a special dinner to celebrate the occasion, and invited the doctor to join them. Not only did Rose oblige with a fine meal, but for the first time ever, she sat with the company and enjoyed her own cooking.

It was an evening which was to prove a turning point in the relationship between nurse and patient. The doctor took his leave, and shortly after Daniel and Rose retired leaving Catrin and Devlin to finish the last of the wine in the comfort of the front room.

She sat close to the fire, gazing into the flames, basking in the glow and seeking pictures in the flames. Devlin sat opposite, watching her face reflected in the glow. She was so pretty. It had been one of the most enjoyable evenings he could remember. A fine dinner, to be sure, and although he had drank sparingly, it was his first taste of alcohol since his accident, and he was feeling mellow and a little sad.

Catrin took advantage of the warmth feeling the meal had made.

"I was wondering what you would be doing now? Are you sure you're well enough to leave?"

"I can't stay here forever, Catrin. I have a lot to thank you for, an' I don't know how I'll ever repay you. I owe you so much."

Catrin extended her arms closer to the fire as if to warm them, before turning to gaze at him.

"You could repay *me* very easily."

He finished his drink and sat twirling the empty glass for a few moments before laying it down gently in the hearth. He clasped his hands in front of his knees.

"It's the Wishing Boy, isn't it? You've never given up, have you?"

"Is there a really good reason why you won't talk about it?"

"Is there a really good reason you should want to know about it?"

"It's not just female curiosity. I knew the first time I saw it there was something special behind it. I had the vibes. I felt the emotions. I wanted to share that emotion, and perhaps let others share it, too."

"It's too personal. People should be allowed to have secrets. I have some that go very deep".

"Has it to do with someone called Shula?"

He looked startled. "Where did you hear that?"

"When you were delirious you called out the name several times. I wondered if it was someone close to you."

"Did I really call out her name?"

Catrin nodded. She knelt before him and extended her hand to his. "Someone close?"

"Once, "he said sadly, "she was the wife of a friend. They're both dead now. It's hard to talk about them."

"I'm sorry. I shouldn't ask so many questions." She freed her hand from his and picked up the wine glasses.

"Let's finish the wine." She rose and replenished their glasses and resumed her seat in front of the fire. The candles on the table flickered in the throes of dying out. Soon there would only be the fire to provide light. The shadows dancing on the ceiling were becoming deeper.

"I'd like to help you, Devlin. You've had a terrible experience, but your body is strong and you have made an amazing recovery, but mentally I think you're scarred. There's something locked up inside you that's not right. I don't know what it is, but I can feel it. I think there's a great sadness within you, and it's been there too long.

"It almost seems you're carrying the burden of guilt for something, but you can't release your feelings. I'm sure it would help if you could only talk about it."

He sipped the wine slowly. He had listened carefully to everything she said, and there was nothing he could argue about. It was strange. His normal inclinations would have been to flare up and deny her, but he felt mellow, relaxed, and for the first time in his life a security greater than he had ever known.

This was the kind of woman he had only ever met once. She had put her finger on his problem and the realisation made the glass in his hand tremble. This was the opportunity his instincts had prophesised. At last there was a shoulder to cry on. The timing was right.

"You're very perceptive. I guess it would help, but you might not like me when I've finished. I'm frightened of that."

"Don't be afraid, trust me."

"I am afraid. Once I tell you, you might — what I mean is – are you sure it's not just the Wishin' Boy you're after?"

"No. I've realised that there's a lot more attached to it.

"I believe it has a lot to do with what's preventing you from having a life outside of what Maguire is giving you. You deserve better." There was a long pause, broken only by the hissing of the burning logs. He stared hypnotically at the flames as if they were helping him compile his thoughts. He sighed wearily and turned away from the fire to face her.

"You may be right. Now that I've had time to think about it, I'm beginning to see things differently. I don't like what Maguire's tryin' to do any more."

"It's a great thing to hear you say that. He is a truly evil man."

"You may think I have been evil too, when I tell you the story."

"Don't be afraid. You can trust me, Devlin. I promise I'll do nothing to hurt you."

He took a long sip of his wine and then set the glass down in the hearth.

"I think it was three years ago. Maybe it was four? I ought to remember but there was a period when I blotted out bits o' my life. There's a lot happened since then."

As he paused to gather his thoughts, Catrin added a few logs to the fire. It would be a long night. She sat facing him, hands clasped across her knees, listening intently as he began to tell his story.

Chapter Thirty-Four

"It was a bad winter that year. Even when Spring came it was unsettled an' stormy. I'd been awake all night. The wind was howlin' like a banshee, an' shakin' the house fit to blow it away. Come daylight it quietened down. There'd been a high tide that night, so I walked down to the beach to see if anythin' interestin' had been washed up.

There was lots. Weed an' flotsam everywhere. Bits o' trees, branches, sticks, fish nettin', and tons o' driftwood but all small bits. Nuthin' that took my eye specially, so I continued to walk further along.

Comin' towards me I saw two people, an' as they got nearer I recognised them as a couple o' students from the University. They were takin' degrees in Science, an' I used to see them in the laboratory. I often helped them set up their apparatus for experiments, and I liked them because they were so easy going and good natured, and she was very pretty.

Turned out they were also lookin' fer driftwood. Somethin' to decorate the house they were sharin'. We got talkin' an' I helped them find a few pieces, an' I told them how I worked on it to make shapes. They asked if they could see some, so I invited them back to Ballanalee.

Everybody liked Liam an' Shula. They must'ave been the most popular couple at the University. He was a fine lookin' lad, an' she was a real beauty, an' it was plain to see that they adored one another, and somehow they looked right for one another.

I showed them some o' my driftwood an' they loved it. Then they noticed some o' my paintin's which they said were good. I'd only been paintin' for two years, an' there wasn't all that much to show, but they said I ought to do more. From then on, I spent as much time on the paintin' as I did on the driftwood.

"Were they the two lovers in The Wishing Boy?"

"I'll come to that. Just let me take it in my own time."

Catrin bit her lip, realising her mistake. She was trying to push him too much. She sensed he was at the first hurdle of releasing pent up emotions and she must be patient. She moved beside him and sat on the floor, her head resting on his thigh. It was a gesture of companionship, of reassurance, and it came quite naturally to her. It had the desired effect. He began to stroke the fringe of her hair, as if it was a faithful dog by his side.

"It was Shula and Liam, wasn't it?" she coaxed.

"Yes. She was the young woman, an' he was the young man. I never saw any man and woman so much in love. She worshipped the very ground he walked on. He was very handsome. All the girls would've fallen at his feet. He could've had the pick o' them all. But he only had eyes for Shula.

She was a mite smaller than you, jet black hair an' big brown eyes. Bright as a button, full o' life. Always laughin' an' smilin'. Never a bad word about anybody. There wasn't a man who didn't envy Liam for havin' her."

"So you were inspired to paint them?"

"Yes. It wasn't just that they were so beautiful. There was a spirit about them that you just had to admire. I wanted to capture it."

"I was at Ballanalee a lot that Spring. They used to walk across at week-ends an' they'd call in, just like old friends. We'd have tay and chat, an' they'd look at the work I'd done. They were always full of encouragement. They made me feel good. I loved havin' them drop in. They showed me what real love was like. I'd never seen it before.

One night I woke up all of a sweat, and I had an inspiration. I wanted to capture this wonderful emotion, an' I had this vision of them sittin' in a shady bower, elegantly dressed, an' lookin' at one another the way they always did.

I rose outta bed an' did some sketches. It came to me so easy. In the mornin' I started to paint."

"Did they know you were doing it?"

"Not at all. I kept it outta sight. I wanted it to be a surprise. Each time they came I'd get another look at their expressions, an' the way they fussed one another, an' I'd try an' work it into the paintin'. I made lots o' changes. After weeks o' tryin' to capture the precise expressions in their eyes for one another, I finally got it. Even their hands looked jest like the way they held each other."

"So why did you not leave it at that? Why did the Wishing Boy come into the picture?"

"That came later. I was so intent on paintin' them, I hadn't noticed how unbalanced the picture was. All the attention was drawn to the one side. I could've filled in the rest with more greenery, but it would've spoiled the effect. That's when I had a second inspiration".

I decided I would paint a young boy who would be so taken by the lovers that he would spy on them. He would envy them, and want to share the same kind of adoration.

I thought of a poor beggar boy. Somebody who had nuthin' an' wanted to have the same as they did. It took me as long to paint him as it did to paint the two lovers."

"So that's how it became the Wishing Boy?"

"I didn't have a title. It was Shula's suggestion."

"I had it ready one Saturday mornin' when they dropped by. They were over the moon when they saw it. She hugged an' kissed me, an' Liam said it was the best paintin' he'd ever seen.

They stood hand in hand an' gazed at it half the mornin'. They wanted to buy it on the spot, but I said I wasn't goin' to sell it. I wanted them to have it as a weddin' present. They had told me they planned to get married as soon as they graduated. They went off, happy as larks.

Shortly after, Professor McCormack told me he had to let me go. His department was runnin' over budget an' he had to save money. I didn't see them quite so often after that, and then, all of a sudden they stopped comin' altogether.

I was troubled. I couldn't understand it. We'd been such good friends. I was worried that I had offended them in some way. I still had the paintin' and I managed to pick up a nice gilt frame for it. I was dyin' to show it to them. But they never came.

Then one day, they did appear, an' I was shocked.

Shula was still pretty, but looked older, her face tired an' strained lookin', and the sparkle had gone from her eyes. But Liam shocked me most. He looked like an old man. His clothes hung on him, his hair had gone grey an' he looked really ill.

I didn't know what to say. When I showed them the paintin' in its frame, they broke down an' cried. Sobbed their hearts out in each other's arms".

"I thought you liked it," I said. Have I done somethin' wrong? Is it the boy I've added that you don't like?"

"It's not that at all," says Shula. "It's wonderful, a real masterpiece, an' the boy— well, he's a masterpiece as well. Isn't he Liam?"

"That he is." His voice broke as he spoke. He was near to cryin'.

I don't remember ever havin' such sadness, not since I saw my Mam and Da kilt. He was so short o' breath he could hardly get the words out "You've a wonderful talent," he says, we always knew you had."

"Have you a name for it'?" says Shula.

"I haven't thought," says I. I wish I had."

"That's it," she says, "The boy looks like he's wishin' ever so hard for something, doesn't he Liam?"

"He does that. She's right Dev. Call it the Wishing Boy. It's a fine title for a fine painting."

"So that's how the name came about, an' the more I thought about it, the better it sounded. I hadn't intended it, but the boy had actually come to dominate the picture. I'd put so much work into him."

"Who did you use for a model?"

"There wasn't anybody, an' I couldn't afford to hire one. So I painted him from the feelin's I had inside me. Whatever his expression showed, it was comin' from those feelin's. The brush was controlled by them. It sounds crazy, but that's what happened."

"Didn't they mind the change in the picture?"

"Shula didn't mind at all, but I think Liam was a bit disappointed. It made me think. Perhaps if I got them to add somethin', it might make them feel it belonged to them.

Know whit I mean? A little touch o' the brush to make a leaf or a twig, or somethin' small."

"I'd spoil it," Liam says. "My hand is too shaky. Anyway, Shula's more of an artist than me."

She looks at him real sad, an' says it's a wonderful idea, but she can't think of anything.

"Tell me," says I, "you've been bright enough to name it the Wishing Boy, an' somebody's bound to ask, what is it he's wishin' for?"

Just suppose you was the boy, what would be your dearest wish in all the world?" I'll never forget the look she gave me. She was so sad, an' the tears runnin' down her cheeks."

"My dearest wish in all the world," she says, "would be for a new heart for my Liam. A heart that would make him healthy an' strong again. That's what I'd wish."

"I felt like cryin', too. I had a lump in my throat. At that moment in time, I'd have given my own heart.

That's when I understood what the matter was. She told me Liam had suddenly developed pains an' was havin' difficulty breathin'. They sent him to Dublin to some special doctor. An' he told them Liam had somethin' very serious wrong with his heart. Nuthin' they could do about it, they said. They only gave him a few months to live. You can imagine how devastated they were.

I couldn't believe God would let such a thing happen to such lovely people. When two people are so much in love, it ought to go on forever. It's unfair to cut it short.

An idea occurred to me.

If I let her paint a little heart somewhere in the picture, it might bring about a miracle. At least it might bring hope. I wanted to join them in the wish, so I helped her paint it under where I had signed my name.

"What about you, Liam?" I asked. "Suppose you were the boy, what would be your dearest wish?"

"I'd wish the same, but for Shula," says he, "I know when I'm taken from her, she'll have a broken heart. She loves me as much as I love her. But I would want her to be strong, and carry on living as the lovely person she is. She'll need new heart. So I'd wish her to have one."

"Help me," he says, "an' I'll paint it next to hers, where it's always been, and where I would like it to be for always."

"So that's how the hearts came to be painted under where I signed it."

Catrin said nothing, merely a slight nod of her head. But tears were brimming in her eyes and she dabbed at them with her handkerchief. There was an enormous lump in her throat.

"What happened after that?"

"They went back to Belfast. Got married. Had a honeymoon in Scotland. They sent me a postcard from Edinburgh. Three months later, Liam died. I had a letter from Shula to tell me everything. They buried him in Stewartstown, the village he was born in. He's in a peaceful spot overlookin' the lough. Liam was right. She was heartbroken. She was never the same again."

"Oh Devlin," she clung to his arm, "you're a hard man on the surface, and you treat life as hard as it treats you, but you're really sentimental underneath. There's a lot of love buried deep inside you, and you won't let it come out. But now that you've made a start, don't bottle it up any more."

"What more are you expectin'?"

"There's still one thing you haven't explained."

"What would that be?"

"You must know. You've only explained two of the little hearts."

"You want to know about the third one?"

"Yes. It may be the most important one."

"I was hoping' I'd told you enough."

"I have to ask. It may be the key to your problem."

"What problem?" It was a sudden burst of anger. She was pushing him into a corner and he didn't like it.

"You don't know what you're askin'. You won't like it. I'm maybe's not the man you think I am. You're the first woman I've ever been able to talk to like this. I don't want to lose your friendship. You've done a lot for me. Can't you understand?"

Catrin reached out her hand and clasped his in hers. "You can trust me, Devlin. If you have grief, I'll share it with you. Don't be afraid."

He looked at her closely, as if he could measure her integrity by means of the tenderness of the firelight dancing in her eyes. His grip tightened on her hand and he sighed deeply, like a swimmer preparing to dive into deep water.

He paused for a long time, struggling with his thoughts, and Catrin began to worry that the ordeal was going to be too much for him, but after what seemed an eternity, he cleared his throat and haltingly began to tell his story.

Chapter Thirty-Five

"When I lost the job at the University, Maguire helped me out. I knew Seamus, and he had told his Da that I knew a lotta things about chemistry from the work I had done in the laboratory.

He sent me to County Mayo to a fellah that who was workin' a still for him. I spent a summer there learnin' all about Poteen. But I applied some o' the things I had learned at the University.

That's how Maguire produced the best precious around. You won't have tasted it, but it's a real man's drink. Maguire's precious has a bite to it that nobody else has ever produced. That's the reason it kept goin' long after many other stills were closed down.

One day he asked me what I knew about electrical things. I'd helped out in the Physics lab at the University, so I knew a little. Next thing he packs me off to Dublin where there's two ex-army fellahs teachin' volunteers to make bombs."

"Oh my God, Devlin! You didn't learn to make bombs?"

"I told you there were things you might not like. Of course I did."

"I never thought you were involved in that."

"I tried to tell you. But you need to know the whole story. Maguire didn't twist my arm to go into it. I had a grudge against the army. I was only fifteen when they kilt my Mam an' Da, an' Keiron, my youngest brother. Kilt in Cork durin' the fighin' in 1922. Innocent folks that just happened to get caught in a crossfire as they tried to leave the city. My older brother Sean had to flee to America. They destroyed my family and I wanted revenge. I had a right to it."

"But making bombs? They hurt innocent people too."

"It seemed a good way to strike back at them. I picked it up quick. I knew enough to make better bombs. They were still using' gelignite an' fuses, blowin' themselves up half the time.

We bombed military targets like barracks, bridges that they used, made land mines and destroyed their armoured cars. I saw nuthin' wrong in that."

"What else did Maguire lead you into?"

"He took an interest in my driftwood. Started to sell it in his shop, even sent some to a place in Dublin. In the summer I was busy on the poteen, an' in the off season he learnt me to drive, an' sometimes I'd do runs for him in the haulage business. Other than that he let me do my own thing, roamin' around doin' odd jobs for folks. To most people I was a harmless tinker. It suited me. People didn't suspect anythin', an' I liked the freedom."

"But there were innocent people being killed by bombs. Surely you didn't want that?"

"Of course not! But innocent people do get kilt in wars. Look at my family! I made bombs to strike at the army, and sometimes the Garda, and the Excise. But Maguire had no scruples. Maguire would issue bombs I made to others. A lot went to Belfast, and Limerick an' Cork, wherever there was resistance goin' on.

His favourite trick was to make up innocent lookin' parcels an' send them to Customs posts with instructions they had to be called for. They were supposed to be timed so that the place would be empty when they went off, but sometimes the timer was set wrong. I didn't like it, but it was all part o' the war. We were fightin' for a cause."

Catrin sighed. She had heard her father and his friends debate the issue many times. The answer was always the same.

"What's all this got to do with the story behind the third heart on your painting?"

"A great deal. It's the part o' the story you'll like the least. I'd give my own life if I could turn the clock back. I've wished that many a time."

Catrin could sense this was going to be very difficult for him to continue, and that it was going to be a long night. But she had to keep him talking.

"Put some logs on the fire. I'll make some tea, and then you can tell me."

The logs crackled and hissed softly as they sat quietly sipping the tea. There was no longer any sense of time.

"After Shula wrote me about Liam, I never heard any more. I tried to keep busy, but I missed havin' their company. To tell the truth, I think I had fallen in love with her.

From the first day I saw her I had this burnin' feelin' in my gut. I used to catch my breath sometimes, she looked so pretty. I had terrible feelin's o' guilt, because I liked Liam. I had too much respect for him, an' they were always so much in love with each other, I kept it to myself.

Odd times she would flirt with some o' the boys, includin' me, but it was all fun, and they'd laugh an' joke about it. I'd never do anythin' to come between them.

"I remember one time, around Christmas, we'd lots o' snow. I was on my way home an' I came across them havin' a snow fight with one another. They were like children, pastin' one another, then they'd chase each other and rub faces in the snow. Then they'd kiss, an' start all over again. I wished I could join in, but it would have been wrong. But whenever I see snow, I can picture them all over again."

"I knew she would grieve deeply, but she would want to do it on her own. I couldn't comfort her. It would've been like betrayin' Liam."

"Did she ever know what you were doing for Maguire?"

"Only the driftwood. She never knew about the bombs, an' yet it was makin' bombs that brought her into my life again."

"Good God!" What happened?"

"I was sent to Dublin. There was a school o' volunteers arranged to train new recruits, an' they needed an instructor. One o' the ex-army teachers had been arrested an' was in jail.

They told me there was to be six trained for possible missions in England."

"In England?"

"Yes. The Council had decided there was more to be gained by settin' off bombs in England instead o' blowin' up Ireland. I thought it a good idea.

In fact, I was keen enough to go myself. But I couldn't believe my eyes when I saw Shula was a volunteer. It wasn't the Shula I knew in Galway. The laughter was gone, she was thinner, almost skin an' bone, and there was a different look about her. Her face was lined and strained, an' there was no shine in her eyes anymore, a haunted look, a hardness that was never there before."

"Was she surprised to see you?"

If she was, she didn't show it. Someone must'ave told her I was one o' the instructors. She behaved like any o' the others. She told me later why she was there.

Seems like her family had always been strong Republicans. She had two brothers, twins they were, who were active members of the IRA. One night they were in a squad assigned to attack a barracks, but they ran into a patrol. They dropped their weapons, but the patrol shot them. Bliddy murder it was!

On top of the grief she still had for Liam, Shula took it very bad. With him gone, an' then her brothers, she was a lost soul. She no longer had any interest in life. She needed to do somethin', so when a friend suggested she join the Woman's IRA, the Cumman Na Mban, she agreed. She wanted a chance to hit back at the bastards who murdered her kin, jest the same as I did.

The women's organisation wasn't a fightin' unit, which was what she wanted. They acted as messengers for the active units, were look-outs, an' provided safe houses for men on the run, things like that. But when they learned she had been to University an' knew a lot about Physics an' Chemistry, so they asked her to join the course in Dublin.

"Shula actually volunteered to make bombs?"

"She jumped at the chance. She wanted to get away from home. It held too many sad memories. She was ideal to be trained to go to England. With her education she would've fitted in to English society dead easy. She believed that by carryin' the war to England, we'd gain more for the cause!"

"Oh, Devlin. Blowing up people and places is horrible, no matter where it is."

There was another silence. A log fell from the grate on to the hearth creating another pause as Devlin used the tongs to replace it on the fire. The candles had burnt themselves out and only the flickering flames of the fire provided light.

"I didn't feel any different at that time. In fact, I was over the moon. The cause brought us close together again, an' I had the feelin' that it was a good thing for her. She started to look a bit better an' take more interest in things. I couldn't tell her the kinda feelin's I had inside me. I decided I would have to be patient and wait for the right moment."

"So what happened when the course ended? She went back to Belfast. She asked me if I'd come an' see her. She hadn't the heart to come to Galway. I could understand that, but I hoped she would come sometime. I wanted to rebuild her back to the same Shula I first knew, an' Galway seemed the best place to do it."

"Did she ever come back?"

"No. Not once," he buried his head in his hands.

"Something terrible happened, didn't it? Yes. I don't know if I can tell it." There was a pause as he fought to keep his composure. His grip tightened on her hand as he sought comfort.

"The Belfast lot put her active straight away. It was far too early. They were desperate to start a terror campaign. She needed to have more experience. It was supposed to be a routine nuisance operation, a bomb placed in a post box. But all bombs are tricky. She should'ave had supervision, like me."

She was to make a parcel of gelignite, set to off by an alarm clock. There's a detonator an' a torch battery that operates when the alarm goes off an' makes the circuit. Sounds simple, doesn't it. I've made dozens o' them."

He thrust Catrin's hands aside and stood up, and began to pace backwards and forwards in front of the fire. He stopped and rested his hands on the mantelpiece, his gaze directed at the fire. It was as if he lacked the courage to look her in the face.

"The bliddy thing went off in her hands! Jaysus Christ! Right in her hands! And I blame meself."

Catrin put her arms around his shoulders, and he collapsed into them. She held him tightly, as the dam broke and the tears came. It took a long time. When the tears stopped, she gently urged him to sit down.

She left him alone for a few minutes and made some more tea. The fire was dying, and there were no more logs to replenish it. Catrin waited until she was sure he had recovered his composure. They sat sipping tea in silence.

"How could you blame yourself? She was trained well enough, surely? You had done your bit. You weren't responsible for what her unit ordered her to do."

"Maybe not, but there was one thing I forgot to drum into her. One little thing."

Once again he buried his face in his hands, running his fingers through his hair as if he wanted to tear the hair from his head.

"I taught her to handle explosives with care. I told her over and over to always wear rubber gloves when she put the bomb together. It was vital, in case the circuit got made by accident durin' the final assembly."

"She didn't wear them?"

"She hated them. Said she became too clumsy and she could do it better and faster without them. She said other people didn't use them. She was right in that. I've seen others not wearin' them. I was too soft with her.

I could never bring meself to shout at her in trainin'. The one mistake I made was not to tell her she must take off her weddin' ring durin' assemblin' the bomb.

I suppose I thought, not bein' married any longer she wouldn't be wearin' one. But she was. When they found what was left of her, the ring was on her hand. They reckoned it must'ave come into contact with the bell wires attached to the alarm clock." He beat his hands against his thighs in exasperation, and fell silent.

"That's when you hit the bottle and went wild?"

"You know about that?"

"Danna told me you went off the rails. He said Maguire got you out of it."

"It's true. He put me through hell. He's good at puttin' people through hell, but in my case it worked. But he never does things without a reason."

"He still required your skills?"

"Of course. He wanted in on the Belfast project. They needed a skilled bomb maker, an' he had one. It gave him power, an' that's what he wanted. He was anxious to get me doin' his dirty work again."

"That almost sounds as if you no longer have enthusiasm for the job?"

He looked at her earnestly. "To tell the truth, I have been havin' second thoughts. All the time I've had to spend here bein' nursed by you and Rose has given me time to think. When I lost Shula, I lost my heart. I didn't care what I did. I wanted to lash out at anybody.

"I thought o' goin' off to America to join Sean. He lives not far from Boston. A little fishing village. He runs a little shop that sells gifts to the tourists who flock there in the summer. Boutiques they call it. He reckons I could do well with my driftwood. I've been thinkin' more an' more about it. But it's hard to get away from Maguire, an' devil take it, I owe him."

"You've paid your dues to him many times over. He doesn't own you."

"Devil he does! Don't get on to me, Catrin! Talkin' to you like this has taken the world offa my shoulders."

He seized her shoulders and looked intently into her eyes. "You wanted to know about the third heart, didn't you? Well I'll tell you now. Then you won't be on my back any longer either."

I wished for a new heart, too. Just like Shula and Liam did. A new heart I could share with someone."

"Have you found someone?"

"I think I have. But I'm still all tied up in knots. I need more time to sort things out. Maguire's chompin' at the bit. He's got plans. He wants me up in Connemara for two weeks. Will you be here when I get back?"

"My parents want me back in Dublin. They want Danna and me to spend Christmas with them."

"In Dublin?" he looked crestfallen.

"Yes. Will you miss me?"

He looked down at the floor as if embarrassed, and then leaned on the mantlepiece, once more gazing into the fire which was now a mass of glowing embers.

"Of course I will. You can't spend two months cooped up so close together without feelin' somethin'. I've told you things I didn't think I could ever tell anyone. Strange I could lay my soul bare to you, isn't it? You from one side o' the tracks, an' me from the other."

"Don't be silly. You're a human being same as I am. You've been led astray due to circumstances you could do nothing about, that's all. But now you do have a chance to change things. If you haven't realised it, you've already started."

"It would help if you stayed."

"I can't, Devlin. I have obligations, too, and I've been here far longer than it was intended. I have to go back to Dublin, but I promise I'll come back, and when I do, I hope you won't be so hard to find. You have so much knowledge of all the country things I want to write about, and you can help me a lot."

"Is that all? He held out his hands to her, and she grasped them instinctively. He spoke with great sincerity. "I know you mean well, but once you get back into the high an' mighty society o' Dublin, I won't blame you if you forget about me. I'll understand."

"I'm not one to break promises. But you have to break away from Maguire. He's destroying you. I can't help you if you continue to be under his thumb."

Her eyes gazed into his, never blinking or flinching, making a promise that made words unnecessary.

"I'll make sure Eamon knows where I am. Ask him if you're lookin' for me. But don't forget. There'll always be a fire in the hearth an' a lamp in the window at Ballanalee for you."

Catrin smiled and ran her hands up his arms to rest on his shoulders. Aware of the tenderness caused by the remains of the bruises, she kissed him very tenderly on the mouth. It was the most tender kiss with the most endearing feelings she had given to any man.

"I'll look out for them," she said with great warmth, "but it's time I went up to bed. It's a wonder Rose hasn't been down to see what shenanigans have been going on."

She kissed him lightly once again and left him standing by the fireside. He watched her leave, a mixture of sadness and relief mingling within him.

He sat down on the fireside chair and lay back in it, tired but not feeling like sleep. He began to reflect on the events of the past few weeks that had led up to the events of the evening.

Something had changed within him. Was it the shock and agony of the beating, or was it the influence of Catrin who had thrust her way into his life?

Was it simply gratitude for the way she had nursed him back to health, or did it go deeper than that? Could he overcome his fear of another unrequited love, and could she resume her place in Dublin society and still keep her promise to return?

His mind seethed with questions and he needed time to find the answers. Now that she had made him tell the story behind the Wishing Boy, perhaps her interest was satisfied, and just like the fire he was looking at, the flames would die, leaving only embers and ash, greying in the hearth, waiting to be swept away in the morning.

He crept silently upstairs and collected his things and wrapped them in a bundle inside a blanket. With great care to avoid noise, he let himself out the front door, and equally silently saddled his horse and led it out of the yard.

Out of sight of the gaunt old house, he gingerly mounted, and stole quietly away into the greying light of dawn.

Chapter Thirty-Six

With the surprise departure of Devlin, Dungannon House settled into its mundane winter routine. Catrin was stunned to find him gone, without even a note left for her, and suddenly time hung heavily on her hands.

"He's always been a wanderer," Daniel tried to console her. "A man like him finds it hard to stay in the same spot for long."

"That's not how I saw it. We talked a lot last night. He told me things he's never told anyone else, and I had the impression he would like to settle down. He even admitted he was getting tired of serving Maguire."

She related the story of the two lovers and the tragic end that befell them both.

"You knew about them, didn't you?"

"Only rumours. But it had to be somethin' like that to make him go on the binge like he did."

"I feel I should go after him and make sure he's alright. He was in a pretty stirred up frame of mind last night."

"Leave him be. He's bared his soul to you. He'll need time to reflect. I'm not blind Catrin."

"What does that mean?"

"I think you've become attracted to him. If that's the case, don't pressure him. You'll lose him. His sort don't take kindly to being pushed. Leave him to sort himself out. For that matter, you need to do the same."

"I'm sure I don't know what you mean," sparked Catrin, but there was a blush to her cheeks. She darted from the room and fled upstairs.

Daniel made to follow her but stopped when he saw Rose standing at the door. He wondered how much of their conversation she had heard.

Rose had heard everything from start to finish. She was amazed to hear Devlin's confessions and found herself with mixed emotions. During the past two months, and the hard work it had entailed to keep him alive, Rose had become fond of Devlin. But she was afraid.

Maguire had placed her in Dungannon House for a purpose, and would be vengeful if she failed to keep him informed. Maguire still retained ambitions to own the house should anything happen to Daniel. She would have to report that Devlin had left the house without giving notice, and spice the information with the fact that he was becoming deeply involved with the Kilpatrick girl.

Seamus inadvertently solved her problem. He had paid his daily visit to see Devlin only to discover that he had left the house, and immediately knew that he would make for Ballanalee. On relaying the news to his father, Maguire decided to take a ride out and see him.

"Glad to see you back," he bellowed as he marched in the door. "Christ! You're still all colours o' the rainbow. They really beat the tasty outta you, sure enough. You know we can take care o' them any time?"

"I told Seamus to leave Dillon to me."

"I did tell him," Seamus protested, "But it doesn't matter."

"Why is that?" Devlin asked.

"He's gone."

"The hell he has! Where?"

"Been sent across to England. Lookin' at new equipment. "There's talk they're goin' to get mechanised"

Inwardly, Devlin was relieved. It was true he was not yet fit for any strenuous activity, but at the same time he had little appetite for revenge. Another month, maybe.

"There's more important things to do besides him, anyway. He'll keep. The joint trainin' session wi' the Belfast unit is still on. The scoutin' party's already on their way. Rafferty'll drive the pair of you up there to-morrow, so get busy an' sort out your gear. He'll be here to pick you up at six in the mornin'."

"Can't you make it a weapons exercise only," Devlin protested, "I'm not in the best frame o' mind for bomb makin' right now."

Maguire exploded. "Don't tell me all this mollycoddlin' you've been enjoying in Dungannon House has made you go soft! I'll have none o' it! It's the bomb makin' that the Belfast boys want more than anythin'. They know more about guns than we do, for Christ's sake!"

"Alright, alright! I'll be ready. But that so called molly coddlin ye're on about saved my life, so don't knock it. And don't try frightenin' Catrin again. She's no threat to you or me. Leave her alone."

Maguire stared hard at him, his blood pressure rising. He was not accustomed to being challenged by those who served him. Seamus saw the danger signs and guided his father out the door.

"See you in the mornin'," he shouted back as he kept his father on the move towards the van. Seamus had been surprised at the outburst from Devlin, but put it down to his nerves still being frayed.

Maguire sat in the passenger seat saying nothing all the way back to Galway. His face was as hard set stone, and he was obviously still fuming over the spark of rebellion shown by Devlin. That young bitch had obviously been at work on his mind. He ground his teeth in annoyance. Only he should enjoy such power.

Catrin caught the train to Dublin the same morning as Seamus and Devlin left for Connemara. There was nothing more to keep her in Galway and with Christmas not far off, there was much more to do in Dublin.

Roderick and Megan met her at the station and drove her home. Without her, the house on Fitzwilliam street had seemed vast and empty, devoid of the excitement she brought to it. Her mother had missed her company dreadfully, and her father was desperate to tell her about a new business idea.

Apart from that, there were a host of social functions building up, and arrangements had to be made. Everyone was asking for Catrin and begging her to attend. Roderick was in hopes that her participation in the social events would rekindle her love of Dublin society, and woo her away from the situation she appeared to be getting into in Galway.

Daniel had given him his impressions of Catrin's behaviour and it had disturbed him. He had his own plans for her.

Catrin was quick to contact Cara. Her sojourn in Galway had been the longest time she had ever been apart from her confidante, and although they had made several telephone conversations, there was no comparison with the intimate personal exchanges they preferred.

Catrin told her about the long spell of nursing she had carried out. It was an achievement she could look back on with some pride and something she could never have imagined possible. She told Cara about the Wishing Boy, and the tragedy that lay behind it.

"So are you really going to write a story about it?" Cara asked.

"Of course! Don't you think it's romantic? I couldn't keep the tears back as he was telling me. If I can capture the emotions he showed, I think it could be a real heart-rending story. Women would love it."

"Sounds to me as if he made a big impression on you."

Catrin deliberated a moment. "I think you may be right. I saw him in a different light. He was so terribly beaten, he nearly died. All my thoughts were focussed on the struggle to save him. I didn't have time to think deeply about anything. Even when he was laying his soul bare to me, I didn't appreciate all my feelings. Now that I'm back home, I think about him a lot."

"I remember you telling me something like that about Anthony. Look how that turned out."

"I did have feelings for him, but they were superficial. He was so good looking and so charming, but, you know, I never did fully trust him. You were the one who warned me, remember? As usual I went my own way. So I suppose I got what I deserved".

"I don't have that feeling about Devlin. He's a bit of a rough diamond, to be sure, but if he could only rid himself of that dreadful Maguire, I think he could be really nice. He has the kindest eyes."

Her resumption into the whirlwind of society life was not difficult. She revelled in it, but several of her friends had the impression that she was not the same Catrin that had left Dublin for Galway.

On the surface she sparkled and glittered, still the belle of the ball, still the life and soul of the party, and captivating the men as usual. But once on her own, the glamour evaporated and there was an emptiness that gnawed at her heart.

She had started to write her story about the Wishing Boy, but found it more difficult to write than she had imagined. If only one of the lovers had remained alive, she might have been able to talk to them and relive through their eyes the true feelings of romance that they shared.

As it was, she kept thinking of Devlin's unrequited love for Shula, and hearing in her mind the anguished cries as he called her name during his bouts of delirium. She found her thoughts straying as she sought to write, wondering where he was, and what he was doing.

The week before Christmas, Roderick decided to drive to Galway and bring his father back to Dublin to join them for Christmas. Catrin seized the opportunity to go with him, and as on the previous occasion, was thrilled to be allowed to drive part of the way.

They arrived in Galway on the Saturday with the intention drive back the following day. Catrin dashed into Galway and made straight for the shop in Eyre square.

Eamon had disappointing news. "He's in Belfast with my Da and Rafferty at a meeting," was all he could tell her.

"I was afraid of that," Catrin sighed. "That's why I've written this letter. Will you make sure he gets it when he returns?"

Eamon took the envelope and propped it up against the side of the till.

"I'll have it in front of me so I won't forget," he assured her.

Christmas itself came and went with any it's usual excitement. She went to the balls at the Gresham and the Shelbourne, the innumerable house parties and dinners, and the flurry of exchanges of gifts. She opened everything that arrived, hoping there might be some response from Galway, but there was none, and she made a poor show of concealing her disappointment.

It did not escape the notice of Roderick, but he waited until the day after New Year to talk to her about a scheme he had been harbouring in his mind for some time. They had finished dinner, and retired by themselves to drink coffee and relax in front of the fire. Megan was busy in the kitchen and would join them later.

Roderick sat gently swirling the Cognac in his glass, warming it and sipping appreciatively. He felt good. The business had been successful during the year and he was in an expansive mood. He looked across at Catrin who appeared to be dreaming.

"You know I've been after you for some time to join me in the business, Catrin?"

She glanced up from gazing into the fire, a wounded expression on her face. Roderick took another sip of his brandy.

"I think I have a proposition you might like. I know you've always been cold on the idea of getting printers ink on your fingers, and I wouldn't want you to. But it is a family business, and it's doing well, and I want to see it moving in the direction to keep it successful. So I've decided to expand into the book publishing business, and you might take a different view.

"You tell me you want to write, so here's a chance to do that, and also look at other writers. Maybe act as an agent to some, or as an editor, or whatever. Don't you think that would appeal to you?"

Catrin was at a loss for words. It did indeed seem like a golden opportunity, but it had come at her like a bolt from the blue, and she had been thinking of other things.

"You mean you want be to run it as a new business?"

"It would be an associate company. I'd be the chief executive, but you'd be the Managing Director. You're well qualified. You've had business management training at College, and you have a love of writing. I think it's a job tailor made for you, and it's going to help the family business grow."

"It sounds good, in fact it's a great idea, but this has come so sudden. I need time to think — I mean when would you intend to start?"

"Not straight away, of course. There's all the rigmarole of starting a new company, premises and machinery to get, and all those sort of things. Probably about six months at least."

"If it will take that long, I suppose I might be able." It was a very condescending statement and it made Roderick angry.

"Dammit Catrin, is that all you can say? It sounds as if you've no interest. This is a perfect chance for you. You've been playing around long enough. Time to think of others now, not just yourself. Your grandfather thinks this is exactly what would be in your interests. He started this business from an office half the size of this room. He's very proud of the way I carried it on, and he wants to see another member of the family carry it on even further. Don't tell me you wouldn't want to do that."

"Oh no. Please don't think that!" Catrin was wounded. Her father had never been so angry with her. "It's just that it's a surprise, and I had been thinking of other things."

"What things?" Roderick drained his glass and banged it on the table.

"I've started to write my story."

"What story?"

"The one about the painting. The Wishing Boy. It'll make a fine romantic novel, but I need time to finish it, and there's more research that I need to do in Galway. Please understand. I have to go back or I'll never finish it."

"For heaven's sake, Catrin, you've been in Galway the past three months. Isn't that long enough?" It was rare for him to get heated with Catrin, but he had expected her to leap at his proposition, and he was disappointed by her reaction.

Catrin explained her reasons, and outlined her ambition to compile another book which would serve to preserve all the traditional country practices that might otherwise be lost for future generations.

"It will become a valuable reference book someday. For example, take Poteen. That precious stuff as you call it, and enjoy. It's all gone now. What stories there are about how it was made, by whom, and where, and all the escapades that went on between the Excise officers and the people who made it.

There are loads of interesting country practices to write about, but I can only do that by being there. Just give me the six months and when I've done that, I'll devote my time to your idea. I'd like to take it on, and I'm sure the extra experience I'll gain in Galway will be of help to make it a success."

Roderick had listened to her carefully. He almost felt like throwing his hands up. No one knew better how to handle him than she did. He had tried to interest her in his idea, and now here she was getting him interested in hers. Having a book like that as one of his first publications would not be a bad idea, and they could build on it. It would take him more than six months to get organised anyway.

"Alright then. It's a deal. Six months. Then I expect to see two manuscripts on my desk, and you appearing for work. That sound alright?"

Catrin sprang across from her seat and flung her arms around him.

"It's a deal," she kissed his forehead, "and I promise to do my best."

As she lay in bed later that evening, Catrin glowed with excitement. Twisting her father around her little finger was part of her usual practice, but this time the victory was much more important. Now she had a mandate to return to Galway, and in order to collect material for her book on country practices, she would have to prevail on Devlin to help her.

The future prospects of running a book publishing business appealed to her enormously. She had always known she would be expected to go into her father's business, but the thought of working amongst the heat and smell of a printing works had no glamour.

Now there was something to look forward to. She turned over and nestled her head into her feather pillow. It had been a wonderful day.

***

About the same time as Catrin finally succumbed to sleep, a dark red coloured Austin 12 cruised quietly into Galway and stopped outside the Maguire house.

Originally there had been four occupants. Seamus had driven back from Belfast with Devlin in the passenger seat, and Maguire and Rafferty in the back, where they had talked incessantly about the meeting with the commanders of the Belfast brigade.

The Southern Command was in chaos and disorganised and there were power struggles between the two commands to determine policies. Maguire saw more prospects of extending the war by following those in Belfast, particularly with their plans to start a bombing campaign in England.

Seamus and Devlin took it all in but said nothing. Seamus was indifferent. He had simply obeyed his father's orders for years without question, but he sensed that Devlin was not happy.

He was the key individual in the plan. They wanted him in England to co-ordinate the cells that would be set up in various parts of the country, and supervise any bomb making facilities. He would lead missions when required and act as the link man with Belfast.

It was an awesome responsibility but there were few better equipped individuals than Devlin and the leaders expected him to conform to the plans. He had angered Maguire by pleading for more time to train people, citing that security would be tighter in England than in Ireland, and there was more risk of detection, but his views were over-ruled and the order to proceed was pushed through despite his protest.

Devlin's objections had little to do with technical experience. He was more than competent to make up for others. The truth was that he had become disenchanted with the leadership. People like Maguire and Rafferty regarded themselves as freedom fighters, fighting for the glory of a freeing Ireland from oppression.

But their war was to be targeted at so called soft targets, where the victims would be innocent civilians rather than military objectives or the police. More effective as a terror campaign they expounded. Letter boxes and left luggage offices. Easier to find and less security. Make the public squeal enough in protest and the politicians would have to listen. Guns and bombs would drive governments to the bargaining tables, and they would get what they sought. Small wonder Devlin was unhappy. He had seen enough of the effects on innocent bystanders.

Since his time at Dungannon House his values had changed. He had seen another side of life where the values were different and he found those values more attractive. He found himself often staring into space and seeing visions of Catrin. He could hear her laughter, smell her perfume, feel the touch of her hands on his. If he went on this murderous campaign to England... he could not bear to dwell on the thought.

They were almost at Ballanalee and Seamus dropped him off. Maguire lowered his window to speak before he disappeared into the house.

"Make sure you're ready in the mornin'. Seamus'll pick you up an' we'll meet at Rafferty's an' draw up a schedule. Forget all that mush about trainin' an' experience. You'll have hand picked men, only the best." He wound the window up and signalled Seamus to drive off. He knew how to handle Dev. A firm hand and a loud voice was all he needed.

Devlin climbed into the loft, tired both physically and mentally. Despite the conflict of emotions raging inside his head, he flopped fully dressed on the bed and was asleep within seconds.

Chapter Thirty-Seven

As he stood at the counter waiting for Eamon to hand, it was Rafferty's job to call at the gift shop each morning and collect any orders that required his delivery service, and also the paper work relating to sales and receipts. Maguire liked to go through them at leisure and ensure he was aware of how the shop was doing.

Over the paper work, he noticed the pale pink envelope propped against the till. He picked it up and saw it was addressed to Devlin. The writing had a feminine slant to it and he dared to sniff the envelope. There was distinctly a light fragrance.

"What's this?" he asked, brandishing the envelope.

"It's a letter for Devlin. Miss Kilpatrick left it at the week-end. Will he be coming in to-day?"

Rafferty thought quickly. The letter intrigued him. He knew how much Maguire hated the girl.

"No," he muttered, "he's at Ballanalee. But I'm goin' over there," he lied. "I'll take it an' I'll drop it off "He slipped the envelope into his pocket and took the paperwork from Eamon.

Back at his office, he sat at his desk and enjoyed his first tea of the morning. He withdrew the letter from his pocket and laid it in front of him. He continued to look at it while he drained the last of his tea, and then having made up his mind, slit it open with his paper knife and extracted the single sheet of scented notepaper from inside. He whistled softly to himself as he scanned the contents, and a faint smile spread across his face. He replaced the note in the envelope, and put it into the drawer of his desk.

Maguire bustled into the office fifteen minutes later and immediately bellowed to one of the clerks to bring him some tea.

"I see you couldn't wait," he said, glancing at the empty mug on the desk.

"I was on the road early this morning," Rafferty reeled off his second lie of the day, "so another one won't go amiss." He shouted for the clerk to bring him another mug.

"I've been to Eyre square an' picked up the paperwork. Picked this up, too." He opened the drawer and slid the envelope across the desk in front of Maguire.

He picked it up and looked at the writing. "It's for Dev."

"I know. But it looked quare to me. I mean, who writes to Dev?"

"He has a brother in America. He sends him money sometimes."

"Oh come on Flann. There's no stamp on it. It's in a woman's hand. I thought you might find it interesting. Read it."

Maguire waited until the clerk brought the tea before he read the note. Rafferty watched keenly as he awaited Maguire's reaction. He did not need to wait for long. Maguire's face went from red to purple, and he crumpled the note in his fist and flung it across the desk at Rafferty.

"The bitch! The feckin' bitch! I knew she spelt trouble for him. That's why I warned her off. An' now the stupid bugger's entangled wi' her. So she wants to see him again, does she? Not if I can help it. You did right. Don't let Dev know."

"Thought you might say that." Rafferty beamed and with a casual sweep of his hand sent the crumpled note into his waste basket.

"In my opinion, Dev's gone a bit soft. Maybe that beatin's knocked the stuffin' outta him."

"It's bugger all to do wi' that. It's her that's softened him up. Bliddy Kilpatricks! Never struck a blow fer us. Just sat back an' made money. Their turn'll come, I'll see to that."

"It's time him an' Seamus were here. We need to get started an' work out a timetable. We'll start on our own." They spent the next ten minutes discussing a provisional action plan and were deep in conversation when Seamus and Devlin made their appearance.

"It's about time," he greeted them. "Half the mornin's gone already. Liam an' I have been busy if you haven't. Sit down an' we'll go through what we've come up with," he indicated the vacant chairs on either side of the desk.

They seated themselves and listened closely as Maguire outlined his proposals. It was an ambitious plan, and well thought out, and there only remained a few minor details to add. Maguire was confident Belfast would approve it.

Devlin had contributed nothing to the discussion, but the expression on his face lacked enthusiasm.

"What's up wi' you this mornin'?" Maguire fired the question at Devlin, "you look as if you'd bit a lemon. Don't you think it's a good plan?"

"It's a fine plan, sure enough," Devlin conceded, "But I'm not happy about goin' to England. I've thought a lot about what was said at Belfast, an' I don't want to go."

Maguire exploded to his feet. "Don't be so bliddy daft! You have to go! You're the key Johnny to the whole shootin' match! It's a great chance to hit back at the buggers. In their own back yard, to boot. Haven't you always said you wanted to rub their noses in it? You've been waitin' a long time for a chance like this."

"I'll tell you why I don't like it," Devlin was on his feet, facing Maguire, his face red with anger.

"Blowin' up these so called "soft targets" is not what I call fightin' for freedom. I'm fed up killin' innocent people. You're right on one thing. I have been in the game too long. Too bliddy long, an' I'm getting' sick o' it. Why not target the military or the politicians?"

"Dev! Fer God's sake sit down an' shut yer gob! We've been all through this yesterday. Why d'ye think they call it a terror campaign?

The tactics are terror. Pure terror. Terror that will have the people bayin' at the government to pull their soldiers outta Ireland and sit around the negotiatin' table an' hammer out an agreement that *we* want. So no more peeps outta you! I'm not havin' this plan scuppered because you're goin' soft all of a sudden. You were right Liam."

"What does that mean?" Devlin had noted the quick exchange of glances between the two.

"It means that since you got involved wi' that young bitch Kilpatrick, we think you're goin' soft. I warned her off before, so don't git me het up about it again. Stay clear o' her or there'll be trouble." Maguire was breathing hard and glaring at Devlin.

Devlin sprang from his chair and made towards the door, but Seamus quickly barred his way.

"Calm down, Dev. Let's talk more. Things are getting' too heated an' before we know it, things'll be said that we'll all be sorry for. You, too, Da. Calm down."

They resumed their seats, but the air was thick enough to be cut with a knife. Rafferty thought a change of subject might defuse the situation.

"I understand your desire to have a crack at the military, Dev. We all hate the bastards, an' you've got more reason than most, what wi' the loss o' yer family an' the beaten you got. What about the lieutenant? We could've taken him out ages ago, but we left him for you, at your request."

Devlin gave him a puzzled glance. "So?"

"Why not act on it? He's a military target."

"He's not around. He's away on a visit to England."

"He was." Rafferty was smiling as if he had played a winning card. "One o' the drivers reported seeing him come off the early train this morning."

"You didn't tell me," growled Maguire.

"I would've got round to it. Dev reminded me o' it when he talked about the military."

"Do it then," Maguire snapped at Devlin. You wanted to have him all to yourself so get on with it. Seamus'll give you a hand. The other matter is closed to discussion. The plan stands. I'm off to the pub now. I'll see you at supper Seamus."

He barged out the door leaving Seamus and Devlin with Rafferty.

"Let me know if you need one o' the vans for the job. Personally I'd drive it right into the very barracks an' blow the bliddy lot up!"

They both looked at Rafferty with disdain and took their leave without bothering to reply.

"He's a slimy toad, that one," said Seamus as they made their way to the van. "Loves to stir my Da up, He's a good quartermaster, but it pays to watch your back when he's around."

Devlin was in one of his sombre moods. He sat in the passenger seat as Seamus drove them to Ballanalee, and said nothing the entire journey. He stared straight ahead, his mind obviously busy with thoughts, and Seamus wisely did not try to make conversation.

Nor did he linger at Ballanalee, for Devlin was clearly not in a mood to talk. As soon as he dropped him at the front gate, he drove straight back to Galway. Perhaps Dev would be more like himself in the morning, and they could make plans to take care of the lieutenant. He'd got a few suggestions.

But he was deluding himself. The next morning Devlin was still uneasy and unsettled. He had slept badly and spent a restless night, glad to get up at first light and busy himself with some chores.

Lieutenant Dillon was very much on his mind. He didn't like pressure put on him and now Maguire was pressurising him to kill the man. Immediately after the attack at the house on the Corrib, he had been angry and vindictive and thirsting for revenge, but in the passing of time he did not feel that way anymore.

In a sense he was prepared to call it quits, for it was he who had injured the lieutenant first, and so the lieutenant was justified to seek revenge. But he had made a clear statement of intention, and Maguire would make him honour it. The bastard should'ave stayed in Dublin where he belonged. He wondered if Catrin was prepared to forgive him.

She had not been in touch and he felt let down. Maybe she had rediscovered where she really belonged, and that life in Dublin was much more interesting than struggling for a living in Galway.

He needed something to occupy himself and stop him from speculating too much, but then he suddenly remembered something Catrin had said, and he walked out into the courtyard and made for the small wooden hut that stood next to the hayshed.

He retrieved the key from under the stone near the door, and unlocked the padlock. He entered and minutes later emerged with a bulky package covered by several layers of hessian. He carried it carefully back to the house and laid it gently on the bog oak table.

As he stripped away the layers of fabric, the dull gleam of a picture frame became exposed. As the last layer fell on the table he held in his hands his masterpiece. The Wishing Boy, the painting Catrin so much admired and had begged him to bring out of hiding. She was right. It was much too good to hide away. It deserved to be seen by others, and be acknowledged as a wonderful example of what true love could inspire.

He looked for the best place to hang it, and decided to place it above the work bench. It took him the best part of half an hour to get it into the perfect position, but when it was done he felt uplifted, and the room suddenly appeared to be brighter. He was surprised that Seamus hadn't appeared and he supposed that Maguire must have found him something to do.

He busied himself making some soda bread and heated some soup for his mid-day meal. The lack of sleep was catching up with him and after eating he sat in the high backed wooden chair in front of the fire and dozed. Sometime around mid afternoon he jerked awake at the sounds of a horse clattering into the yard.

He raced to the work bench, dragging his revolver from the drawer, and running to crouch down at the window. His fear was that it was one of the military patrols coming to take him in for questioning.

He was completely unprepared for what he saw. Catrin was dismounting from her grandfather's grey Irish cob, and running towards the house. He dropped the gun and ran out the door to meet her, and in the middle of the yard they literally ran into one another, to fuse into an embrace that no mortal could have pulled apart with a team of wild horses.

When the kissing was all over, they were still locked in the embrace, nose touching nose, and their eyes searching for messages that only lovers can find.

"I was beginning to think you'd forgotten me," his voice was hoarse with emotion. "I thought Dublin had reclaimed you. I can't believe it. You're actually here." He kissed her again.

"Why did you sneak off in the middle of the night? I was hurt when I found you had gone. Not even a note"

"I hated doin' it, but at the time I felt shame. For another thing, I hate goodbyes. I wanted to crawl away an' lick my wounds. I was hopin' you'd understand."

"I didn't, but Danna did. He tried to explain. But didn't you get my letter?"

She explained how she and her father had arrived the week before Christmas to take Daniel back with them, and had dashed into Galway hoping to see him. "I left a letter with Eamon to give to you when you returned from Belfast. I told you I would come back when it was Danna's time to come home."

"I didn't get a letter. Perhaps Eamon forgot." As he spoke he remembered the strange looks Rafferty and his Da had exchanged when on the subject of Catrin, He remembered Rafferty was a regular caller at the shop. The pieces fell into place, but he was too happy to care at that moment. Maguire and Rafferty could go to the devil.

"Go inside where it's warm. I'll put the horse in the stable in case the patrols spot it. Put the kettle on an' you can tell me about all the goin's on in Dublin over Christmas."

Catrin entered the house and looked around. So small and sparse compared to Dungannon House and her own home in Dublin, yet it had a cosiness and a homeliness that neither of them could boast. She gasped as she saw the painting above the work bench and walked towards it as if drawn by a magnet.

Even in the dimness of the light, it radiated the quality of love she had first recognised. She was still standing entranced when he came back into the house.

She looked round at him. "You did hear me. You decided to bring it out of hiding. It's just as wonderful as the first time I saw it. Thank you for hanging it up."

"I only did it this morning. Must'ave known you were comin'." He stood behind her and clasped his hands around her waist.

"You were right. It needed to be shown. Since I put it up, I do believe the room looks brighter."

"I'll be able to do my writing here. It will inspire me I know. I'm going to write such a wonderful story. I know I am."

Over a mug of tea at the fireside she told Devlin of how her father had agreed to give her six months grace in Galway so that she could finish the books she had in mind. She did not add that there were conditions attached. Six months was a long time, and there would be occasions later on.

She related all the events that had taken place over Christmas and the New Year in Dublin, and made him laugh at the story of Daniel imbibing too much of his favourite tipple and having to be carried upstairs.

"I do believe Maguire's precious stuff was the cause. I know my Da's got some he keeps hidden from Mam."

"There was a few drams o' precious knocked back here at New Year. Maguire throws a party for his cronies in the pub he owns. I used to go an' get a skinful, but not this year. There was too much on my mind."

"That's funny. I had similar feelings. I enjoyed all the parties, especially when there were dances. The Gresham has a wonderful ball at New Year. But I was glad when they were all over. I thought quite a lot about you, wondering what you might be doing."

"Really? I thought Dublin would reclaim you, make you appreciate how hopeless things are here. Are you sure you want to spend as long as six months away from your folks?"

"It's all settled. I've already made a start on writing the Wishing Boy, and you're going to tell me and show me as much of the old time country practices as you can. Apart from writing I'll need to research for old drawings, pictures and diagrams of the kinds of implements and machinery that were used. I'm going to be very busy, and probably very happy."

It all seemed so cut and dried, and so unbelievably wonderful. For a strange reason probably associated with his dreadful childhood in Cork, Devlin was troubled by a shadow that hung over their relationship. He had to lay the ghost to rest.

"Did you see anything o' the lieutenant? He was in Dublin over Christmas."

"No. I did not! Catrin was shocked. "Even if I had known, I certainly would have ignored him. He probably has another lady friend by now. You know he was a terrible womaniser."

"He looked the type."

"Would you believe he actually flirted with Mauguire's daughter?"

"That can't be right. She would never dare. Maguire would'ave killed her an' him both."

"Well it's true. I interrupted them in the shop one day. Looking for a birthday present for me, he said. But I knew he was lying. My instincts are never wrong. He was damn well flirting. He admitted to me later that he found her attractive. I don't believe he could resist any pretty girl. When I look back now, he was a real rake if ever there was one."

"Sweet Jaysus," Devlin muttered softly. His face had gone ashen.

"What is it? What's the matter?" Catrin was horrified by his expression.

"Is it possible he found out?"

"Devlin! Snap out of it. What are you saying? Who found out about what?"

"I always thought there was somethin' strange about the way Maura died. It didn't seem right somehow. Maguire never said a word, Seamus an' Eamon didn't even talk to me about it. It was all kept so quiet, he even had her buried in Limerick. That was strange. She lived most of her life in Galway.

"It shocked me too. Seamus told me when I came here looking for you. I remember when I told Anthony he went very pale."

"Seamus was there when the accident happened, but he never spoke. Maguire did all the talkin'. Eamon was shutaway in his room. I felt there was somethin' strange about the whole business. That's why I'm wonderin' about the lieutenant.

"Oh Devlin. Stop playing guessing games. It's all in the past now. Forget it."

"Everythin' in this country's in the past," Devlin blazed, "that's it's biggest problem. It can never forget the past, and any crimes committed have to be accounted for. Did you know that it was Dillon an' his boy's that beat me up? As soon as Seamus told me I told him to leave him for me. I was goin' to nail him for what he did, and it wouldn't be a fish hook this time."

"Don't speak like that. Surely you wouldn't do something terrible?"

"When I was flat on my back, sufferin' pain like I was in every bone an' muscle in my body, all I could think of was to get well enough so I could kill him."

"What would you have done?"

"Shot him. One bullet. Back o' the head. All traitors go that way."

Catrin was horrified. "Is that what you intend to do? You can't. It's murder."

"I know. At one time it wouldn't have bothered me. But since I met you I couldn't do it an' look you in the face again. When I had time to think, I realised what a stinkin' business this is. I was tryin' to tell you that night we sat by the fire in

Dungannon House. I was hopin' he'd gone back to Dublin for keeps, an' I was prepared to let sleepin' dogs lie."

"So you're not going to do anything terrible to him after all?"

"That's the problem. He's arrived back in Galway. Maguire knows. He expects me to deal with him. I don't know what to do. I feel like packin' up the whole business and runnin' away. But I can't."

"Why not? Oh I wish you would. Making bombs and killing innocent people is a dreadful thing. It's cruel. Where does it get you in the end?"

"I had a row with Maguire about it. He's got plans to send me to England to start bombin' them. I don't want to go, Catrin, but he insists. He's mad enough to kill me if I don't."

Catrin stood up and place her hands on the mantlepiece and gazed down at the turf fire. It was a gesture she remembered Devlin using at Dungannon House when he had to face up to a difficult confession.

"You have to get away from Maguire, Devlin," she said gravely. "He's poisoned you with his beliefs and malice. He's the most evil man I've ever come across. You do his dirty work, and take the risks; he takes the credit and the glory. You've got talent that's wasted here. You deserve another chance in life. I'll help you. I'll do everything I can if you'll try."

"Would you come with me if I made a run for it?" He searched her face anxiously for the truth.

"We have to see how it could be done first of all. Where would we go?"

"To America. My brother Sean is out there. I told you about his little shop that night. Remember?"

"I've always wanted to go to America," Catrin admitted. "But there's my folks. It would be difficult to leave them."

"I understand that. Gettin' away from the IRA is even more difficult. They never let you off the hook without good reason, an' they'll follow any traitor to the ends o' the earth."

"But you're not a traitor, Devlin. You've served them for more than half your life, surely that's enough? You ought to be able to give it up if you no longer feel able to serve them."

"Doesn't work that way. If you possess special skills, they never let go."

"There must be a way. We have to find it. Let's act normal for the time being while we think about it. I'm going back to Danna now, but I'll be back in the morning and we'll make a start on the things I want to do. Whatever happens, I promised my Da I'd have two books ready for him by the time the six months is up, and I always keep my promises. Just remember that." She kissed him firmly.

Back at Dungannon House she retired to bed early and, as she often did, lay quietly reflecting on the events of the day. New horizons were appearing, and new feelings were stirring within her. She had always known there would be special feelings arise within her when the right man would come into her life, and these were the feelings she had now. But she could not fully rejoice.

The shadow of Maguire hung over them.

Chapter Thirty-Eight

The next few days proved blissful. Maguire and Rafferty were called to Belfast, and Seamus went with them. From Belfast they took the ferry to Liverpool with a view to make contacts and scout the territory for the proposed campaign. It would occupy them for a week, and a week is a long time for lovers to explore their feelings.

Catrin left Dungannon House early each morning and rode over the moor to Ballanalee where she would arrive to find breakfast awaiting her, after which she would settle into a domestic routine, almost as though they were husband and wife.

She would wash up and tidy the room whilst Devlin brought in the daily water supply and turves for the fire. Between the chores there were intervals for flirtations which usually ended in passionate embraces. In the afternoons they applied themselves to their individual artistic tasks, Catrin to her writing, and Devlin to his driftwood.

She wrote at the bog oak table, occasionally stealing a glance at the work bench where he so cleverly fashioned his driftwood, and above it hung the painting. The story of the Wishing Boy was flowing from her pen, inspired by the scene surrounding her. Sometimes he would catch her in the act of looking at him, and he would smile and wag a finger in admonishment.

He was as anxious as herself to see the story completed.

Each day, Catrin marvelled at the changes in her life. Her natural beauty and vitality had always attracted men. During her college years she had a stream of admirers. As the daughter of a successful business man, and mingling constantly in Dublin society circles, she received several proposals of marriage.

She had been in and out of love so often, it had become a game, and it was a game she loved to play, and she played it well to the despair of many a prospective suitor. But hidden under the veneer of her flirtatious behaviour, lay a heart which would recognise real love when it came, and she would give herself to no man until that time arrived.

She loved the novelty of acting the part of a housewife, and the fact that she had nursed Devlin all through his illness gave her a unique insight into his life.

He loved the presence of someone who looked after him, and who took pleasure in doing it. Since his early teens, when his family had been taken so tragically from him, he had become accustomed to fending for himself. To have someone pamper him, who not only gave out love, but joyously received the love he had held back for so long, was a source of wonderment.

With each passing hour his love for Catrin grew. The scars of his unrequited love for Shula healed and the memories of the past were replaced by new found pleasures.

This was a tangible love. It was no longer the stuff of dreams. As their affections deepened, it was inevitable that the forces of nature would act to consummate their feelings. The weather supplied the catalyst.

Daniel had not wanted her to leave that morning. There was a heavy mist and the rain fell steadily.

"Wait 'till it fairs up," he advised her, but she would not listen. She borrowed his yellow slicker and sou'wester and set off for Ballanalee. She was riding into the rain, and there was a steady wind, and as a result arrived at the farm thoroughly soaked. Devlin pulled her inside, concerned at the state she was in. He dried her face gently with a soft cloth, and kissed her lovingly.

"I didn't expect you," he said hoarsely. "Have you no sense woman? You're soaked to the skin, so you are."

She shook her head, laughing as his face was showered with raindrops from her hair. She took the cloth from his hand and wiped his face.

"No weather was going to keep me away. Time is too precious. We can't afford to waste it." She returned his kiss.

"Well you'd better get outta them clothes. You're like a drowned crow like that," he laughed at her shocked expression. "Get you close to the fire an' I'll fetch somethin' dry to wear." He stirred the fire into a blaze and then climbed into the loft. He came down with a bundle of clothes that he tossed to her.

"Get these on while I go an' put that poor beast outside in the stable. He'll need dryin' too an' some feed. "That'll give you plenty time to change."

He returned ten minutes later, sprinting across the yard and dashing inside. The downpour had increased and even in the short distance from the stable his shirt was saturated. He stood, back against the door pushing it shut, panting with exertion, his eyes widening at the sight that met his eyes.

Catrin stood facing him, her back to the fire, but the bundle of clothes was lying at her feet. She was smiling provocatively, a woollen patchwork quilt draped around her, which she had obviously fetched from the bed in the loft.

There was a gleam of mischief in her eyes.

"Look at you," she laughed, "you're the one that looks like a drowned crow now. It's you that'll need these." She stretched a pointed toe at the bundle of clothes. "Come nearer the fire and get into them. I'll help you."

He advanced slowly towards her trying not to let his gaze stray to the shapely ivory white leg that her movement had disclosed. As he drew closer, the sensory messages exchanged by their eyes were mutual. Nature would wait no longer.

He cupped her face in his hands and kissed her deeply, a kiss whose fires rapidly increased in intensity. Both hearts were racing and their breathing becoming muted gasps as the fervour of the embrace increased. He was aware of her hands undoing the buttons of his shirt, and the tug at his belt as it was unfastened.

In the same moment the quilt slid from her shoulders, exposing her breasts. As she pulled the wet shirt from his body the quilt dropped to the floor and they stood, inches apart, and they both knew there was no going back.

"You now. Off with those trousers. I'll spread the quilt out."

"But the bed's in the loft."

"I know. But it's warm here. It's fine. I can't wait any longer."

He dragged the wet trousers from his legs and kicked them aside to lie in the hearth beside his shirt.

"Are you sure this is what you want?" his eyes were roving over the body of the most beautiful woman he had ever seen. The ravages of the wind and rain had only served to make her more beautiful.

"Of course. I always knew there would be a right time, and my heart tells me this is it." Her eyes had also been busy, devouring his well-proportioned body, lingering briefly at his groin, her eyes widening as she saw his erection.

She knelt down on the quilt and pulled him down beside her. They lay side by side, their lips fused, his hands seeking the firm softness of her breasts and teasing the nipples gently into rigid peaks. His heart beat faster and he sighed as he felt her hand slide over his belly. Her fingers explored it's contours in a delicate manner that enraptured him.

"Do you... I mean, have you... the question died on his lips as the caressing fingers explored his groin still further.

She shook her head. "No. I've never allowed anyone. You are the first."

"You're sure about this?

"I only know I want it to be with you. I know the time is right."

"It's serious Catrin." He tried to ease her grip, but she held on tightly.

"I have to be certain. I wouldn't want to hurt you." She relaxed her grip.

"Stop worrying, Devlin. I know what I'm doing. I love you or I wouldn't be lying here like this. I've heard it hurts a little, so I won't be shocked."

She turned over and lay on her back. He gazed at her body, marvelling at the skin like alabaster, the delicate features, and the perfect proportions of her breasts.

She took hold of his hands, pulling him on to her body, and spread her legs open to allow him to lie between them. There was no wild rush to copulate.

For several moments they were content to lavish kisses on one another and allow their hands to explore the intimate parts of their bodies, and all the time the stored up passions slowly began to boil. Finally nature could wait no longer.

The twinge of pain she felt as her hymen parted was not as painful as she had expected, and was quickly forgotten as she responded to his gentle rhythmic movements. He moved his lips from hers and fastened them on her nipples, sucking greedily and running his tongue around them, sending a tingling sensation through her whole body.

Her hands were around his back, hugging him ever closer as the rhythm increased and tingling sensations began to flow from other sources.

She could feel his excitement mounting as his breathing became heavier and more passionate, and she found herself following the same pattern. She began to encourage a faster sequence of thrusts that had them both heaving, gasping and writhing in a fury as they strove to obey their basic instincts.

In one wondrous, blinding moment, there was a sudden scalding fusion of passion that left them both paralysed, unable to stir, or to comprehend fully what they had achieved.

They lay helpless, in rapture, relaxing slowly in each other's arms, basking in the glory of their union, and as they lay in their ecstasy, a strange symbolic happening that could have been taken as approval of the consummation of their love took place.

The rain soaked clothing, lying next to them in the hearth, slowly began to steam.

Chapter Thirty-Nine

For a few moments they remained locked together. As the fires of their passion gradually diminished, he slid off her body and they turned in towards each other. The warmth of the fire on her back increased Catrin's pleasure. She was in a trance. He stroked her hair.

"Was it what you expected?"

"Better. I've never felt anything so wonderful. I didn't expect it to be so frantic, but I couldn't help myself. I was frantic, too. I was frightened I wouldn't satisfy you. Now I feel a real woman."

"You were marvellous. I wanted to love you so much, an' yet I didn't want to put you off." He kissed her tenderly. "Now I have the courage to say I love you. I really love you."

They remained closely together, gently unwinding and soothing one another, exchanging little kisses of gratitude, and as the fire settled down into a warm glow, they drifted off into a luxurious sleep.

It was the start of a pattern that followed for the next few days, and their love making was transferred to the comforts of the bed in the loft. The pleasure and passion remained the same. She learned much in such a short time, and as she became bolder she took the lead in the love making.

It was lustful, but there was always tenderness and love, and when their exertions were finished, they would lie clasped together and talk quietly about the wonder of it all.

Daniel saw the change in her as she returned to the house each night. She had always been a lively girl, full of vitality and ambition, but now there was also a glow to her. He put it down to her daily horse riding, and the enjoyment of her writing, and said so in his conversations on the telephone to Roderick. Mrs. Donavan saw the same changes, but she was not as naive as Daniel. Her womanly instincts suggested that Catrin was learning more about life than as good for her.

The newly found contentment could not last forever. Catrin had ridden over from Dungannon House as usual that morning, and was enjoying breakfast with Devlin, when the car suddenly rattled into the courtyard.

Devlin jumped to his feet and looked out the window.

"Oh Jaysus!" he exclaimed, "its Seamus an' his Da. They must'ave come back last night."

"Should I hide in the loft?"

"No time. They're at the door. Stick close to me. I'll handle him." They stood holding hands, backs to the fire, facing the door. Catrin's legs started to tremble and he tightened his grip on her hand.

Seamus banged on the door and entered. His eyes took in at a glance what the situation was, but there was no time to do anything. Maguire thrust Seamus aside and bustled into the room. He glared at them both, his displeasure plainly evident.

"Well. Well, what a lovin' sight," he said sarcastically. "When the cat's away the mice do play. That's it, isn't it? What are you doin' here?"

"She's payin' me a visit," Devlin answered defiantly.

"I didn't ask you. I asked her. She can talk for herself, I'm sure." He stepped forward and surveyed the breakfast spread on the table.

"I hope you're not up to what I think you're up to Dev." He turned his attention to Catrin.

"Didn't I give you fair warnin' to keep away. It's foolhardy to ignore such warnin's"

"So it was you who abused me?"

Maguire's face flushed. "I knew about it," he roared in an effort to hide his mistake, "I know everythin' that moves in Galway. I make it my business to know. But I never expected this. Get outta here before I lose my temper completely, an' let Dev be. He has important work to do."

Devlin thrust himself in front of Catrin, his fists clenched, and a determined look on his face.

"Catrin's a guest under my roof. I'll not drive her out."

Maguire glared, his fists clenching and unclenching in fury.

"Does little miss Goody two shoes know what kinda business you're in? Do you suggest she sits down at the table an' joins in our plans, especially when her former boyfriend is involved. You know who I mean. Lieutenant Dillon."

"You bastard!" Devlin sprang forward. "You feckin' bastard, Maguire." He had almost reached him but Seamus swung himself between them and held him back.

"That's enough. Back off Dev. You, too Da. There's no need for this."

Devlin retreated and once again stood beside Catrin, his hand clutching hers in a clear challenge.

"There's important developments to discuss Dev. With all respect, Catrin, could you please leave us alone for a little 'till we talk. Please Dev, it's better if she leaves us alone. It won't take long."

Catrin looked at Devlin and nodded agreement. "It's alright. I'll go for a walk along the beach. I'll be fine. Don't worry." She kissed him on the cheek and put on her coat and walked out into the outside air.

"Very touching," Maguire's sarcasm was heavy. He sat down at the table.

"Make us some tay, an' we'll git down to business." He spoke sharply as if nothing had happened, and began to relate the experiences of his trip. It had not gone as well as he had hoped.

One of the cells had been broken up and the leader arrested by the CID and the command felt it wise to postpone further activities until the fuss died down.

"That should suit you. It'll provide more time for extra training."

Devlin nodded agreement. It would suit him. He was already formulating a plan of escape and the breathing space would be to his advantage.

"The more training the better. Some o' them need it badly."

"That's more like it," Maguire slapped him on the back. "I'll get Rafferty to make the arrangements for transport an' gear. But keep that girl away. I don't want her interferin'."

"I don't want her mixed up in this business either, but don't ask me to give her up, an' if you dare lay a finger on her, Flann, I'll pack the whole thing up an' you can do your own dirty work."

Maguire held his temper with difficulty. Such defiance was unknown to him. But the man had him over a barrel. The whole plan was at a critical stage and it was vital to have Dev on board. But he suffered no threats from anyone, and he would take his revenge once the time came.

"Just do your job, an' Keep her outta it. What have you been doin' this past week, anyway, or need I ask? Nuthin' on your explosives research, I'll bet."

Devlin ignored the taunt. He dared not antagonise Maguire further.

"Busy on the driftwood. There's quite a few pieces for the shop. I'll bring them over afore the week's out."

"What's the progress on your plans to dispose o' lieutenant Dillon?"

"I thought about it, but I've decided to let things be."

"What! What the hell are you talkin' about? You wanted him specially for yourself an' I gave you the chance. You better have a good reason. Has that bitch persuaded you to call it off? Has she softened you up that much?"

"Stop calling her a bitch! She had nothin' to do with it. As a matter o' fact I'm declining the mission because I think it's your duty, not mine."

"For Christ's sake! You're the one he beat up. Why is it my duty?"

"Think back Flann. Think back to a personal tragedy."

Maguire's face remained devoid of expression, only his eyes flickered with annoyance. If he knew what Devlin was driving at, he betrayed nothing. It was Seamus who spoke up.

"Maura. You mean Maura?"

Maguire was on his feet in an instant, his powerful hands leaning on the table as he bellowed at his son.

"What in hell's name has Maura to do with Dillon? Your pushin' things too far this morning Dev. I'll smash your face in if you dare even mention Maura again. So be careful."

"Catrin knows there was somethin' goin' on. He used to visit the shop often, early mornin' usually. She caught them flirtin' one day she went early. He confessed to her he found her attractive. He was an out an' out womaniser. Catrin never did trust him for that reason. Look what he tried to do to her."

"I mighta known that bitch would be behind this. An' you think just because she fed you a load o' shite like that, there was somethin' goin' on?" Maguire spat in the hearth to show his disgust. Seamus unexpectedly joined the argument.

"There's somethin' in what Dev is sayin'. Remember when —

"Shut yer gob," Maguire cut him off. "The idea is crazy. Maura an' a lieutenant in the Free State Army. Jaysus Christ! You might as well accuse her o' treason."

"It's not so crazy," Seamus had memories flashing through his mind and he could not hold back the urge to speak."In fact the more you think about it, the more reason to wonder why she refused to name the...

Maguire cut him off, reaching across the table and hauling Seamus to his feet by the lapels of his jacket.

"You bliddy eejit! Have you gone off your head?

Sit down and shut your gob. You've said enough already."

He pushed Seamus back into his chair, and sat down glaring murder.

Devlin glanced from one to the other, stunned by what Seamus had just said.

"You were goin' to say father, weren't you Seamus? Sweet Jaysus! She was pregnant! Is it true?" One look at the guilt on Seamus's face was sufficient confirmation.

"That was it. An' you with all your bad temper an' threats couldn't drag it outta her. She'd sooner die before she would confess to you."

"I've had enough o' this shite, "Maguire shook his fist at Devlin, "You say nuthin' o' this to anybody or by God I'll put your lights out, so I will. Don't make me do it! C'mon Seamus, we're outta here."

He strode aggressively to the door, banged it open, and stormed into the yard.

Seamus made to follow him, but paused at the door. "Mind out. Watch your step. You've really upset him this time. I'll catch up with you later, when the heat's died down."

A minute later the car drove out of the yard and headed back to Galway. Peace descended on Ballanalee once more, but there was no peace in his mind. Devlin placed a few turves on the fire and sat down on the high backed chair to wait for Catrin to return.

Seamus was right to warn him. He had opened up a big can of worms. What must Maguire feel like?

Now he could understand why everything about Maura's death was kept so low key, and why so little was said at the time. Maguire would have been beside himself to find out she was pregnant, and to seek vengeance on the father would have been his first reaction. Maura would never have confessed if it was Dillon. The shame would have been far too much for her. So she had died.

He shook his head sadly, and he now knew for certain the sooner he escaped from Maguire's clutches the better. He would write to Sean in America and ask him if he would help him start a new life together with Catrin. He would find out from his contacts in the North, outside of Maguire's control, how best to make arrangements.

Chapter Forty

Seamus was normally the first up each morning. His customary duty was to mash the tea for his father, but on this occasion he found Maguire already seated at the kitchen table, surly and tired looking, nursing a mug of tea in his hand.

"Be Jaysus!" Seamus expressed his surprise. "What the hell's got into you?"

"Been awake all night, thinkin'. Thinkin' the unbelievable."

"Dev wouldna say anythin' he didn't believe in. He was as fond o' Maura as anyone. I can't believe it would be that feckin' lieutenant either, but little things keep croppin' up in my memory, things I thought nuthin' of at the time, but now... his words trailed off into silence.

"I want you to work with Rafferty on this. Two heads are better than one. Delve into that bastard's movements around the time we found out. If there's evidence that ties in with what Dev says, then by God it is me who'll have him, an' it won't be a quick death".

"I want you on it right away, an' I don't care how you do it. Just get the evidence."

Ten minutes away from the Maguire home, two other individuals were enjoying their morning tea. Anthony had invited his sergeant to share his break with him, to go over the orders for the day, and also to take him into his confidence about his recent visit to Dublin.

"There's exciting plans in the offing," he told McNulty. "The top brass want to send observers to Spain and monitor the

Civil War. Pick up some tips on how modern armies will need to equip and operate in the future. It's on the cards I might be considered.

Bad news for us is that it looks as if the cavalry units are finished. Tanks and armoured cars are standard in most armies now. There's lots of developments going on in the air forces. Planes are no longer just to spy for the artillery. They can carry bombs, hundreds of pounds of them, and they can knock out key targets better than artillery."

"I'll be sorry to see the horses go, Surr. Will we get tanks in their place?"

"Not for a while, but if war breaks out in Europe, we might get something. Perhaps an armoured car."

"Just one? We couldn't do much with that, could we?"

"No, and the way things seem to be going with this bloody de Valera government, there'll soon be no army anyway. Another five thousand men are to go shortly. It's crazy! Just at the time they should be recruiting, they're reducing our strength."

McNulty finished his tea and left Anthony studying some of the documents he had brought back from Dublin. He was looking particularly at the pictures of new models of armoured cars manufactured by Rolls Royce and wishing it would be possible to have one for the unit in Galway. But he knew their chances of getting one were very slim.

***

At Ballanalee, Catrin had just sat down to breakfast with Devlin. He had already told her about the scenes with Maguire the previous afternoon.

"I've thought a lot more about it, "he told her, "my mind is made up now. You were right. I have to get away from Maguire. I'm goin' to write a letter to Sean in America and ask if we can come. I can do my craft work an' I know there's great scope for paintin'. America's a great place for anybody with talent to get on in the world, an' I know we can do it together."

"Have you thought more about it? I mean, can you bear the thought o' leavin' your folks?"

"I have. It's not an easy choice. It's going to be a big wrench. They'll be very hurt especially my Da. He's expecting me to join him in the business in six months time. But I need to help get you away from Maguire before he destroys you, or gets you killed. I love you too much."

"You must love me a lot to be prepared to do that"

"You know I do. But how will you escape Maguire? You said they might track you down, Can they really?"

"They have spies everywhere, but I'd take the chance. If we can make it to America I think we'll be alright. But we must be careful in the next week or two. We must act completely normal and not give anything away of our plan."

"Does that mean I should be staying away for a while?" Catrin asked tearfully.

"That's probably a good idea. I hate to be left alone again, but it makes sense. If you're back in Dublin, Maguire won't need to be checkin' on me so much. He'll think he's frightened you off."

"Why can't I just go to Dungannon House?"

"Go home, Catrin. If you're prepared to leave your folks at short notice, you should stay with them as much as you can. Once I've got the way organised here, I'll send for you."

The decisions made, and their emotions stirred, it was only natural that the rest of the morning was spent in love making. It would be their last opportunity for the foreseeable future and Catrin threw to the winds any inhibitions she had left. It was a tearful parting when she finally left to return to Dungannon House.

Two days later Maguire called at the transport depot and stomped into Rafferty's office.

"I hear you've got some news for me," he snapped in his usual gruff manner.

"I have that. Better sit down."

"Is it about Dillon?"

"It is."

"Well, get on with it. I haven't all day. Is it true what Dev says?"

"Looks that way."

"Rafferty," Maguire leaned forward menacingly, "for Christ's sake just tell me in simple words yes or no."

"Probably that red haired bitch Kilpatrick."

Rafferty dropped his patronising smile. "I had a little talk with the orderly in Dillon's office. Bought him a drink and greased his palm a little. He tells me Dillon used to get a number of telephone calls from a woman who said he was his sister. He thought it queer that a sister should be callin' so often."

"Does he have a sister?"

"Yes, but that one always announced her name when she called and she had a definite Dublin accent. The other who said she was his sister had a Galway one."

"Could'ave been anyone," Maguire growled, "you'll need a lot more than that to convince me."

"There is more. The orderly then finds out from somethin' the sergeant says that Dillon has only a brother. There's no sister."

"Jaysus! "

"I asked Seamus to check with Annie at the local exchange and list all the calls she put through to the barracks. She has every record. She wasn't goin' to tell him at first, but he eventually twisted her arm and got the list. Sure enough there was several calls, and guess where they came from?" He leaned back in his chair, the sly gloating smile reappearing.

Maguire looked daggers at him. "Go on then. Spit it out"

"They came from the shop in Eyre square."

Maguire was crestfallen. He rose wearily from his chair and crossed over to the window. He said nothing and appeared to be surveying the yard below. There was a van departing out the gate. He was suddenly crushed, his faith crumbling and, like the van, fast disappearing.

"I never could have imagined it. What could have possessed her? Jaysus Murphy. No wonder she wouldn't tell me."

"Tell you what?" Rafferty queried.

Maguire turned on him furiously. He had suddenly realised his slip. Only Seamus and McCrimmond knew about the pregnancy.

"His name, ye bliddy fool, that's all."

"So what now?"

"Take him out. I swore I'd hunt him down, no matter how long it took or wherever he was. I'll make the plan, and it'll be me personally who finishes him off. I'll tell you when I'm ready."

Rafferty continued to lean back in his chair. It was a change to feel superior to Maguire, but the fact that he had accomplished the mission Maguire had ordered, and the results had deflated him so much, made him realise that Maguire was vulnerable after all, and that made him feel good.

Maguire had turned his attention to the large map of Galway district that hung on the wall. He had no particular interest in it, he merely wanted to hide the faint traces of moisture that lay in his eyes. Rafferty had further news for him.

"There's a message just in from Belfast. From the quartermaster. He's askin' for some stuff."

"What do they want?"

"Everythin' we've got. Gelignite, Cordite, detonators, timers an' some o' that fertilizer stuff Dev's been playin' about with. They want to smuggle it into England."

"That'll clean out all there is at Ballanalee."

"They want to disguise the load as a return delivery that's goin' back to a factory in Liverpool."

"They want to use *our* lorry to go across the ferry?"

"Why not? Our lorries are in an' out the docks nearly every day. Customs never bother with the regular users."

"I'll think about it," Maguire muttered. An idea was beginning to germinate in his mind. He turned his attention back to the map. Rafferty's curiosity got the better of him and he left his desk to stand beside Maguire.

"What's on your mind," he asked.

"Nothin' growled Maguire. "just thinkin' that's all. I'll let you know about Belfast when I've decided, not before. First off, I have to decide what to do with that bastard o' a lieutenant." He stalked out of the office leaving Rafferty to speculate.

It was a quieter than usual supper table at the Maguire house that night. The housekeeper had left immediately after the dishes had been washed and cleared away. Seamus and his father remained at the table, but Eamon had fled upstairs, fearful that the silence was prelude to one of his father's stormy lectures.

Maguire painfully related what Rafferty had said. "Bliddy gobshite! He looked as if he wis enjoyin' himself. He said the real information came from Annie at the exchange."

"I got it from her. But there was somethin' else that finally clinched it."

Maguire looked up sharply. "What?"

"I'll tell you on one condition."

"For Christ's sake Seamus. It's your sister we're tryin' to sort out. We're both out for vengeance, aren't we? What the hell does it require a condition for?"

"I don't want another Maura disaster. You can't control your temper. You know full well you lose all sense o' responsibility when you fly off the handle."

"Alright. I'm sorry. No outbursts. Just tell me."

Seamus inclined his head towards the ceiling. "Eamon knows somethin'."

Maguire clenched his fists as he fought to control himself. "Will he tell me?"

"Yes. As long as I'm with him, an' you promise not to fly off the handle."

"I've said I'll stay cool. Fetch him down."

Seamus brought Eamon into the room and sat him down. He sat alongside him to give him confidence, and placed a protective arm around his shoulder.

"There's nuthin to be frightened about. Da's promised. Just tell him what you told me last night."

Eamon began in a faltering voice, his eyes downcast, fearing to look directly at his father.

"It was a few nights before the accident. Maura went back to the shop. Catchin' up on some bookwork she said.

She said she wouldn't be long. But she was away for two hours, and I started to worry, so I went out to see if she was alright. The shop was in darkness, so I went round the back and saw a light in the office. I was about to knock on the window when I heard voices. Angry voices. They were arguing. One of the voices was Maura's, the other was a man. Maura was cryin'."

"For Christ's sake. Why didn't you do somethin?" Maguire could contain himself no longer.

"I was frightened, that's why. I was going to run back to the house and see if you or Seamus was there, and I would have fetched you back. I snuck back to the front and just as I was going up the street, I heard the shop door slam shut and this man came out.

I dodged into a doorway and watched him pass by. It was him. The lieutenant. He wasn't in uniform but I knew it was him. I'd seen him before in the shop."

Maguire slumped on the table, his head in his hands. He had never been so humbled. "Get you back upstairs Eamon," he muttered from beneath his hands, "not a word about this to another livin' soul. Do you hear me?"

Eamon scrambled to his feet and ran from the room. The ordeal had made him want to cry, but that would have been too much for his father.

Seamus waited until he heard Eamon close his bedroom door.

The last time he had been so humbled was to hear Eamon say, "Sorry Da. But you had to know."

"Leave me be. I need to think. Dillon'll pay fer it, as God is my witness." He waved Seamus to leave him alone.

He sat brooding over the fire, stirring it occasionally to promote a flame. humiliated was years ago, in the Curragh. Stripped naked, in front of a burly sergeant major who screamed insults and obscenities in his ears. He had hoped never to experience the same feeling ever again.

His train of thought was interrupted by the telephone in the hall ringing loudly. He was inclined not to answer it, but there was a persistence about the ring that made him get up and pick up the receiver.

It was Mrs Donnavan calling from Dungannon House. She had overheard Catrin talking to Daniel. She was leaving for Dublin on the early morning train, but she had indicated that Devlin was fed up with his present life and wanted to start a new life somewhere else. She thought he ought to know.

He groaned aloud as he put the receiver back on the hook. Now he had two problems. The lieutenant and Devlin. He went to bed, deeply troubled, but by no means beaten. He had handled two problems and more at the same time before, and he would find a way.

As far as these two were concerned, the timer was set, and the sand already running.

Chapter Forty-One

It was unfortunate that Father O'Donnell was hungry. As a priest of the parish he held a position of considerable influence, but as a domestic servant held a much less exalted rank. His housekeeper had gone to visit a sick relative in Limerick, leaving him to fend for himself, and he was making a poor job of it. His tea looked pathetic.

A single poached egg laid on a slice of blackened toast, and to compound the misery, the yolk had broken due to his clumsiness. Never the less, he was about to sit down and eat when there was a thunderous knock at the back door.

"Dear God," he blasphemed, "is a man to have no peace?"

He shuffled to the door in a fit of temper. The door was stiff and he had to yank it fiercely to pull it open. His look of irritation was quickly replaced by a practised sickly smile.

"Saints be praised," he gushed, "'tis the Maguire himself. An unexpected pleasure to be sure. I was about to eat. Would you join me in a cup o' tay?"

Maguire strode past him into the kitchen, as imperious as the bishop. He looked in disgust at the plate on the table, where the egg lay in an ugly yellow splotch on the burnt toast.

"I take it Mrs. Donnachie is away?"

"Aye, more's the pity."

"So we won't be disturbed?"

"No. Not at all, at all."

"Fine. I have somethin' in confidence to discuss. But sit down an' eat. I'll mash us a brew an' then we can talk."

The small black kettle was already spouting steam on the single gas ring as Maguire busied himself. He poured the boiling water into the teapot and set it down on the table, and selected two mugs from several lying on the draining board. He sat down opposite the priest.

"I take it this is not just a social call?" Father O'Donnell asked the question despite his mouth full of egg, and yolk dribbling down his chin. "'Tis something' important, is it?"

Maguire did not reply. It was one of his traits to keep people in suspense. He neither liked or disliked the

priest, but had no respect for him. Pompous little bastard, full of his own importance. With his dark oily hair cut short and fringed around his large head, he was small and portly, reminding him of a picture he had once seen of Friar Tuck in a school book about Robin Hood.

The silence was too much for the priest.

"So what is it you might be after havin' this visit for?"

"In a minute, Father." Maguire began to pour tea into the mugs. He passed one over to the priest who wrapped his hands around it as if seeking to warm them. He added milk and stirred three spoonfuls of sugar into the mug, and proceeded to drink it with loud slurping noises. He smacked his lips in appreciation. The whole performance irritated Maguire and confirmed his lack of respect. Greedy little bastard as well, he thought.

"'Tis a fine brew there. Fine indeed. I'll take a drop more if you please."

Maguire refilled the mug and shoved it back to the priest for a repeat performance. Father O'Donnell smacked his lips for the second time and let the mug rest on the table.

"So, this matter you want to talk about, is it for the country or for the Church?" He was well aware of Maguire's Republican activities, and he also knew he had powerful connections in the Diocese, and was a generous benefactor into the bargain.

Maguire continued to sip his tea. His cold grey eyes stared out from his smooth ruddy complexioned face. He might have been a handsome man, but for his eyes. They were too small for the rest of his face, like those of a pig, an indication of a bad temper, and they had an ability to pierce into the soul of whoever became subject to his scrutiny. He was doing that to Father O'Donnell, and it made the priest nervous.

"You could say it was for both," he said at last. He folded his arms in front of him and leaned on the table. "That's the reason it seems fittin' to involve you. I'm after havin' your help."

"That word "involve" you just said. What exactly does that mean?"

"Don't look so worried, Father, 'tis not much I'm after askin'. 'Tis a service that will benefit the church. As he spoke Maguire reached inside his coat pocket and took out a long white envelope. He laid it on the table and tapped it lightly with his fingers.

"There's four nice new five pound notes in there, Father, crisp an' white as if they were newly off the press, so they are. That's a great deal more than you get in the collection plates in many a day, is it not?"

Father O'Donnell licked his lips nervously and nodded. His eyes were fixed hypnotically on the envelope. It looked so white and pure, but he sensed trouble.

"'Tis indeed. But what has it got to do with the Church?"

"Encouragement for your work, Father." Maguire had a malicious smile and his eyes continued to bore into those of the priest.

"You'll have to tell me more."

"Of course Father. Finish off your tay an' I'll tell you."

Maguire waited while the priest drained his mug, his fingers tapping on the table intimidating.

"It's very simple. A matter o' communication. I need the church to do its job. I'm after wantin' you to arrange a Confessional. That's not too much to ask. Is it?"

"A Confessional? For who? Surely not himself?"

Maguire laughed as if it was a good joke, but the laughter was not sustained.

"No. Someone who needs it a great deal more than me. A certain Army officer. You've probably seen him around. He's the young lieutenant that's taken over at the barracks. His name's Dillon."

Father O'Donnell pushed back his chair and rose to his feet, his arms waving.

"In the name of God, what are you trying to get me into? You know the situation between the Church and the military. And why should I even think of it? He hasn't made a request. He hasn't even been near the Church!"

"He's no devout Catholic, that's for sure," agreed Maguire, "but I'm sure he'll attend if you ask him nicely. Sit down and listen. It's important."

Father O'Donnell resumed his seat reluctantly. "What makes you so sure he'll come. Has he sins to atone for?"

"No doubts about that Father. I know of one grievous sin for sure, but the church doesn't need to deal with that one. That's between him an' me. God doesn't come into it. That's not why I want him to see you. It's a matter of service to the country."

"I don't know where this is leading, but I don't like it." The priest pushed his chair back making a loud scraping noise against the stone flags, and tried to get to his feet. "I think you should go. I'll forget this took place."

"Sit where you are," Maguire commanded, "sit down an' listen to me." As the priest hesitated he brought his large ham of a fist crashing down on the table.

"I'm after havin' you arrange this confessional, not for Dillon to confess his sins. He wouldn't own up to them anyway. I simply want you to pass him some information. It's the kind o' information I can't give him me self. He mustn't know where it comes from. He wouldn't trust another source. He'll trust the Church."

"What's so special about this information?"

"Information that will benefit the country. It will save innocent lives. That's all you need to know."

"So how am I supposed to give him this information if I don't know what it is?"

"I'll give you an envelope, like the one on the table. The information will be inside. All you need do is slip it under the screen. That's worth twenty pounds surely?"

"What if he won't take it? He'll be suspicious."

"He's no fool. But that's where you earn your money" Once again he fingered the white envelope that lay between them. "Money for the Church Father, and the information's for the good o' the country because it will save many innocent lives. That's a Christian gesture is it not?" He pushed the envelope further towards the priest.

Father O'Donnell shrank back. "I don't like it. I've told you already the Church and the military are at odds with each other. We cannot be seen to be involved with them."

"You must insist he can't attend in uniform. We'll arrange the Church won't be disturbed while he's there. It will only take a few minutes."

"No, no, I don't like it. There is an evil purpose behind this. I don't want any part of it. Keep your bribe." He pushed the envelope away from him.

Maguire stood up abruptly, his face flushed with anger and he glared at the priest. "I didn't come to here to waste my time. Sit down again and I'll try an' provide better motivation." Maguire resumed his seat, but the priest remained standing, desperately trying to keep his defiance from evaporating.

"I said sit down, Father. Now!" He banged the table with his fist again. One of the mugs toppled over and rolled over the edge to smash on the floor. The noise made the priest jump. He wilted and sat down, his legs beginning to tremble violently.

"I didn't think this would be so difficult." Maguire's tone of voice had changed. It was a quieter voice, but there was malice in it, a steel-like menace calculated to set the nerves on edge.

"I had hoped to avoid this. I was thinkin' the Church might be grateful for help. Spiritual help's all the easier with some financial help, surely? I didn't mean to press you more than I had to. But you're not givin' me the chance."

"What does that mean?" Father O'Donnell once again licked his lips nervously.

"I had hoped to avoid mentioning your little mistakes or, how should I put it?... your little financial problems."

The Priest sent his chair toppling over as he sprang to his feet, his face pale and his arms trembling. "What are you talking about? What are you accusing me of?"

Maguire half rose, his hands gripping both sides of the table with a force that caused the other mug to fall off and shatter on the floor. He ignored it, and the priest was too terrified to move.

Father O'Donell was clearly upset. "Get out of here. You're just trying to scare me into doing some of your dirty work." He was on the verge of panic. You have no proof. I'll deny everything."

"Not so Father, I have it on the best o' authority. From the horse's mouth so to speak. I had a little bird that told me there was a discrepancy in the Church's income recently. Apparently a difference of twenty pounds, would you believe it?"

"What do you mean? What are you talking about?"

He sat down and motioned the priest to pick up his chair and do the same. Once again he pushed the envelope across the table.

"It would seem that the income collected in the Church collection boxes recently was not the same as was the deposit you made to the Bank.

The Father started to panic. "There must be a mistake."

"There certainly is, a big mistake, and I know who made it" Maguire sat back in his chair looking pleased at the effect on the Priest. "I also know what you did with it".

Father O'Donnell started to sweat. He was being driven into a corner and was sick with fear.

"Get out of this house! How dare you accuse me of such a thing! You're just trying to blackmail me into doing one of your evil plans."

Maguire kept his beady eyes fastened on the panicking Priest. "I know very well what you did with the money. I'm not just out to scare you. Pifirin' the Church funds is bad enough, but usin' it to gamble at the Galway Races... the

Bishop will go ballistic, if he gets to know. The congregation might well tar an' feather you and drive you outta town".

Father O'Donell sat down in a daze, and looked frightened. He had witnessed some thieves being tarred and feathered, and it was most unpleasant.

"Alright! Alright! I did overspend that month, but I had every intention of paying it back. The Races offered a hope. I thought with luck I could get back the twenty pounds, and possibly a bit more."

"What a pity your horse didn't win. Some would commiserate with you, but not the Bishop. He's a stickler for well kept accounts, and with the quarterly audits due at the end of this month, you're headin' for real trouble."

But the Priest did not collapse in shame. He jumped to his feet and pushed his chair away. There were tears in his eyes, but he steadied himself and squared up to Maguire. "You're an evil man, Maguire! Even more evil than people think. I'm not the only person with skeletons in their cupboard! Yours are far worse than mine!"

Maguire was on his feet in a flash, and roared "Whit the Devil are you talkin' about?"

"I know about your Maura!"

Maguire was stupefied. For a brief moment he seemed lost, then his complexion turned red. "Whit the Devil are you talkin' about? Whit do you know?"

"She came to me for a Confession two days before she died. She confessed that she was with child. She was nearly out of her mind, frightened to death what would happen when you found out. I thought I had

What do you mean by that?" Maguire was recovering his usual fighting spirit.

"I thought it strange. She had lots of friends in Galway. So called tragic accident, and no mention of the fact that she was pregnant. Seemed it was all being as quiet as possible."

"You gobshite! You know nothin'. I never knew she had been at a Confessional. I wanted her name kept clean. Watch what you say!"

"Calm down Maguire. You know full well that a Confession is shared only by the Priest and the individual. "I'm making the point that you should not be trying to force me to do something I don't like the sound of."

"Now please go, and do not threaten me – there are skeletons in your cupboard too."

Maguire exploded out of his seat and charged round the table, scattering the broken china on the floor, his fist raised to strike. The priest fled to the other side and they faced one another across the table.

"What the hell are you insinuating'," Maguire roared, "Out with it!

O'Donnell's mouth was bone dry and his knees were like jelly. "I know about your girl, Maura."

Maguire's belligerent look suddenly disappeared. His face went white and his eyes narrowed. "You know what?"

"She was pregnant. Father unknown. She wouldn't tell me."

"Tell you?"

"She came to confession the day or two before she died. She told me she was with child. She was nearly out of her mind with fear, frightened out of her wits because of what you might do. I tried to calm her down, but she was too upset. Two days later she was dead. You had me read the last rites over her body yet you had her buried in Limerick instead of the church here, I began to wonder."

"Wonder what?" Maguire's face was returning to the angry red he had displayed throughout most of the conversation.

"I just thought it strange, that's all. Tragic accident, but the unborn child was never mentioned. For all you knew, it might have still been alive inside her."

"You bliddy little gobshite! Who are you to speculate? I never knew she had been to confession. This better not be mentioned to anyone. I want her name kept clean, d'ye hear?"

"Of course. A confession is always confidential between the priest and the individual. But I'm only making the point that you shouldn't be trying to force me to do something I don't like the sound of. Now please go. I'll say no more about it."

Maguire did not move. He leaned on the table with both hands and looked straight at the priest. It was the hint of a threat to come.

"Don't think you can wipe away your sin by playin' that card, Father. If I thought you would be so stupid as to tell anyone what you've just told me, the Parish would be havin' a vacancy for a new priest to-morrow."

Father O'Donnell blanched. His trump card had failed.

"Let me try another tack," Maguire adopted a more conciliatory tone. This pompous little bastard was tougher than he expected.

"Perhaps it's because I don't go to Church enough. Perhaps I don't understand God any more. After all, look at the state the country's in. Starvation, poverty, sickness, no work an' no support for almost half the population. Tell me Father, what does God do for them?"

The priest remained silent. He was not going to be led into any traps.

"That's why you an' I have different Gods, Father".

"Don't be stupid! There is only one God."

"Is there now? It depends what you stand for. Let me tell you Father, I've been a Republican all my life. I was in Dublin durin' the Easter risin'. I saw innocent civilians shot. Where was God an' his mercy when the valiant leaders were lined up an' shot by firin' squads in Kilmainham jail?

Was he around in the Civil War? I didn't see him. I served with the Limerick Brigade in 1921 right through to the end, when fathers fought against sons.

Where was he then? When the Black an' Tans were lootin' murderin' an' rapin' our women, burnin' their homes an' puttin' them out in the streets with nuthin' but what they stood up in. When we were on the run an' starvin', hidin' in hedges, an' the wounded crying for help. Where was he? Tell me that."

"God was always with you," the priest mumbled miserably.

"Well if he was, Father, he needed to be more in evidence, like my God."

"What do you mean, *your* God?"

"My God is very much in evidence. He's a Republican leader living in Dublin, or Belfast, Limerick or Cork. Wherever needed, he's always close to his people. He doesn't work in the palatial splendour of a church like yours. His temple is a squalid room in a back street. No carpets on the floor or pictures o' Saints on the wall. It stinks o' piss an' horse dung instead o' incense.

"He's a strong God. Doesn't believe in turnin' the other cheek jest to get smacked on it as well. He fights persecution. Protects his flock. He believes in an eye for an eye, an' a tooth for a tooth. He doesn't forgive or forget."

He has many disciples, an' they're jest as devoted as Christ's. My God gives them more persuasive means than the Bible to spread his gospel."

He reached into his pocket and tugged out a heavy revolver, and laid it on the table with a dull thud.

"Ye'know what they call this gun in the Wild West, Father? They call it the Peacemaker. That's exactly what it is. It settles arguments."

"In the name of God, put it away."

Maguire ignored him, but placed his hand over the gun.

"Tell me somethin' Father. Did you ever wonder why there was so little crime around here?

"Why should I? They are friendly people, good people. The Church provides guidance which they respond to. The Garda keeps a watchful eye. Why should there be crime? That just shows how much outta touch you are. Let me educate you a bit, Father. Firstly they're all too poor to be able to steal from one another. But the real reason is fear. The Garda doesn't control crime.

There's too many blind eyes in that lot. It's *our* army that keeps law an' order. We take care o' our own, an' see that they're not preyed upon by those who step out the bounds o' common dacency."

"I've heard of your so called "peoples courts". They're no more than an excuse to settle old scores. I don't call it justice."

"Better not say that in one o'your sermons, Father. You're wrong. Our system is simple, not cluttered up with red tape or legislation that nobody but a Philadelphia lawyer can understand, or politicians that move the goal posts every time it suits them. Things are either black or white. You're either for the people or against. A parasite is a parasite and is dealt with accordingly. The penalties are severe an' understood by everybody. No lawyer gets rich off us. That's the real reason crime is low here."

Maguire picked up the gun, swinging the muzzle in the direction of the priest, and spinning the chamber, allowing it to come to rest so that the priest could see the lead tips of the bullets in the chambers. He replaced the gun in his coat pocket.

"Does that make things clearer, Father? Can you appreciate the seriousness of your position? You're faulty expenses? That's a new crime for us to consider, but I think it would be classed under those dealt with as parasites".

"Now can you see the sense in the choice I'm offerin'?" For the last time he pushed the white envelope closer to the priest.

"Aid for the Church, Father, not just spiritual platitudes, and the chance to perform a small deed that will help the country. I'd say that wasn't a bad deal. Better than the Bishop comin' down on you like a ton o' bricks, or facin' a people's court.

Father O'Donnell slumped on to his chair, his face ashen, and his body trembling. His hand shook as he picked up the envelope. It felt hot to the touch, and he wished he could throw it back on the table, but it seemed to stick in his hand. He stuffed it awkwardly into his waistcoat pocket and sat with his head bowed.

"So. Tell me again. What is it you want me to do?"

"Now you're seein' sense," Maguire was almost jovial. "Tell you what, Father, I'll make us another brew o' tay an' we'll discuss it."

"Let me make it," the priest pleaded. He picked up the teapot and carried it to the sink. He had to distance himself from his tormentor.

He flushed the tea leaves from the pot into the sink, some of the brown mash splashing on to his hands. In the dim light of the solitary gas mantle, the leaves looked like blood. He took a long time to rinse the sink, running the water continually over his hands as if to wash his sins away. And all the time he could feel the envelope in his pocket. He felt wretched.

Maguire's words haunted him Where was God?"

Chapter Forty-Two

Anthony was sitting idly at his desk when the call came through. It had been a morning of low activity, and he was bored.

"Call fer you, surr," the orderly shouted from the outer office.

"Who is it?" he shouted back.

"Father O'Donnell. He says it's important."

Anthony was surprised. He hadn't been to church since his arrival. The army was not popular with the clergy, so there was no incentive to attend. He was reluctant to take the call but curiosity got the better of him.

"Put him through," he shouted. He picked up the receiver and leaned back into his chair. He swung his legs up and planted his boots on the desk, and prepared to listen to a boring sermon.

"Hello Father. This is a surprise."

"Is it yourself lieutenant? Good of you to take my call. "'tis a busy man you are for sure."

Anthony smiled at the flattery. He surveyed the bare expanse of desk in front of him, and the empty in-tray that furnished it.

"Are you by yourself lieutenant? This is for your ears only."

"Just a minute." He swung his feet off the desk and crossed the room to close the door.

"This sounds very mysterious, Father. Have you a problem?"

"No, not at all, at all," the priest assured him, "'tis you that's got the problem. But I think I can help."

"I'm not aware of any problem, certainly not one that needs the help of the Church. Come straight to the point, Father."

"Patience my son. I'm carrying out God's work. I'm after askin' you to attend for a Confessional to-morrow. ''Tis important that you come.

"Are you serious Father? I'm an active soldier. I can't pop into church any old time. You said yourself that I was very busy. Besides, I don't think I've anything to confess to. Sorry! I can't manage,"

"Please lieutenant. Hear me out. 'tis not a normal confession. 'tis specially arranged for you. There will be no one else in the church."

"You're sounding even more strange, Father."

"I have some very important information to give you, military information. It could be of great help to you. It is so valuable that it must be handed over to you in person. 'tis why I want you to attend the confession. I can pass the information in the secrecy it requires."

"Smells fishy, Father. What would you be doing with military information, and where did it come from?"

"Let's just say it came from a very reliable source that must remain confidential. You have your own intelligence scattered everywhere. You might say this came from a similar source."

"You mean from an informer?"

"You said that not me.""

"How do I know if this information is reliable? How do I know it is not a trap of some sort?"

"I wouldn't get the Church involved if I didn't believe it was genuine information. The party that gave it to me has similar interests in mind to those of the church.

"He is being watched all the time, and it is impossible for him to hand it over to you in person. You must understand that."

"What can the Church have in common with military matters? I've heard about priests that are forever condemning the army."

"Of course." admitted the priest, "but only when the forces of law and order have inflicted sufferin' on innocent people, which they have, many a time."

"Let's not go into that, Father. Just exactly does the church have in common with this particular information?"

"'tis the saving of innocent lives that's involved. This information will do that." The priest spoke with such gravity that Anthony was very curious. The fact that the priest had emphasised saving lives, made him speculate hurriedly if a possible uprising could be close at hand. He dismissed the idea.

"Alright," he said after the pause. "I'll think about it. What do I have to do?"

"Come to the church at noon to-morrow. Come to the door on the West side. All the others will be closed. Don't wear your uniform. Someone will admit you and you are to come straight to my Confession Box. It is the last box on the same side as you enter. My name will be on it. I will hand over the information and you will leave by the same door. That is all. After that it is up to you to decide whether to act on the information or not."

There was a loud click as the phone was hung up. Anthony waited a few seconds before replacing the receiver, to make sure the call was finished. It had seemed a very abrupt ending to the conversation. He opened the door and instructed the orderly.

"Ring the exchange and verify where that call came from. If she gets uppity about it, tell her is important and I'll contact her superior if there's any trouble."

He returned to his desk and waited. He heard the orderly pose the query.

"Surr!" the orderly shouted. "The call came from the Parish church. She says it was Father O'Donnell for sure."

He spent most of the afternoon in conflict with himself. He debated informing Gallagher, the Chief Inspector of the Garda, but decided against it. There was too much sympathy towards the local Republicans.

In the morning he briefed sergeant McNulty to take over The Father had mentioned benefits. What did that mean? It couldn't be money, the Church had none. Promotion for him? That was possible. If he succeeded in breaking up a rebel project, it might get him promoted and back to Dublin. He continued to debate all the possibilities and ultimately decided to attend for Confession.

He informed MacNulty and told him he would be going out for a couple of hours on some private business. He changed into civilian clothes and decided to wear his long trench coat. His main purpose in wearing the coat was not for the weather, but so that he could take his revolver. He could keep his hand in the deep pocket and have it ready for instant use. If he was walking into a trap, he would be prepared.

He strolled leisurely across the Weir bridge and turned up the street leading to the church. The morning rain had practically ceased and as if to celebrate, the clouds parted and a watery sun made a brief appearance. The orange coloured rays caught the side of the church steeple, making it glisten. In the reddish light, rivulets of rain meandered down the sides reminding him of the sight of blood running from a wound. He gave an involuntary shudder. Someone had just walked over his grave.

The main door was closed, and there was a wooden trestle that declared no entry due to emergency repairs. He found the door on the West side and entered into the gloom. His hand tightened around his revolver as he could make out a figure standing in the dark, but it was an unnecessary precaution. A pronounced Galway accent spoke from the shadows.

"Straight ahead into the nave and turn left. Father O'Donnell's box is the last one down on the same side."

It was too dark to identify who it was, but whoever it was looked tall and lanky. He proceeded into the knave, his footsteps echoing hollowly in the vastness of the empty church.

Without the sunlight, the stained glass windows behind the chapel at the end looked cold and lifeless. The damp chill of the air reminded him of boyhood experiences when he had been dragged to church against his will. He was only six and wore short trousers, and wriggled and fidgeted as the horse hair stuffing of the seats irritated his bare legs. The minister always seemed to be angry, and shouting at him.

As he approached the Confessional box he recalled the stark fear he had when told he had to go and confess his sins. What sins? He was only playing. It was real fear. Fear of the unknown. Fear of the dark. Why was it so dark inside? He remembered how his heart had leapt into his mouth when the shutter door slid back without warning, with a thud that echoed through his head to this very day. He disliked the church.

The priest's name was on the door as he had been told. He paused before entering, scanning the nave to check no one was watching. The silence was intense, only the faint sounds of water dripping from somewhere. He closed the door firmly and stood facing the screen. No need to kneel. He was not there for his sins. The shutter slid open and he could just make out the faint outlines of the head and shoulders of the shadowy figure behind it.

He tightened his grip on the revolver, his thumb ready to ease off the safety catch if he had any hint of danger.

"Thank you for coming, my son."

"I am here at your request, Father. I believe you have something for me?"

"'tis so. I have it here". He slid a long narrow envelope partially under the screen, but kept his fingers on it as if reluctant to part with it.

"You will use it wisely, I hope. Bear in mind the purpose. It is to save innocent lives."

"Of course, Father. But this is most unusual. What guarantee do I have that the information is genuine? How do I know for certain that it is not a trap set by enemies of the State? I doubt if you would class army personnel as innocent lives?"

"The information is highly reliable, to be sure and there is further proof. The envelope contains a map of a certain location. You will have ample time to check it out and satisfy yourself that it is genuine. Of course, if you do not trust the information, you need do nothing. But that would certainly cause innocent lives to be lost. In that case any benefits to you are unlikely to happen."

"What benefits?" His voice rose as he felt angered.

"Not so loud my son," admonished the priest. Think of it. If this information was to foil a certain party from committing a foul deed, it can only be good for you. Good soldiers are valued by their superiors. Success with this will help you. Now go my son. There's no more to say. It is up to you. Do as you must." He pushed the envelope from beneath the screen and closed the shutter quickly, leaving Anthony alone in the gloom.

He thrust the envelope into his inside pocket and made his way back to the West door. There was no sign of the individual who had let him in, and the barrier had disappeared from the front door. Whoever was responsible had organised it well.

He returned to the barracks immediately, surprising McNulty who had not expected him for at least another hour.

"Any messages, sergeant?"

"Nuthin' at all, surr. I t'ink H.Q.'s forgotten all about us."

Anthony removed his coat and hung it on the peg behind the door. He would change into his uniform later, but for the moment he was more interested in the contents of the envelope.

"See that I'm not disturbed for the next ten minutes, sergeant." He closed the door of his office. McNulty had time to see the envelope in his hand.

Another letter from the girlfriend in Dublin, he thought. Must be a passionate one for him to want such privacy.

Anthony slit the envelope open and extracted two sheets of paper, one of which had a map drawn on it. The other sheet had been written in block capitals and was addressed to him.

TOMORROW NIGHT BETWEEN NINE THIRTY AND TEN THIRTY THERE WILL BE A MOVEMENT OF A LARGE QUANTITY OF REPUBLICAN ARMS FROM A SITE IN GALWAY TO A NEW SITE IN CONNEMARA. THE ARMS WILL BE TRANSPORTED IN A CATTLE TRUCK BEARING THE NAME OF MAGUIRE & SONS ON THE SIDES. IT WILL BE DRIVEN BY TWO MEN, BOTH OF WHOM ARE KEY PERSONNEL OF THE GALWAY BRIGADE. BOTH WILL BE ARMED AND ARE DANGEROUS MEN. THERE IS A MAP ENCLOSED WHICH SHOWS THE ROUTE THEY WILL TAKE. THERE IS A PARTICULAR LOCATION ON THE MAP WHICH INDICATES A SPOT WHERE INTERCEPTION COULD BE MADE VERY EFFECTIVELY.

THE PREVENTION OF THIS CARGO REACHING ITS DESTINATION WOULD SAVE MANY LIVES IN THE FUTURE AND WOULD DEAL A MASSIVE BLOW TO THE REPUBLICAN CAUSE IN THE GALWAY AREA.

Anthony read the note several times. The wording suggested an intelligence source, and the way it was phrased and spelt correctly had a ring of military intelligence. The Priest had said the informant was being watched all the time. Could a government agent have infiltrated a Republican group? The government had loads of spies up and down the country. It was very possible.

He sat deep in thought, tapping the paper between his hands. He knew what his gut instinct was, but it was an enormous risk. Should he phone H.Q. in Dublin? He shook his head. They would take too long to react, and probably tell him to remember his orders and let the Gardai deal with it.

The Gardai would do precious little. His thoughts returned to the last words of the priest. The benefits.

If he succeeded in nipping this project in the bud, he would undoubtedly be promoted to captain. More than that, he had a score to settle with Maguire.

He made up his mind to take the chance, but not without precautions. He would have time to check the information out before charging head first into danger, and he would call on the experience of McNulty to help him.

Chapter Forty-Three

Anthony called McNulty into his office.

"Take a look at this," he handed him the note. "Tell me what you make of it."

The sergeant studied the note. He looked up once as if to query something, but carried on reading. He put it back on the desk.

"D'ye think it's genuine, Surr? It's a bit suspicious to me. Where'd it come from?"

"From an intelligence source." It was only a white lie. Father O'Donnell could loosely be described as an intelligence source.

"I think it may be genuine. There's a sketch of a location along with the note. It's worth investigating. Bring out the Ordinance Survey map of the Galway West area, and we'll make a comparison."

Together they pored over the map and quickly found the area that corresponded to the sketch. "There's the old Drovers track they mention," he traced it with his finger.

"It runs for about four miles to meet up with the main road on the other side. You can see it saves a few miles, and it also takes them away from the Garda patrols on the other road."

"It makes sense," McNulty agreed, "an' they won't be seen by anyone at that time o' night. What's that mark fer?" he indicated a heavily pencilled cross on the sketch map.

"That's the spot they are recommending we can stop the truck. That's what makes me really suspicious." He refolded the map and put both sheets back into the envelope, and then slid them into his briefcase.

"Get the small van ready, we're going on a little scouting mission. We'll check the whole thing out and then make a decision on what to do."

The rain had ceased when they drove out of the barracks and they headed north-west, skirting the lough. McNulty drove whilst Anthony followed their progress on the map. The Drovers track was no longer sign -posted, but they picked it up easily enough. It was still used by the occasional farmer, and there were two farms a few hundred yards from the entrance, but on the far side of the road.

"On our way back, we'll take a closer look at those." Anthony was already mapping out a plan in his head. They proceeded to drive up the track, finding it slightly bumpy, but in surprisingly good condition. It had taken many thousands of cattle and sheep hooves to wear it down over many years. The building of new road had rendered it redundant, and it was only the occasional local who still made use of it.

The ground on the right rose steeply to a crest about three hundred feet up. On the left it fell away sharply, forming a deep ditch, before levelling out into open ground which was thickly covered by huge clumps of reeds and marsh grass. Scattered throughout were pools of stagnant water making it a totally useless piece of ground.

It was obvious the track had been dug out of the lowest part of the slope, high enough to clear the marshy ground, and not high enough to meet resistance from the limestone rocks that lay above. There was just one spot about a mile up the track where nature interfered.

McNulty braked to a stop as they saw it, and they exchanged significant glances. This was the spot marked by the cross on the map, the suggested place to stop the contraband.

"Now we know why they picked the spot." Anthony climbed out of the passenger seat and advanced a few feet. He climbed the slope and stood surveying the scene, one leg pushed forward, hands on hips, like an explorer seeing new land for the first time.

He was looking at a gully cut through a large mass of limestone. It made a natural boreen, framing the track on each side, higher on the top side and lower on the opposite side.

It ran for forty or fifty feet before resuming the normal track. On the downward slope, the rocks formed an uneven wall almost three feet high, a natural safety barrier to prevent slipping into the marsh below. The upper side was more than twelve feet high, and over the years young saplings had sprung up spreading their branches to form a screen that was gradually extending over the gully to complete the appearance of a natural boreen.

"Looks like they started to make the track an' then came across the rocks," McNulty observed.

"Probably," mused Anthony. "They couldn't go round it because of the ground below and more rocks up above, so they hacked their way through it."

"Must'ave been a helluvah job. All picks an' shovels. Christ, it must'ave taken weeks."

"They made it surprisingly wide for just driving cattle. There's room to get a small truck through there."

"They had to make it reasonably wide. It probably wouldn't have been stable enough if they had made it narrow. They were just unlucky to meet such a large bit o' rock. Good job it was limestone and not granite."

Anthony continued to look at the layout. "Are you thinking what I'm thinking?"

"Very likely, surr. Dead easy to stop anyone there. A barrier at the front, and a couple o' men on each side, an' you could hold off an army. The lower ground's too marshy to come that way, an' there's no cover for anyone tryin' to come down from the top."

"Let's drive up the rest of the track and see what's on the other side."

They drove the other three miles to meet up with the main road without finding anything suspicious. One solitary farmhouse stood at the end of the track close to the main road, otherwise it was clear of habitation and any obstructions.

As they made their way back towards the boreen, Anthony noticed a discarded wooden gate lying in the ditch at the side of the track.

"We'll use that. Couple of oil drums and that across them will form a check barrier. Not much of a barrier, but it'll make them slow down at least."

They found their way back to the main road where Anthony had McNulty stop at the two farm houses whilst he made a quick inspection.

"Might have a use for them," was all he told McNulty as he resumed his place in the passenger seat, leaving the sergeant to ponder what was going on in his mind.

Back in his office, they spread the map out on his desk and resumed a discussion on their findings.

"Surely this is a matter for the Garda, surr'. They're supposed to be in charge o' security. They won't take kindly to interference from us, will they?"

"Of course not. But we are here at their request. They called in help from the army because they couldn't cope. What have they let us do so far? Nothing! You know what they're like. They turn a blind eye to half the going's on because they know too many of the people they should be locking up.

"Why do you think the informant gave the information to us and not the Gardai? Because he knew we might do something with it! You said you and the men were bored, didn't you? Well, here's a chance for some action."

It was logical and McNulty had no questions.

"This is between you and I, sergeant. I have a plan, but we'll only brief the men at the last minute. I don't want any loose tongues blabbing before we make our move."

He spent the next half hour outlining his plan.

"We'll have to be in position before nine o' clock. That will give us the opportunity to inspect the location and make sure there are no booby traps or other surprises in store for us. Then we make sure everything is out of sight and wait."

As he was speaking, Anthony was scrawling out a list of items on a pad. He ripped off the page and handed it to the sergeant.

"That's a list of the gear you need to requisition from stores. We need both vans. We'll take all the men except the orderly clerk, he'll stay on guard here. We'll split into two groups. Make sure there's a driver for each van."

"McNulty looked up from the list he had been reading. "You want the Lewis gun, Surr? Isn't that a bit strong?"

"I'm taking no chances. These men are said to be armed. Probably killed more people than our whole lot put together. I want all the firepower we can muster. We have to be sure this plan is a success. If we mess it up, the Gardai will fling the book at us. I'm not going to give Gallagher the pleasure.

Now get busy and draw the equipment. We'll brief the men straight after breakfast."

McNulty left clutching the list and still looking concerned. He marched across to stores, and on the pretext of conducting an impromptu inventory check, accounted for all the equipment required, including the Lewis gun.

It was still in its box, wrapped in an oiled cloth as it had been since it was first issued to the unit, and had never been fired in action. McNulty knew the responsibility would fall on his shoulders and he was not as thrilled with the prospect.

Chapter Forty-Four

Sergeant McNulty's order for the men to parade came as a surprise, a shock that increased when they were marched into the orderly room and not on to the barrack square. Anthony appeared from his office holding a large sheet of paper which he proceeded to pin up on the notice board.

McNulty recognised it as a large scale version of the map showing the ambush site, and he also noted Anthony had added the two farm houses he had been so interested in.

Anthony stood the men at ease and asked them to group themselves around the drawing. He had a wooden pointer to help identify the various features. There was a buzz of conversation as speculation mounted about what was to follow.

"Quiet," snapped McNulty. "Pay attention to the lieutenant."

Anthony nodded his approval and began his presentation.

"I have been given information that later this evening the IRA is planning to move a shipment of arms out of Galway to somewhere in Connemara." A buzz of voices broke out again. Anthony waved his pointer at them and it ceased as quickly as it had begun.

"Wait until I've finished, then you can talk, but keep quiet until then and listen carefully. We are going to intercept it and capture it together with those involved. If we succeed, as I'm sure we will, we will have struck a severe blow against the Galway Brigade of the IRA.

The plan the sergeant and I have prepared is to ambush the truck they will be using at this point here", he indicated the boreen marked with the large red cross. It's the perfect spot for an ambush. Correct sergeant?"

"Yes surr. Couldn't be more perfect." He was pleased to be consulted.

"The truck will be coming up this track towards the boreen which is about a mile up. It won't be able to travel fast because it's an old Drovers track that hasn't see a lot of use since the new road was built.

We will make a check point at the mouth of the boreen and halt the truck, just as if it was a routine check point. But we know the two men in the truck will be armed and are dangerous, so we plan to do this.

I will signal the truck to stop, and I'll have one of you with me to cover me. The sergeant will allocate you to your positions once we are on site. There will be two men to cover the lower side, and on the top side sergeant McNulty will be stationed with the Lewis gun and a mate to help him. We will only open fire if the van fails to stop.

As a back up, I want the remainder of you to be in our second van and stationed in the yard behind these two farm houses here," he pointed them out.

"You must be out of sight from the road. Once the IRA truck has turned off the road on to the track, you follow about half a mile behind it so they don't see your lights too easily. This will cut off any escape they may try to make. Is everybody clear what we're trying to do?"

"Just one thing, surr," McNulty interjected, "what happens to our van once we've unloaded an' set things up?"

"I want the driver to park it about twenty yards up from the end of the boreen, so that it will block the track. The driver can stay with it and in the unlikely event that someone makes a run for it through the boreen, he can shoot him." McNulty was satisfied. It was a sensible safeguard, but with the firepower planted so strategically, he was confident nothing would get through.

"Any questions?" Anthony asked, but there was no response. "Very well, no one leaves the barracks from this moment on."

"Prepare your gear and make sure your rifles are cleaned and oiled. We set out at eight o'clock. That gives us plenty of time to check out the site and set everything up. Sergeant McNulty has drawn kit and ammunition from stores."

He took down his drawing from the notice board and told McNulty to dismiss the men. "Be on parade fifteen minutes before we go. I want to inspect them personally. I want no slip ups."

He retired to his office and sat down at his desk feeling drained. He felt his plan was quite sound and he had presented it effectively. The men had seemed excited about the prospect of action after the long weeks of inactivity, but despite all the positive factors, he knew he was taking a big risk. If the plan failed, he would have both the Garda and army commanders howling for his blood.

He opened the bottom drawer and took out the half bottle of Bushmills that lay under some papers along with a small medicine glass. He poured himself a generous measure and gulped it down. It was a comforting feeling and eased his tension. He sat for a few moments twirling the empty glass between his fingers, reviewing the forthcoming action and trying to find any weaknesses that might exist in his plan.

He refilled the glass, and commenced to sip it slowly and then set the glass down to pull out his gold cigarette case from his top pocket, and lit a cigarette. He swung his legs and planted his boots on the desk. He could see no problems provided the men stuck to their training.

He puffed contentedly at his cigarette as he relaxed, and looked fondly at the cigarette case before he replaced it in his pocket. It was his most valuable possession and he loved to show it off, but he never allowed anyone to read the inscription that adorned the inner lid.

He indulged in a little speculation. If his plan succeeded, and a promotion followed that would get him posted back to Dublin, would she still find him irresistible?

Both vans loaded with men and equipment left the barracks at precisely eight o' clock. The streets of Galway were deserted and there were no witnesses to see them leave.

When they reached the two farmhouses at the side of the road, both vans drove into the rear yard and Anthony and McNulty leapt out and roused the occupants.

They were all from one family of farmers and shocked when they saw the army uniforms.

"There will be military action on this road to-night," he warned them brusquely, "for your own safety stay indoors and keep out of sight. Some of my men will stay here to make sure that you do."

He left the van with his corporal and four men whilst the other van with himself, McNulty, and five privates proceeded up the Drovers track. They stopped fifty yards from the proposed check point whilst Anthony swept the area with his field glasses.

He could see nothing out of the ordinary. They inspected the boreen minutely, eyes combing it for any signs of booby traps, and after a thorough inspection, were satisfied that the area was clean.

"Looks like our informant was correct," Anthony told McNulty. "Get the men allotted to their positions and set the Lewis gun up at a point on the high side where you can cover both entrance and exit. Give me one man who's a good shot. If for any reason the driver is stupid enough to charge us at the entrance, I want someone who'll pick him off first. Get that old gate we saw set up at the front. It's not much of a barrier, but it'll have to do."

By nine o'clock everything was in position and Anthony was satisfied he had an impregnable position. He ordered no smoking and the men to keep well hidden. Dusk was falling and he wanted to ensure there were no signs that would give them away. Surprise was a big element in his plan.

McNulty had found a useful position on the rocks on the top side of the boreen, but could not cover both front and rear from a fixed position. On his own initiative he decided to cover the exit only. He could not imagine a truck breaking through the barrier and surviving with three rifles and the lieutenant's pistol firing at it, but if it did get through, he would blast it before it reached the exit.

For the umpteenth time he checked the elevation and squinted through the gunsight, checking his arc of fire. It might be difficult to get a good shot at the tyres, but if it came to that he could fire from a standing position.

"Pass us a drum o' ammo," he asked his mate, "we'll load it now an' be ready in plenty o' time. The private prised open the ammunition box and swore softly.

"What's up?" asked McNulty.

"We've got tracer bullets instead o' the normal.303"

"Check again. All the drums can't be the same." He looked for himself and cursed.

"Some eejit put these drums in the wrong box. They're all the same. Bliddy hell! I'll have that storeman's guts fer garters when we git back."

"What'll we do sarge?

McNulty was devastated. Everything was supposed to have been checked meticulously, but no one had thought to look inside the ammunition box. They had assumed the bullets were the standard issue because the code number on the box indicated it was. The lieutenant would be furious.

Tracer would give away their position the minute they opened fire, but that was not his biggest concern. At such close range the bullets would be flaming and would act like incendiaries. Supposing the truck was carrying explosives as well as guns?

"What'll we do sarge?" the private continued to badger him." Will it be OK to load it?"

McNulty was sweating. His stomach was turning over, but he made his decision.

"It's all we've got, we'll have to use it. With any luck we may not need to open fire. The boys below will probably stop them. If we do fire, at least we'll see where the bullets are hittin' the target." He did not bother to explain his misgivings about the possibility of explosives being in the truck.

McNulty crouched low against a rock, trying to make himself comfortable. In the gathering twilight the excitement was building. It was becoming cooler as night fell, but he was sweating profusely. The waiting was always the worst, and his responsibility with the Lewis gun had now increased tenfold.

Anthony checked his watch. It was almost ten o'clock and something should be happening soon. He lit the oil lamp he had brought to use as a signal, and hid it behind a rock covered with a blanket to conceal it.

He drew out a Very pistol from its box and loaded a flare. Once the van was within fifty yards, he would signal it to stop using the lamp, and then fire the pistol. The flare would illuminate the truck and its occupants and give them little chance to escape.

He explained all this to McNulty and to Private O'Leary, who the sergeant had assigned as his cover at the barrier. O'Leary was not one of the brightest, but he was a good shot.

"I'll be covering the driver with my revolver, and you cover the fellah in the passenger seat. I'll only fire if they refuse to stop, so don't fire until I do. Understand?"

If possible he would prefer to capture them alive.

Intelligence could possibly extract information from them which would make his contribution all the more valuable.

The group were getting restless. It was five minutes past ten on his watch and still no sign of the truck. Darkness had fallen and his eyes strained down the track seeking the signs of approaching lights that he hoped to see.

He silently cursed Father O'Donnell. Had they been sent on a wild goose chase? Suddenly he caught his breath. In the distance he saw two pin pricks of light, swaying unevenly as they negotiated the uneven track towards them.

"Get ready everyone," he commanded. "Check your weapons. Remember don't fire unless I do."

He laid the Very pistol on the rock beside him and took his revolver from the holster, and for the second time in as many minutes checked that it was fully loaded. He snapped the chamber shut and replaced it in the holster and lifted the Very pistol.

His mouth was dry, and his hands shook slightly. He could hear the engine now, a steady growling noise as it toiled in low gear over the track. Only four hundred yards now. The headlights were brighter, the engine noise increasing. He calculated the point fifty yards from where he was standing and prepared to fire the Very pistol when it reached that point

He was eager to identify the two men who would be in the cab. Would one be Maguire himself? He raised the Very pistol into the air and prepared to fire.

Chapter Forty-Five

Maguire and Rafferty had arrived at Ballanalee shortly after eight o' clock and found the van parked in the yard. It was a thirty hundred weight vehicle, substituted for the original truck which had developed an engine problem at the last minute. They entered the house to find Seamus and Cassidy, the driver, seated around the fire with Devlin, drinking tea and chatting, obviously in good humour.

"The pot's still warm," Devlin greeted them.

"No time for that," snapped Maguire, "it's time you' started to load. This place has gotta be cleared an' quick at that."

"You haven't explained what's goin' on an' where are we takin' all the stuff anyway? What's Rafferty needed for?" Devlin made no attempt to hide his scorn.

"I've told you nuthin' for your own safety. Rafferty's here in his capacity as quartermaster because we're taking a stock check as we clear out everything. It's all bein' shifted to Connemara. That's all you need to know."

"Isn't it safe enough here?" Devlin asked.

"Not any longer. That bliddy lieutenant is becoming too curious about this place." Maguire found the lie easy to make, and it sounded convincing.

"That gobshite! We should'ave taken care o' him after he beat up Dev." Seamus spoke bitterly.

"Don't fash yourself. I've got plans for him," Maguire answered. But this comes first. I want all the ammunition, gelignite, and the bomb makin' stuff loaded first. Be very careful, especially wi' the box o' detonators. Cushion it between these sacks o' fertilizer that you've been experimentin' with Dev."

"I don't know if that's a good idea. Some o' that's already converted to Nitrate. It's highly explosive. Do we really have to move it?"

"Yes. Everythin's got to go. Pack it as you see fit. You're the explosives expert. Just take care. Rafferty will take the inventory as you load it. You're to hand the load over to the boys from Mayo. They'll transfer it an' take it to Belfast. You come straight back here after the drop."

"Where do we meet them?" Seamus asked.

"I've a map here." Maguire spread it out on the table. "You'll go from here on the main road as if you were headin' for Ochterarder. About two miles from the village, you turn on to the old Drovers road. It cuts across country and comes out on the main road the other side o' the Cross. You've used that track Dev. It's still good an' it avoids the Garda check point at the Cross."

"It's a good way to avoid the check point, but I'm not sure about takin' a van. There's a pretty narrow boreen on it which will be a tight fit."

"This is only a thirty hundred weight. It'll make it easy. You'll be travellin' slow anyway."

"Who's drivin'?"

"You are. You know the track. Mick can swop for the return."

"You mean I'm not goin'?" Seamus was shocked.

"Not this time. I need you for other things."

"But I always go wi' Dev. We're a team. We know each other's thinkin'."

"Maybe so. But Mick's goin' this time. I've got other plans I need you for."

Devlin joined the protest. "I'm not happy. I'd rather have Seamus. Mick's a clumsy ox."

"Shut your gobs the pair o' you!" Maguire was building into one of his tempers, "I'm givin' the orders, an' am tellin' you Mick is goin'. Now shut up. We need to outta here before ten, so get loadin'"

He handed the map to Devlin. "Once off the track, keep headin' north. Watch out for the junction to Westport. About a mile after you fork off, you'll see a sign for a farm called Ballycraig. Turn in there an' you'll find the boys waitin' for you.

Make sure they know all the safety precautions to take. Then head back here. I reckon it'll take about two hours each way, maybe a little more if you take it real slow."

The territory was familiar to Devlin, so he had no further questions, but he was still smarting over the loss of his usual companion. He was at a loss to understand what other work he could want Seamus for.

But there was no time to dwell on the matter. Maguire hustled them into loading the van. It was already nine o' clock and the dusk had commence to fall.

They emptied each outbuilding in turn, Maguire supervising and Rafferty compiling his inventory. The gelignite was sandwiched carefully between two large sacks of fertilizer, and the detonators packed between two other sacks well away from the gelignite. There were several sacks to load, each one weighing a hundredweight, but difficult to handle because of the bulk. Mick found it the hardest because of his hefty paunch.

One of the sacks had been placed on a low shelf and he had grasped it awkwardly, trying to secure it better by hugging it tight as he could. He was moving backwards when the sacking caught on a protruding nail.

He wrenched brutally to free it, and the canvas ripped, sending him off balance to crash to the floor still clutching the sack. There was a sickening crack and a scream of pain as his arm took the full weight.

"Mother o' God," he screamed, "me arm's broken. Git this bliddy sack offa me. Hurry up fer God's sake."

Seamus rushed to heave the sack away and gasped when he saw the blood flowing and part of the bone sticking out of the sleeve. Mick continued to scream.

Seamus looked to his father. "You'll need to get him to McCrimmond. It looks bad." As he spoke he ripped a strip of cloth from Mick's shirt and wound it round the top of his arm to stop the loss of blood. He looked again at his father.

Maguire stared back, his face expressionless, but his eyes glared annoyance.

"Just what we could'a done without," he said sourly, "bliddy fool!"

Mick lay at his feet whimpering and moaning. "Shut up moanin' for God's sake. We'll get you to McCrimmond."

"I'll go with Dev then," Seamus said.

"I said I wanted you elsewhere, didn't I?"

"Well there's only Rafferty or me. Dev can't go on his own."

"I'm, not goin' with Rafferty," Devlin was adamant.

"I want Seamus."

Maguire looked at them both, seemingly lost for words. His brain was racing trying to cope with a dilemma he had not foreseen. His well nurtured plan could not afford to fail. The fiendishness of it had him trapped. He had to go ahead or be exposed. He struggled to answer.

Seamus took the decision out of his hands.

"Let's get this last sack on the van Dev. Then we're off. Himself an' Rafferty can get Mick to the doctor."

They lifted the bloodstained sack and closed the tailgate. Maguire watched in stony silence. His brain was in total confusion. He walked to the outbuildings and made a quick inspection, satisfying himself that they were all clear. They were waiting around the van when he came back, his face still grim and impassive.

"Right then. It's seems to be all there. Nuthin' left in the house?"

"Nuthin' at all," Devlin answered.

"You leavin' that lamp lit?" Maguire indicated the light in the window.

"Always do. Makes it look occupied."

"On your way then. Keep your eyes skinned. Did you give Dev the inventory?" Maguire fired the question at Rafferty.

"I did. There's enough nearly a ton in that load. Enough to blow up half o' Belfast. For Christ's sake be careful."

Devlin climbed into the driver's seat as Seamus moved to the front of the van where he placed one hand on the radiator and seized the starting handle in his large fist. He swung the handle several times without success, but on the fifth swing the engine burst into life.

He clambered into the passenger seat without a backward glance at his father. Devlin released the handbrake and put the engine in gear, moving slowly out of the yard.

Maguire stood motionless watching it disappear through the trees, his arms by his side, as if at standing to attention. Rafferty thought it strange.

Maguire motioned him into the truck and they set off for Galway without a further word being exchanged. Only the continual moaning of Mick in the back of the van broke the strange silence between the two men.

Now and again Rafferty stole a glance at Maguire, expecting him to say something, but he continued to stare ahead as if in a trance, occasionally biting his lip as if suppressing a comment.

Rafferty put it down to anxiety. Shipping a load of explosives was always a risky business, but in Seamus and Dev the load was in good hands.

He was not to know the battle that had gone on in Maguire's mind, nor the attempt still going on to salve his conscience. In the end he consoled himself by recalling that many a brave man had died for the cause. Posterity would remember his son as one of many brave martyrs and the credit for that would be reflected on him. His conscience began to ease.

Chapter Forty-Six

They had not spoken a word from the moment they turned off the main road on to the Drovers track. Both had their attention concentrated on the terrain. Seamus watched the off side, where there was a steep drop into the ditch that bordered the marshes, and Devlin concentrated in keeping as straight a course as he could. He was familiar with the track, for his excursions to the north often required him to use it.

His only real concern was the boreen. He was thankful that they were using the smaller van instead of the original truck. There would be more clearance, and with a load of this nature extreme care was necessary, especially as the darkness increased and they were relying on the headlights to see the way.

They were stunned when suddenly a light appeared roughly a hundred yards ahead and, in the same instant there was a flash, and a flare arced into the sky, illuminating the scene like daylight.

In the light they could see an Army officer swinging a lantern and hailing them to stop.

Immediately behind him stood a soldier with his rifle raised to his shoulder.

There was a barrier that appeared to be an ordinary field gate placed in front of the boreen.

"Jaysus Christ!" Seamus swore. "It's the feckin' army. What the hell are they doin' here?"

"Christ knows, but it looks like a check point. They're never on this road. We've been set up."

He switched off the headlights and let the engine idle. The lamp continued to wave and the voice called upon them to come out of the van with their hands up and approach the barrier. The flare above sputtered out and fell to earth. In the illumination provided by the flare, Devlin had recognised the officer as Dillon and had seen the glint of the gun he held in his hand. The army had no business here. The Garda normally manned the road checks. If Dillon had taken the law into his own hands, he had no doubt the lieutenant was prepared to use his gun.

"What are you thinkin'? Seamus asked. He pulled his revolver from the waistband of his pants. "Should we take them on?"

"We don't know how many there are for one thing. I bet that boreen's full o' them. They couldn't have chosen a better spot. We wouldn't have a chance."

"What then?"

"I can reverse. Slip out an' let the tailgate down, so as I can see better. Drop into the ditch and cover me. Shoot if they open fire and keep alongside. You can warn me if I get too near the edge."

Seamus opened his door and slid out cautiously. He undid the tailgate and slid on his belly into the ditch. He felt it was a desperate idea, but he had no alternative, and Dev was one of the best drivers he knew. Perhaps they could distance themselves enough to make a run for it. If there were more men in the boreen, they'd have to come out, and that gave them a better chance in a stand off. He cocked the revolver in readiness to fire, but as he crouched down to shout guidance, he froze.

There were headlights coming up the track towards them, no more than two hundred yards away. He scrambled alongside the cab.

"Hold it Dev. There's more o' the bastards. There's another van comin' up the track. They've boxed us in. Let's make a run fer it."

"Across the marsh? No chance. They'd pick us off like rabbits. Same thing if we tried to go up the rise. There's no cover anywhere."

"Oh, Jaysus. Sweet Jaysus! This is a feckin' mess."

"This is a well planned trap. Somebody's shopped us an' no mistake. Listen Seamus, I want you to do what I tell you. No arguments, right?"

Seamus nodded agreement even although he did not know what Devlin had in mind. His loyalty was such that he would have followed Dev to hell and back.

"Stay in the ditch. Keep low an' start movin' towards the boreen. Go as fast as you can without bein' seen. That barricade's only an old gate. Wouldn't stop a baby's pram. I'm goin' to smash through it. I think I can make it.

If you make a dash for it, loose off a couple o' rounds at these two. It could put them off long enough for me to crash through. Run like hell to the far side. If I make it, be ready to jump on the runnin' board as I come through. Then we'll high tail it smartly."

"That's crazy, Dev. Let's jest shoot it out from here."

"That's even more crazy! With a ton o' explosives on top 'o us?"

"One o' us has to get back an' find out who shopped us. Catrin will be at Ballananlee, waitin' for me. She needs to get outta there in a hurry! This is the best chance. For Christ's sake go, Seamus. We can't stop here arguing about it." The approaching headlights were drawing closer and it was clearly another small military van. The odds were now overwhelming.

At that moment a shot rang out, and Seamus dived hastily into the ditch. Impatient with the lack of response from the van, Anthony had fired a shot into the air. He could see his other van advancing steadily and he hoped the two men would realise the hopelessness of their situation, and come out with their hands in the air.

Seamus floundered for a moment. The coldness of the water took his breath away and he could feel his boots filling up. He managed to hold his revolver clear, and started to claw his way along, sliding and slithering in the glue-like mud that clung to his boots. He was desperate to try and get within range and take a shot at the barrier, but he had not appreciated the difficulty.

He heard the engine roar and Devlin moved forward slowly. It appeared he was approaching the check point as if to stop, but suddenly the engine roared and the van surged forward, increasing speed every second.

The headlights came on catching Anthony in the glare. It was an unexpected act, so suicidal that he had a hard job to accept that it was really happening.

More by instinct than speed of thought, he raised his revolver and loosed off two shots at the windscreen as the van careered towards him.

Devlin ducked in time as the windscreen was punctured. The first bullet whizzed past his head, but the second caught him in the shoulder causing him to yell in pain. The van swerved, but he held it in control. Coupled with the swerve, Seamus managed to loose two rounds that whistled close enough to Private O'Leary to put him off aim.

Anthony screamed at him to fire, but he was slow to react and in another instant the van was almost upon them.

Anthony shot wildly as he realised the van was not going to stop. He leapt aside, scrambling to hold on to the rocks on the side as the van thundered past, smashing into the flimsy gate and sending the splinters flying as it crashed through. On the opposite side O'Leary was less fortunate as he lost his footing and plunged into the ditch.

Anthony regained his feet and ran after the van firing until his gun was empty. The two men stationed on the lower side were shooting at the van in quick succession as he screamed at McNulty to open fire with the Lewis gun.

Whose bullet found the fatal mark would never be known, but with less than twenty feet to go before clearing the boreen, the van suddenly swerved and hit the lower rock wall and cannoned off it to slam into the other side.

The impact raised the rear wheels off the ground, in the same instant as a deadly stream of flaming tracer bullets from the Lewis gun sped into the load in the back of the van.

The military enquiry that later followed concluded that the tracer bullets had hit the petrol tank and the fire had set off the explosives. Whatever the actual cause, the impact of the tracer was catastrophic.

Anthony gaped in disbelief when he heard the Lewis gun open up and saw the stream of tracer bullets fly into the back of the van. He was only ten yards from it when there was a blinding white light, followed instantly by a huge ball of fire and a deafening explosion which echoed for miles around.

Had the explosion taken place on open ground, the effects would have been less drastic. Much of the blast would have dissipated upwards and outwards, but confined in the narrow walls of the boreen, the effects were catastrophic.

The huge blast was propelled back through the narrow channel which acted like a funnel to concentrate the effects. Anthony was the first victim, engulfed by the fireball that turned him into a pillar of fire and sent him flying to smash against the rocks. The two privates on the lower wall were struck by a hail of splintered rocks like shrapnel and blown twenty yards to land in the marshes. Senseless and badly injured, they drowned in a few inches of water.

On the top side, McNulty was lucky. He had flung himself behind the rocks on which he had mounted the Lewis gun and escaped with a few cuts from flying rock splinters. His mate was less fortunate. He had been slower to react than the sergeant and was blown yards away to die through the loss of blood from a severed artery.

The reserve van with the corporal and four privates had just reached the entrance to the boreen when the blast hit them. It lifted the front of the van several feet in the air and threw it like a toy against the upper bank where it flipped over and fell back on its roof. The soldiers in the back were thrown clear into the ditch and escaped with broken limbs, but the corporal and the driver were trapped in the cabin and died in the fire that followed.

Seamus was only yards off the entrance to the boreen when Devlin smashed through the barrier. As he stumbled through the cloying mud he heard a cry and saw a figure floundering in the ditch a few yards ahead.

It was a soldier, on his knees, blinded by mud and desperately searching to regain his rifle. Seamus raised his revolver and fired. A single shot and the look of surprise on the soldier's face as he slowly sank back into the ditch was a picture he would remember for a long time.

He continued to slosh forward as fast as he could clear his feet from the mud. Devlin could not afford to be held up. He gasped as he heard the Lewis gun open up and in the same instant the sky lit up with the sudden burst of intense white light. Instinctively he flung himself down and flattened himself against the side of the ditch. He felt the searing heat of the blast as it tore through the boreen above his head. He screamed to relieve the pressure on his ears of the explosion and covered his head with his hands as pieces of rock showered all around him. One fragment flew into his face, causing a gash in his cheek and blood flowed.

He screamed again knowing the worst had happened. He scrambled to his feet and once again desperately clawed his way through the mud. His heart sank as he beheld the blazing mass, the flames leaping thirty feet in the air. Ammunition was popping off erratically like firecrackers. Only the chassis of the van remained, twisted into an unrecognisable tangle, and it was obvious that Devlin had stood no chance of survival. There was no time to mourn.

He raised his head cautiously over the top of the ditch and recoiled in surprise as he saw an army van parked in the middle of the track no more than twenty feet from him. It was facing the opposite way.

"Be Jaysus," he muttered softly, "how many more?"

He crouched low and crept forward, and risked another glance. Only one soldier in the cab. At that very moment the driver's door opened and the private stepped out and started to advance cautiously towards the boreen, his rifle held across his body. His gaze was riveted on the inferno. He was completely unaware of Seamus's stealthy approach from behind. The single shot that disposed of him went unnoticed in the explosions of stray ammunition that continued to go off.

The keys were still in the ignition. A minute later he was speeding down the track, away from the boreen, racing to get to the main road before the Garda appeared on the scene. The whole of Ireland must have heard the blast and already there could be someone on the way to investigate.

He was on the main road in minutes and turned back towards Galway. There was a short cut known only to locals, a single track road that would lead across country to Ballanalee. A road that was difficult to drive on in the dark, even with the faint moon, but there would be no traffic to contend with at that time of night.

It was a pulsating race, but his knowledge of the road was good and he negotiated the tricky turns with expert handling. He slowed down as he got closer to Ballanlee, and stopped completely at the entrance to the yard, attempting to gather his wits and compose himself for the dreadful news he would have to give Catrin.

The oil lamp in the window glowed a welcome, just as Devlin had intended, and a pang of regret passed through his mind as he realised it would welcome him no more.

He drove cautiously into the yard and drew up facing the door. He shut off the engine and switched the headlamps off, and sat quivering as the enormity of the disaster finally hit home.

He tried desperately to gather his thoughts. He should have stayed close. He should have killed the two at the barrier. The bile rose in his throat. He should have done more to save Devlin.

He was not prepared for this. All he wanted at this moment was comfort and sanctuary, the things he had been denied most of his life. He staggered to the door and pounded upon it with all his strength.

He felt no pain. It helped ease his mental agony to beat something, but the effort drained him and he slumped against the door in his misery, the tears flowing down his cheeks as emotion overcame him and he sobbed his heart out.

Chapter Forty-Seven

In Dublin, Catrin had been on pins for several days awaiting word from Devlin. When the call finally came, it was alarming.

"You have to get here right away. There's a job on to-morrow night. Maguire's given no details, but I believe it's a quick trip to Connemara. Once it's over, it'll be a good chance to sneak away. Everythin's laid on. We'll probably be back in the early hours. You be in the house an' ready to go an' we'll be on the water before they realise we're gone."

Catrin had expected to move quickly, but this almost too sudden.

"Can't we go from Danlogaire? It would be easier to meet you there."

"No, sweetheart. Time's against us. Besides there's too many eyes watchin' there. The route I have is safer."

"I'll have to get the early morning train. Can you meet me?"

"I can't. Maguire's too close to me, an' Seamus doesn't know about this, so I move without questions being asked. Could you get Daniel instead?"

"Of course. But he'll be suspicious."

"You can handle him. He worships you even more than I do."

"I know, but I hate taking advantage of him."

"This is for our future, Catrin. We may never get another chance. Maguire's already planning for England. I want out before that happens."

"I understand. I'll work something out."

"What about your parents?

"They're not here. They've gone to England for a few days. There's a big printing machinery exhibition in Birmingham. Da wanted me to go but I said I needed to work at my writing. There's no problem getting away, but it means I won't be able to say goodbye."

"Our goodbyes will have to come from America, otherwise we'd never get out of the country. I'll leave the lamp in the window as usual. Seamus will drop me off, an' as soon as he's gone we can be off. I've arranged for transport an' everthin' else is organised. Take care. I'll see you soon."

Catrin put the phone down, her mind in a whirl. The lesser of her immediate problems was her parents. They would be away for another two or three days and she would simply have to leave them a note.

Her grandfather was no problem. She telephoned and asked if he would meet her off the train, and although he was surprised, he readily agreed. Her next problem was what to take with her. She managed to cram what seemed the most practical choice into one large suitcase.

A taxi took her to the station in the morning and just after lunch time she was in Galway and found Daniel at the station waiting for her. For once Mrs. Donavan was pleased to see her. Their combined efforts to nurse Devlin had changed her attitude, and they were on a first name basis with each other.

It was after tea when she summoned the courage to tackle Daniel.

"Danna," she said demurely, "would it be alright if I borrowed the trap to go over to Ballanalee?"

"Of course. When d'you want it?"

"This evening. I'd like to see Devlin before he goes off for a few days. I'm at a critical place in my story about his painting, and I need to ask him a few things."

"Oh Catrin. You've only just arrived. Does it have to be to-night?"

"You'll need to go before it gets dark. I can drive "I'm sorry Danna. But he's to be off early in the morning."

It was the only plausible excuse she could think of, although there was a glimmer of truth in it. Daniel could be twisted around Catrin's little finger very easily.

Catrin convinced him to let her go on her own, and daringly suggested that it would be better for her to stay the night at Ballanalee rather than have him worry about her returning in the dark.

Daniel had been aware of the relationship building up with Devlin for some time, ever since the fine job she had done in helping him recover from his beating. There were many cases of the nurse falling in love with the patient, and vice versa, but they usually came to an end once recovery took place. This affair did not seem like that to him. What he would have to explain to Roderick and Megan was the thing that troubled him most. It was much later when Catrin drove the trap into the yard at Ballanalee, and the last part of the journey was in darkness.

She unhitched the pony and turned it into the field beside Devlin's cob and the donkey, and pushed the trap into the hay shed out of the way.

The oil lamp in the window gave the house a homely look. The door was on the latch and she pushed it open and entered cautiously. She found the matches on the mantle shelf and lit the lamp on the kitchen table to provide more light.

The peat fire glowed softly and she swung the kettle over it to boil water for tea. She sat in the high backed chair and reviewed her thoughts. What would her parents think, especially her father who had pinned such hopes on her joining the business?

She could only imagine the shock when they discovered the purpose behind her sudden visit to Dungannon House. They knew very little about Devlin. They would never understand how much she loved this man, and how desperate she was to save him from the evil forces that would destroy him.

The silence inside and outside was intense. She was not sure of the exact time Devlin had left on his mission, but he had suggested it would be in the early hours of the morning before he returned.

The temptation was to go to bed in the loft, but she decided to sit and cat nap by the fire instead. Devlin would not want to linger when he returned in order to be well on their way before Maguire had the chance to find out.

Her emotions were strained to breaking point. She needed sleep. She blew out the lamp on the table and put a few more turves on the fire before settling back in the chair. She was fast asleep in minutes.

It was a deep sleep, and how long she has slept she did not know, but she awoke with a start to hear the sound of a vehicle rattling into the yard. The rays of light from the headlamps shone through the windows and then the engine stopped and the lights went out.

An agonizing silence followed. Her heart started to pound. Instinctively she knew something was wrong. It couldn't be Devlin. It was too early and he would have been rushing to meet her. She rose from the chair and crept towards the door.

She was almost there when she heard a door slam shut and footsteps that appeared to stumble towards the house. They did not sound like Devlin's steps, and her panic increased. A voice startled her.

"Catrin, are you there? It's Seamus. Let me in, please", he sounded in distress.

As she opened the door he fell into her arms, dishevelled, covered in mud, his eyes staring wide, his face white and strained. Dried blood caked his temple and there was a nasty bruise on his cheek.

"Oh my God!" she cried, "what's happened? Where's Devlin?" She hauled him inside then wedged her shoulder under his armpit and struggled to get him to the seat by the fire. She ran to the cupboard in the recess and brought out the small bottle of spirit she knew was always there. Her hands trembled as she poured a measure into her empty teacup and thrust it into his hands.

"Sip this. Take your time, Seamus. When you're ready, tell me what happened." She knelt down by his side.

He ignored her advice and gulped a mouthful, but then sipped the remainder before lowering the cup and handing it back.

"Thanks," he mumbled.

Catrin was close to screaming. He had said nothing about Devlin. Surely he must know how anxious she was. But Seamus leaned back wearily in the chair and his eyes were closing.

"Seamus," she shook his arm. "Seamus don't go to sleep, please. Please answer me. Please, please!" she pleaded, "where's Devlin. Why isn't he with you?"

He sat up and opened his eyes, hunching towards the fire, staring into it as if it would help his memory.

"I don't know how to tell you Catrin."

"Something's happened to him? Is it bad?"

He nodded. "He's dead Catrin. He's gone. We were set up. Ambushed by the Army. We tried to get away, but they had us trapped."

She screamed and burst into tears, all the pent up tension released in one agonizing shriek, her head pressed against his leg, her nails digging into his flesh as if to transfer her pain to him. He placed his arm gently around her and pulled her closer to let her sob her heart out. She cried helplessly for several minutes and he waited patiently for her to regain her composure.

"They were waitin' for us, about a dozen o' them, all in position, even a machine gun. I was for leavin' the van an' shootin' it out, but Dev said it would be hopeless. He told me to jump out an' make for the end of the boreen while he would drive the van straight through the check point. He reckoned he could do it. He was countin' on takin' them by surprise."

"What happened?"

"He was almost through. Another few yards an' he would've been clear. Then this bliddy machine gun they had opened up. It hit somethin' in the load an' the whole lot went up in flames."

"It blew up and Devlin was still in it?"

He nodded, his eyes downcast, afraid to look at her. She staggered to her feet and fled into the yard. He stumbled after her and found her leaning over the yard wall, retching and vomiting.

He held her head to support her and waited patiently until she had exhausted herself. He led her back to the house and sat her by the fire. She lay back in the chair, her eyes closed, and whimpering softly.

"Take a sip o' this," he said, offering the teacup. She shook her head.

"C'mon now. A sip. It'll settle your stomach."

She reluctantly allowed herself a small sip. She shuddered as the fiery spirit bit at her throat, but it masked the foul taste of vomit in her mouth. She took another tiny sip and handed him back the cup.

"Tell me more," she begged in a shaky voice.

He related their disbelief at finding a check point at the boreen and how they had found themselves boxed in. Devlin realised it was a planned ambush. He told her how they had recognised the army lieutenant who commanded them to surrender.

"A lieutenant?" Catrin asked, an awful thought flashing through her mind.

"Aye. The one... the one that beat up Dev"

"Anthony. Oh my God! "

He explained how Devlin had ordered him to get back here and to get you away before the Garda or the Army came lookin'.

Catrin began to sob again. Through the tears she asked,

"Why couldn't he have made a run for it too?" she sobbed.

"Like I said, he thought he could make it. He wouldn't have tried if he didn't think he could do it. He came close. Only a few yards more an' he'd have made it."

"So you think someone told the army?"

"For sure. They'd never have set up a check point there, nor would they have had so many men. They knew we were comin'. Dev told me to find out who set us up."

"Have you any ideas? Not yet. I still can't believe it's happened."

"So who knew about the mission?"

"Dev an' meself only knew about it yesterday. Da told us he had a tip off that the Garda would raid the place, so all the explosives had to be shifted. There was Mick Cassidy, who fetched the van, an' Rafferty the quartermaster, that's all."

"So it has to one of those three. Could Mick have done it?"

"No. Mick's as thick as two planks. He hates the army. They kilt his father."

"Could hardly be your father. That leaves Rafferty."

"I never liked that gobshite."

"Did he know the route you were going?"

"Maybe Da told him. I dunno." He rose from the chair and began to pace the floor, trying to muster his thoughts.

"Da wis the only one with the map. He said he'd kept everythin' secret for our safety. The only time Rafferty could'ave seen the map was at the same time as us."

"Perhaps they discussed it when the travelled over in the car?"

"Even if they did, he couldn't have contacted the army in time... he stopped abruptly as a sudden thought struck him. His face went very pale.

"What's the matter?"

"He acted so queer. He knows I always go with Dev. We're a team. Always have been. But he kept tellin' me not to go on this trip. Said he had other plans for me."

What sort of plans?"

"He wouldn't explain. Then Mick broke his arm, so he couldn't drive. Dev refused to take Rafferty, an' said he would only go with me."

"And your Da agreed?"

"That's what was strange. He just stood there cursin' Mick. He never said anythin'. It was gettin' late. Dev was anxious to get on the road. So we just finished loadin' and shot off. He never tried to stop us. He was still standin' in the yard. Never even waved us off."

His face was a mixture of grief, disbelief, and slowly turning to anger.

"Sweet Jaysus! I can't believe it. But it starts to make sense."

"That's a terrible thing to think Seamus. How could a father send his son into a deliberate trap?"

"His bliddy cause is the most important thing to him."

"Is there any way you could verify this?"

He thought deeply for a moment, and suddenly slapped his fist against his thigh.

"Yes, by God! I've just remembered somethin'. I'll need to leave you a while Catrin. I need to get back into town an' check somethin' out. I'll only be an hour or so. Put all the lights out an' stay outta sight. I'll be straight back, an' we'll high tail it outta here."

"Can't I come with you?"

"No. If it was my Da, I need to be the one to confront him. Listen now, keep this for me." He handed her his revolver. "If I should be stopped by the Garda I don't want them to find it on me. Keep it close by, but if the Garda should get here before I get back, hide it somewhere. In the soup pot if you have to."

He placed his hands on her shoulders and looked into her tear filled eyes. "I'll be back as soon as I can, an' I'll know the answer for sure."

He kissed her gently on the forehead and made his way out the door.

She stood watching the van disappear into the night and then turned back into the room. She sat at the fireside, a picture of complete misery, and the crying started all over again.

Chapter Forty-Eight

Catrin waited until the noise of the engine faded into the darkness. She was exhausted and felt a compulsion to lie down. She added turves to the fire and decided to climb into the loft and rest on the bed.

She took one oil lamp, leaving the downstairs in darkness, and climbed wearily into the loft, setting the lamp on the bedside table. She looked for a place to put Seamus's revolver, but there was no room on the small table. She pushed it out of the way under the pillow.

She sat on the edge of the bed, struggling to hold back the tears, wanting to lie down, and yet reluctant to do so. They had made wonderful love in this bed, warm magical events that had drawn her into a realm of pleasure that had enriched her soul.

They had given their love freely and joyously, and had in turn received each other's love with unfettered passion. She could not imagine she would ever love again. Her head throbbed and her whole body ached. It was not physical pain, but sheer stress as she fought to overcome her grief.

She summoned the strength to blow out the lamp and threw herself face down on the pillow, sobbing until she could sob no longer. She had no recollection of falling asleep.

A noise awoke her. There was a car entering the yard. She sat up, struggling to open her eyes and disperse the fog that clouded her brain. Her fuddled mind thought of Devlin. Then the shock. Devlin was not coming back. Not now. Not ever! It must be Seamus.

She groped for the matches to light the lamp, but her fingers were clumsy and knocked the matchbox to the floor. She was on her knees fumbling to find them when she heard the front door open. It banged heavily against the wall, then nothing but a silence, stark and foreboding.

Footsteps sounded on the hard floor, heavy steps with a measured tread, full of menace. She shivered. She had heard these footsteps before. The hairs rose on the nape of her neck, and her mouth went dry.

The footsteps halted and she heard the sound of a match being struck, and a ray of light indicated the intruder had lit the lamp on the kitchen table. The light moved as if the room was being explored.

She remained on her knees, sweating and fearing to move. Her heart was pounding and the palms of her hand were moist. She stifled a sob.

The intruder was searching for something. She cringed as she heard drawers ransacked, cupboards opened and crockery scattered. Under cover of the noise she crept to the hatch and peered cautiously into the room below.

The figure was across the room ransacking the work bench. He swept aside the brushes and paints, and sent the driftwood and tools to the floor. He threw paintings and frames after them, and then to her horror reached up and plucked The Wishing Boy from the wall.

He held the painting to the light as if seeking something, then hurled it to join the jumbled mass on the floor. As he turned around she saw his face in the lamplight and gasped in horror. It was the sight she feared most of all. Maguire was searching for something.

It would be a matter of minutes before he investigated the loft. She had to escape, and she was on the point of panicking.

The only escape was the tiny window that overlooked the lean-to. The roof was only two feet below the window sill, and if she could lower herself on to it, she could scramble on to the knoll at the rear, and escape across the field, or make her way down to the estuary and take the road to the village.

She inched towards the window, sweat beading her brow and her heart beating so loudly she thought he must hear it. She grasped the sill and levered herself to her feet. The noise downstairs continued as Maguire rummaged through the work bench and under cover of the noise she grasped the handles of the sash and tugged hard.

Her heart sank. It scarcely moved. The frame was swollen with damp. In desperation she attacked it more fiercely and this time it moved, slowly and reluctantly but not high enough. She was almost in tears as she made another effort, exerting all the strength she possessed and a prayer in her heart. The frame yielded, but there was a hideous squeal of tortured wood.

At that very moment Maguire paused to leaf through the set of papers in his hands, and the noise could have been heard a mile away. He moved swiftly to the foot of the ladder, pulling a gun from his coat pocket as he did so.

"Who's there? Come on now. I know you're up there. Better come down, an' be quick. I've a gun! I'll give you five seconds. Come down or I'll fire."

She remained rooted to the spot, struggling to control her bladder. The roar of the gun made her jump. As the bullet splintered the floor a few inches from her feet and zipped into the thatch, she screamed.

"What the hell," Maguire exclaimed, but he now had a clue. He climbed the ladder cautiously, the lamp in his left hand, and the gun in his right. He paused near the top, his ears straining for the sounds of movement.

Catrin had seen the light advancing up the ladder, and scrambled from the window to the opposite side of the bed where she crouched as low as possible.

She was petrified, and in desperation groped for the revolver under the pillow. It was heavy and cumbersome and required both hands to hold it, but if Maguire had been responsible for the death of Devlin, she would happily use it.

He set the lamp down on the floor, scanning the room cautiously and then climbed through the hatch. He lifted the lamp shoulder high to look closer.

"Come on Catrin. I know it's you. Come out where I can see you. Don't be frightened. I only want to talk." His voice was full of syrupy menace. She made no response.

"Damn you woman! Don't make it difficult. I don't want trouble."

She crouched lower. From under the bed she could see his feet moving towards her.

Maguire's patience snapped. "I haven't got all night. The Garda could be here at any moment." But the silence continued.

"For Christ's sake come out you stupid bitch! Enough playin' about."

He advanced closer and smiled grimly as he made out where she was. She raised herself on her knees and rested her arms on the bed, the revolver held in both hands, wavering slightly, but trained on him.

"That's near enough," she warned, "don't come any closer."

He froze. "Where did you get that?"

"Never you mind. I've got it and I'll use it if you come a step nearer."

Maguire slid one foot forward. Testing her resolve.

"I'm warning you. I know how to use it." As she spoke, a wave of panic surged through her. Seamus had not shown her anything. He had simply given it to her for safe keeping. She had never fired a handgun in her life.

The momentary glimmer of panic in her eyes was enough to convince Maguire to take the risk. He ignored the warning and stepped closer so as to illuminate her better. His trained eye took in the detail of the revolver and he breathed easier.

A Webley, army issue, but the safety catch was still on. He remained cautious. He was aware she was a determined and resourceful young woman, and a pretty one to boot. His lips moistened.

"Put the gun down, Catrin. It's far too heavy for such a delicate lass. Come on now. I'm not goin' to hurt you." He carefully set the lamp down on the table, his eyes glued to the wavering revolver which followed his every move.

But there was no move to lift the safety catch. A faint smile flickered across his face. She doesn't know.

"Why are you ransacking the place?" she asked.

"I'm making sure there's no incriminating evidence been left for the Army or the Garda to find."

"Are you expecting them?"

"It's very possible. They're active at the moment. Your former boyfriend is desperate for glory. He wants promotion."

"How do you know that?" She was stalling for time. How long had Seamus been gone? The gun wavered a little more.

"I know about him. People talk. He wants promotion that'll get him back to Dublin where he belongs. Galway's no place for him. We're too much like peasants for him," he spat the words out.

"So you made plans for him," her tone was scathing.

He moved cautiously to the side of the bed and knelt down opposite her. With great ceremony he laid his gun on the bedside table. Catrin straightened up in suspicion as he raised his hands in surrender.

"There now. How much more do I need to do to get you to trust me? Why not put your gun down? Then we can talk."

"I wouldn't trust you an inch. You're a slimy devious toad!"

His temper flared and his face was purple with rage.

"Why couldn't you leave it to Devlin to clean up?" she went on, "he could have done it without wrecking the place?"

Maguire was too enraged to think clearly. "You stupid cow! He wouldn't have done it. I had to do it. Devlin wasn't... he broke off as he suddenly realised what he was saying.

"Yes, you bastard! You knew Devlin wasn't coming back. You sent him into an ambush, didn't you? Not only that you sent your own son with him. May you rot in hell," she was crying again and fumbling with the gun but nothing happened.

Maguire sprang across the bed, grappling for the gun with one hand and chopping at her wrist with the other. He pulled her across the bed still struggling to free the gun. As he brutally wrenched it from her hand, he lost his grip, and it flew in an arc over his head to thud on the floor. It skidded along the floor boards and disappeared through the open hatch. It clattered and banged on every rung on the ladder on the way down to hit the floor. Miraculously it failed to go off.

He pinned her face down on the bed and held her firmly despite her struggles. He grabbed his gun from the table and jammed it against her temple.

"Now then, you bitch. Hold still or I'll blow your brains out."

She ceased to struggle. He wound his fingers around her hair and moved off the bed, yanking her around to lie face up. She screamed as he straddled her legs and held the gun barrel under her chin.

"Now, you red haired bitch. You've some questions to answer. What d'you mean by sayin' I sent Dev into an ambush?" He waved the gun under her nose.

"Answer me, dammit!" He struck her cheek savagely leaving an ugly red weal. She screamed with pain and struggled to free herself, but he was too heavy and had her in an iron grip.

"Don't try any more tricks. I'll ask you once more. How did you know about the ambush? Tell me dammit or I'll hit you again. I haven't got all night.

Who told you?" He raised his hand again to strike.

"I did." The voice came from behind him. His hand froze in mid air. He knew that voice.

"Seamus?" His question brought no response.

There was the unmistakable sound of a gun being cocked. It was his turn to sweat.

"Drop the gun. Drop it carefully on the floor. Do it now." The voice was calm and deadly serious. It couldn't be Seamus. He would never threaten his Da like that.

Maguire was in a bad position, sitting across her legs, his back to the threat. It would be difficult to turn around and fire. He shifted his weight from her legs and leaned over as if to drop the gun carefully to the floor, but then swivelled quickly to fire at his challenger.

Catrin felt the weight shift from her legs and in the same instant she heaved them upwards to throw Maguire off balance. He sprawled to the floor, his shot passing harmlessly into the wall.

Seamus gave him no chance to recover.

He fired with practised calm at the sprawling figure, and Catrin screamed as she heard the bullet thud home. It brought a sharp cry of pain. She scrambled from the bed and stumbled towards Seamus. He put one arm around her shoulder to comfort her, but the still smoking gun and his gaze were fixed on his father.

Maguire lay on his side, his face a picture of incredulity and pain. His left hand clutched his abdomen and blood was seeping through his fingers.

"For God's sake, Seamus. It is you! You've hurt me bad. Have you gone mad?" he groaned and lay on his back.

"Thank God you're alive! How did you get here? How did you manage to get away? What about Dev?" he sounded weary.

"I've been away doin' a little research, "Seamus said coldly. "I also managed to ditch the army van I escaped in from the ambush we walked into. That answer your questions?

I sunk the van in the old quarry and walked the rest of the way. Lucky I did, otherwise you might have heard me comin'. I saw the car in the yard an' then I heard Catrin scream".

Damn nearly tripped over my gun at the bottom o' the ladder. I know all about your plan for the night. I had a little chat wi' Father O'Donnell."

"What the hell would that little gobshite know?"

"Quite a lot. I remembered you got me to go to the church an' direct the lieutenant to his Confessional Box. I watched him go in."

"So what does that mean?" there was another groan.

"You gave the priest an envelope to pass on to the lieutenant. Bein' a curious man, he read it before he gave it to him. He hates your guts, so he does. He was very willing to tell me what was in it. A fine map you drew him an' all, with its little cross marked specially."

Maguire lay still, his face grey, clutching his abdomen and moaning softly. "The little gobshite," he muttered. He struggled to sit up and prop himself against the bedside table.

"I had to do it." He opened his eyes and looked at Seamus for sympathy but there was none. His right hand inched towards the bed where he had dropped his gun. The butt protruded slightly from underneath. The move was noted, but Seamus allowed it to continue as Maguire laboured to talk.

"Dev was goin' to run off with this bitch. The Command in Dublin would've ordered him kilt anyway. He knew too much to let him go. He could'ave sent us all to the gallows. You wanted the lieutenant dead as much as me. It was him who did for Maura. Doin' it this way was goin' to take care o' them both. I did it to save all o' us." I did it for the cause."

He was getting desperate as his weakness grew. The pain was excruciating and the pool of blood was growing.

"You and your bliddy cause! What about me," Seamus asked, "what did I do to deserve bein' sacrificed?"

"For God's sake, I tried to prevent you goin', you know that. I kept tellin' you I had other plans for you. I wanted you to stay put. If that stupid gobshite Mick hadn't fucked things up breakin' his arm, you'd have stayed. You'da been safe."

"Don't give me that shite," Seamus exploded, "you could'ave called it off. There wasn't goin' to be any raid on Ballinalee. I don't suppose there was any boys from Mayo either. You made it up so as to run your plan. You could'ave kilt the lieutenant any time you wanted. You wanted to do it in grand style an' have everyone think it was a great blow for the cause. Dublin an' Belfast would'ave liked that, wouldn't they?"

Maguire merely groaned, but his groping fingers had almost reached the gun. Seamus moved towards him.

"Dev would never have betrayed us. He was sick o' all the petty little bombin's an' killin' innocent people. He found other interests. He was runnin' off wi' Catrin to start a fresh life, that's all." He stepped forward and kicked the gun out of reach. Maguire looked at him with cold fury.

"Jaysus Christ! Have you no feelin's? You need to get me to hospital. For God's sake I'm hurtin' bad an' bleeding. You've got to do somethin' for me. I'm your own flesh and blood for Christ's sake. Hurry now. There'll be all hell let loose out there. The Garda could be here at any time. Get me to hospital an' then make a run for it."

Seamus ignored him. He turned to Catrin.

"Go down an' make some tay," he told her, "put a drop o' precious in it for me."

"What are you going to do? Can you get him to hospital?"

"Just make the tay. Leave him to me," his face was cold and expressionless.

He waited until she had disappeared down the ladder.

"Get up on your knees," he commanded.

"I can't. You've hurt me real bad."

"Then I'll help you." Maguire screamed with pain as Seamus wrenched him on to his knees, and swung him to face the wall.

"Seamus, for the love of Jaysus! I'm your father, for God's sake. You can't kill your own Da. You can't."

"Shut your Gob! A few hours ago you were quite willing to sacrifice me an' Dev for the sake o' the cause. What sort o' a father would do that? A father?" he snorted, "all you ever did was terrorise us. Put the fear o' God in us an' thought blind obedience was enough to make us good. When did you ever show us some love?

The only love you ever had was for the bliddy cause. Well, if you love it so much, be happy to die for it."

"Don't do it Seamus! You're disobeying orders. You know the rules! You need to have the authority o' Dublin for an execution. They'll court martial you."

"Get on with your absolution. You're a bloody traitor an' you know full well there's only one penalty for treason."

Maguire's head sank. He closed his eyes and began muttering his absolution beneath his breath.

Seamus had waited long enough. He thrust the revolver against the back of the drooping head and pulled the trigger.

The noise was deafening, and he winced as the mixture of blood and brains spattered against the wall.

The noise of the gunshot frightened Catrin, sending her staggering against the table. There was the thud of an object hitting the upstairs floor, and for the second time she felt like vomiting.

Up in the loft, Seamus felt no remorse. He had been brainwashed about the cause since childhood and the rules were plain. He had obeyed the rules. He pulled the blanket off the bed and laid it flat on the floor. He rolled the body on to the blanket it and wrapped it up. The feet protruded from the end and he removed the laces from the boots and used them to tie the ends of the blanket.

Removing the body posed a problem. The passage from the loft down the ladder was too difficult. He looked at the partially open window and decided that would be the only way.

He climbed down and joined Catrin who had a mug of tea waiting for him. She was crying.

"Did you shoot him?" she asked.

"Aye. He's dead. He would'ave died anyway."

"But he was your father."

"Makes no difference. He was a traitor. Treason is the worst crime of all. He deliberately sent us out to be kilt, knowin' we 'd probably take some army with us. He was right about that. I guess we got five o' them at least including the lieutenant. Dev'll be a hero. They'll talk about him for years, maybe even write a song about him."

Catrin began to cry again. It was all too much for her.

"I'm sorry," he put an arm around her shoulder. "You've had a bad night. I'll say no more about it."

He waited until she composed herself. "We have to move, Catrin, it's possible the Garda will come."

"What about him?" she glanced up to the loft, "he can't just disappear.

"I've had an idea. Accordin' to Father O'Donnell, the army was told there were two men in the van, but it didn't say who they were. There's only two others that know it wasn't me an' Dev. I'll make sure they won't talk. If I put it around that it was him that was with Dev. that will explain his disappearance."

"It'll make him a hero."

"I don't care. Better he be known for that and not a traitor. Neither Eamon or I deserve the shame on the family that would bring."

"How will you get rid of him?"

"I know a deep bog up country where I can bury him. They'll never find him.

Don't be frightened. I'm going to knock the window outta the loft and take him out over the roof o' the lean-to. I'll load him on the donkey and head north.

"I'll be back before daylight. Be ready to go an' we'll skip from here double quick." He patted her gently on the back and climbed back to the loft.

Catrin busied herself clearing up the debris that Maguire had scattered on the floor, trying to ignore the sounds of breaking wood and glass as Seamus battered and wrenched the whole window frame from the wall.

She heard the sound of Seamus bringing Devlin's horse into the yard and watched him complete the saddling. He returned to the paddock and fetched the donkey with its gruesome burden tied to its back. A spade was strapped to its side, and he attached the donkey with a length of rope to the saddle of the Cob.

"Mind what I told you. Keep the place in darkness. Scatter if you hear a car comin'. Burn all them papers he was lookin' for an' don't leave anythin' that might help the Garda. I'll be back as soon as I can. Take care now."

He nudged the Cob into motion, and as the slack of the rope was taken up, the heavily laden donkey followed. She waited until they had disappeared down the track before returning to the house.

The rain had held off and there was an occasional glimpse of the moon behind the clouds. Seamus would have enough light to see where he was going. She shivered as she thought of his dreadful mission and closed the door to retreat to the warmth of the fire. It had been the longest and saddest night of her life, and it would take a long time to recover from it.

Chapter Forty-Nine

A silence descended upon the house, so deep and so intense, it was as if the world had come to a stop, and everything on land, sea, and air was in mourning. Catrin had never felt more alone.

Her dreams were in tatters, blown away like cobwebs in the wind. The wonderful plans for a new life in America were in ruins. She had never experienced such a void. The very thought of his name was enough to start her crying.

She longed to be able to run next door and seek compassion from Cara. But there was no next door, and no Cara with a shoulder to cry on. She paced the floor aimlessly, trying to piece her world together. It was a time for soul searching and she found herself ashamed. Perhaps this was the retribution.

It was providential that she would have time to get home before her parents arrived back from England, and she would be able to destroy her farewell note before they had a chance to read it.

She had lied to Daniel. Once he got news of the catastrophe he would not take long to fathom out why she was so desperate to visit Balanalee that night.

She was becoming morbid and feeling sorry for herself. She needed to find something to do. The mess made by Maguire needed tidying up, so she decided to tackle that. The painting of the Wishing Boy lay where he had flung it, and she stooped to pick it up.

Miraculously it had survived the ill treatment, although one side of the frame was damaged. She used the hem of her dress to wipe away the film of dust that masked the surface, and cradled it her arms for a few moments as if she was nursing a child who had fallen and injured itself.

This was Devlin's tribute to love. He had created it out of the warmth of his own love, just as surely as he would have created life within her, and she had so much wanted to share that love. She clasped it to her bosom and tried to feel the radiation she knew was there, but it felt hard and cold. She hung it back reverently on its place above the work bench and turned her attention to clearing up the rest of the debris.

The papers that Seamus wanted destroyed consisted of training manuals and electrical drawings. She stirred the fire until it burst into life, and fed the papers one by one into the flames.

It was a bizarre feeling. Each page represented something in his life that she had never shared, pages that she would probably have wished him never have to have read, and now she was presiding over their destruction.

The waste saddened her. She had lost a lover; the world had lost a talent. Her tears were bitter. It was difficult to believe there was a God. She carried on, labouring in a purely mechanical fashion until the room was restored to a presentable state.

She had gone beyond the stage of tiredness, and had no inclination to sleep. To have climbed back to the loft was unthinkable. The thought of the bloodstained chaos that remained there made her shudder. She was sure Maguire would have murdered her had Seamus not intervened, and it might have been her blood running from the walls and not his.

She had no means of telling time. The clock was in the loft, but outside the sky was becoming paler, broken up by fleeting glimpses of the moon. She judged it was nearing dawn and Seamus would soon be back.

She sat down by the fire and raked aside the charred papers that clogged it, coaxing a little warmth from the smouldering turves.

Across the room the Wishing Boy hung in his frame and seemed to be staring at her, but it was only a trick of the lamplight. She dabbed her tears, marvelling at the way Devlin had captured so perfectly the emotions of love.

From nowhere, a dreadful thought struck her. Could Devlin have loved Shula as much as he professed to love her? He had taken her death really badly, even although she was the wife of a friend he respected.

Love between herself and Devlin had sprung up so quickly, far faster than she ever imagined possible. The huge wave of pity she had felt when she saw his badly beaten body had been the catalyst to start the romance, and the constant daily attention required love and devotion of a different sort to restore him to fitness. It was an environment that nurtured emotions.

But was it just a hospital romance? Was his love genuine, or just born out of gratitude, or maybe even a rebound from his unrequited love for Shula?

She remembered how plaintiff his cries of her name had been during his period of delirium.

Her mind was suddenly besieged by all kinds of doubts. Why did she feel this way? She put it down to her depression and the fact that her nerves were too frayed. But the feelings persisted.

She crossed to the work bench and took down the painting, carrying it to the kitchen table where the light was better. She traced his signature with her finger, trying to find reassurance by the simple act of stroking it.

Her gaze fastened on the three little hearts painted below it. The delicate pink symbols represented symbols of love, but of loves that were tragic. They were broken hearts, each one representing the wish of a grieving lover. Now it was her turn to grieve and she also had a broken heart, and a wish that it could be healed.

The realization roused her from the mire of confused emotions that were hounding her, and she knew what she must do. She searched the work bench to find a tube of paint and a brush. With great care she added another little heart to the existing three. Her heart stood out plainly because the only paint she could find in the litter was a brighter shade of red, and she could not find any black to enable her to paint the fine jagged line that signified it was a broken heart.

But the painting would belong to her now, and she would always know what it represented. No matter the difference, they belonged together. Each one of them represented a wish by a lover to have a new heart, one that would bring them relief from suffering and hopefully encourage a new life.

As she surveyed her work once again, yet another dreadful thought flashed through her mind.

Liam had died. Shula had died, and now Devlin. Could the heart she had just added signify another death? She realized it was her heart that she had painted. It was yet one more broken heart. She recoiled with the shock. It was a collection of broken hearts, all associated with the Wishing Boy. Were they trophies? How many more hearts would it wish to collect?

She re-examined the painting, her gaze fastened on the boy, studying the expression on his face in great detail. In the poorer light of the lamp it appeared to have changed dramatically.

It was not adulation that shone from his eyes. It was greed and envy. The sensual mouth was not begging a kiss, it was demanding it, begging for a heart to be given to him. She dropped the painting to the floor and fled in horror to the window where she sat on the low sill praying for Seamus to appear.

She cried bitterly. Not only did she nurse a broken heart, but her beliefs had been shaken and she was confused.

The Wishing Boy could possess another meaning, and it had shaken her. She had spent the past year obsessed to discover the story that lay behind the painting, and she thought she had achieved her objective, and found love in doing so.

The real truth was like the stab of a knife in her heart. The Wishing Boy was a depiction of how Devlin must have felt when watching the devotion of Liam and Shula.

She should have realized long ago who the boy was. Hadn't Devlin told her that he did not have a model, that he painted from the feelings that were from his heart.

He was the Wishing Boy!

The deep blue of the night was fading, being replaced by the greying light of dawn. It acted like a signal, and the clouds that befuddled her mind cleared like the rise of a curtain. She was calm now, and her mind aware of what she had to do.

She crossed the room and once more looked at the painting, but this time she had a different interpretation. The tears streamed down her cheeks. The mouth she once thought was so sensual and craving affection portrayed jealousy, seeking to swallow her heart and destroy her. Four hearts had been victims. There must be no more.

She gathered all the papers that had not yet been burned and heaped them on the bog oak table together with pieces of driftwood, picture frames and any other debris that would burn.

She dragged the work bench from the wall and tilted it on its' side, and cast the chairs around it.

She pulled the loft ladder away from its position and flung that on the pile surrounding the table. It still did not look enough.

From the hay shed she brought in several bundles of rye thatch that had been cut and dried for the next thatching, and stacked them in various places amongst the debris. She surveyed the heap she had created and felt it was sufficient.

The Wishing Boy had demanded sacrifices. Now it was his turn. She placed the painting on top of the pile on the table and left it without a backward glance. From the store in the lean to she found the large stone jug that contained lamp oil.

With considerable effort she proceeded to scatter oil amongst the debris, concentrating most on the mass surrounding the table. She hurled the jar into the stone hearth where it smashed into pieces. The dregs of the oil ignited within seconds once the heat of the fire took effect.

She watched in fascination as the trail of oil slowly followed suit, and the flames spread, darting like hungry serpents amongst the saturated debris, all of them making in the direction of the table.

She pushed the door wide open and walked into the yard. The morning air wafted through the open door and fanned the blaze rapidly. In a few minutes the flames were leaping towards the ceiling and the smoke was thickening.

She wheeled out the trap from the hay shed and called the pony from the field and within minutes was hitched up and trotting out of the yard. She passed Maguire's car, parked where he had left it, a stark reminder of her terrifying ordeal at his hands. She had no pity for him.

The first rays of the sun produced a yellow glow as the new day advanced, and she headed back to Dungannon House. It would be but a temporary sanctuary, for she would have to get back to Dublin before her parents, and destroy the evidence of the terrible thing she had been about to do.

Danna would understand and help her. Behind her, the first signs of the blaze were evident, and a coil of black smoke rose slowly into the greying sky. As the blaze grew, bursts of fiery sparks erupted spasmodically, illuminating the rapidly spreading cloud. It would soon be visible a long way off.

Not once did she look back. Her eyes were fixed on the horizon. What she had left behind was the past, and she had to move on. One decision at a time was all she could contemplate. Perhaps later in the day she might think more clearly.

There was a dull ache in her heart, but her tears were drying, and there was the old spark of determination in her eyes. She had learned a great deal about human emotions and experiences she would never have learned otherwise. With such a gain in maturity she could look forward to being a help to her father in the role he wished her to take up.

Her first task would be to complete the story that had brought her all these emotions and experiences, and to share them with others. She could tell them of her relentless pursuit of an object and how persistence achieved her ambition. But she would also add a caution.

"Never wish too much for something – you might get it!"

In the future she would always remember her grandmother's advice.

The End